"A powerful, poignant journey of discovery."　　　—*Library Journal*

"Greg Belliveau has written a terrific novel. There is surprise, terror, and a testimony to the providence of God. *Go Down to Silence* will entertain and encourage every reader."

　　　　　　　　　　　—Paul Dixon, President, Cedarville University

"A refreshingly unpredictable Christian novel."　　　—*Publishers Weekly*

"This wrenching story of tragedy, grace, and reconciliation is told with the deft pen of a creative wordsmith. The tale's intriguing arrangement grabs the reader's imagination and does not relent until the resolution of the final pages."

　　　　　—Eric Mounts, Pastor, Southgate Baptist Church, Springfield, Ohio

"A deeply felt, sad, but somehow affirmative odyssey."　　　—*Booklist*

go down to silence

A NOVEL

Multnomah®Publishers *Sisters, Oregon*

G . K . B E L L I V E A U

GO DOWN TO SILENCE
© 2001 by Greg K. Belliveau
published by Multnomah Publishers, Inc.

International Standard Book Number: 1-57673-736-5

Cover images by Tony Stone Images
Cover image of man with cane by Akira Nagamatsu/Photonica

Unless otherwise indicated, Scripture quotations are from:
The Holy Bible, New International Version © 1973, 1984 by International Bible Society, used by permission of Zondervan Publishing House

Multnomah is a trademark of Multnomah Publishers, Inc., and is registered in the U.S. Patent and Trademark Office.
The colophon is a trademark of Multnomah publishers, Inc.

Printed in the United States of America

For information:
Multnomah Publishers, Inc.•Post Office Box 1720•Sisters, Oregon 97759

Library of Congress Cataloging-in-Publication Data
Belliveau, G. K. (Gregory Kenneth), 1965-
Go down to silence: a novel/by G. K. Belliveau.
p. cm.
ISBN 1-57673-736-5
1. Holocaust, Jewish (1939-1945)—Fiction. 2. Fathers and sons—Fiction.
3. Jewish men—Fiction. 4. Aged men—Fiction. I. Title.
PS3552.E533727 G6 2001   813'.54—dc21   00-010211

01 02 03 04 05 06 07 08 09—10 9 8 7 6 5 4 3 2 1

To Patricia and Kaitlin

It is not the dead who praise the LORD,
those who go down to silence;
it is we who extol the LORD,
both now and forevermore.

PSALM 115:17–18

ACKNOWLEDGMENTS

First and foremost I want to thank Nathan Lypsic, whose life inspired me to write a novel about the Holocaust in Belgium, for his interviews. Thank you to my father and mother for telling me about Nathan and his story; that night at the dinner table started it all. I am indebted to Yvonne de Ridder Files for her informative book *The Quest for Freedom: Belgian Resistance in World War II* and also to George Watt for his book *The Comet Connection*. Thank you also to the Belgium Tourist Bureau for their helpful packet of maps and material. Special thanks to Les Stobbe, my agent, and to Rod Morris, my editor. And of course, thank you to my wife, Patricia, for keeping me sane, focused, and encouraged through the whole process of writing this novel.

PART ONE

1

H urry up, Pop. If you poke any more, you'll miss the plane." Asher Horowitz glanced again at his watch and then back at the old man before him. "Let me help you with those." Asher reached down and lifted the heavy bag and scurried to the car.

But Jacob Horowitz hesitated at the mirror, staring at his complexion. It reminded him of an old riverbed, creased and worn—perhaps a piece of leather sun-scarred and brittle. And for a brief second he raised his large hand to touch it, to establish contact with the other in the mirror, the self that had been transformed. Yes, this was he—Jacob Andre Horowitz—the Belgian Jew who nearly lost his life fleeing from the Nazis. Yes, yes, indeed. The car horn forced him into the present once again. He rubbed the smooth cherry table with his index finger and slowly walked out to his son.

The trip to the airport was slowed by the rain, torrents of water splashing across the windows, lines of cars, taillights like red burning eyes suddenly blinking open.

Asher gripped the steering wheel tighter than usual, then suddenly smacked it with both hands. "You'll never make the plane at this rate."

"I can catch another." Jacob turned to gaze out the side window, thin streaks of water like fingers spreading across the entire glass.

Silence.

A large truck pulled in front of their black Mercedes and with it a blizzard of thick mist, rendering the already frantic wipers useless.

"They should outlaw these—"

Asher suddenly swerved the car into the other lane. A set of headlights approached, and he swerved back and slowed down to get away from the oily spray.

Jacob was resolute about his decision and he knew his oldest son did not understand. He had made all the arrangements months in advance, had written all the letters, made long distance phone calls. It had taken time, this plan, yes, time. And that was something Jacob Horowitz had precious little of. And even as he thought of this, he smiled. Somehow traveling to Belgium with Isaac was the right thing to do. How could he tell Asher about such an absurd idea. He knew it to be absurd, but something deep inside convinced him it was right. Yes, Isaac would have to do, was the only one to do it, the only one who could. And so, as Asher swerved once again out into the other lane, passing the truck and speeding toward the airport, Jacob silently stared out the window.

"He won't show, Pop. You know that deep inside. I mean, you haven't even seen him for what—ten years? It's crazy, Pop. I told you this before. You're only setting yourself up for a complete let-down." Asher glanced over at the old man still looking out the window. "Are you listening to anything I'm telling you?"

"Yes, yes, Asher. I am listening. I am always listening to you, Asher." Jacob faced his son. "I listened when you told me not to call him. I listened to you when you told me he wouldn't call back. I listen to you even now." Jacob turned his face back to the streaked glass. "But he did call back, Asher." Jacob's voice was a whisper. "He did."

They drove on in silence for a time.

"Why are you going to Belgium? Why now? I mean, to go and visit your old garment factory is one thing, but to take Isaac. Pop, it doesn't add up."

"I am patient with you, my Asherel. I will tell you one more time. I am going to the old garment factory in Antwerp. I am going to take your brother, Isaac, because it is my wish. We should all know our roots, Asher. It is good to know from where we came. This changes the future."

Asher shook his head.

"Have I not taken you there many times, Asher? Yes, when your mother was still alive, I took you and your family. Yes, to the garment factory in Antwerp." Jacob stared for quite some time out the window, houses and cars blurred by. "Now is the time to take Isaac."

Jacob remembered that phone call from Isaac. It had been late; he had exhausted himself playing handball with his friends at the club. Seventy-one years old and still playing handball. Three Jewish associates and one Gentile—a retired carpenter, big, burly, and extremely adroit with his kill shots. The other three he had known for quite some time, ever since he moved from New York to Cleveland. Harvey Spellman was a saggy body mounted on two bad knees. After each game Harvey would hobble and swear all the way to the locker room. Melvin Braun, thin, rail-like, was a miserable and self-deprecating handball player. Melvin was a garment store manager who wished to be a part of Jacob's world—more to the point to learn Jacob's business savvy. And of course,

Herman Bergman, a huge fat man who was as nimble as a gymnast, crouching down like a sumo wrestler before each return. The Gentile's name was Raymond Lereau, a newcomer who had ingratiated himself into this Jewish world through his skill and athleticism. Lereau was a born-again Christian, who at every turn witnessed and questioned the other three about what they believed and why—nicely, politely, but with a sense of urgency Jacob could not understand.

Now that he was seventy-one, now that he had seen the doctor, these things he began to think about. So he had called Isaac. The doctor had been very clear: Get your things in order, Jacob. Yes, yes, indeed. So he had called his son and left a long and surreptitious message.

Idiot! he thought to himself afterward. What kind of father would ask such a thing on an answering message?

And so, a day or so later, when Jacob walked into his large house in the east suburbs of the city—well established, old money—when he pushed the button on the answering machine and heard the messages, his knees gave way, and he sat at the counter rubbing his furrowed brow.

The first message was of no importance. The second was from Asher: "Pop, I'm closing the Ferguson account for good this time. They are cheating Gentiles who only want to run us out of business! I know you like them, but I am making the decision to shut them down. I just wanted you to hear it from me. Love ya, Pop. Ruth and I will be over for the Sabbath." The third message was of no consequence. And then Isaac's voice came on. There was a hesitation, a clearing of the throat:

"Hello." Pause. "This is Isaac Horowitz returning your call. Papa? I will be at the airport at Gate 37. I don't know why I'm doing this, but for some reason I think it's a good thing. I'll be flying in from New York the day before, not until late. The book signings have gone better than I had hoped." Pause. "Well, okay then." And the phone message abruptly cut off with a synthesized voice: *That was your last message.*

That night Jacob wept. Sitting at the counter, in the middle of a large empty house, he shook with an emotion he had not felt since Belgium. Once again he found himself scared and alone. So he rubbed his forehead, rubbed it and allowed the tears to find their way down his cheeks and onto his arm.

Asher pulled the car up to the airport terminal and abruptly stopped between a yellow taxi and gold Lexus. He jumped out of the car and opened the trunk, pulling out his father's heavy suitcase. A skycap came over with a luggage cart.

"Good day to you, sir," said the lanky, black man. "Let me take your bag for you." He reached down and heaved the bag onto the tarnished, flat surface.

"Thank you." Jacob peered closely at the attendant's identity badge, "Lawrence. If you take my luggage, I am sure I can make it the rest of the way by myself." The attendant nodded and wheeled the cart toward the ticket counter.

"I should really call you one of those service carts, Pop," Asher said, looking around for someone to wave down. But Jacob had already walked inside.

"Welcome, Mr. Horowitz," said the spunky woman behind the ticket counter. "You'll be traveling first class on flight 417 from Cleveland to Chicago. And then nonstop to Brussels." She smiled at him just as Asher scurried up behind.

"Miss," Asher said, a flustered look on his face, "can my father get a cart to take him to gate 37?"

The women nodded politely and picked up the intercom. Jacob shook his head and smiled at the woman.

"That will not be necessary, Miss…" And Jacob looked at her badge. "Jane. I can manage the walk all by myself."

Asher pulled on his father's arm and leaned forward. "You don't want to miss the flight, Pop."

"I will be fine, Asherel. Just fine. You should not leave the car parked where it is. You might get a ticket."

Asher asked, "Is flight 417 on time?"

Jane checked her watch and looked at the computer screen.

"From what this tells me, it is. If you hurry you should have no problem."

Jacob smiled at the woman and fast-walked toward the gate. Asher followed behind. They passed the food court, a bustle of commotion, and joined the large and snaking security line. Inch by inch, they stepped toward the gate. Jacob walked through first and Asher followed. The alarm went off.

"Step over here, sir," said a security guard. Jacob turned around and then motioned he was going on ahead.

"I'll catch up to you, Pop."

Asher stepped through the gate again, and again the alarm went off.

"Step over here, sir. Any metal objects on your person?"

Jacob could hear his oldest son complaining about the service, the rush, and the immediacy of his situation. Jacob passed a small bar, filled with people and smoke. He walked past a nice bookstore, trimmed in dark cherry, an entrance of elegant glass. He turned instinctively—as he did every time he passed a bookstore—and peered into the front display window. He shook his head in recognition and moved quickly on. There was a small coffee shop to his right, and then gate 34. He walked on, a sense of dread, of hope, of urgency filtering through his thoughts. Was he here? Would he be on the plane? Gate 35. A horde of people streamed out into the waiting area: hugging, squeezing, shaking hands, some empty and hollow on their way to the next airport. Gate 36. The hub was empty, a sole attendant behind a desk scribbling on a piece of paper. Gate 37.

The hub was packed with people, rows and rows of frustration. Jacob stopped, scanned the crowd. Several people huddled around a tall thin man. Was it Isaac? He walked toward the group, and the man turned around. No, it was not Isaac. Again Jacob scanned the mass of people. He sighed and made his way into the line of impatient passengers waiting for a flight update. The group inched forward and by the time he was in earshot, he had guessed the situation. Flight 417 had been delayed due to weather. It was still stranded in New York. The thunderstorm front was massive and unrelenting. They would make their announcement shortly. Jacob stepped out of the line and waited on the fringes.

"There you are," said a familiar voice. Jacob turned around and once again scanned the crowd. "I told you," Asher said. "I told you he wouldn't be here."

"The plane has been delayed. He has probably called ahead."

They both scanned the crowd again, and Asher shoved his hands in his pockets. "What did you expect, Pop? I told you he would hurt you."

"He will be here," said Jacob calmly. He took one more look around and then turned to Asher. "You may go now, if you want. I know you are busy today." He suddenly put his hand up and stopped Asher before he could speak. "I will call you if I need you. Have a safe trip home, my Asher. Give my love to Ruth and the kids." He smiled. "I will call you when we get to Belgium."

Asher hesitated, shook his head, and then hugged Jacob good-bye.

"Yes, my Asher, yes," Jacob said. "I will call you if he does not show." And with that Asher walked back to his illegally parked car.

A heavy burden suddenly settled upon Jacob's shoulders. He sat near the large rain-streaked window and looked outside. Alone. This was the single word spinning around in his head. His precious Liza, of blessed memory, wife of thirty-six years, had died five years ago. The years since her death had taken their toll on Jacob. The empty house in Pepper Pike was harder and harder to come home to. Asher, now a successful businessman in his own right—a bit of an ogre at times, but a businessman in the nineties had to be—he had launched out on his own long ago. He had recently expanded his father's garment empire, opening more and more stores across the country. And that shift in power, that stepping down process had also taken a toll on Jacob. But it was the letter from Belgium that seemed to suck his marrow dry.

When he received the letter, postmarked Brussels, his heart fluttered just a moment, and once again a feeling of dread, a darkness he could not explain settled upon him like a mist. The writing was small, beautifully scripted French:

My dear Tany,
      Pierre is very sick and will not last the month. Please come.
He so wants to see you.
      Sincerely,
      Micheline

The tether that for sixty years had secretly bound Jacob to his roots was beginning to fray. Jacob sat staring out the window and suddenly grunted so that a little boy next to him looked on with curiosity. He stood up and scanned the crowd for Isaac.

Yes, there was still Isaac, enigmatic and odd. Isaac did not want anything to do with the garment empire, did not want to be Jewish; and one day he proclaimed quite emphatically he was going to New York to be a writer. Isaac succeeded. He wrote furiously for two years, wrote and by a sheer act of will transformed himself from a rich Jewish man from Cleveland into a struggling artist living in Greenwich Village. But then Jack Oxford, Isaac's pen name, became synonymous with action adventure novels. His picture was prominently displayed in windows—a gangly cardboard frame, one arm at his side, the other relaxed over the stack of his latest release. They were written at just the right time, said the critics, tapping into the social conscience of the complacent nineties America. And best of all, they were perfect for the movie industry. Jack Oxford was wealthy, was a celebrity. And Isaac Horowitz had not seen his father for more than ten years.

Jacob rubbed his brow. Still no sign of Isaac. Why should he show? Hadn't Jacob neglected his son? Hadn't he confounded him at every turn? You want to do what? But certainly, Isaac, you want to work for the family business. Your roots demand that you do. We must keep the business in the family.

But the response fell on deaf ears. So off his son went. Oh, there was a letter here, a letter there—Papa, can I borrow some money for this idea? Papa, can I borrow some more money for this idea? Papa, my bills are due, and I cannot pay them, may I borrow some more money. This time I promise I will pay it all back, everything, the whole lot, and even with interest. Jacob didn't mind sending his son the money, didn't mind the late night pleas. No, what Jacob did mind was when he received a package in the mail, a package from New York, Isaac's first published novel. But Isaac Horowitz was not the author—no, Jack Oxford had written this action thriller: *The Moon below the Earth.*

That had been ten years ago. In one draconian act, Jacob banished Isaac from his home, his life, his world. This sent Liza to an early grave, created a palpable hatred between Asher and his brother, and was slowly draining Jacobs's life away.

And when Jacob received the letter from Micheline, the letter begging him to visit his dear friend Pierre before his death, this trip became the balm of Gilead that would somehow fix the wrongs he had done, would lift the terrible darkness that seemed to march around him day and night. If Isaac would only come, would risk the anguish and fear of the first meeting, Jacob would tell him everything, tell him about the Nazis, the hiding, the fear and the pain; would tell him about the righteous Gentiles God used to save him and his family. Yes, he would tell him everything—no, he would *show* it all to him in Belgium. He would take him from house to house, from family to family. And Isaac Horowitz, son of Jacob Horowitz—not the Gentile Jack Oxford—could see where he came from, the price that was paid. And then, once that boundary had been crossed—then, just maybe—reconciliation was not far off. *What is a man's life,* thought Jacob, *if he dies without ever telling the only thing he has: his story.*

Jacob walked the perimeter of the crowd. Isaac was nowhere to be seen. Once again he felt darkness, a hollowness settling down upon him. He will show. He must show.

2

It is May 10, 1940. Eleven-year-old Jacob Horowitz sits in the backseat of his father's car with his sister, Sarah. She is nine years old. They have been stopped in traffic for twenty minutes, and Jacob stares out the window at the passing lines of refugees. A man, gaunt and withered, strides by with a huge basket strapped to his back, stooping from the weight. Jacob has stopped waving at the passersby for he is scared, frightened by their hollow stares, their anxious and stern faces.

"Mama, when will Papa come back?" pleads Sarah.

"Hush now, sweetie," replies Jacob's mother. She too looks anxious. "He will be back shortly. He has gone to find out why we have stopped."

Jacob continues to stare out the window. A woman rides by on a rusted bicycle, her baby strapped to her front. Again the hollow look. A horn beeps just ahead of them, several times, angry shouts follow. Jacob can hear his father calming the man down, telling him of a broken-down car up the road.

"They will kill us here if we don't hurry!" cries the man in the car ahead. Jacob's father walks back to his car and steps in.

"Who will kill us, Papa?" Jacob asks.

His father turns around shaking his head in disgust. "No one will kill us, Jacob. Now let us be patient." He turns to Rachael, his wife. "There's a car with a flat tire up the road." He looks around at the chaos, the lines of people fleeing from Antwerp toward Paris. A businessman he knows wanders by with his family. He hails the man.

"Hello, Isaac. Any news?"

"Ruben? Ruben Horowitz?" says the startled man, his thick, gray beard unkempt and wild. "If Ruben Horowitz is leaving Antwerp, then the news is true. The Germans are closer than they say."

"Better to be safe, Isaac." Ruben looks about again. "So many people."

The old man looks around as well and then with a resolute expression on his face says, "Good-bye, Ruben Horowitz. May the Master of the universe be with you." And he hurries away.

The cars begin to inch forward once again. Jacob hears his mother's sigh of relief, sees his mother and father clench hands, briefly, but with a strong emotion. Again, Jacob looks out the window. Lines and lines of people. A little girl no more than five years old, red bloomers sticking out past her soiled dress, cries for her family. People pass her by, their one goal: get to Paris. Paris is safety. An old man lumbers past Jacob's window, a white walrus mustache, browned near his nose from cigarette smoke, droops over his lips. Still the little girl screams. Jacob loses sight of her, and then shifts in his seat to face the back window. A frantic man walks up to her and picks her off the ground. He pats her on the back to soothe her, but she cries harder. The mother screams something at the father in Flemish and then sternly walks back to the other children who patiently wait ahead. They have a cart, a wagon, and a small pony. Jacob wonders what they will do with the pony in the city of Paris.

As far as Jacob can see, the road is blocked, stuffed full with people and cars, all heading from Antwerp, from the threat of invasion, from death. He shifts again and turns forward to get the line and the fear out of his head. But as long as the line is in back, it is the same ahead. The fear remains. The cars inch forward and time passes—thousands of pictures collide and merge, pictures of desperation, of fear.

At twelve o'clock that same day, Jacob's mother passes out sandwiches and a piece of fruit. Sarah asks if they will ever go back to Antwerp. Jacob's mother looks at her husband and then back at Sarah. "Perhaps someday, sweetie. Now eat your lunch." They drive on, on and on, slowly crawling toward Paris and freedom. Jacob is sad he has left his friends. He thinks of them in turn, and wonders as his sister had if he will ever see them again.

It is now evening and the signs for Paris have been visible for several miles. They are still in Belgium, in the French speaking part, past La Louvière and Hainaut, now near the city of Mons. The traffic is stopped dead. Jacob's father gets out to see what has happened. The people too have stopped, some eating their dinner, some crouching on their haunches talking with each other. Jacob's father has not returned.

"Mama? Where's Papa?" Sarah asks.

"He will be back shortly, sweetie. Jacob, are you hungry?"

Jacob does not hear her, for he is busy watching the people outside his window. There is a sudden look of panic, faces peer toward the evening sky. Jacob cannot see what they are looking at. And then there is a sudden and terrible roar, close to their car—a whining surge of power. The car shakes from the unseen object above. Jacob can see the fear on his mother's face. The crowd of people dash in all directions as the sound returns.

"Out of the car, children!" Jacob's mother screams. "Out of the car!" Jacob can hear the terrible noise closing in on them. He grabs Sarah and pulls her from the car. His mother scoops them up and nearly drags them to a ditch near several large trees. The ditch is filled with people, some crying, some searching for their children, some huddled down with their hands over their heads. Jacob looks at the road, a long line of cars, some with people, most empty but still running. He stares up into the sky at the terrible whining sound.

The Stuka swoops down and skims across the road, only two hundred feet above. Then Jacob hears the shredding of metal, of tires, of humans as the German fighter pilot unleashes his machine guns upon the fleeing refugees. The plane disappears into the air. The crowd hums to life. Questions and groans. Some run back to their cars to untie their belongings and drag them to the side of the road. But the Stuka returns, the machine guns blazing and shredding once again. A storm of bullets sprays close to where Jacob and his mother and sister lie. Jacob's mother screams out and wraps her arms around her children. "What is happening?" she cries out. And she suddenly thinks of her husband. "Ruben!" she screams, and she stands up, hands to her lips. "Ruben!"

People are pushing and running in every direction. The Stuka swoops down for another attack. Jacob's mother cries out, covering her children with her body. Sarah weeps uncontrollably. The white leprous fear has returned to Jacob and he is unable to speak, to see, only hear the terrible whining of the fighter, the shredding bullets, the desperate cries of the people. And on the next pass by the fighter, the Horowitzes' car shudders and then disintegrates: tires erupting and hissing, glass exploding into shards. The car in front and behind are also hit by the bullets.

"Oh no! No!" Jacob's mother cries. She stands up in panic. "Stay here, children! Stay here!" She releases Sarah, who grabs onto Jacob, and runs toward the car. She grabs several bags and pulls them to the side of the road. She goes back. The whine of the fighter returns.

"Mama!" Jacob screams. "Mama, the fighter! Mama!" But she reaches into the car and pulls out another bag, this one bigger than the rest. Jacob calls out again. She looks up into the sky and goes for one more bag. The terrible roar increases and the machine guns release their destruction. "Mama!" Jacob screams again. And she drags the bags across the road. The machine guns fire, dirt, and pavement; metal and glass spray about Jacob's mother. She huddles on the ground with the suitcases around her. Then the fighter disappears again into the evening sky. Jacob looks at his mother. She is motionless. He runs out to her in the street and finds her sobbing uncontrollably. Jacob pulls the suitcase from her and lifts her to her feet. They pull the cases off the road and cling once again to each other.

The people around them are in disarray. There are shouts and screams as family members try to contact one another. Thousands and thousands of people mass along the side of the road. A group of men appear around the Horowitzes' car. One of them, with his back turned to Jacob, places his hands to his face and shakes his head with grief. He turns around, wiping his eyes, and searches the shattered and mangled car.

"Ruben!" Jacob's mother screams. "Ruben, we're over here! Over here!" He does not hear her. "Jacob, go to your father and tell him we are over here." Jacob runs to the group of men. One of them spots him. Ruben turns around and lifts Jacob in the air, hugging him tightly—father and son. Jacob points to the side of the road, past the throng of people now making their way to their cars. Ruben puts Jacob down and runs to his wife and daughter. The men near the car are familiar. It is Jacob's Uncle Benjamin

Horowitz and his oldest son Samuel. They walk over to the side of the road.

"Paris has been taken," Ruben says to his wife. "The Germans have skirted Belgium. Paris is not safe for us."

"Our safest bet is to travel back to Antwerp," Uncle Benjamin says. "Our own government will protect us. In Paris, who knows what will happen."

"But how can we go anywhere now?" Jacob's mother says. "Our car is—"

"We will travel back with Benjamin and his family. He has room. His truck is about a mile down the road."

"I have plenty of space," Benjamin says. "Antwerp will be safe."

"Just like Paris?" Jacob's mother says. "What are we to do, Ruben?"

"It will be okay, Rachael. We will be protected. Or next step is to go back, to get away from these fighters and this crowd. So let us take our things and go."

They walk with the masses, through the masses, against the masses until they reach Uncle Benjamin's truck. It is one of the trucks used to transport garments across Belgium. They load in the back with Benjamin's family, Ruben and Benjamin in the front seat. The truck turns down a side road and they make their way back to Antwerp just as night settles upon the border.

Leaving Antwerp was very hard for the Horowitz family. Ruben had considered long and with great deliberation what to do and when to do it. His decision was agonizing, but final. They would leave the business to his partner Hans Kraemer. Hans would transfer funds to the family once they were established in France. "It will be a good thing," Ruben said to Rachael one night in bed.

"We always wanted to expand." He smiled, but she saw the emptiness, the concern just below the surface. His father's father had started the store, at that time just a simple garment maker. Now it would have to go into the trusted hands of Hans Kraemer.

Jacob is happy to go home, but there is a strange sense of urgency. Uncle Benjamin's news about Belgium has been disconcerting. The Germans now occupy the government and the major cities. No Jew is safe. The garment truck drives through the night, and Jacob drifts in and out of a restless sleep, wrapped in blankets, huddled with his mother and Sarah and Uncle Benjamin's family in the back of the truck. The trip is monotonous, and the crowds that once fled now slowly reenter, disbelief and panic drifting across the entire country. Jacob thinks of his home. It will be good to get back to life as normal.

But it is not life as normal. The truck is stopped several times on its journey back into Antwerp. Guards ask for papers, check the back of the truck—a flashlight, bright and menacing, lingers on the huddled family in the back. Then the truck moves on. The city of Antwerp is transformed over night. Large red and white flags hang from windows and poles, the swastika bold and black. The truck stops once again. Jacob can see the fear in his mother's face, a hollowness, a panic deep within the eyes.

Ruben climbs into the back of the truck. "We shall go back to the house. We need time to find out what has happened, and how deep the poison runs in our city." He jumps out and converses with Uncle Benjamin. The truck has stopped near a forest near the suburb of Hoboken—east of the city next to the Schelde River.

"Mama?" asks Jacob.

"Yes, my lamb."

"What poison is Papa talking about?"

"Shh. We must not think of such things now. Cover your sister up with the rest of this blanket."

The truck starts with several jerks, and soon they pull up to their house. The driveway is empty, as with all the driveways near it. Ruben comes out and tells his family to stay in the truck until he returns. He is gone for only a few minutes.

"It is safe, Rachael," Ruben says. "Let's get the children inside and cleaned up. This has been a night they will not soon forget."

Jacob helps his sister out of the truck and they walk up the driveway. Ruben stays behind to talk with Uncle Benjamin. "Yes, it will be good to call us later tonight. Let us both find out what has happened." The truck jerks forward and then slowly pulls away.

Most of the day has vanished with the excitement, with telephone calls to Hans Kraemer, to relatives. The majority of them with no response. The house feels strange and different. All of their possessions still remain: Jacob's bed, his dresser, his toy box with its soccer ball forcing the lid open. And yet, Jacob fears this place. He walks to his bed and searches the covers for the poison his father has talked so much about. He turns on the water at the bathroom sink, but decides he will not use it, just in case it is contaminated. His mother tells him to take a bath, but instead he closes the door and fills up the tub, huddling naked, staring at the clear water, wondering if the Nazi poison has seeped its way into it, expecting at any moment the red and white flag with the strange black symbol to somehow pour from the pipes. No, he did not like this house anymore.

"Jacob?" his mother calls. "Hurry up in there. Your sister must bathe as—" And as Jacob's mother opens the door, she sees her scared and naked son shivering and crying, staring at the clear bath water in fear. "Oh, my baby," she whispers grabbing him and wrapping a towel around him. "Oh, my little lamb. It's okay. It's okay, my sweet little lamb, it's okay." Jacob can't control his sobs, can't control the terrible fear that has suddenly seized him. He holds his mother for all of his life. That night Jacob and Sarah sleep on a mattress next to their mother and father's bed, a small light on in the bathroom.

That same night Jacob dreams of fighter planes and terrible red and white flags. A huge figure with a metal helmet screams at him: *"Ihre papieren! Ihre papieren!* Show me your identity card!" His voice is guttural and harsh, eyes red and demonic, pupils in the shape of a swastika. And then he sees that horrible flag dropping down around him, around his father, his mother. He hears his father screaming out, "Run, Rachael! Run, children!" But Jacob's feet are as heavy as lead balls. He looks back and the flag has bound his father so only his face is showing. Jacob screams at the flag, but his voice is silenced. He hears his father cry out, "Run from the poison, Jacob! Run from the poison!" And then the flag covers his face, and his father is no more.

Jacob sits up in his bed with a start. Sarah grunts something and turns over, pulling the covers from Jacob. He realizes his parents are in the bed next to him. They stop whispering and his mother reaches down and strokes Jacob's sweating head.

"Go to sleep, my little lamb. Go to sleep. Everything is okay." Jacob lies back down and listens to his parents' conversation.

"The children are scared, Ruben."

"Yes, I know. They will be fine, my love. We must be strong for them."

"But how can I be strong, Ruben? How can I be strong when I am as afraid as they are?"

"I will be strong for all of us, my love. I will carry you and the children on my back if I have to." There is silence. "We are in

God's hands now. He will not let this poison infect us."

"What are we to do now, Ruben?"

"I will travel down to the store tomorrow morning. I will talk to Hans Kraemer and find out all I can. It may be this occupation will be harmless, that it will be no more than a discomfort." Ruben is silent again. "We should not have fled in the first place. It is better to stand our ground." There is silence again. "The morning will bring clarity to our situation, Rachael. The morning will make things better."

The light turns off, and Jacob is left in darkness.

The morning brings no certain news as Ruben has hoped. The occupation has begun, but nothing has really changed save for increased presence of German soldiers in the city. May ends and June begins. June ends and July begins. The months go by with little effect on Jacob and his family. That all changes in 1941.

Ruben receives the letter in his mailbox at the store:

"No Jews shall be able to own a business or be hired by a Gentile. If they are caught doing so, all property will be confiscated by the government and the offender will be prosecuted to the highest extent of the law: death."

It is as simple as that. The store that had been handed down from generation to generation is to be dissolved or sold. Ruben's knees give way and he sits down against a large cutting table. Hans Kraemer sees the pale complexion of his partner and drops his scissors to rush over to him. Ruben hands him the letter.

"It is beginning, my friend. It took some time, but now it is beginning. The rumors were true." Ruben looks out the window at a beautiful fall day. "And there is nowhere to hide or to run."

"We can fight this!" Hans says. "We shall take it up with the officials. They cannot just take from someone what they want. This cannot be."

"Who will we complain to, Hans?" Ruben replies with a simple smile. "Those who wrote the law are in charge. We have no recourse."

"Perhaps they will not—"

"No. No, they will come. Read the bottom. They will be checking all suspected proprietors within the next few weeks."

Ruben sits around the table with his family that night. The meal is meager, but they eat thankfully. Since the occupation, food has been harder and harder to come by.

"I will sell the business to Hans," Ruben says to Rachael. "He is a good man. He will maintain it until this whole thing is cleared up. Once I sign the business over to him, then—" But Ruben cannot finish, and Jacob sees his father break down in front of him. His mother stands up and walks over to him. She lifts his head in her hands.

"You must be strong, Ruben. You must carry us now. Now is the time," she whispers so Jacob can barely hear her.

Ruben wipes his eyes and smiles at the children who are stunned at the display of emotion. "Eat your dinner, children. We must eat up, for we do not know what is to come. Not now or ever." He turns to Rachael with a smile of reassurance. "God is good, my wife. He shall see us through."

She clutches his hand tightly, and Jacob remembers the same gesture on their way to Paris nearly a year ago.

"I must see you, my brother," Benjamin Horowitz calls his brother one evening. "I have a plan. I must see you."

That night, Benjamin comes over, the yellow Star of David

around his coat sleeve, a law that was passed only a month ago. The night is cold and a fog lingers about the fallen snow. Benjamin stomps his boots and takes off his coat. He is given a hot cup of coffee. Jacob hugs his uncle hello, but the scene is soon transformed into business. Ruben and his brother walk into Ruben's study to discuss what must be done. The meeting lasts for an hour. Jacob hears loud outbursts, a pounding on the desk, and then continued whispers. When the two men immerge, they are resolute. Uncle Benjamin shakes Ruben's hand and smiles at Rachael. With a quick rub of Jacob's head, his uncle walks out into the cold.

Ruben gathers his family around the table; such gatherings are beginning to frighten Jacob and Sarah. He patiently explains to the children they are going to go into hiding. The rumors have spread that the Nazis are taking Jews away. Jacob knows this first-hand; just last week his friend Moshe came home from school to an empty house. Yes, the poison was pouring out all over Antwerp and Belgium. They would be okay, however, Jacob's father explains, because Uncle Benjamin has located an apartment building on the outskirts of town where other Jews are hiding out. It is a secret building where mainly Gentiles live, sympathetic Gentiles who hate the Nazis. Soon all of this will be over. All of Europe is involved with the effort to defeat the Nazis. Even the Americans are involved. Yes, there is nothing to fear. Hiding will be the best way to wait out the war.

Jacob remembers his dream, the dream of the flag and of the horrible German soldier. Yes, it will be best to leave this house. His father would protect them from the Nazis. If not his father, then who?

And so, Ruben and Benjamin Horowitz, stripped of business, wealth, and pride, take their families to a small apartment complex on the outskirts of Hoboken, near the boatyards on the Schelde River. Here they will wait out the war. Here they will stay hunkered down in seclusion until Hitler is defeated by the Allies, or Belgium somehow overthrows its oppressors.

3

C leveland Hopkins International Airport was very busy. Planes from every carrier were delayed by the torrent of water, the thunder and lightning that passed over Ohio. Jacob Horowitz would be here for quite some time, for the plane scheduled to take him to Belgium had not even left New York.

Asher was a good boy. Oh, how much like his father, thought Jacob. Yes, indeed, Asher had achieved what his father had achieved in half the time, less than half. He had a mind for business and a temperament that exuded confidence. Everyone knew from the beginning Asher was the rightful heir to his father's fortunes. Even from the early days, he was working in the shop, learning the trade, cutting garments, sewing, shipping, and boxing merchandise. Jacob saw his willingness to learn and promoted it. He had always been tough on Asher, for the next in line would have to be more of a businessman and more of a political animal, more of a tyrant than he had ever been—more of a success.

"Listen to me, Asher," said Jacob to his son on his eighteenth birthday. "I am sending you to Harvard for a reason. Do you know what it is?"

"Yes, Papa."

"Tell me."

"So I can learn about business and run your company when you retire."

"And?"

"To meet people, Papa. To connect with others who are successful Jews."

"And what do I expect from you, Asher?"

"To be the best in my class. To get the highest grades."

"And if you do not?"

"You will send me home in shame, and I will pack merchandise with the unskilled laborers who work for you."

"And what do I always tell you, Asher?"

"Come home *with* your shield or *on* it."

Yes, Jacob Horowitz had been tough on both of his sons. Asher would fetch the stick no matter how far Jacob threw it. Jacob would throw it so outrageously far sometimes he would never expect his son to bring it back. But Asher always did. Oh, but at what price? Harvard was a success—Asher made summa cum laude, graduated in two years with a BA and received his MBA at the age of twenty-one. Farther and farther would Jacob throw the stick, and always Asher would bring it back, always a little more resentful, a little bit more worn, a small gleam in his eye that protested ever so slightly. The long hours, the fetching, cost him dearly. His wife, Ruth, nearly divorced him, his children were estranged. And then came little Rebecca.

It was a troubled birth right from the beginning. Ruth had thought she had miscarried, but the baby was still alive. The doctor said she would have to take it easy, that bed rest and regular checks would be the only way of maintaining the pregnancy.

"Why don't you abort it, Ruth," Asher said one night. "You don't need this anxiety. Our family is just too, too...busy for this."

"You mean *you're* too busy!" she screamed. "How dare you say such a thing to me. I run this house. I cook. I clean. I wash the clothes, feed the kids, get them off to school. What do you do, Asher? When are you ever around?" She stopped and sat down on a couch, rubbing her now bloated stomach. "Since when are you even a part of this family life?"

"I am giving you options, Ruth. You can do what you want." He paused and grabbed his coat. "I guess I'll tell Papa the kids can't come for supper tonight." But they did come, they did eat with Jacob, and the perfect family acted perfectly.

Ruth began to take on an enormous amount of fluid, bloating up as though her stomach would burst at any moment. On the day of her delivery, with Asher in California negotiating the opening of a new store, Ruth gave birth to Rebecca Ann Horowitz. And on that day Ruth cried. She cried that her husband was not there, that he did not want the child. But most importantly she cried that Rebecca Ann was diagnosed with Down's syndrome. From the day Rebecca was born, Asher would have no part of her. Ruth had tried to make contact between baby and father, had tried to force Asher to hold her, feed her, bond. But each time, Asher would do only what was required of him.

Jacob had seen this all before. Yes, his own life had been in such a fashion—close off the past, drive toward the future, you don't have time for the casualties. Oh yes, he had seen the signs, knew them all too well. The reasons were never clear cut. Jacob had once tried to analyze his own life, who could truly know all the machinations behind such cold actions? There was always other hidden and diabolical ones lurking just below the surface. He suspected Asher was like many fathers with a special needs child—place up a barrier so that when the worst happens the mind engages, separating itself from the emotions—the mind engages and commands by sheer will that all this has been planned from the outset—the great and terrible "I told you so." It could have been the conditioned response Jacob had stamped onto his warm and malleable wax: Come home *with* your shield or *on* it. So said the Spartan mothers to their sons who were off to war.

There is no room in the Horowitz family for outsiders. No room for the unwanted, the unlovable, the outcast. No father would confess to such an attitude, but Jacob knew from his son's early statements and his inattentiveness to Rebecca that it was so. And Asher knew it as well. He dove headfirst into his father's business and further and further from his uncomfortable situation at home.

Jacob was not concerned with Rebecca at first, but when he found out she was different than other children, that before her was a life of struggle, he started to get headaches. Liza had died just a year before. They had been married thirty-six years, and the absence was palpable. Maybe that is why Jacob took such interest in Rebecca. Maybe it was the long nights up in the attic, pulling out old pictures of his life in Belgium, of his mother and father and Sarah. Or maybe it was the pictures of the Delvauxs, of his best friend Pierre Chabot, or the old curmudgeon Gaston Delvigne. It could have been the wedding pictures of Yvonne. He would lay them all out like a card game. On one side his life in Belgium—on the other his life in America. The mountain that separated them was immense, a stone barricade Jacob had pieced together one rock at a time. But the rocks were tumbling down, and the pain and sorrow, the forgotten heroism, the terrible fear swooped about him and made his head throb.

Jacob had come to the hospital to see his new granddaughter. She was tiny and pink, creases across her limbs where joints bent, her face a rash of blotchy red. The signs of Down's syndrome were pronounced: flat neck, lowered ears, squinty eyes with the extra fold of skin. And the long thick tongue jutted out as though the mouth was inadequate to contain it. He saw her and his heart broke. A man who had shown little emotion soon wept over this little baby. He held her in his arms and rubbed her head.

"I was not around much for Asher," he said to Ruth as she lay in the hospital bed. "Those were hard times indeed. Nor was I truly there for Isaac." Jacob fell silent and smiled at Rebecca, her tiny socked feet pushing out into the air. The statement was neither sentimental nor emotional.

Ruth smiled and rubbed the bruise on her forearm from the intravenous tube. Jacob gave Rebecca back to her and walked out without saying another word.

A week later, Jacob showed up on Ruth's doorstep, and she invited him inside. He awkwardly gave her a wrapped gift for Rebecca. A small, red dress with a frilly hat.

"It's adorable, Jacob."

The old man's face brightened red, and he would not look at his daughter-in-law.

"Since Liza passed away, I really don't know what is in style or not. The woman at The Gap said this should fit Rebecca."

"Oh, it's precious," Ruth said.

Jacob walked over to Rebecca who was sound asleep in her bassinet. She was so tiny, her blotchy red face and hands a miracle. He stared at her for a long time in complete silence. Ruth offered him some tea. They sat quietly at the kitchen table.

"The other children? Are they around?" Jacob asked.

"No, they're at school." Ruth paused and sipped her tea. "I'm alone with Rebecca."

Jacob looked out the large bay window. He was ready to leave, ready to call off this stupid idea of spending time with his daughter-in-law. What in the world was he doing here? What could he possibly do to help the little baby. No, he had tried too late. Tried and failed. He gulped down the rest of his tea and began to rise.

"You know, Jacob, I have some vegetables in the garden that need to be picked, and I dare not leave Rebecca."

Jacob looked out the window again, this time focusing on the garden. He excused himself and went outside. The garden was large and rectangular: rows of beans, tomatoes, asparagus, lettuce, beets, melons, and long gangly corn stalks. The tomatoes were ripening beyond what Ruth and Asher could use, and so Jacob set about picking them and placing them in a wicker basket. He checked the beans, and the leaves of the melon plants for parasites and disease. He knelt down and pulled a weed from between the beds. Then another and another. Time passed and before he knew it, Ruth was calling him in for some lemonade. He stood and looked at the small, neat piles he had made. And this forced a memory. No, he would not think of the past, not those nights when he took out his boxes of pictures, placing each photo one next to the other. The neat piles of weeds reminded him of Pierre, of the enormous garden the Chabot family had cultivated.

He turned from Ruth's garden and walked inside. This was not the time to reflect. He would wait for Isaac. Isaac would understand it all, he would write it down. And he began to think more of his plan. The lemonade was sweet with a slight lemon bite. Jacob thanked Ruth for the refreshment and then drove around the rest of the day. He dare not go back to the empty house, the stacks of pictures. It would be too much.

Jacob placed the keys on the counter and walked into the kitchen, a large open expanse, oak island in the middle, stainless steel pots dangling off the overhead rack like a jester's crown. He pushed the message button on his answering machine. One message: "Pop, Ruth tells me you stopped over again. Is there something bothering you? Maybe we need to talk. Are we still on for Saturday's dinner?"

He walked over to the laundry room and shuffled through his sport bag for the sweat-soaked clothes. It was a good match. He had beaten Lereau one out of the three games. Jacob squeezed his hand into a fist, did this several times. His fingers were a bit arthritic, the knuckles showing a bulge. Old lady hands, he called them. It was hard to see one's life drifting toward its end. He opened the washer lid and tossed in his jock, his socks, a T-shirt with his store's logo in the upper right hand corner, and the soaking sweat bands—head and wrist.

What a game! The second one he could do no wrong. Lereau, a big man in his own right, carpenter paws, the pinky finger on his left hand crooked and twisted slightly—*Gives me that extra spin,* he said—Lereau could sense Jacob in the zone. Every shot was a kill. Bounce off the front wall, pick up the serve and send it to the side wall so it triangulates and drops in the corner near the back wall. Perfect. Everything he did was exact, precise. Come on baby! Come on! And then a quarter of an inch off the floor, front wall and dribble back to Lereau.

"You're hot, Jake." Lereau smiled and shook his head, sweat beading on his hooked nose. "Untouchable, baby."

Lereau was an interesting character with an uncanny resemblance to...

Jacob pulled the knob and hot water rushed into the drum. He poured the soap and softener into their appropriate places, then closed the lid. His head began to throb.

Lereau reminded him of...yes, of Pierre Chabot.

Lereau had played football in Florida, Tampa University. He had all sorts of awards including Little All American. He had a chance to play in the NFL, the San Francisco Forty-Niners, but chose to take another path. He had nine children and a happy life. Well, it was happy now. He had worked middle management with several paper companies—shipping trees here, lumber there. But the wealth he aquired was not making him happy. His family was in disarray during the seventies. His oldest son, a hippie, became unmanageable, punching Lereau, kicking holes in the walls, threatening the kids. What a story. Jacob was always shocked when Lereau recounted those horrors. Lereau began to hit the bottle, only on weekends, then too much all together—sneak some here; hide it there; honey, I'm working in the yard.

One day Lereau's oldest son came home and said, "Dad, I've been born again!" What was that? Jacob always loved to see Lereau's face as he mimicked his oldest son's expression—a cross between Bing Crosby and a sixties love child. And after all the mess settled down, his oldest son proved out this strange new experience, this amazing claim. He had been changed! Lereau listened to his son and his friends, at first from a distance, then one on one. He too made this commitment to Christ—an unfathomable thing to do, in Jacob's mind. And Lereau's life changed as well. Soon the whole family was going to church every Sunday, Bible studies, the whole shootin' match.

Jacob stood before the washing machine and listened to it hum. He rubbed his pounding head. Mrs. Chabot was like that—an unwavering belief in God, in the salvation of souls, praying for those who persecute you. Pierre's fervor was altogether different —his passionate belief in the good of man and the overthrow of the Nazis.

What a game, though! thought Jacob again, trying desperately to shift the boat in midstream. He had been unstoppable. Well, at least until the third game when Lereau came back with a strategy quite different than the first two games. Jacob had shown his mettle the second game, had shown the Gentile who was boss. That was all that mattered. He squeezed his hands into fists over and over, allowing the dull pain in his joints to work itself out. He cracked his knuckles, rubbing his hands and thinking of Belgium—all the while standing in front of the thumping and humming washing machine. Then he turned around and stepped into the kitchen.

He had all sorts of wonderful meats in the freezer—fillet, porterhouse, fresh walleye from Lake Erie—but he opted for a sandwich and some chips. Cooking was just too much trouble, too much energy for one person anymore. He thought of Liza, of her roaming the large kitchen like a machine, every cabinet, every drawer, its contents known, organized, and labeled. "Could you get me the ginger, honey," she would say. "Over to your right. Keep going. Keep going. Stop. There. No, up one. Yes. It should be in the fourth row." Now, it was a maze of confusion. If he was honest with himself, it was a terror.

One night shortly after Liza died, Jacob decided to make a dinner for himself, a consolation dinner—a porterhouse, large salad, baked potato. As the steak cooked on the grill, he frantically searched for the salad tongs. Drawer after drawer, cabinet after cabinet. The grill smoked, and he ran outside to flip the steak over. He ran back in the kitchen—so many drawers, so many places for the thing to hide. The grill smoked, and he frantically began pulling drawers open, leaving them open. A salad tong, that was all he wanted. A stupid salad tong, and the porterhouse burned up. A simple salad tong rushed him headlong into his wife's death. He smelled the carbon as the steak sizzled and smoldered. Just a stupid salad tong, and he was suddenly lost in a rage of confusion, torment, and unbearable grief. He ripped the drawers out, letting them fall to the tiled floor. Utensils and various objects bounced and skidded upon the slate gray tile, and still he raged, until he was exhausted. Then, huddled on the floor, convulsing in silent sobs and horrible gasps of air, he looked up. In a white marble container, along with wooden spoons and spatulas, there all along, were the salad tongs.

So, on this night—after his evening handball game—Jacob pulled out the sliced roast beef, the cheese, and the hot mustard. He knew where they were, for he had put them away. He placed his sandwich on a paper plate and piled some chips into a heaping mass. Why he did that he didn't know, for chips always fell onto the floor as he walked into the living room. He set the flimsy plate on the coffee table, clicked on the TV, and surfed through the stations: CNN—too liberal, CSPAN—only for sleepless nights, MSNBC—what was that anyway? There, Fox News. Jacob enjoyed losing himself in the discourse of the evening. It was easy television, mindless. Attach like a lamprey to the conservative, identify the liberal enemy, and munch the sandwich—as easy as that. Hour after hour, the spinning, flip-flopping world of politics. And all the while he could forget about his dead wife, Belgium, and his sick little grandchild.

But these days, like some insect caught in a scent loop, he would eventually find his way to the attic, to the boxes of pictures, to his long forgotten past. The procedure was almost ritualistic, a sacred right. First carry the boxes downstairs one at a time. Then, with a cup of coffee neatly placed on the coffee table—the brewing time, the delay between opening the boxes and that first cup of coffee was crucial—he would pull the first box to him, between his legs, like a child at Christmas opening a present. His puffy hand would rub across the smooth paper top. This had been done so many times there was no dust. A pause. A deep breath. Then Jacob would remember the coffee. He always remembered it at this time. And with a trembling hand he would sip the steaming cup and place it back on its saucer. The ritual would start again: a rub, a pause, a deep breath, and then he would open the box.

The boxes were a talisman, a mysterious oracle that drew him. If he was one to make connections, he would have drawn a line directly from his wife's death to Rebecca's birth and then straight to his secret past. But he was not one for connections, not now. And so as he pulled the envelopes of pictures from the musty boxes, he recounted the reasons why at this time and this moment in his life, these pictures captivated him so. The answer was always the same: a void with no response. Each envelope and every picture was placed in chronological order. Each part of his separated life was placed on one side of his legs or the other: America to the right, Belgium to the left. And then he would once again remember his coffee, now cold, on the coffee table. This was the perfect time to take a break and warm the cup in the microwave. His joints were stiff from the hours at the boxes, and the surge to his feet placed an intolerable pressure on his prostate—pain, then relief as the buttocks once again absorbed the blood back into its muscles. The whole house was dark, silent, a single light above the sink casting shadows on the floor. With several presses of a button, the microwave spun the cup around in a soothing circle. Never mind that an entire pot of coffee was still steaming on the coffeemaker. No, this was the routine; don't think, just do. Beep, beep, beep. Take the coffee from the little box and go back to the pictures. But by this time the fascination had worn off. He was tired, mad that he had once again succumbed to the boxes in the attic. And like every time before, he would shuffle the pictures up with a humph of rage, place them in the boxes and carry them back upstairs.

But this time he picked up the phone and dialed the airlines. "Two tickets to Belgium, please. Yes, Brussels. I want to leave from Cleveland." He gave the man a departure date, his Visa number and then hung up. Yes, yes indeed. He would go back. But this time he would take Isaac. It was an absurd plan. He laughed out loud as he turned off the bathroom light—always going to the bathroom these days, would be going all night because of the coffee. He would have to call his son. That would be the hard part. Yes, Isaac would be the one, must be the one, the only one that could.

He pulled the covers across the queen-size bed, placing various pillows on his wife's side, then stacking some up near his head. The empty void suddenly stretched out before him. He could feel the terrible pain in his head returning, a throbbing, piercing into his skull. He rubbed his forehead and found he was sweating. This would be a hard night, convulsions of sobs lay just beneath the surface. He reached over to the nightstand and set his alarm (as though he planned to get some sleep). He needed to pick Ruth's garden in the morning, weed it, maintain some order. Then, he picked up the remote control and turned on the television. Tonight would be a night for CSPAN.

Asher had sat in the restaurant waiting for his father. He was now fifteen minutes late. Asher ordered a martini and stirred the olive around until it dipped below the ice. At twenty-five after the hour Jacob walked through the door, and Asher watched his father smile politely to those waiting to be seated. He had thrown a suit coat over a polo shirt, khaki pants, and tennis shoes. Asher gulped down the remains of the drink. Jacob searched the room for his son and sauntered over.

"Sorry for my tardiness," Jacob said reaching out his hand for a shake. "There were just too many vegetables in your garden. You would not believe how the tomatoes have come on. And the corn—"

"At least you could have washed up before coming here, Pop."

Jacob pulled back his arm and looked at the dried dirt in his fingernails and across his palm.

"Well, I guess I had better wash them before lunch."

Jacob smiled and headed to the restroom. That was a blessing anyway. He suddenly needed to relieve himself. The medication was not working as the doctor had hoped.

Jacob returned and sat across from his son. The waiter appeared to take drink orders.

"Another martini for me. Add extra olives," Asher said. "Pop, can I get you a mixed drink?"

"Oh no, no, no. Uh," he paused searching the menu, "do you have lemonade?" The waiter nodded. "I will have a nice tall glass of that. Uh, with plenty of ice. Thank you." Jacob smiled at the waiter as he walked away. "You know, Asher, Ruth makes the most marvelous lemonade. It pokes at the taste buds just enough to make the juices flow. Do you know what I mean?"

Asher rubbed his empty martini glass with thumb and forefinger. "Yes, Pop. I've had her lemonade."

"I never realized how much I missed simple things like that. Just the right amount of sugar and just enough to—"

"I get the point, Pop."

The waiter returned with their drinks and the two ordered lunch. There was an awkward pause as they waited for their food.

"Your melons are beginning to really grow, Asher," Jacob said finally. "You should see them. The kids are all excited about the pumpkins for Halloween. Sometimes we sit out there in the afternoon and play guessing games over how big they will get."

"Yes, Pop, I've seen the garden."

"And how about those cucumbers. Did you notice the ones on the far right are just not as green and as ripe as the others? I bet it's the soil mixture. Perhaps it needs a bit more nitrogen. And let me tell you, the corn—"

"Stop it. Just stop it." Asher lifted his glass to his mouth and gulped his drink.

"What? All I'm doing is talking about your garden."

"What is happening to you?"

"What? I can't talk about your garden? I talk about the garden and this offends my son? Can I talk about the weather? Would that be less offensive?"

"Ruth calls me up and tells me you're over at the house, outside, weeding the garden. That you come every day."

"Should I stop coming, Asher? Does Ruth mind me coming? I'll stop coming over. I didn't know I was bothering her. I thought she enjoyed having me over. She tells me she enjoys me being there."

Asher nodded. "Yes, yes, yes. She does enjoy you over there, Pop. She thinks it's great you're spending time with the grandkids."

"Then what is the problem?"

Asher gulped his drink again. Jacob smiled ever so slightly, enjoying his son's panic. They munched on their salads in silence.

"I think I will take Ruth and the kids to the lake next week some time," Jacob said. "She just seems so cooped up in that house."

"What are you doing?" Asher hissed.

Jacob lifted his arms, hunching his shoulders as if to say, "What?"

"This! This coming over all of the sudden. This, *Have you seen* the garden, Asher? Have you sat with your kids by the garden, Asher? When was the last time you took Ruth and the kids anywhere, Asher?" He gulped his drink and there was no more liquid in the glass. He ordered another one.

"That stuff will kill you, Asher."

"What do you mean, that stuff? You used to put me under the table at our power lunches. You were the king of the martini!" Asher stopped and pointed his finger at Jacob. "That! That is what I am talking about."

Jacob hunched his shoulders again in reply.

"No, I mean it. What is that-stuff-will-kill-you all about? What is going on with you? You never used to spend any time with us, let alone without me there, and suddenly you're telling me about my garden, about my wife, about my kids. Well, I don't need it from you. *Especially* from you!"

The waiter returned with another drink. Asher fell silent. As soon as the waiter was gone, he started up again.

"You of all people have no right to barge into my life like this. Pointing your finger at me, accusing me of neglect. How dare you! *You* of all people! For heaven's sake, Pop! Where were you when I was alone with Mom? Where were you when Isaac left? *You* of all people should not be throwing stones!"

Jacob rubbed his forehead, looked earnestly at his son. "I was wrong and I want to change, Asher."

Asher shook his head. "Oh no, Pop. It's not that easy. Oh no. No. No!" He sipped his drink, but his hand was shaking. "You can't just come in here one day and decide once and for all that you, the great Jacob Horowitz, made a mistake with raising your children. It's not that easy, Pop. Oh no. You are not going to sit across from me and tell me how to run my family. The man who all but abandoned his for the almighty dollar, the one who told me to bring my shield home or don't come home at all, that man has no business telling me *anything!*"

Others in the restaurant turned to see what was the matter, then went back to their eating and talking.

"I can't change, Asher? A man who has lived all his life as a lie, a man who focused on the wrong agenda all his life cannot say he was wrong and he wants to make amends?"

"Yes, other men perhaps. But not Jacob Horowitz to his son. No, I cannot accept those words from you." Asher leaned across the table. "You made me, Pop. I learned it all from you, every phrase and every action. What one learns in a lifetime cannot be taken back over lunch. No way."

There was silence. Jacob's head was throbbing again.

"I am going to Belgium," Jacob said in a whisper.

"When?"

"I leave in a month."

"Why are you going to Belgium?"

Jacob hesitated. "I need to go back. That's all I can say. I want to take Isaac."

Asher suddenly gulped down his drink and shook his head.

"No. I will not hear this from you. I am through talking to a crazy man."

He stood up, pulling out his money clip and three twenties. He threw them on the table in disgust. He was about to say something else but the words would not come. And then, like a father to a son, he said, "I'll see you at dinner on Saturday." And Asher walked out of the restaurant in a controlled rage.

Jacob ordered another lemonade and sat quietly for some time sipping it, allowing the bitterness to distract him from his headache. The waiter came by to ask if everything was okay. Yes, it was okay. Here is the tip. Thank you.

It was crazy to do what he just did, Jacob thought. It was crazy to explain to his son what was happening in his life. How can anyone apologize for a lifetime of wrongs? He suddenly felt a weight in his abdomen working its way downward. Soon there would be no time to say anything at all. Then what? And Jacob stood up and walked out of the restaurant. He would not go back to the house, not just yet. Ruth's garden needed watering. And he rubbed his head as the pain beat against his skull.

4

It is 1942 and the Horowitz family is in hiding. Ruben, Rachael, Jacob, and Sarah along with Benjamin Horowitz and his family are hiding out in an apartment complex on the outskirts of Hoboken, near the boatyards on the Schelde River. The Horowitz family is not the only Jewish family in the complex. In fact on several occasions, late in the evening or early morning, Jacob has seen young Jewish children wandering in and out of dark hallways and into other apartments close by.

Jacob wakes early in the morning and looks out the window at the Schelde River, at its wide girth and the tugboats slogging their way toward the docks. Sarah is asleep near him, wrapped in a blanket, her thin face peaceful and lost in the world between heaven and earth. Jacob has not been able to sleep very well since the family's return to Antwerp. A tugboat's whistle, low and melancholy, fills the salty air around the apartment. Here they are safe from the poison Jacob's father keeps mentioning. Here on the outskirts of the world, they will wait out the German occupation. Jacob knows this to be false. Deep in his heart he fears for his life, for the life of his family. This is how he spends his nights. But the sun coming over the horizon, red and orange, the chill of the fall and the swooping seagulls bring hope to his mind. Today is market day, a chance for him to escape the confines of the apartment and the tension building between Uncle Benjamin and Jacob's father.

The previous night was like so many others. For quite some time, Ruben has been putting out fires as fast as his brother Benjamin lights them. The argument smolders during dinner.

"What is this?" says Uncle Benjamin, throwing up his arms in disgust.

There is silence as the soup is poured into his bowl. Several pieces of potato plop into the thin broth. Jacob looks at his mother and then over to his uncle. Jacob sees his father lifting his hand ever so slightly to wave off his wife's response.

"Is there a problem, Benjamin?" Ruben asks politely, taking spoon in hand and dipping it into the broth.

"Is there a problem, my brother asks?" Benjamin puts down his spoon next to his bowl. "Is there a problem?" He picks up the spoon and stirs around the small hump in the middle. "This is the problem, Ruben. This!" He stabs the potato and severs it in half. "This, my brother, is the problem."

"You don't like the soup, Benjamin?"

"Like the soup? Like the soup, my brother asks? I sleep and wake, sleep and wake, sleep and wake all for potato soup! This is what I wake up for. This is what I go to sleep for. Potato soup!" He places his spoon down again and looks across the table at Jacob's mother. "Just once would I like to see some meat, some vegetables, something different."

Jacob's mother sips her broth, but her anger is boiling up to her face, a rose color now appearing on her neck and cheeks.

"You complain every night, Benjamin, and every night I tell you this is the way it must be. I tell you every night, dear brother, that meat and vegetables are precious, and we cannot afford to buy any. To get them is to risk something I do not even dare think about." Ruben pauses, rubs the table with his hands as though allowing the anger to ease its way out through his fingertips. "Now, we eat our soup and be thankful we have this to eat, that God is merciful to us, that we have our families."

The families sit in silence, each in turn allowing the tension to disappear, to evaporate somewhere in the small dining room, through the peeling plaster and dingy, smoke-stained ceiling. Sarah is looking pale and undernourished. The children need meat and fresh vegetables, but the streets are filled with Brownshirts.

Just last month a letter came for Jacob's father—a letter from Hans Kraemer, their friend. Hans enclosed a note that was posted in all government windows. A rumor had circulated that the SS was rounding up all male Jews and taking them off to concentration camps. Hans had written that many Jews were rounded up that week. Now in this follow-up letter, Hans had enclosed a note from the SS stating "it was all a mistake. Only foreign Jews were taken, Jews that had come illegally from other countries. All native born Jews are in no danger whatsoever. It would be good for Belgian Jews to show themselves, so the SS can separate the foreign Jews from those who belong in Belgium. Food is scarce and provisions are going to be handed out to Belgian Jews only." Hans Kraemer had urged Ruben to come out of hiding, that he thought the worst was over, that finally some order was being restored to Belgium.

Ruben thought over the letter long and hard. He discussed it with Benjamin after breakfast one morning. Benjamin thought it was best to be counted in the census, that it was the right of every Belgian Jew to receive the food that was due him.

"What if this is a trap?" Ruben says.

"How can it be a trap?"

"I have been talking to others. Relatives and families have been secretly rounded up. They are gone—suddenly, without warning. I do not trust these letters."

"And what do we do, my brother?" Benjamin sighs. "The world is righting itself and we starve in our hole, watch our children waste away before our eyes? No, I say we leave this place and go back to our houses where we can get food and proper treatment. Enough of this potato soup!"

"What have we to change our minds, Benjamin? Why should we suddenly trust the very people who tried to stop us from fleeing the country? No, I disagree completely. Time is our greatest friend, time and secrecy. If we go out from here, then we have limited our choices. And choices are the difference between life and death."

Benjamin rubs his hands over the worn wooden table. His brow is furrowed with thought, and Ruben understands what he is thinking.

"No, my brother, I cannot let you jeopardize my family."

"How can our leaving jeopardize your family?"

"If you are caught, if this is another trick, then you will be forced to give us away. No, we must all be here together."

Benjamin knows this is true, knows this to be right and is silent and sad for it. Jacob sits in a corner and listens, thinking himself a mouse—staring out of the hole at the cheese in the trap, staring, gaunt and weak, wondering if one bite of cheese is worth even death.

It is not long after that discussion that Hans Kraemer sends another note. Thousands of Jews showed themselves, came to the cheese—and the trap closed. They had vanished like all those before them.

Today is market day. Today will be the first day Jacob leaves the apartment and goes to the butcher for some meat and to the market for fresh vegetables. The tensions have been high in the apartment, and Benjamin has convinced Ruben that Jacob will not be in danger, for he is below the age of identification. He does not have to have Jew written on his identification card.

Jacob stands before his father and mother, Rachael showing fear, face creased and eyes wide.

"Do you have the list, Jacob?" his father asks.

"Yes, Papa."

"And the money? Ruben, did you give him the money?"

"Yes, yes, he has the money." Ruben turns to his son. "You do have the money I gave you, Jacob?"

"Yes, Papa."

"Now what are you to say to the clerks at the store?" Rachael says, rubbing Jacob's hair with her slender hands, stroking her son like a pet, calming him down—or calming herself down, reassuring herself more than her son. "What are you to say to the clerks?"

"That I need these groceries from the list. That my mother is unable to come today. My mother asked me to buy these items on the list."

Ruben stands tall before his son and holds his wife's hand. He squeezes it firmly. "He will do just fine, Rachael. He will do just fine."

Jacob is about to walk out the door when Uncle Benjamin runs up to him. "Jacob, buy me some cigarettes like a good little boy. And buy yourself a piece of candy with the change."

"No," Ruben says. "No, Benjamin. He is only going to buy the essentials, only what is on the list. We dare not risk anything else for now."

Benjamin shrugs his shoulders—a shrug Jacob will forever use, a free wheeling gesture that indicates, "What? What did I say? What is the problem? What?"

"You know he is to buy only what is on the list, Benjamin," Ruben says.

"What is the problem with a pack of cigarettes? What?" And Benjamin shrugs his shoulders again and looks directly at Jacob for some sort of reply.

"Keep your money, Benjamin. Jacob is not buying anything but what is on the list."

Benjamin retracts the money, as if it is dirty, as if he were caught sneaking a dab of icing from a birthday cake. And Jacob wanders out the door.

He is familiar with the route, for he has been to downtown Antwerp many times with his father. He tells the cabdriver to pull off several blocks from the center of town, pays his fare, and walks the rest of the way. The wind is cold, becoming colder as fall approaches winter. He puts his hands in his coat pockets and decides not to think too hard upon what he is about to do. But something happens. He sees the empty streets, the German guards standing and smoking on street corners, the large rippling red and white flags with the swastika in the center. He steps up to a crosswalk. A German guard, young, probably about eighteen, sucks on a cigarette. He is standing with his buddy, and their voices sound harsh and mean.

Jacob looks one way and then the other. The street is empty. He is focused on one objective: cross the street and move as fast as he can from the two German guards. They are laughing about something. A car appears and then zooms by. Finally, it is time to go.

The Germans are spouting off something harsh now, something more biting than the conversation just a moment before. He dare not look over, but he can sense that the mood on the corner has changed. He begins to think about all his parents told him. He lists the options in his head, trying to find the appropriate response. But he cannot find the appropriate response, for he has not been asked anything. He begins to panic. He feels as though a secret sign has suddenly appeared in the air above his head: *Jew! Jew in hiding! Jew!*

The German voices are louder now, but Jacob is ready to cross the street. And then somebody grabs his shoulder. He turns around and is face to face with the German soldier, mouth drawn down in anger. It is the German from his dream. He cannot tell the difference now, for the two images have blended into one. Jacob is frozen with fear. The German is shouting something at him, putting out his hand and asking for something: *"Ihre Papieren! Ihre Papieren!"*

If Jacob could just breathe, just clear his head, he would see that the question is calm and even a bit aloof, as though the young German soldier is saying it out of habit more than anything else. If only he could clear his head, he would realize the other German soldier is still talking about the girl he met last night, the fight he had with her, and the slap that came as a result. They are both laughing, but Jacob cannot see this. He is trapped in his head, in a world of horrible poison with evil men who wish to kill all of his family. And just like that, Jacob bolts across the street, just missing a car, runs for all of his life and does not turn around until he reaches the market place.

It is early morning and the merchants have flooded the streets. Jacob races into the throng and darts behind a cart on wheels. It is a man selling assorted chops. Jacob bends down as though tying his shoe and looks up half expecting the two German guards to race into the market square. But they are not there. They will not be there, for they were laughing at the scared Belgian boy with his hands in his pockets and his eyes large and round with fear. Jacob lifts his head and pushes it above the row of chops, ribs, and pigs' feet. He is staring directly into the lifeless, black orbs of a severed pig's head with its pink leathery skin and a reddish jagged trunk. He hurries toward the butcher shop where his mother has told him to go.

The small store is full of women—women in fine clothes, women with hats, some poor women, some with dark drab clothes. He pushes his way in line, but soon realizes he has lost the list. A panic seizes him. He turns directly into a rather round woman with rosy cheeks, thick chin, and bright hat. She smiles at Jacob, but he responds only by moving past her and standing near the back. She follows him. Jacob reaches into his pants: empty. He reaches into his back pockets: empty. He frantically searches his coat again and finds only the small rolled up wad of money his father has given him.

"What seems to be the problem, young man?" says the fat woman with the bright hat and the thick chin. She kneels down to his level and her face changes. She stares long into his eyes, probing, searching his thoughts. She whispers: "You have lost something, sweetie?"

Jacob nods, does not know why he nods, but feels a force beyond himself pulling him down this undiscovered road.

"You have lost your money?" the large woman questions, a bit of warmth that was there all along but now detectable for the first time to Jacob.

Jacob shakes his head, no.

"You have lost the list your mother has given you, haven't you?"

Jacob nods. The large woman looks around and then her face stiffens. There is a tall, thin man standing on the doorstep of the store. He is smoking a cigarette and wearing a dark black hat and leather Gestapo overcoat. The woman leans toward Jacob once again, this time in a whisper, warm and full of compassion.

"Your mother is sick, isn't that right? She has sent you to get your food, for you haven't eaten any meat or vegetables for quite some time, isn't that right?"

Jacob nods his head, a small tear streaming down his left cheek.

"Oh, now, now, sweetie, we mustn't make a fuss." She looks across Jacob's shoulder at the man in the doorway. "Not with such bad people around. You understand? Do you understand what I am telling you, sweetie?"

Jacob nods again.

"Come with me." She suddenly stops and bends down once again. "What is your name, little one?" Jacob is about to answer, when she cuts him off. "No, no, don't tell me, my little darling. It is better that such things are not said. I will call you Edward. Do you understand—Edward. You are my nephew, and I am buying groceries for us. Do you understand, Edward?"

Jacob is not clear about what has transpired. He is scared and his legs feel like heavy steel rods. She walks up to the counter with him at her side. She begins to pick out cuts of meat.

"Having a party, Mrs. Tupa?" says the butcher with a smile.

"Yes, I'm having special guests tonight at my table. Guests who deserve the very best cuts, special guests indeed." She hesitates and taps the glass, choosing this and declining that, testing the thickness of this steak and that one. Jacob watches as the butcher wraps up the beautiful pieces of meat and puts them in a paper bag for Mrs. Tupa. Jacob follows her out of the butcher's shop and past the man in the dark hat and leather overcoat. He pays them only a passing glance. They wander together through the throng of merchants, Jacob doing all he can to keep up. Mrs. Tupa purchases several bags of fresh vegetables, some Jacob has heard of, others he has never seen. With three large bags filled, Mrs. Tupa takes Jacob to her car and driver. Jacob hesitates and then sits down upon the rich leather seats. The driver loads the bags into the back of the car, and Jacob remembers the money his father gave him. He gives the wad of bills to Mrs. Tupa, but she refuses it. "You will need your money later. This is a special gift from those who care." She stares at Jacob for quite some time and then taps the glass that separates her from her driver. She pauses. "What part of the city do you live in—be careful not to tell me exact locations." Jacob tells her it is close to the river. She taps the glass again and tells the driver where to take them. "I will drop you off several blocks from where you live so as not to raise suspicion."

After several minutes the car slows to a stop. "Now, my Edward, it is time for us to part. I hope your family enjoys this, and that this small token will encourage them." Mrs. Tupa takes out a piece of paper and hastily writes a message on it. "Give this to your parents, it will explain everything." She reaches over and pats Jacob on the head. "God bless you and your family, Edward." She smiles warmly and Jacob leaves the car, never to see her again.

There is stunned disbelief as Rachael takes the food out of the bags. Ruben is concerned, Benjamin delighted, for contained in the bags are several packs of cigarettes.

"But she said nothing to you?" Ruben asks. "This is not good—or this is too good to be true. Of which, I don't know."

Jacob gives his father the note from Mrs. Tupa. It is a warm and encouraging note that has no signature. Again, Jacob tells the story of losing the list and the large woman with the pretty hat coming over to assist him.

"All this food, Ruben," Rachael exclaims with bewilderment. "I will separate it into smaller portions and we can save it as long as possible."

Ruben sits down with the roll of money he gave Jacob. He sits in silence for quite some time. "There is still good in the world, Rachael. The darkness has not yet fallen completely." He rubs the money with his thumb. "Tonight we shall celebrate this goodness. Tonight we shall thank God and eat well."

That night the Horowitz family does eat well, and there is a breath of fresh air with each bite of the meat, with each fragrant whiff of greens and onions that erodes the fear and anxiety that has settled upon them. It is a feast to remember.

5

J acob stares at his sister, her eyes wide, tears welling up and leaking down her face. Jacob is frightened as well, but he wraps his arms around Sarah's thin body and pulls her close. The voices are louder. Ruben watches through a crack in the window as two German guards talk with the superintendent of the apartment complex. The guards are laughing and pointing off to the river. A German staff car pulls up, Nazi flags on either side of the front end, stiff, ominous. A man steps out, a tall thin man with long dark boots and black leather overcoat.

This incident is no surprise to the Horowitz family, for they have been planning for something like this. All of Belgium is dangerous now. More roundups have occurred, secret roundups, taking the victims by surprise. The horror stories are many. Hans Kraemer has been in touch with a father and son team, Jules and Andre Biset, in Brussels. These two Belgian citizens are the conduit for the British intelligence and the lead contact for all of the Belgian Underground. As the noose tightens around the strangled country that separates France and Germany, "a new man has been brought in," warns the Belgium Underground, "a new man to take care of the remaining Jews. He is highly trained in the sciences of detection and hates all Jews indiscriminately." With the Wolf leading the searches, the German forces have systematically captured and murdered hundreds of families.

One evening when Ruben is out meeting Hans, a neighbor pounds upon the Horowitzes' door. Rachael runs to it and responds with the secret password. She waits for the reply and then lets the young man into the apartment.

"We have just gotten word: The Germans have started another roundup on the west side of Antwerp, in Deurne." Rachael thanks the man and then bolts the door behind him. There have been several roundups in the last year but none making their way as far as the Schelde River. Rachael hurries over to Jacob and Sarah.

"Now, children, you know what we must do. You remember what Papa has taught us, what food to gather and where to hide." She hesitates as there is a dog barking out in the yard. "Let us make haste and do what we have practiced." Jacob takes Sarah and they both gather up their bedding. Rachael talks to Benjamin and his wife. They too gather up their essentials and begin to make their way into the secret room Ruben and Benjamin have built, a room that once was a closet, now looking no different than the papered wall that lines the hallway. Everyone knows the drill, but fear grabs at each of their legs, their stomachs.

"What about Papa?" Jacob asks.

Rachael looks worried, and she strokes his head. "Papa will be okay, my lamb. He knows what to do." She looks out the window expecting at any moment to see German trucks and solders with machine guns. There is only darkness. She whispers a prayer for her husband.

An hour goes by and Rachael and Uncle Benjamin wait by the window, lights off, all the others hidden in the secret room. When they see the Germans or when they hear the three-knock code from downstairs, they too will enter the hidden room. Another hour goes by. Rachael looks out the window and sees the night sky, the myriad stars. Such a beautiful night, such a beautiful country, such evil in the world. Uncle Benjamin lights a cigarette.

"You should not smoke, Benjamin."

"What? What will happen? How long has it been, Rachael? Nothing." He sucks in the smoke with a sense of pleasure.

Suddenly, a car pulls into the parking lot, lights flashing across the building. Benjamin ducks into the shadows while Rachael surveys the scene. She searches the road: no lights. She looks again at the parked car and realizes it is one of the tenants of the building. Benjamin revives his smashed out cigarette and sucks it back to life. Another hour passes with not a stir.

By now a strange sense of peace and panic has settled upon the family. Rachael leaves to check on the others in the room. When she appears fifteen minutes later, Benjamin is fast asleep.

"Wake up! Wake up!" she hisses, shaking Benjamin. "All we need is one slip up like this—just one—and we are lost! Our children taken from us!" Benjamin starts up and wipes his face with his hands. "Do you understand me, Benjamin?"

"Forgive me, Rachael. I only dozed for a moment. Just a moment. Forgive me, it will not happen again."

Rachael looks at Benjamin and then back to the room. "This time we are lucky—God be praised—this time." She hurries over to the secret room and tells the others it will be best if they stay there for the night. She closes the door partway, Sarah and Jacob already asleep with their cousins.

Several hours pass and Ruben has not returned. Rachael and Benjamin are worried. Then, just as the two begin to nod off, the door opens and Ruben walks into the room.

Rachael hugs Ruben and kisses him on the lips. "You are freezing, my husband. We have been so worried!"

Ruben calms her and walks her and his brother over to the kitchen table. Rachael makes some coffee, and Ruben tells his story.

Hans and Ruben had met in the town of Borgerhout in the heart of Antwerp. As Hans was telling him about the latest movements of the allied troops, the latest hot spots for Germans, the roundup began. They noticed Gestapo and SS troops flooding the streets demanding to see identity papers. Hans decided he and Ruben should separate and join up south of the city on a road they both knew and where Hans would be waiting with a car.

Ruben knew his only hope of escape was the nearby woods. The woods, a small island in the middle of several blocks, would be the easiest route to the designated location—the fastest and straightest route to safety. But Ruben was sure SS troops were there. It would be very dangerous. He scurried into the darkness of the wood, tree by tree, shadow by shadow. He could hear the chaos of the roundup, knew the fear and terror in the poor Jewish families. Up against a tree, on the ground, then into the shadows of another tree. Soon he was perfectly still, heart pounding, heightened senses—hearing, feeling, smelling. A movement on the fringe told him a soldier was nearby. A sudden glow of a cigarette proved it. He crept slowly, step by step, backwards toward the heart of the wood, using a large oak as a shield. And then, with a quick burst of speed, he darted down a narrow dirt path.

As he moved toward the end of the wood, he froze and pulled into the shadows. Five or six SS men were walking the border of the forest. He crept up to a large oak tree and squatted in the hovel of an immense and winding root. The dampness of the night, the coming of winter bit into his face and hands. A German shepherd barked in the distance, and Ruben pushed even further into the tree. He thought of his wife, of his children—who would carry the family if he were taken? He forced his mind to focus on the here and now, using the fear to clear his thoughts of anything but the present and looked out at the guards one more time. Hans's car was off in the distance. Several trees blocked the guards from the car. He darted from the seclusion of the wood and to the first large maple. Then again, and again. He could hear the guards talking about something. One of them was calling for the dogs. "Let's comb the woods! Quick! Quick! Check the perimeter! Quick!" Ruben could see Hans waiting for him in his car. One more tree to go. And then with one last burst of energy, Ruben dashed toward the shadow of the car. He could hear the weeping of young children, the rapid fire of the German machine guns, the screams of the mothers. The car door closed all of this out, and Hans slowly moved the car—lights off—down the winding road that would take them both toward safety.

"Oh, my husband," cries Rachael, again hugging and kissing Ruben. "What would we do without you?"

Benjamin rubs the sleep from his eyes and sips his coffee. "What news from Hans, Ruben?"

Ruben cups his hands around his mug of coffee and looks long and hard at his wife and then over to his brother.

"There is a new man heading up the roundups. I have seen firsthand his style. He leaves nothing unturned. They call him the Wolf." Ruben sips his coffee, and his hands tremble. "I fear this is evil tidings for us, my brother."

"But we have made it so far," Benjamin says. "We have the secret room, the room we made together. It is a safe place, Ruben."

"A secret room will not hide us from this monster," Ruben whispers. "We are at great risk here."

Rachael grabs his arm. "But fleeing the country now is futile, my husband."

"No, no, we can't flee. That is for certain. This is the safest place there can be right now. Perhaps they will overlook us. Perhaps there are too many Gentiles here for them to worry about us. Perhaps, perhaps, perhaps."

There is silence, and all three stare at the table in thought. Belgium is getting smaller, suffocating, soon it will become a tiny dot in a sea of terror.

"They have taken out the communications network in Brussels," Ruben says. "Jules Biset and his son Andre have been caught. Andre was beaten to death during the interrogation." Ruben rubs his eyes briefly, trying to contain the emotion. "Jules was murdered during the raid—in front of his son."

There is silence again.

"The underground is strong, Ruben," says Benjamin suddenly with great emotion. "There is a vast force, unseen and powerful working against such evil."

"Yes, Hans has told me about a police chief in Charleroi who is networking an Underground railroad system. There is strength in the south. Someone near La Louvière has taken control of the Belgian Underground. Yes, there is strength, but it is not in Antwerp. Not here. And that is where we are."

The Wolf tightens the noose around Antwerp, arrests more and more Jewish families, Jewish families who had thought for all the world they were safe.

Benjamin is cranky, for they have been forced to eat potatoes once again. He is irritable and his cigarettes have run out weeks ago. Tensions are high and the dam breaks one afternoon when Jacob is sent out to get cigarettes and candy. Uncle Benjamin, unbeknownst to Ruben and Rachael, sends him out under threat of punishment. Jacob returns several hours later. After Rachael has nearly come to blows with Benjamin, and after a good scolding from Ruben, Jacob is sent to his room.

There are Brownshirts everywhere; the Wolf uses them as his primary force to root out hiding Jews. While Jacob is out getting cigarettes, he is questioned by a Brownshirt. He is asked for his identity papers, and asked where his parents reside. He lies and is eventually released, but Ruben knows how the trap works. Jacob was probably shadowed for quite some time. Jacob swears he was not.

And one morning all of their fears come to fruition. The Wolf has shown up at their apartment complex. He wears small round glasses, which give his long narrow face a sinister look. His lips are thick and wet, and the tip of his cigarette is soggy. He questions the apartment owner and searches his face.

Ruben stares out the curtained window, sweat beading and dripping down the side of his face. The children and his brother hide out in the secret room—a room that seems so inadequate now, its promise of defense laughable. A thought races through Ruben's head: Give yourself up to this monster, save your family. But the voice of reason takes over, and he stays put, pulling back from the windowpane.

Jacob squeezes his sister, calming her fear. Rachael helps Benjamin and his wife calm their children. Before the guards appeared, there was the sudden knock from below, the secret taps that warned them danger was imminent. In a calm panic, they grab food and blankets, and all of them hurry to the secret room. Jacob is old enough to feel the fear, a fear he will never forget, a fear he will know for the next several years. He looks around at the panic on his uncle's and aunt's faces and the darkness of the room. He thinks if only they could vanish, like ghosts, creep down the stairs past the guards, past the barking dogs, float away to the horizon and to somewhere safe. But the screams of the soldiers and the frenzied dogs wake him from this dream, pulling him back into the tiny room hidden behind a thin veneer of paper and paste.

Ruben stays by the window as a lookout. And when he sees the Wolf and the SS guards with their dogs, his mouth goes dry. Several tenants come out and talk with the Wolf. He calmly stares at the building, adjusts his glasses and turns to his officers. There is a strong protest from one of the tenants, a baldheaded man, but the Wolf ignores him. The baldheaded tenant disappears into one of the buildings.

The Wolf points to part of the complex farthest from Ruben and his family, building D, and commands the SS guards with the dogs to start their search. Ruben feels as though this is the end, for the hiding place will not withstand the nose of trained dogs. He dashes back to the secret room and warns them to be quiet, not a word, not even a whisper. He rushes back to the window and sees the Wolf calmly smoking a cigarette. There is a loud commotion in Building D, knocking and shouting. Tenants file out and stand in the driveway. Some are furious, cursing at the guards, demanding to see the superior officer. Ruben knows Building D is safe; no Jews are hiding there. Buildings A and B are not so safe. The Horowitz family is hiding out in Building B. The papers are shown, and the tenants move back into their building. One man, in a bathrobe and slippers, shouts in the face of the stone-faced guard, then turns and walks away. An SS guard reports to the Wolf and he points to Building C. The guard salutes and then hurries off with his force of soldiers and dogs. Another commotion breaks out, shouts and stomping. The tenants from Building C begin to stream out.

Never has Ruben felt such fear. He cannot move, just watches as more tenants come out of the adjacent building. He is about to dash from the window to his family when he takes one more glance. He gasps.

The baldheaded tenant has returned with a fat, well-dressed man. He is pointing his finger at the Wolf, who does not move, but watches as his troops check the papers of Building C. The fat man points at the Wolf, then points back at the tenants from Building C. The Wolf hesitates for a moment, inhales from his cigarette, then extinguishes it on the pavement. And then the Wolf calls to the officer in charge of the interrogations. The man rushes over to him. The Wolf barely moves his mouth. The officer rushes back to his SS guards, those with the dogs, those who had begun the search for hiding Jews. Everything is put to a stop. The Wolf turns toward the fat, well-dressed man and tells him hiding Jews is punishable by death. The fat man points his arm as if to say, "Get out of here! Now!"

And just like that, the Wolf walks steadily over to his staff car, his attendant opening the door for him. And the car pulls out of the driveway followed by the rest of his elite forces. Ruben leans his head against the wall and slumps to the floor sobbing.

6

airports become a world unto themselves when flights are delayed. They are small cities with shopping centers in the basements, hotels just off to the side, and various restaurants to soothe any craving. Jacob had waited at gate 37 for over an hour. He was bored and wanted to get away from the tumultuous thoughts raging through his mind.

Isaac will not show, not now. I don't have to think about the future or the encounter—only the present.

And so he stood and slowly walked down the long concourse, perusing the shops for something that would catch his fancy. A cup of coffee would be very nice, so he walked over to the small café. The line was long, people impatient from the plane delays. He could hear the boiler hissing as the steamed milk foamed and churned into a mound of froth. A cappuccino, that was what he wanted. When did he first discover the pleasure of a cappuccino? The answer crashed down upon him: It was with Pierre. Pierre had taught him to love the bite of the espresso and the soothing fluff of milk. Jacob rubbed his forehead, the memory bringing on the headache once again. He stepped up to the counter and ordered plain coffee, decaffeinated; the caffeine would play havoc with his prostate.

Jacob made his way to a seat at an abandoned gate, a window seat positioned for two views: one where he could watch the thunderstorm, the dark mass of clouds rumbling overhead, and the other so he could watch the passengers arriving and departing through the long concourse. This particular concourse was emptying quickly, impatient travelers looking for any flight out of the airport, others wandering down into the food court in the hub. Jacob watched a young couple pushing their child in a stroller. The child was red with grief, tears streaming down her face, mouth open and screaming. The father, an overweight man with a dark blue polo shirt and khaki pants, looked around impatiently as if to see who was watching the tantrum. The mother, a large woman in her own right, suddenly forced the man to stop the stroller so she could see to her infant. But the baby did not stop. Hoisted from the seat, one leg sticking while the husband frantically tried to untangle it, the baby still sucked air and gasped out high-pitched screams.

"Will you just help me get her out of this," scolded the woman. "That's the least you could do."

The man finally was able to release the young girl's foot, and the mother lifted her to her shoulder. The little baby was not at all satisfied. Hisses and whispers came from the impatient mother's lips as the father tried to console the baby, now making a face, now touching her little leg.

"You're obviously not helping, dear," the woman said.

"Fine. I'm going to get us some coffee."

The man hurried off toward the hub, and as the mother walked her daughter around the empty gate, the little girl relaxed and finally calmed herself into a sleep.

Jacob thought of little Rebecca. How tiny she was, how delicate and pink. When he saw her in the hospital she had been taken to ICU for observation. The small head with the white hospital knit cap, the small dainty booties, contrasted dramatically with the clear tube snaking into her groin. She was having problems breathing, her heart rate unstable. Such a fight for life!

Much like Jacob during the war. Maybe that was the connection that plunged him head long into this little girl's world. She was a survivor. She had the will to live beyond anyone's expectations and hopes.

When the doctor gave Ruth the fact sheet, the Xeroxed copy of information every parent of a Down's syndrome child must know—when Ruth was handed that blackened and smudged paper, she silently wept. Jacob talked with the doctor on his own, and he too was given the paper, blackened and nearly unreadable on the edges. And this made him more angry than the facts themselves. The risk of mental retardation, the high percentage of heart conditions, even the age expectations did not affect him as much as that simple presentation of the blackened paper with the rounded and tiny margins. "Quick, make a copy of this, Marge. Yes, page 456 in the *Genetic Disorder* textbook." And voilà! Another parent dismissed into the world of chaos and confusion. At least the doctors can't be sued watering down the facts. Jacob crumbled the paper into a wad as he stared at his grandchild fighting for life. She would be on her own. This was her time to make it. She would have to fight against all odds, and even then the world would deal her a heavy blow: special needs child.

And so, after that conviction of the heart, that moment when grandfather and granddaughter secretly bonded, made the pact in that ICU through the glass—the pact that said, if you make it out of here, I will do whatever it takes to give you the life you deserve—after Rebecca came home, Jacob committed himself completely and selflessly.

At first, Asher was unaware of his father's passion, but after Ruth began to receive package after package containing literature and articles, pamphlets from international and local organizations, addresses for Internet chat organizations, after this Asher started to get the message: Pick up the ball, or I will! It still had little effect on his son, but Jacob was now in a new world, a world he had closed off years ago—the world of the underdog, the child who beats the odds and succeeds. And suddenly Jacob thought of the Wolf, of his relentless pursuit. Now the Wolf was pursuing his granddaughter, and she would make it too! Yes, she would make it too!

Jacob shook his head and realized that for twenty minutes he had been somewhere else. His head pounded with the last memory. The couple had walked away long ago. He looked out the window at the storm still raging, wind blowing the trees, bowing them toward the ground. He took a sudden and deep breath and decided to walk the long concourse to clear his head.

It is not that Jacob had not thought long and hard about why he sealed off his past, why he remained silent about it, why he was living two lives. These thoughts visited him often after Liza's death. He had watched the documentaries on Holocaust survivors, had read several books about his condition—what makes a man who has experienced so much trauma as a child close off all access, hermetically seal it, compartmentalize it into the realm of fantasy. Like veterans of war—those who landed on the beaches, those who struggled in the jungles, those who saw the depravity of man in themselves and in others—Jacob experienced hell and cut it off as though it had never happened. He left Belgium, left that world and never once looked back. He raised his children as though it never happened, married his wife and loved her as though she were the only one. The horrors that had once been imprinted onto his soul had now been forcefully, minute by minute, closed off, bricked up, sealed. He convinced himself with great effort that Asher was no different than Isaac; that Liza had been his only love. Day by day he took another step, and each step took him further and further from Belgium and his past. Until the distance became an impassable chasm. Well, save for those moments when he found himself in that other world.

It would happen with the smallest trigger. He would suddenly feel the tremor of grief, the overwhelming sensation that would ultimately cast him into the abyss. And at that moment, he would silently close the bathroom door behind him, turn on the exhaust fan, and huddle in the shower a sobbing wreck of a man. Oh, he tried to wipe the tears away, tried to force that terrible surge of emotion into submission, staring at his reflection in the mirror, trying to intimidate it. But to no avail. And this made him angry, angry he could not control it, angry it would surprise him at the most inopportune time, angry that all of his world, the world he had so diligently created, could not withstand a single jolt from the past. But then, when it had worked its course, when it had writhed his body like a seizure, then the bricks were stacked up again, the wall was reconstructed, the one world was once again two separate entities without any correlation or contact with each other.

But now the two worlds were colliding regularly. When Liza died, they collided, for he had never told her about his past, about Belgium and the war. Oh, she knew he had spent his childhood in Belgium, but he never talked about Yvonne or about Pierre and the other families. And when Liza died, the guilt so overwhelmed him he nearly did the unthinkable, razor inches from his wrists. And then came Rebecca, that precious gift of humanity, and the worlds collided again. But the event that tore up the foundations of the barrier, ripped them from their footings and lay them jumbled and jagged was the letter from Micheline: Pierre is dying. He needs to see you. And so, he decided to finally and without fear head himself straight into the storm, meet it head on, take what it could dish out and, no matter what, be free.

With cup of coffee in hand, Jacob strolled down the concourse and into the food court. Most of the seats were taken. He stood for some time just staring at the masses of people, not deciphering one from the other, but seeing them as a Renoir: blobs of dots and color. Snatches of conversations here and there writhed up like smoke, dialogues about the weather and the "what ifs" of further delays. He was glad for the delay, glad he could escape somewhere that would keep him away from the encounter that must take place. In this mass of throbbing life, he was just another human, another disgruntled person thinking of the present. He sipped his coffee again and decided to get a bite to eat.

The bakery seemed clean and well kept, so he stood in line to order a muffin. There was an assortment, but he knew his doctor's orders: bran this and bran that. Oh, but the cookies, so big and so elegantly layered one on the other. *What would it hurt?* he thought. *What could a stupid cookie do to me that the cancer has not already done? If it were laced with cyanide, it would make little difference.* And yet, when the young woman with clear plastic gloves asked him what he wanted, he ordered the bran muffin. He took the muffin and some napkins and walked around until he found an open seat on the fringes. A businessman dressed in a well-tailored Italian suit (Jacob immediately noticed the beautiful lines, the strong stitching) stood with his *Wall Street Journal* and asked if Jacob wanted his place.

"I'm off to the bar," said the man, his face creased from too much sun. "A Bloody Mary and a cigarette is all that will salvage this trip now."

Jacob smiled and nodded, then sat down with his muffin and

half empty cup of coffee. The large top of the muffin was crunchy and sweet, the inside a moist web of bran and raisins. He sipped his coffee again and looked at the crowd. A husband and wife were trying to maintain order with their four children, all under the age of ten. He watched as the mother frantically grasped this and caught that while the father tried to unwrap a burger before the little girl burst into tears. Jacob sipped his coffee and then tore another piece of the muffin from the crusty top. He looked over at a woman next to him, young, long hair pulled over one shoulder, small round glasses masking her thin face. She had soft tones and well-defined cheekbones. She was dressed in shorts and a sweatshirt with a college logo across the front. Jacob watched her as she sat silently engrossed in her large hardback novel. She was close enough he could smell her perfume, a fruity fragrance that was quite pleasant.

The young woman reached up, still reading her book, and tried to locate her coffee. She misjudged it, and soon coffee poured over the table and onto the floor. Jacob immediately got up and pulled napkins from the counter.

"Oh, thank you," the young woman said. "I'm such a klutz sometimes."

"Don't think twice about it." Jacob handed her some napkins and wiped up the table with her. "A good book is worth a spilled cup of coffee every now and then."

The young woman smiled politely. The mess was soon cleaned up, and Jacob made his way back to his seat.

"It's some storm out there," the young woman said.

"Indeed it is. It certainly has screwed up people's plans, I'm afraid."

"Well, it certainly has made my trip a bit more exciting than it otherwise would have been." She smiled and lifted her coffee cup to her mouth, then jiggled it with an embarrassed sort of laugh.

"Why?"

"Well, like you said, a good book is worth it sometimes. I picked this one up here at the airport earlier today. I heard about it on the radio and have seen the advertisements for it, but never really gave it the time of day. It really is a good read."

Jacob looked at the unmistakable cover, the picture of the author on the back. He sipped what little remained of his coffee. "What is the title of the book you're reading?"

The young woman placed the bookmark between the pages and closed it. "It's some adventure novel. *The Tombs of Anakim.*" She turned the book over to show the picture of the author. "It's by this guy, Jack Oxford. I must say, we professors don't give such books the time of day—too pulp fiction for our tastes." She adjusted her glasses and smiled. "I teach English literature at a small college on the east coast. I thought I would be able to imbibe my passion secretly, but you have found me out—" She paused, and the pause was meant for Jacob to fill in his name.

"Jacob Horowitz is my name."

"Hi, Jacob. My name is Betty Withers. I'm pleased to meet you. Have you read anything by Jack Oxford?"

Jacob looked around the food court as if expecting his son to appear at any moment. "No, no, I don't believe so."

Betty jiggled her empty cup again and stood up. "I need a refill. Can I get you one while I'm up there?"

"Yes, yes, that would be wonderful." He watched Betty's slim body as she made her way past the chairs and tables filled with people. And as she waited in line, he reached over and picked up the hardback book. The cover was black and glossy, and across it were scrolled the letters: *The Tombs of Anakim.* Below it was a rendition of a gothic crypt of some sort, and below that—in larger font than the title—was Jack Oxford. Jacob turned it over and looked at the back and the full-spread photo of the author—leather jacket with collar pulled up, Indiana Jones hat, and safari boots. His hair was blowing to the side, one hand holding his hat resting on his knee, the other against the side of a large rock. Jacob recognized the rock. He unconsciously rubbed his hand across the picture. Betty returned with the coffee.

"He's some guy," Betty said as she placed the cup of coffee on Jacob's table and then pulled up a chair next to him. "I think most of his international audience is comprised of women."

Jacob looked again at the author's chiseled features, the hypnotizing eyes. They had done a bang-up job with this shoot. "Yes," replied Jacob giving the book back to her. "Yes, I'm sure you're right."

There was an awkward pause before Jacob said, "Where are you headed when the storm blows over?"

"I'm on my way to the east coast; back to the college where I teach."

"Would I have heard of it?"

"No. It has only three thousand students or so." Betty sipped her coffee and then realized she had some packets of creamer in her pocket and placed them on the table. "Almost forgot those. I'm always doing things like that. Losing this, forgetting that. Once I walked off without paying for a dinner. The waiter ran after me, all the way out to my car. He probably still thinks I was going to D and D."

"D and D?" responded Jacob smiling.

"Dine and dash."

"Oh, I see." Jacob pointed at the book. "Do you teach Jack Oxford at your college?"

Betty laughed with delight, then stopped when she realized Jacob's question was serious.

"Oh no, Jacob. Jack Oxford is basically scorned in my profession. Oh sure, some scholars have attempted to write articles about his style or his popularity, but nothing truly serious. In my profession, we stick to the obscure. There's more gold to mine in those than in these." And she patted the book that was on the table.

"But I don't understand," Jacob said. "If so many people are reading an author like Jack Oxford, doesn't that mean maybe he has hit upon something?"

"Some would say so. In fact, in his case, the critics have begun to side more with him than against him. He's trying new ideas, new ways of expressing the old clichés, the old used-up tropes... I mean, Oxford is saying it differently than the other mass market writers. He seems to be pushing the envelope of what's expected."

Jacob sipped his coffee and finished off his muffin. He knew the coffee was not decaffeinated by the way it surged straight to his bladder. Betty continued with a sudden passion.

"You see, Jacob, take Oxford's latest release. By the title you would think it was just another run of the mill adventure novel— Clive Cussler, Benjamin Stone, Margaret Singer. But from the very first sentence the informed reader knows Oxford is a highly gifted wordsmith." Betty grabbed the book and opened up to the first page. "Listen to this: *In the heart of madness, in the very depths of chaos, Lawrence Fairborne found the strand of sanity that would keep him alive.* That, Jacob, is good writing. The whole novel is tight like that."

For his part, Jacob thought the first sentence overwritten, a bit much. He preferred: *It was the best of times, it was the worst of times.* But for Betty's sake he nodded in agreement.

"So," Jacob said, "I take it you are one of those scholars you mentioned earlier. The ones trying to prove that Jack Oxford is not a pulp fiction writer after all?"

Betty looked embarrassed once again. "You've got me, Jacob. In fact, I'm the only one who's writing anything on his stuff at all." Betty pulled her chair closer to Jacob and screwed up her face as though what she was about to say was deadly serious. "I've read all his books, all of them. From the very first one, *The Moon below the Earth*, *The Taloned Necklace*, *Buried*, and even the obscure, hard-to-get *The Hills behind the Mountain*. I've read them all—*Terror in the Dark*, *The Golden Calf*, all of them—and now I'm halfway through this one. I have read and studied these texts and have found connections no one has yet discovered. He's a genius! He's the next Shakespeare!" She leaned toward Jacob again and whispered, "I call it subversive textualization."

Jacob nodded and rubbed his chin. "What does that mean, subversive textualization?"

"Well," said Betty, clearing her throat and pushing up her glasses, "it's a phrase I coined that means: Oxford is using the genre to subvert the forms. He is playing with the language in such a way that he revisits the old forms with irony and displacement."

"Oh," said Jacob nodding his head. A thought flashed through his mind: *I hope my tax dollars aren't supporting such trash.*

"It is my firm belief, after studying all of his novels, that Jack Oxford is not who he pretends to be."

"He's not?"

"No. No, indeed. I think hidden in his novels are a range of..." Betty was once more diving deep into the abyss of jargon and technical hubbub. She resurfaced about ten minutes later. "I tried to contact him, but he has not responded or returned my calls."

Jacob thought, *Good for him*, but said, "Who?"

"Jack, Jack Oxford. I've tried to get in touch with him, but he lives in a veil of secrecy. I even tried to find his wife and kids and make a connection that way—nothing."

"Oh really."

"But I don't need his personal interview. The text does not lie. Did you know that even in his latest novel he uses subversive textualization to…" And once again she dove into the abyss.

Jacob listened politely, but his bladder was full, and he was desperate to excuse himself. Finally, he just said, "Excuse me, Betty, for interrupting you, but I have a condition where if I don't go to the men's room, we might both have a problem."

Betty frowned and looked a little annoyed, then caught herself and smiled. "By all means. I get talking sometimes and don't even realize where I am."

Jacob excused himself, creaked and grunted to his feet, and lumbered his way toward the restroom. He dallied at the sink for some time, hoping that when he returned Betty would be back to her beloved novel. It was better than he expected. She was nowhere to be seen.

He sat down at the table and sipped his coffee. The headache was once again making itself known, and he suddenly looked up and surveyed the food court for his son. But Isaac was not there. Jacob grabbed his coffee and started walking away from his gate and toward another concourse with less risk, one where he could once again be anonymous.

The shops in this concourse were the same, and he mingled for some time in a small storefront that sold Cleveland Indians paraphernalia. The baseball team was doing well, leading their division by five games. They would probably win the pennant. He looked at the hats, the shirts, the mugs, thinking maybe one of his nephews would enjoy them. But then he realized he would be carrying the object, no matter what it was, throughout Belgium. No, he wanted to escape Cleveland, escape all of this. And for a fleeting moment he nearly decided to forget the whole affair. Isaac wouldn't show. Besides, who needs such struggle and pain at his age? But that too faded, and he continued down the concourse eyeing the next storefront to come along.

As he passed the bar, he noticed how crowded it had become. Passengers of every kind had suddenly become friends, alcohol the great mediator between social status. He walked over to the drinking fountain, but decided against a quick sip, for the fountain was tarnished with a brown stain and a lump of green gum, teeth marks still visible. He noticed the businessman with the well-cut suit talking in the bar to a blond bombshell. Did he care about his wife? Did he have a wife? Was that his wife? These questions lingered for a moment, then were replaced by another shop where more paraphernalia hung on the walls. He entered and bought a Snickers bar. The bridgework would suffer, but the taste and the distraction were well worth it.

And then he came to the end of the concourse, a bubble of windows streaked with rain. The torrent was not letting up. He noticed a thin male in an ill-fitting blue airport jacket talking on a cell phone. Jacob sat next to a window and munched on his candy bar.

Subversive textualization. Jacob laughed and shook his head. Wait until Isaac hears that one. "Oh, by the way, son. I haven't seen you for ten years, but have you ever heard of subversive textualization? Did you know you do that?" He chuckled again, but the headache was coming back. He looked at the candy bar and then took another bite. His mind began to reel and he knew he must move, move somewhere else, move to open space. In here was claustrophobic. Jacob threw the wrapper away and rubbed his forehead. The pain was intensifying, and he walked up to the large glass window and placed his burning cheek against it. He could feel the wind as it throbbed and pounded the window. And this pounding made him relax. Yes, soon it would all be over. Soon he could unload this heavy burden and step away. But when?

"Excuse me, sir. Excuse me. Sir? Are you okay?"

It was the desk clerk in the ill-fitting jacket. His voice, feminine and calm, broke through Jacob's rush of thoughts. He stirred from the window and pushed himself away.

"Yes. Yes, I am fine, thank you."

"Can I get you some water? Or perhaps you would wish to see our medical personnel?"

"No, no. I am fine. Thank you. I was just thinking..."

Jacob lumbered back toward the food court. To his left was a small café, and just past that was the ornately trimmed bookstore. He decided it would be a good distraction to browse through the magazines.

7

The Barnes and Noble in the airport was a miniature of the larger stores: dark hardwood trim, immense glass windows looking out into the concourse, and it even had a Starbucks coffee mini café. Jacob entered through the glass doors and was immediately greeted by his son—a life-size replica of Jack Oxford, one hand over the display of his latest release, the other with hand on knee, Indiana Jones hat. Jacob did not give it a second glance, but walked over to the periodicals. As he searched for the parenting magazines he stumbled upon one for senior citizens. On the cover was a warning: *You may have prostate cancer and not know it: the importance of yearly rectal exams.* He pulled it from the rack and paged through it. What could he learn from a magazine? He was the expert on prostate cancer. Since the very beginning, he had ignored the warnings; now it was too late. He skimmed the article and it condemned him:

Prostate cancer is an easily detectable and treatable disease if caught early...

Jacob closed the magazine and put it back on the rack. What ifs once again surfaced and resurfaced.

He sought refuge in a parenting magazine, and soon he was skimming through it looking for articles on Down's syndrome children. Most issues ignored special needs children as Jacob discovered soon after Rebecca was born. But the Internet provided much more than the mainstream presses, and the library down-town had everything he could want. He had made connections with scholars at Ohio State University and closer to home at Case Western Reserve University. He soon forged a relationship with the head of the department for Early Childhood Development, Dr. Bob Tanner. Dr. Tanner at first was not really interested in helping Jacob, but after a social event, a fund-raiser for the university, Tanner soon realized who Jacob was and his importance in the city. Jacob knew the routine and did not blame the man—he did that type of deferment himself all the time. But after several lunches, Jacob and Dr. Tanner began to speak frankly with each other. Dr. Tanner told Jacob where he must go for the best help, and who he must see. Tanner was a big gun in a field of big guns, and as soon as Jacob mentioned his name, people responded immediately. That was where Jacob found out about early intervention for Rebecca, the latest in vitamin supplements and physical therapy routines.

The magazine was fluffy, which didn't surprise him, and he soon returned it to the rack. He stared at the variety and desperately wanted to find something to distract him from why he was really there. His headache resurfaced, and so he decided to browse the bookshelves for comfort.

So many books, so many authors, so many topics. Every year more displays and more sections, and yet all the time more publishing house mergers, more focus on the big sellers. Jacob followed it all, and this too was another secret he kept deep within. A prodigal son is still a son after all.

He started the way he always did with new releases. First fiction and then nonfiction. He scanned the As, Bs, Cs, picking up the competition and reading the inside flap, the first page and if really intriguing, the first chapter. It always amused him the new marketing gimmicks: Oprah's Book Club, the Imus book of the month, *New York Times* bestsellers, *Publisher's Weekly* top ten. On one occasion, Jack Oxford had made every single one of them—the same month. It was Liza who popped the Dom Perignon and invited her friends over for a party. Jacob drank reluctantly and retired to his study, but he really was the first to know; he had followed his son from the very beginning. But to deny one's heritage! To walk away and become someone else! To act like a Gentile, to be a part of their world and not even acknowledge his roots! This was too much.

He skipped over the Os altogether and moved straight to the nonfiction. He recognized several names, people he knew as powerful businessmen, those who had written books to boost their company's image, to promote the latest marketing trend, the latest twelve-step program for success. He had been approached to write a book on how he became so successful. It was just one of many ploys Asher developed to promote the family business. But Jacob declined. He was humble, ruthless when he had to be, but humble all the same. A man's stature was based on character, who he was inside, and that could never be marketed or transferred by a twelve-step program. Jacob moved down the list and suddenly found himself in the Fiction/Literature section.

So many novels! It always amazed him as he scanned the faces of the books—yes, the faces, not even counting the thousands tucked away, spine out, only a name and a title. If a writer was lucky enough to get his book published, that did not mean it would sell. What a ruthless game. What an occupation for Isaac to desire. And yet Isaac had accomplished the impossible. Nearly every Jack Oxford book was selling over a million copies now. All but three books had become major motion pictures. It was truly incredible.

Jacob had tried to dissuade his son from a writing career as soon as Isaac had graduated with an MFA from the Iowa Fiction Workshop. (Why not Harvard, like Asher? Jacob could never understand.) He sat down with Isaac at an upscale restaurant. Jacob had invited a friend to accompany them, a successful local fiction writer. The man was middle-aged, slightly overweight, his appearance disheveled, a look cultivated with effort. He liked his wine, talked loudly, and looked about for anyone who would recognize him. When a man came up to the table, the writer reached into his jacket pocket and pulled out a fountain pen, expecting to autograph his latest work. But alas, the man was there to say hello to Jacob. After a strange silence, Jacob introduced the writer. "No, I don't believe I've heard of you," replied the businessman politely. "What have you written?"

They ate together and the writer asked Isaac what his plans were, what he was writing, all the precursory stuff that set him up for the hammer drop—the big fist of reality that would somehow knock sense into the boy before his move to New York City. The facts stunned even Jacob.

- 90 percent of all books published go out of print after their first printing.
- The number of writers who make their living off of their work is in the three to four thousands.
- Even if you get a book published, chances are it will never make it to the stores.
- If it does make it to the stores, it has a three-month shelf life or less before it is returned to the publisher.
- The percentage of authors who consistently hit the bestseller lists can be counted on two hands.

- Even if a writer is published once, that does not mean he will be published a second time.
- Do the math: a dollar a book if you're lucky. How many books would you have to sell in order to make a living, raise a family? First printings were four thousand to ten thousand copies.

And on and on and on and on. Jacob looked at the writer and then at his son with a sense of sorrow. But Isaac calmly listened, interested in the minutest details in the author's life. Did he not hear that horror? Soon the two men were talking about reputations, about writers Isaac had met at the workshop (some of them friends of this man), about the creative process—what was supposed to be a time of chastening became a love fest. Isaac promised to send some of his latest stories to the man for review, and the man even said he would put in a word for Isaac with his agent in Manhattan.

And just like that Isaac was gone. The son of a prominent businessman soon became—by choice—a starving writer in the bowels of New York City. Jacob had spoken at length with his writer friend about Isaac's chances. The writer was emphatic: He's good. He's very good, but good does not make you a selling writer. Luck and good connections do. And like everything else Jacob did, he threw himself completely into helping his son. Jacob had all sorts of friends in New York, his relatives (those who survived the Holocaust) were all around that area, some established quite firmly in the literary scene. He did all he could, and soon received a letter from Isaac.

No more! I don't need, don't want, will do without your connections! P.S. If you really want to help, send me some cash.

So Jacob sent Isaac money every month. Several years passed, and Jacob heard nothing save bits and pieces from his contacts in New York. No call was returned, nor letter either. Liza's brother, Moses, had seen Isaac waiting tables at an upscale restaurant. Two more years passed and Jacob received that package in the mail. The author pictured on the book jacket was Isaac Horowitz; the name was of someone Jacob had never known.

"What is this?" cried Jacob to Liza who was making dinner in the kitchen. "What is this I have in my hand? It shows my son, but says he's someone else! What trickery is this?"

Liza came over and held up the book. A smile beamed from ear to ear. "Jacob! Oh, Jacob! Our son has published a book! He has really done it!" She was so happy she hugged Jacob around the neck to the point of pain.

Jacob pushed her away.

"No. No son of mine has written a book. No, this is not my son. This is an imposter." And he shoved the book across the large center island.

"Oh, Jacob, don't be a fool. Isaac is using a pen name. He probably was told to do it by his agent or somebody." And Liza walked over to the book and picked it up as though it were a piece of fine china.

"What is wrong with my name?" Jacob said. "What is wrong with Horowitz? Plenty of Jews are writing. Plenty of Jews publish books like this. I don't understand."

Jacob refused to read the book, refused to sit in the same room as the book. And soon he demanded that it not be in the house. Liza kept the book in her closet, and when Jacob would leave for work, Liza would pour a cup of coffee, sit in the sunroom, and read with great enthusiasm. Her son had become a writer. She shook her head in astonishment and admiration as she found herself trapped within her son's world of make believe.

One night several days after he sent the book, Isaac called home. Liza answered the phone and screamed with excitement.

"We got your book! Oh, honey, it is wonderful! We are so proud of you."

"Did Papa read it yet?"

There was a pause on the other end.

"Mama?"

"Yes, dear, I'm here."

"Did Papa read the book yet?"

"Well, no. He just hasn't had the time yet. You know how busy he is."

Jacob came downstairs and was getting something out of the refrigerator. "Who's on the phone?" he asked with a tilt of his head.

Liza looked panic-stricken.

"Who's on the phone?"

She covered the mouthpiece. "It's Isaac. He's calling about the book."

Jacob set down the Coke and walked over to the phone. "Let me speak to him."

"Jacob," said Liza sternly, pulling the phone out of her husband's reach, "he is happy and very excited about his book. You be kind to him. Now is not the time—"

But Jacob grabbed the phone from Liza and proceeded to bawl out his son right there and then. He called the book a "travesty," a "sellout." He yelled into the receiver and stormed about the house like a madman. "Is that what being a Horowitz means: embarrassment and shame?" Isaac did not respond, and then suddenly a dial tone was all Jacob heard. "Hello! Hello! Isaac?" And he turned off the small portable phone and flung it onto the couch.

"How dare you!" Liza shouted. "How dare you speak to your

son that way, when he has worked so hard. So hard! You should be ashamed of yourself!"

"Ashamed? Me? I am not the one who sold out to the Gentiles. I am not the one who changed my name. No, my name is still Jacob Horowitz!" And he pounded the countertop with his fist. "The Horowitz name is worth more than this! It is worth everything! Everything, I tell you!" Jacob grabbed his coat and like a little child stormed out the door, slamming it behind him.

Liza could not understand what had come over her husband, and from that day until her death she began to construct a wall between them.

Jacob not only cut his son off from all money but also from any family contact. But he did not stop there. He began to plant the seed in Asher: Isaac was a traitor, a betrayer of the family. And Asher took the seed and watered it, fertilized it with anger and made up stories until the division was as wide as the ocean.

Liza became a secret confidant to her son. She wrote him letters. She begged for reconciliation between father and son, but neither one budged. Isaac married. Jacob and Liza did not attend. Isaac had a son. Jacob refused to have anything to do with him. Liza wept at night, wept that her own flesh and blood was an exile for no reason. She tried to understand her husband, tried to see through the wall of stubbornness. But every time she inquired into the reason, Jacob became silent.

One night after dinner, Liza said, "You never speak about the war. Why don't you ever tell me about it?"

Jacob adjusted the *Wall Street Journal* and turned the page.

"We have been married for thirty-two years and I still do not know about your childhood. I mean, some things are better left unsaid, but maybe if you spoke to me about—"

Jacob crumpled the paper to his lap. "What is this about? Why do we need to talk about this tonight?"

"I just thought maybe if I understood you more, I may understand..."

"You may understand why I am acting the way I am acting toward my son?"

Liza was silent. She sat in her chair facing the crackling fire. She was losing weight, her face gaunt and eyes filled with worry. Jacob chose not to think about it. And he lifted his paper to block her from view.

"He is my son too, Jacob!" Liza said suddenly with great force, so much so that Jacob pulled the paper down in surprise. "He's my son too. He is my flesh and blood, from my womb. I carried him and held him when he was young, fed him from my own two breasts." Liza leaned forward toward Jacob. "I have seen our lives crumble but have said nothing. I was silent when you complained that he didn't want to go to Harvard. I was silent when you complained that he wanted to write novels. I was even silent—God have mercy on me—when you banished him from this family. But he is not just *your* son, Jacob. No! He is not just yours! He is *mine*, and I am forbidden to see or hear from my own flesh and blood."

"You are tired, dear. Let's not talk about this now. We can talk about it when we are both—"

"No. No, I will not talk about it another time. Can't you see, Jacob? Can't you see what is happening to. to our family...to us?"

"We have a problem? Now you are telling me we have a problem? What are you telling me, Liza? What are you telling me you want?"

"I want my son back," whispered Liza as her head fell into her hands. "I want my son back, Jacob." And she began to sob.

Jacob stood up. "Enough of this. I have told you why it cannot be that way. I will not hear this any more."

"What have you told me?" responded Liza suddenly lifting her head and staring at Jacob. "What have you told me? That our son has disgraced his name? That our son has betrayed us? What has he betrayed, Jacob? How has he disgraced our family? You have told me nothing. Tell me now, tell me so I can understand."

"There is nothing but what there is."

"That is not good enough!"

"That is all I have to say. It is final. You are either with me or against me."

"No, it is not that simple anymore." Liza stood up, her legs suddenly so weak she had to lean against the chair. "I want my baby. You cannot take away my own flesh and blood!" And as she stepped forward she collapsed onto the floor.

Liza was admitted into the hospital, and the doctors diagnosed her with lymphatic cancer. It had spread throughout her body and she was given a year to live. She lived for five. Jacob watched as her frame decayed into a skeleton, face sunken in. They never spoke of that night again. On the day Liza passed away, Jacob was by her side. He held her hand and cried, asking her for forgiveness, asking her to tell him everything was okay. Liza smiled a shallow smile, her face already showing her departure, and squeezed his hand ever so slightly. Jacob grabbed her body into his arms and sobbed in a loud moan, an animal yelp. And just like that his wife of thirty-six years was no more.

The evening after the funeral Jacob sat alone in the house staring at the backyard, the woods, the changing leaves. He stared and hated his son Isaac with all that was in him. Isaac did this. Isaac killed Liza, killed her with his selfishness, with his betrayal. Were it not for such a traitor, Liza would still be alive. The cancer was the poison Isaac had inflicted with his rebellion. Jacob sat and drank his scotch. He rubbed the moisture on the glass and balled up his other hand into a fist, the knuckles white with rage. Isaac killed Liza! That was what happened. Jacob gulped down the remains of his drink and stood up, glass in hand. It was Isaac! Isaac! All of this could have been avoided. He thought of the casket as it was lowered into the earth, the terrible green carpet surrounding it like a lake of algae. He heard the rabbi's speech, heard the grief from the guests. This was Isaac's doing. Jacob walked over to the window.

What man could make such terrible choices, thought Jacob, *such selfish choices that would destroy a family.* He clutched the glass tighter and tighter. *How could a person act with such little conscience, such reckless abandon to pursue a dream?* And then he shouted out in anger, "Who is such a man! Tell me! Who?" And suddenly his own voice whispered back, "You are that man." Jacob fell against the window, then collapsed into a nearby chair. He put his hands to his eyes, pushing them so tight he saw white splotches. "Yes," he sobbed. "Yes, I am that man."

Jacob moved through the shelves of fiction and kept thinking about those early days when Isaac's reputation was not taken for granted. He looked at the names on the shelves and knew that his son knew many of these famous and some not so famous people. No scholar—besides Betty—gave Jack Oxford the time of day. Most called his work pure adventure stories. Jacob remembered an interview with *Publisher's Weekly* where the interviewer asked how he dealt with the unfavorable critics. Isaac responded: *"I think of my three houses, of my boat, of my next royalty check—and then I think of the critics and their critiques. What did that bumper sticker say: Revenge is living well."*

Jacob had laughed when he read that, but he knew his son considered him in the camp with the critics.

Soon he stumbled upon the Os, and there in front of him were all of his son's novels, some hardback, most paperbacks. All of them, every one Betty had mentioned, were lined up in a row like sentinels. Jacob had read none of these, would not permit any of them in the house. And yet he knew every one by heart, had kept the clippings and reviews for each one. Every book had a separate folder and in each folder he kept all the news from book signings to critiques. Jacob spent hours scouring the periodicals looking for mention of his son's books. All in secret, of course. All of this a smoke and mirrors ordeal so as to keep his reputation and his word intact. What good had any of that done him? What reputation? What invisible power is worth a wife and a son? It was so easy to see now, but not then.

For the first time in his life he reached down and picked up one of the hardbound copies. He read the glowing reviews on the back and opened up the cover to see the picture on the dust jacket. His son was young then, a fire burning in those eyes. The picture was not as professional as his latest one, but at this point in Isaac's career, he had neither the reputation nor the money he soon would have. Jacob closed the book and rubbed the spine. He opened it up again and started to browse through the first several pages.

"Excuse me, sir."

Jacob looked up in surprise. A young woman was standing next to him.

"Could I just reach behind you here and pick out one of these?" Jacob moved to the side and the woman reached for one of Jack Oxford's books.

"Are you a fan?" asked Jacob smiling.

The woman stood up and pulled the book to her chest. "Oh, you bet. I'm in the process of reading all of them over again. You see, we just moved, and the movers sort of took off with several of our boxes. Well, my collection of Jack Oxford books just so happened to be with the stereo equipment. So now I have to buy them all over again."

"Really. You are going to read them all over again?"

"Absolutely. I live and die by this guy's stories. It's like he takes you right there with him." She smiled. "And to have him right there with you isn't all half bad, if you know what I mean." She flipped her copy over and pointed to the picture.

"You know he has a new one out."

"Oh yes, I know. *The Tombs of Anakim*. I was one of the first ones in line when I heard its release date. I'm about halfway through it right now."

Jacob looked at the row of books and then back up at the young woman. "I was wondering if you could do me a favor. I have a son who I know would love to read Jack Oxford's books, but I am not sure which book to buy him. Which one do you think is the best one—there are just too many for me to choose from."

"Well, what has he been reading?"

"I really don't know. You see I am going to see him for the first time in quite some time."

"Hmm. Let's see." And soon she was critiquing and summarizing each book out loud. It was truly a remarkable lecture. "If it were my son, I'd buy him the latest novel, *The Tombs of Anakim*, and see if he likes it. From what I've read so far, I think it will be his best book ever. There's something about the way he's writing now—more...more beefy or something."

Suddenly another person entered the discussion. It was a

Barnes and Noble employee. He was balding and bearded, with a nose like a bent finger.

"I think his writing is really maturing," said the man in an effeminate voice. "If you read his early stuff and then this latest, there is really no comparison."

"Really," Jacob said.

"Oh, absolutely," said the employee sniffing with satisfaction. "Take for example the protagonist, Dr. Cory Witherspoon, from his first novel, *The Moon below the Earth*. If you read that novel and compare it to say, well, any of the other later novels, especially *The Tombs*, then you'll see what I mean."

"But when he killed off Thomas in *The Hills behind the Moon*, don't you think that was a little too much?" the young woman said.

The employee sniffed again. "Yes, I see what you mean, but there is the issue of integrity. There is definitely the artistic integrity issue."

"I don't know what you mean by that, but I do have to say I love the way he develops his women characters." She turned toward Jacob. "But not just the women characters. Your son would still enjoy reading it…I mean his books aren't girly in any way."

"Oh, I see," Jacob said. "This very helpful woman explained to me which one of Jack Oxford's books my son would like."

The employee sniffed again and then rubbed his beard in contemplation. "*The Tombs* is by far his most mature work." He paused and then reached over and pulled a Jack Oxford novel from the shelf. "Here is a most intriguing book, however. In fact, I think one of his most interesting novels: *The Golden Calf*. It was his last book, and it didn't sell very well, but I think it is one of his high water marks."

"Oh no. I didn't like that one at all," the young woman said. "It's too deep, too much heady stuff for my taste." She turned to Jacob. "Your son wouldn't like that one as much as the others. He spends too much time on Jewish history and not enough on developing his women characters."

Soon, the employee and the young woman were in a deepening debate. Jacob edged his way backwards and then hobbled toward the front of the store. Yes, he had known all about *The Golden Calf*. He had read the reviews, the praises from the Jewish community, the praises from the critics on his seemingly abrupt turn away from the adventure genre. But sales plummeted, the fans complained, and Jack Oxford gave them what they wanted with *The Tombs of Anakim*. And this change in direction, this testing of the waters—writing *The Golden Calf*—this was also an indication Isaac would be the one to carry out the ludicrous plan revolving in Jacob's head.

Jacob stopped at the cardboard display of his son. He stared at his features, so much like Liza: her nose, her lips, her chin. Ten years. And soon Jacob felt his headache returning, a thumping in his chest as he picked up *The Tombs of Anakim* and carried it over to the checkout counter. It was a heavy book, many pages. Jacob scanned the cover again. He didn't much like the covers with glitzy, catch-your-eye type, which this was certainly one. The man at the counter called "next," and Jacob hobbled forward.

"Oh, you are in for a real treat with this one," the cashier said, his nose ring bobbing up and down as he spoke. "I think it's his best ever." The man paused and looked at the computer screen. "That will be $28.75 please."

Jacob handed the man his credit card and waited as the employee swiped it through the machine. "Here's your card, Mr. Horowitz. If you could just sign at the bottom for me please."

Jacob had a sudden urge to sign "Jacob Oxford" as a joke. But he signed his own name and carried the bag out to the food court. He checked his watch and then looked at the crowd. And for the first time in a long time, his headache dissipated, vanished without a trace. Jacob pulled the book from the plastic bag and threw the bag away. He clutched the book in his arm and smiled. This would be a good time to get a cappuccino.

8

It is late fall, 1942. The Horowitz family is restless, all of them: Benjamin and his wife, Ruben and Rachael. The food is running low, and the market where Jacob has gone for the past month is now swarming with Brownshirts and Gestapo. And yet, for all of the fear, the crisp November wind combined with the bright afternoon sun seems to lighten the mood in the apartment. The Horowitz family, with Ruben's lead, has learned to take each moment for all that it is, each conversation a nugget of joy. And everyone in the small apartment dares not think beyond this.

Ruben and Jacob are playing chess in the corner. Rachael is rereading a letter from her brother, a letter smuggled in from Argentina through the Belgian underground. Benjamin and his wife are resting on a sofa, while Sarah, thin and with dark rings around her eyes, sits leaning against the wall, face absorbing the warmth of the afternoon sun.

Ruben smiles. "You are improving, Jacob. Soon I will not be able to beat you." He rubs his chin, scanning the board for potential moves. "You hide your thoughts so well. Each move carefully calculated." Ruben places his hand on his rook, then decides not to move it. He rubs his chin again. "It's almost as if you have learned to shut them up until you need them." Ruben places his hand upon his queen and then withdraws it once again. "Yes, my son, you have developed your skills quite nicely." Ruben places his thumb and forefinger back upon the queen and slides the piece across the board. "But, my little lamb, you have not quite outsmarted your papa yet." He pauses, lifts his hand from the queen and pronounces with triumph, "Checkmate!"

"Please, Ruben," exclaims the startled Benjamin who is dozing on the couch, "keep your voice down." He rolls over and is silent.

Jacob is not willing to give up, but soon he realizes his father has beaten him once again. There is sudden anger and frustration. Ruben walks Jacob through his moves and the moves of his son. He patiently shows Jacob where he made his fatal error. "Remember, my little lamb, chess is a game of stages: the beginning game, the middle game, and the end game. Each stage you have a chance to redeem yourself or plummet further into defeat." He stops and looks at his wife and then outside. He whispers as if to no one in particular, "Much like life."

Rachael stirs from her thoughts. "My brother and his family are in dire straits in Argentina. They have no food, nothing. I am fearful for their lives."

Ruben comes over and sits down beside her at the kitchen table. "Much like Belgium."

"But at least we can still eat. They have nothing. And this letter is dated three weeks ago. You know him, Ruben, he is not likely to complain and ask for help if he was not desperate."

Ruben nods and looks outside at the beautiful day before them. He looks at his daughter by the window and smiles, but the smile is weak and he knows something will have to be done soon to keep the family from the Nazis. "Why don't we send them a package filled with food, some notes—a package for encouragement," Ruben says suddenly.

"You mean it?"

"Yes, indeed." He squeezes her hand. "The children can make

cards for their aunt and uncle, and we can provide some extra food, canned goods, whatever we can spare."

Sarah turns from the sun and gets to her feet with excitement. "Oh, Papa, I could make a nice card, color it and everything."

"You sure can, my little Sarah." He smiles seeing her demeanor transform before his eyes. Jacob stands up as well and walks over to the table.

"Mother," Ruben says, "get the paper and pencils for our little artists, and I will see about a box."

Soon the apartment is turned into a production center. Sarah and Jacob and Benjamin's children draw pictures on white pieces of paper, while Ruben asks the neighbors if they have any boxes. Rachael spends her time meticulously writing a letter of hope and encouragement. Ruben returns a little while later with a box and some tape. He places it on the counter and then walks over to his brother.

"Let's celebrate, Benjamin."

"What are we celebrating, my brother?" says Benjamin, staring out the window. "Another day closer to death?"

"No, not at all, Benjamin." Ruben pulls out a pack of cigarettes from his coat pocket and gives them to his brother. "A present from the neighbors. Let us celebrate that we are still alive, and that we have our families and each other."

Benjamin opens the pack and lights a cigarette, and soon the whole Horowitz family is humming and deep into preparing the gift they will soon send to Rachael's brother.

Benjamin walks to the opposite side of the apartment with his brother. "Our families will not last here much longer," Ruben whispers. "There is a sense of dread coming upon me I cannot shake."

"I feel it too. Maybe it's the confinement. Maybe it is nothing," says Benjamin, sucking on his cigarette with noticeable joy.

"I think it might be time to get out of here."

Benjamin nearly gags on the smoke just inhaled. "What!" he exclaims.

Ruben quiets him down and they face the window once again. "I have been speaking with some others in the apartments. There are rumors of an Underground system run by the Gentiles. A system whereby we could escape into France, and then to England or America."

"How can we risk everything on a rumor?"

"I don't know. If it is there, it will be our salvation."

"If it is not, we will die."

Ruben looks again at his wife and children. They are diligent, so content for the moment. He knows the joy is fleeting, and by tomorrow they will be back to the harsh realities of life. How long?

"We cannot sit here forever. It is only a matter of time before the Nazis discover us. No, we cannot stay here any longer. It will be better for everyone to finally face our fears, to do something and not just wait until they come for us. We must have something to shoot for, or we will be lost. I feel it here," and he suddenly strikes his chest.

Jacob is busy writing a letter with pictures to his uncle and aunt. He has learned to write well in school and it is very pleasurable for him to place one word next to the other, to control each phrase, to place each comma and period where it belongs. He finally has control of his universe, this universe of language and structure. No Nazi can catch him in this place, no Nazi can suddenly appear and destroy his sentences, take the commas away, erase the periods and choice of words. Here is freedom, and he wallows in it with abandon. If he chooses to paint a house red and the sky yellow, to make the grass purple and the trees bright orange, he can—and he does. All the while he keeps glancing up at his father and uncle who whisper in the corner.

The joy of this afternoon is one Jacob will never forget. He will remember later in his life the vibrant colors of his picture, of all the pictures, the concentration and meticulous effort he put into each object. He will remember that freedom and that day, for its edges are stark.

Rachael carefully inspects and comments on each and every homemade card. She is delighted, and her face beams with a joy that has been lost, hidden away for months on end. Ruben sees all of this and is reminded of the little moments that suddenly appear and just as quickly vanish: a simple smile, the touch of his child's hand, the blue sky so impenetrable and infinite, a piece of music that stirs the heart. There are millions of such thoughts and images racing in his head, but he knows that this moment, this simple act of kindness will do more for his family and their spirits than all of the others combined. For a moment, the dead are resurrected—a breath of God moves through the tiny apartment.

Jacob watches as his mother takes his card and smiles with delight at his choice of colors. She carefully takes the cans of peaches, peas, and a small canned ham (bought and secured at such a high price)—takes them all and gently folds a piece of cloth around them. Jacob stares at the box, as does everyone, as Rachael closes the flaps and seals it with tape.

"A very special gift," she whispers. And she looks up at everyone. "A special gift from very special people." Ruben walks over and places his arm around her, squeezing affectionately.

Later that afternoon, with Ruben and Benjamin sleeping on the beds, the rest of the children quiet and subdued, Rachael decides to go out to post the box. She writes a brief note to Ruben:

I have taken the children for some air while I post this box to my brother. I hope you don't mind. The children need to stretch their legs, and the fresh air will do Sarah some good. I will not be gone long. And I will be careful.

Yours forever,

Rachael

She grabs Sarah's hand and tells Jacob he can carry the box if he is careful. Jacob is so excited he nearly leaves without his coat.

The fall wind is biting, tossing the leaves about like abandoned feathers, swirling them and collecting them, piling them into mounds. Rachael stops and pulls Sarah's collar up further around her face. She notices the sky, dark and foreboding, a threat of rain. It is about four-thirty when they leave the house. Rachael is cautious, knows how to keep near the trees and the wooded areas for protection. With the coming of dusk, she knows prying eyes will be less observant. Even the Nazis have to eat. There is another reason she feels secure at this moment. The Belgian Underground has proclaimed: 90 percent of Belgium is against the occupation. Belgium seems infinite when 10 percent must watch it all.

The walk to the post office is not long, near the river, a pleasant smell of water and life drifting across the land. Jacob and Sarah hold hands and stick close to their mother. Jacob scans the houses on his right and then glances over at the ever darkening wood on his left, searching for any sign of danger—a shadow, a snapping twig, anything. Rachael quickens her pace, for she too feels something. As they near the post office, she notices several townspeople waiting in line outside the small building. She gives her son money for the package and then hurries him over into the line.

Jacob steps into the line and patiently waits while each in turn posts letters, collects stamps, receives packages. He smells the pungent pipe smoke from the man in front of him, lingering about the man's shoulders and his thick black coat and drooping brimmed hat. The man turns and smiles at Jacob.

"Big box there, son," says the man, larger grin now, several front teeth missing.

"Yes, sir."

"Mailing it to—" The man is interrupted by the postmaster.

Jacob smiles at the man as he leaves, then posts the package. It is not long until Rachael and the children are making their way back to the apartment.

"The air is so fresh, children," says Rachael, breathing in deep and with a large smile. "But winter is coming, that's for sure."

A dog barks in the distance. By the sound it is a large dog, a German shepherd probably. The darkness settles fast, faster than usual, for there is a mandatory blackout across Antwerp. Allied bombers are crossing frequently over Belgium and France. Rachael looks up into the sky. There is still time to get back before the dark moves in. As they approach the last road to the apartment, woods on the right and houses now to their left, an open field catty-corner to the road—as they turn the corner, they are stunned to see what is before them.

"Quick, into the woods, children!" Rachael hisses. All three of them dash into a thicket, huddling behind a large oak. A Nazi truck rumbles by, and another, and another. German shepherds bark and growl into the rapidly cooling night air. "Come with me. Hurry." They rush through the forest, near the edge of the wood but deep enough the Nazis will not notice them. Rachael pulls them to another tree and forces them to sit down on its large roots. "Stay here."

She creeps up ever so slowly to the edge of the woods, small branches poking her and snapping into her face and neck. Nazis are all over the road, forming lines and waiting patiently for orders. She pulls the final few shrubs from her view and gasps. The apartment buildings are surrounded.

"O God of the universe," she whispers covering her mouth. "O Ruben, my Ruben." She watches as the soldiers with the dogs scurry into formation and then rush forward, all at one time, into each building. Other soldiers follow, shouting orders and pointing to the upper stories. "Ruben, O my Ruben," whispers Rachael again, blinking away the tears in her eyes. She jumps as machine gun fire erupts in one building, flashes of light, like bolts of lightning illuminate the darkening sky. She waits and waits. Yells and screams, shouts and wailing come from the rooms above. Still Rachael waits, eyes wide. There are more shouts and then another blast of machine guns. Guards emerge from the buildings, and before them, lines of people. Rachael knows them by name. Somebody gasps near her. She looks over and sees Jacob. He has been watching all of this.

And then the unthinkable, like a nightmare, a sudden surge of terror tearing through her body—Ruben and Benjamin and the rest of the Horowitz family hurriedly make their way to the other prisoners.

"Papa!" Jacob cries out, but Rachael covers his mouth with her hand. Jacob watches as the butt of a gun knocks Uncle Benjamin to the ground. Ruben bends to help his brother, and he too is knocked to the ground. Rachael yelps like a struck animal, muffling the sound with her arm. She watches as her husband lifts his hands in submission then helps Benjamin to his feet. They are hurried into a line with other Jews. Several more machine guns go off inside the buildings, terrible flashes of light. Jacob wants to pull his mother's hand away, wants to run to his father, wants to scream his name. But Rachael holds him tighter and tighter to her trembling body, watching with open mouth as her husband and his brother are loaded into a covered truck. A Nazi officer shouts several commands. It is the Wolf. More soldiers line up, and then they pile into several other trucks near the one Ruben is in. And suddenly, just like that, the truck rumbles to life and rolls out of the complex. Darkness now seals off the evening, and Rachael hears the trucks disappear into the night.

Three guards nearby suddenly burst out with laughter. A fourth is telling them a joke.

Rachael sweeps her children further into the forest. Sarah stumbles on a root and falls to the ground, crying out in pain, the noise stark against the silence. Rachael gathers up Sarah, and the three cower against a large tree. One of the Nazi guards quiets his friends and steps up to the edge of the woods. A bright light penetrates the darkness. Rachael again places her hands over her children's mouths. "Shh. Shh." Her mind is racing, her heart a steady thump, so loud she is convinced they can hear it. The light scans across the woods, sweeping past her and then back again. It goes off, but Rachael keeps her hands over her children's mouths. Five minutes pass like fifty, her ears straining for any sound. Nothing. The emptiness, the silence now pounding and pounding. And then, one of the Nazi guards laughs, a nervous and guttural laugh, almost a relief. Another one shoves his comrade and then a blaze of light illuminates his face. He lights his friend's cigarette and then his own. The four of them walk to their nearby car and drive away.

They are alone. Rachael breathes a deep breath, shuddering her body, trembling her arms. She leans her head against the tree and closes her eyes—mind numb. After several long, deep breaths she realizes her children are in her arms, and she releases her hands from their mouths.

"Now listen to me, children," she whispers. "You must be completely quiet. Not a word. You must follow me. Here, grab my hand. Jacob, take your sister's hand."

"Are we going home, Mama?" Sarah asks.

"No, my lamb, not yet. I need you to be very quiet now. Not a word. It is not safe here. There are bad people everywhere."

Jacob grabs Sarah's hand and then grabs his mother's. He sees the screaming Nazi from his dream. He remembers the terrible flag covering his father's body.

"Come with me, children. Not a word."

They scurry deeper into the woods, every now and then stopping to listen.

9

Rachael does not remember now the scene where Ruben was beaten and taken into the truck; no, that will return in the quiet moments, a stamp forever upon the wax. She now thinks only of her children, survival, hide from the enemy—the next step. She rushes them further and further away from the river, further into the woods where they will be safe from the dogs, from the Nazis.

They find shelter in a gathering of trees, Rachael pulling the children close to keep them warm. "Try to sleep now, children. Shh. There now. It's okay. Try to sleep for a while." Jacob keeps his eyes open for as long as he can. Sarah has fallen into a restless sleep. Jacob hears his mother's heart racing and pounding. He feels her fear, and then a soft touch of her hand upon his hair, stroking it with compassion and a gentle rhythm. The animal life begins to move about, rodents scurry for food. Sarah is shivering in her sleep and Rachael pulls her tighter to her side. Late into the night Jacob and Rachael are still awake, both thinking about what has happened and what will be. But eventually the mind closes off that route, and sleep comes to the Horowitz remnant.

In the morning, early, they awake, and Rachael leads her children through the woods. She has an idea where they are, but is not sure where to go. The woods is large and it heads away from the river, east toward Antwerp. The children are hungry, and

Rachael decides to venture closer to the border of the wood to gauge where she is. A field juts up against the woods, and off in the distance is a farmhouse, a small chicken coop, and a pen full of goats. The day is overcast and threatening to rain. Rachael and the children walk closer to the farmhouse, then Rachael hurries them to the fence that keeps in the goats. Quickly, she enters the barn and hides her children in the mounds of hay.

"Stay put," she says to Jacob. "I'm going to get some food for us. Keep your sister warm until I return." And just like that she is gone. Jacob pushes further into the hay, covering his chilled and damp body with the golden, dry strands. His feet begin to warm up, then his arms, and soon he feels the drowsiness creeping over him. Sarah is already sleeping on his arm. He can hear the goats moving about the pen, the chickens scratching and clucking for food, a moaning wind as it fingers its way though the dilapidated siding. And this becomes a rhythm, a hypnotic siren that forces his lids to droop.

Footsteps and voices startle him awake. Rachael has returned with the farmer, a large man with a burly mustache dipping way below his lips.

"Children?" Rachael whispers. "Children, come out." Jacob rouses his sister and they appear from their hiding. The man holds bread and fresh milk. Rachael breaks off portions of the bread and hands it to her children.

"You can't stay here," the man says with a deep voice. "The Germans are throughout the town looking for Jews. If they catch you here, it will mean the camps for my family. I have to consider my family, if you know what I mean."

Rachael nods and eats her bread.

"The city is just up east a bit. You can make it most of the way through the forest. I will give you some more bread and a canteen of water. That's really the best I can do." He shakes his head and rubs the ends of his moustache. "That's all I can do. The Germans are everywhere. I have to consider my family." Then he is quiet for some time as he watches Sarah and Jacob eat the bread and drink the milk. And he walks out of the barn and back to his house.

Sarah looks up from her milk. She is sickly and pale from the night. "Mama, why aren't we going back home?"

"The Nazis are there," Jacob says in anger.

"Where's Papa and Uncle Benjamin?"

"Well, my little lamb—"

"He's gone, Sarah," Jacob says. "That's all. The Nazis took him and Uncle Benjamin, everyone. They're all gone. There is no one left but us! Just us!" And suddenly he walks over to the side of the barn, squatting on his haunches.

Rachael consoles Sarah and tells her to eat up for the journey ahead, and she walks over to her son. She bends over him and begins to stroke his hair, but he pulls away.

"Your father once told me I could depend on him, that in a pinch, when all seemed lost, he would carry us if need be."

"Well, a lot of good that did him. A lot of good it's done us all."

"We are alive, Jacob. That is the good it has done. We are safe from the Nazis."

"But he is not," says Jacob, beginning to cry. "They have taken him away, and…and they will kill him. They will kill them all."

"Shh, my little lamb," quiets Rachael, now holding her sobbing son in her arms. "Your father is strong. He will survive. Don't worry about him. He and his brother are smart, survivors. They will make it out." She pulls Jacob's face toward her own and wipes his tears from his dirty cheeks. "You are your father's child. I see his strength in you, in your eyes." She holds his face in her hands. "I need you to be like your father, Jacob. I need you to be strong no matter what happens to us. I need you to carry your sister and me." She smiles warmly at him. "You are the man of the house now, Jacob. I need you to be strong, for my sake, my lamb. I need you to be strong like your father."

Jacob looks into his mother's eyes, sees the worry, the fear, but also the strength to take the next step, whatever that next step may be. "I'm sorry, Mama," he says, wiping his eyes with his coat sleeve. "I'm sorry. I will be strong from now on. I will be like Papa."

Rachael hugs him and then they walk back over to Sarah who is still munching on the bread. The farmer returns with a knapsack of food.

"You must leave here as soon as you are able. This food should take care of you for a few days. Head east toward the city. Stay in the woods as long as you can."

Rachael thanks the farmer and assures him they will go soon.

He rubs his mustache with his hands. "God be with you," he says, and walks out.

The day is overcast, a light drizzle descending from the heavens. Rachael and her children have a knapsack of bread and cheese as they disappear into the wood that borders the farm. It runs east and west around Antwerp, sections of it moving right into the heart of the city. The morning turns into midday, the sky still dark and full of rain, a cold wind blowing through the forest, trees creaking and swaying. Rachael finds a thick canopy of brush and makes a small shelter from the dampness. The children huddle around their mother and silently eat their slice of bread and cheese.

The dampness has begun to saturate the clothing, a mildew-like odor engulfing them. Rachael concentrates on the pungent taste of cheese, not allowing her mind to journey anywhere but the present. It is a constant battle to control her thoughts. At every turn they are desperate to fling her over the abyss into the darkness that borders everything she does. No. She will not allow it to win. *The Nazis will take no one else,* she says to herself. *We shall survive.* And with every internal dialogue she strengthens her heart and soul, smiles at her children, and thinks about the next step.

Food and water is the priority, day to day, control the thoughts—food, water, and shelter from the rain, this is all: the next step.

Rachael stops and looks about the woods for limbs and branches. She tells Jacob to take his sister and gather firewood. "But stay close," she commands.

Jacob is cold and hungry, wet, and feeling the effects of their travel. He is not so much worried about himself, however. He has recognized, as has his mother, how Sarah's health has precipitously fallen. She is running a low grade fever now, and is silent for long periods of time. Jacob gathers several sticks, small ones, and gives them to his sister.

"Go ahead, Sarah. Take these and go back to Mother. I'll get the rest." She leaves, face blank and pale, and Jacob ventures further into the woods. He collects a large bundle of dead limbs, and slowly makes his way back to the shelter. As he walks he hears the wind groaning through the branches above. The dampness filters through the trees in the form of a mist, clinging and seeping into the very marrow of his bones. He walks further, and then suddenly he hears a rustle and a breaking of twigs. He looks around but sees nothing. He leans against a tree, waiting for the sound again, but there is only the swaying of the trees, the creaking of the limbs, and the dampness. He returns to his mother and Sarah in the makeshift shelter. Jacob sets the wood down as his mother begins to light a fire with matches the farmer gave her. She takes some paper she has found in her pocket and tears it into strips. After some anxious moments, a small crackle and flame emerge from the logs. Soon they are huddled around it, rubbing their hands over the heat.

Rachael hands out another small portion of bread and cheese. She has to force Sarah to eat, for all she wants to do is sleep, huddled next to the fire, eyes closed. Jacob wonders if he should mention the sound he heard to his mother. He watches her gently stroke Sarah's head and cheek. No, he will not bother her right now. Not now. It was probably just a deer or a falling branch. He munches on his cheese in silence.

Later that night as he is gathering more wood, he hears the noise again. Darkness has surrounded the forest, so it is impossible for Jacob to see anything but a few feet in front of him.

"Who's there?" he whispers, but his voice is small and void of power. He waits in the silence, thinking about the Nazi guards who stood outside of the forest the night his father was taken away. He draws the bundle of sticks closer to his chest and slowly creeps back to the shelter—a terror just behind him, reaching out, out, out.

"Mama," he whispers, "I think I heard someone in the forest."

Rachael strokes Sarah's face. "It was probably only an animal. They come out at night."

Jacob pulls his knees up further to his chest and rubs his hands over the fire. He does not smell the mildew on his clothes any longer, does not notice the disheveled look of his mother or sister. He feels the heat and is thankful for that, and the scant cheese and bread. He forces his mind to focus on his mother gently stroking his sister's pale and sallow cheek. No one speaks, and Jacob drifts off into that silence, into the freedom of his mind where everything is warm and dry and where there is a storehouse of food.

Jacob wakes from his sleep. It is early morning and Rachael has stood up to face the solitary man walking toward the campfire.

"Don't come any closer!" she cries out. "I said stop!" Rachael walks out to the man in defiance. The mist is coming down hard, a thick and oppressive curtain of moisture. Rachael approaches the man and stands in his way. "I am the only one here. What do you want?" But the man walks around her and stands before the children and the fire. Sarah does not stir. Jacob stands over her in defense.

"What do you want?" Rachael says. "We have only some bread and cheese. If you want something else, take me. Do not hurt my children, please. Take me. I will do whatever you want, just don't harm my children." The man is wraithlike, baggy coat and disheveled, thick black hair. His face is dirty and unshaven. Jacob notices the thick and pungent smell of mildew and dampness coming from him.

The man lifts off his knapsack and pulls out a pan, fills it with water from his canteen, and sets it on the crackling fire.

"Please," Rachael says, "we have nothing for you here. My children are very sick, and we barely have enough food for ourselves."

The thin man sits silently stirring the coffee grounds in the water. "Yes, your daughter is very sick," he says in a whisper. "She needs more than coffee if she is going to survive."

Rachael crouches down next to Sarah and places her hand against her cheek. It is hot with fever.

"How long have you been out here, Mother?" says the man as he lifts his long face and looks at Rachael.

"We have been two nights in the woods," she says.

The man nods his head and rubs his hands together over the fire. Rachael looks at his face and realizes this is but a young man: twenty-five at most.

"I have been hiding since the first roundup," the man says in his whisper voice. "I don't even know how long that has been."

The coffee boils and the man takes out two tin cups from his knapsack, pours the coffee, and gives one cup to Rachael. She palms the warmth in her hands like a precious stone.

"Thank you."

The man is silent. They drink their coffee, and the man pours her another cup. Still they are silent. Then the man speaks in his whisper voice.

"They say there are no Jews left in Belgium. They say all Jews have been taken to the death camps." He drinks his coffee, tosses out the grounds, and pours another cup. "Is that true?"

"I don't know. I truly don't know."

The young man pulls out his canteen and pours a cup of water for Jacob. They sit in silence again.

"My father and mother were taken from our house. My wife with them. We have been married for only one month. I came home from work and they were gone." He says this in such a matter of fact way that Rachael, at first, does not understand. He sips his coffee again and looks at Sarah. "She needs medical treatment. If she doesn't get it, she will die."

"She has a fever, that is all. All she needs is some rest."

"I am a dentist by trade, but by the looks of her face and the sound of her breathing, I would diagnose her with pneumonia." This too is matter-of-fact, in the whisper voice—void of emotion.

Rachael feels Sarah's head again as if there will be a sudden change.

"I have more supplies over at my camp. It is deeper in the forest, but you will be safer there." He looks around the woods, looks out into the mist. "You are still too close to the border for safety. I have seen German patrols out here before."

They sit in silence for quite some time. Then suddenly, the man stands up. He dumps out the coffee grounds from the now empty pot, and places the pot and his cup back in the knapsack. And he begins to walk deeper into the woods.

"Mama," Jacob says. "Mama, he is right. Sarah is going to die if we don't get her to a doctor. Mama? Mama, the man said we are not safe here."

Rachael turns and looks into the woods, the man has disappeared. And then she looks at Jacob. "Go and stop him," she says, her voice empty.

The camp Dr. Aaron Feldman has made—that is the wraithlike man's name—is part of a rock formation, a shallow cave. Its entranceway is covered with branches so it is barely detectable from only ten feet away. The shelter overlooks a deep ravine where at the bottom flows a small stream.

Sarah is placed against a rock ledge and covered with a musty blanket. Aaron stoops over the fire and places several more logs on it. On one side of the cave is a rock where he has placed several candles and many cans of food. The bottom of the cave is covered with dried leaves to keep out the moisture. Rachael watches as Aaron gives Sarah several pills to control the fever. He puts the pill bottle into his black doctor's bag and closes it up.

That night they eat rabbit Aaron has caught—the meat a savory treat—and drink coffee. Aaron lights a cigarette and offers one to Rachael who declines.

"Fourteen years of schooling to live in a cave like an animal," says Aaron with a smile, the first sign of emotion Rachael has seen. "It is better than the camps or a bullet, I guess." He pours another cup of coffee for himself. "Your little girl should feel the effects of those drugs soon. It will stave off the fever, but the pneumonia is getting worse, I'm afraid."

"Where is the nearest town?"

"Antwerp is all around you. Two miles straight that way," and he points into the darkness. "The problem is not where is the town, but whom can you trust?" He puffs on his cigarette. "I have made raids in the town, taking food and stealing what I can, but I trust no one anymore. The Black Brigade is everywhere." He spits with disgust into the fire. "Belgians turning in fellow Belgians. We are in dark times." After this he falls silent and then steps out of the cave.

Jacob huddles close to Sarah, using some of her musty blanket. Rachael sits near the fire, her back to her children. Aaron steps into the cave and closes the makeshift door behind him. The quarters are very cramped, and Rachael is forced to sleep up against the wall. Aaron leans against the other wall, near Sarah, and pensively looks at Rachael.

"My wife was beautiful like you," he says in his whisper voice and reaches out to push back a strand of Rachael's hair that has fallen across her face. She instinctively pulls away. Aaron smiles. "I am not going to hurt you. It is just good to have someone else in my world for a while. When I first saw you, I was shocked at the sudden surge of emotion I felt for my wife. I loved her very much."

"I too miss my husband." Rachael pauses, once again trying to reign in her emotions, harnessing them with great effort. "But now I must think of my children. They are all I have left."

Aaron closes his eyes and falls asleep. Rachael stares at the fire and watches as it slowly burns itself out.

In the morning, Sarah's breathing is raspy and shallow. Rachael decides they must make their way into the city no matter what the consequences. Aaron agrees but urges her to wait until evening. He gives her food and a large overcoat. He tells her she does not look like a Jew, and her beauty may help her in the city.

Evening falls and a steady rain is coming down. They set out from the forest and make their way to the border on the eastern side of Antwerp. The town is completely dark, no lights, no lamp-posts, nothing but darkness. With the children by her side— Sarah barely able to walk, Jacob holding her up most of the time—Rachael makes her way out of the woods and into the city streets. She stays close to the buildings and watches out for any patrols. The rain picks up and saturates them to the bone. Rachael begins to hear that nagging persistent voice, "You have lost. It is the end. You have come from safety into the very mouth of the lion. Fool!" She sees a street sign, one she thinks is familiar, one she remembers her husband mentioning on occasion. Maybe it is familiar, maybe it is just a delusion. Sarah begins to cough so loudly Rachael pulls her into an alley and covers her mouth. Her daughter is dying, and this forces her to go on. Soon they come to a crossroads, the rain coming down so hard now she can barely see in front of her. The children are soaked through, Jacob nearly carrying his sister.

Rachael looks down the deserted street and sees a small light coming from a door several houses down the road. She hurries them forward through the rain and walks up to the front gate. The door is ajar, for someone is standing in it. Rachael bends down to Jacob and whispers, "If I am taken, run for your life. Save yourself if you can." Rachael leaves her son, now huddled over Sarah, who has slumped onto the sidewalk. She stumbles forward through the downpour and walks up to the startled man in the door.

"Please, sir," she cries out, "can you tell me if you know a Hans Kraemer?"

The man turns around and looks stunned at the wretch of a woman before him. He does not say anything.

"Please, sir. Do you know a man named Hans Kraemer?"

The man moves away from the door as another man steps to the threshold. "Yes, I know Hans Kraemer…" But the man's voice suddenly catches in his throat. "Mrs. Horowitz? Rachael, is that you?"

Rachael cries out as Hans Kraemer rushes out toward her. They embrace, Rachael sobbing uncontrollably.

Hans looks toward the fence and sees Jacob and Sarah now lying on the ground. "O my God in heaven!" he says and runs to them. He lifts Sarah in his arms and carries her into the house, Jacob and Rachael following close behind. The door is shut behind them, the rain and cold whipping against the glass in protest.

PART TWO

10

When Jacob left Belgium for the United States in 1951, he had determined in his heart to forget the past. That was easy for a twenty-two-year-old father of one to say, but nearly impossible to do. As he boarded the *St. Martin* en route to New York, he wrapped a small white blanket tighter around his newborn son. The wind was blowing across the harbor in twenty mile an hour gusts. *It will be good to be closed up in my cabin,* he thought, *closed up with Asher in a small cabin where I can rest and shut out the world.* And that is what he did. He ordered room service and stared out the tiny porthole. Every once in a while he walked over to Asher and caressed his cheek, but the child brought back the terrible memories, and he walked back over to the porthole and stared at the infinite sea. Soon the gentle swaying of the ship hypnotized him into a restless sleep. And that was how every day of the crossing went.

Jacob had married Yvonne in 1951. It was one of the easiest decisions he had ever made, for she had been the love of his life during some of the darkest times he had ever encountered. By the end of the war, Jacob had established himself as a diligent worker, and soon he was running a small garment shop in De Panne, a small coastal city just east of the French border. Yvonne had followed him there after the war hoping to cement their relationship, but Jacob had changed. He was becoming closed off, as though what had happened to him and his family, to Belgium, to the world had never happened. She saw him slipping into an isolation of the present—a world where no plans could ever be secured, for the future did not exist. Jacob left Liège, left Brussels, left it all and tried to make a new life for himself. Yvonne followed close behind.

One day while Jacob was stitching a suit coat, he looked up and saw out his large glass window, Yvonne! Yes, it was Yvonne walking to the post office. He had not seen her for nearly three and a half years. Then, back in the days at Liège, she was lanky, almost boyish in appearance—short, dark brown hair and brown eyes, large and doelike. When Jacob saw her in the coastal town of De Panne, in a place of seclusion from all he had known—when he saw her out that large glass window—a secret part of him suddenly burned for life. He put down his needle and thread and walked over to the window. Her blue skirt and tanned arms swung in that awkward gesture he had grown to love during his youth. She was filled out, her teenage gangliness transformed into a beautiful young woman. Her once short-cropped hair, hair she cut herself, now flowed down her shoulders, swaying from side to side as she walked. Yvonne, here! And all that day Jacob stood by the window hoping to see her walk by, sat in his chair half expecting her at any moment to walk through the door. She did not, and Jacob began to brood once more.

And as the days passed in his little garment shop, Jacob wondered if the woman he had seen weeks before was really Yvonne at all. Soon he was closing the shop early and walking the streets, hoping to confirm the vision he had witnessed. Soon his life was filled with one thought: Yvonne. He closed the shop for days on end and walked the town: out on the pier, on the beach, through the streets. She was not to be seen. And after many days like this,

his mind clicked again into the present, squashed all thoughts of the future, all thoughts of hope, and dove back into his work making custom suits at a reasonable price. The present, the present. This is all we have.

Twenty-two years old is the prime of life, the vibrant and dreamy time where young men can do anything. Jacob had become an old man at twenty-two. The flower that had appeared on that spring day was nipped in the bud. Next time he would control such emotion, such excess of hope and joy. Day to day, this was life.

And one day, just like that, Yvonne showed up at Jacob's little shop. She walked over to the empty desk and rang the small metal bell. With a mouthful of sandwich, Jacob walked out to the counter, not a little upset with the impatience of his customer.

"I am coming. Coming. Just a minute—" His voice was cut short by Yvonne's presence, and he nearly choked on the roast beef.

"Hello, Jacob," she said with an awkward smile, face flush with embarrassment.

Jacob wiped his mouth and took up his yellow measuring tape. "Are you here for a fitting or to pick up a garment?"

"Jacob Horowitz, it is I: Yvonne Chabot—Pierre's sister—from Charleroi." She paused and then put her hands on her hips. "Surely you have not forgotten me?"

Jacob looked at the counter, trying to suppress the terrible hope flowering within him. He looked up at her.

"I was never in Charleroi. I don't know you."

Yvonne looked at him with a blank face. Then, after a long stare, she said, "I am sorry. I have made a fool of myself. Please forgive me." And with hand over mouth, she rushed out the door.

Jacob sat on his chair and watched her disappear around the

corner. He bent over the piece of clothing that lay on the counter and began to fold it up. Five minutes passed, and Yvonne appeared once again at the window, then the door, stopped, shook her head and walked away. Another five minutes later Jacob noticed Yvonne slowly walking past the storefront window, glancing in as if looking at the clothing. She disappeared from view. Then, he thought he saw her across the street talking with the butcher, pointing at Jacob's store. She disappeared again.

Not more than twenty minutes later—while Jacob was patiently measuring an old man's arm length, writing the numbers down in a small notebook—in stormed Yvonne, flinging open the door and allowing it to bang the shelves behind it. She marched toward Jacob and his customer. The old man's eyes were wide with fear, his white droopy whiskers sagging. Jacob continued to measure and then write in his little notebook.

"I am not leaving, Jacob Horowitz, until you acknowledge me!" Yvonne shouted. He was about to respond when she suddenly grabbed the tape from his hands. "I have come too far and waited too long for you to be so impertinent." She threw the tape to the floor. "How absolutely rude of you to make me walk in here and play such a game. To pull my emotions around like you were some silly adolescent boy! I will not stand for it, Jacob Horowitz! Do you hear me?"

The customer, a pudgy old codger, backed against the counter as Yvonne unleashed her fury. Jacob deflected her accusing eyes by stooping down to pick up the tape measure.

"Please, Yvonne," he said standing up and then ducking again as she grabbed a long measuring stick and threatened him with it.

"Oh, so it's Yvonne now, is it, now that I confront you, now that you are forced to face me? Well, Jacob Horowitz, the only way I am leaving is if you tell me where and when we shall have dinner tonight." Yvonne raised the measuring stick to strike, and Jacob looked up helplessly and stuttered for an answer.

"The Rose!" the old man shouted suddenly from behind. "The Garden Rose on Main Street, for heaven's sake! Six o'clock at the Garden Rose!"

Yvonne hesitated for a moment, then turned around, and calmly placed the stick on the counter.

"Well then," she said with an air of dignity, "the Garden Rose at six o'clock. That sounds very pleasant indeed." And she sauntered out of the store, daintily closing the door behind her.

Jacob stared with open mouth as she walked out. And then the old man with the large whiskers started to cackle, even snorting with glee. "Son," he continued, "if you don't marry that woman, I will!" He bellowed out another spasm of laughter and then slapped his knee with complete joy. "By heaven, what a woman!"

That night Jacob and Yvonne ate dinner together for the first time since the war. Jacob watched as she smiled, as she shook her head, as she waved with that awkward gesture that had become synonymous with Yvonne. Every time she spoke, he watched her and remembered all their experiences, remembered the secret blood oath, their first kiss. They did not talk about their past, but sat content in each other's company. Jacob spoke of his store, his customers, his future plans. Yvonne divulged little of what she had done after the war. She also focused on the present. At times the conversation lagged, and each stared out at the ocean beyond.

It was as awkward and wonderful as any reunion can be, but there was a chemistry here that hovered about them, lingered on the border of every spoken word. Jacob was young and vibrant, strong willed and—after all he had been through—invulnerable. Yvonne was carefree and strong willed as well. The first meeting ended with Jacob holding out his hand to shake good-bye. Yvonne, spontaneous and full of life, suddenly grabbed his hand and kissed him on his right cheek. And then, like a butterfly, she dashed into her house.

That night Jacob tried to think about his work, about anything but the past and Yvonne. But nothing doing. Yvonne was that tiny flame that ignited the dried and brittle past, the memories of love and terror. Was it safe to stay in such memories? Could he dare to share an emotional bond? The war had taught him, with thunderous fists—blow by blow—that life was fragile, relationships weak, emotions dangerous. But Yvonne made him want to try, made him want to wish for something better. She had forced her way back into his life, forced him to dare the dream of love—real love. And as Jacob lay in his bed, he decided that with Yvonne he could dare. And for the first time since the war he actually looked forward to the next morning.

They saw each other nearly every day, shared time in the evening together, and talked of the war, of the death, of the terror. Jacob began to shed the scales, the layers of protection that caused him to act twice his age. Soon they would take picnics on the beach together—fruit, cheese, and wine. The expanse of ocean became an avenue for dreams.

"Do you see that horizon, Yvonne?"

"Yes, dear."

"Some day I am going to cross over that horizon, cross over it to America."

"And leave me here?"

"Maybe." Jacob smiled and ducked as Yvonne faked a slap. "My aunt lives in New York City. I think very soon, I will board a ship and travel to New York. I will step off the boat and look at the Statue of Liberty, the Empire State Building, Wall Street. I will look at them all and then start my business."

Yvonne sat and listened to Jacob dream big dreams, stacking one idea on the other.

"If I could make it to America, where people are willing to take risks, I could become a wealthy man."

Yvonne leaned over to Jacob and caressed his hair, then snuggled her head on his shoulder. "Tell me about your plan again, Jacob. Start from the beginning and tell me all about it." They both looked into the setting sun, the large expanse of water, and Jacob told the story.

He would come to America and settle first with his aunt in Yonkers. Then after a year, he would rent his own apartment. His idea was simple: make quality suits the average man on the street could buy. He would create a warehouse of suits, a discount place where even the rich could be frugal and look good. He had experienced some of that here in De Panne, but Belgians were too stuck in their old ways. America would be different. The overhead would be minimal, for he would make the suits himself, and soon, if God was good and peacetime held, the Americans would make him a wealthy man.

Jacob stroked Yvonne's hair and talked about America. He could invent and create, embellish and revise as he told the story. His father had been gifted in such a way. The stories of America were elaborately detailed, filled with Dickens-like characters: fat bankers chomping on their soggy cigars, snobbish customers coming in with mink coats and Italian suits—"Oh, indeed, these are very nicely made." He imitated them all, giving them caricatured names: Mr. and Mrs. Snobsneeze, Mr. Greedbeetle, and so on. Yvonne sat and listened, smiling and chuckling, lost in her lover's imaginary world of America. And all the while they stared into the darkening sky.

It was like this for quite some time. One evening while they sat staring at the ocean, at the orange and reddish hues of the setting sun, Jacob told his story again, but this time all of the Is were suddenly Wes. That night Jacob took his wife-to-be across the ocean and to New York. She saw the Empire State Building, saw Wall Street, and the Statue of Liberty. Jacob took her to the promised land.

Jacob had it planned from the beginning. He would tell her the story, and then ask her to marry him. He would even tell her about the money he had saved for their new adventure. The night was magnificent and forever etched into Jacob's mind. He asked Yvonne to marry him, and she cried in his arms. Two people, two people who have experienced so much—so much terror, so much pain, so much joy—could not have been happier. And Jacob thought on his way home that night, *Now I can live. I have been given a second chance to blossom. Now I will live!*

They were married early in 1951 and honeymooned in Paris. The world was at their fingertips.

One day Yvonne walked into the clothing store and stepped over to Jacob, who was busy sewing the sleeve of a suit coat. Jacob looked up and smiled, then started to sew again. Then he stopped and looked up again.

"What is it, dear?" he said with concern.

"Well, my love," Yvonne whispered and then rubbed her stomach, "there will be more than two Horowitzes on that ship to America." And she smiled, large and full, her narrow face aglow.

Jacob did not understand at first, then with a sudden panic, then an explosion of joy, he leapt over the counter and hugged his wife.

The world was spinning in such harmony, thought Jacob as Yvonne closed the door behind her, *that maybe, just maybe the pain and terror of the war could be forgotten forever.* And he hummed while he sewed, hummed and laughed out loud with joy. *Yes, he thought, yes indeed. This is how life heals itself. The pain of the past is consumed by the life of the new; the seed of the living expunges the sins of the past.* And he hummed and laughed again.

The joy and astonishment of her swelling, of her enlarged breasts, of the incredible miracle of new life soon superseded everything else. The story of America now included Asher or Sonya. Asher or Sonya would travel the world with them, would work at the store, would take it over some day, become wealthy in a land of plenty. Jacob and Yvonne would visit him or her and his or her children, would chuckle and smile with delight as the children grew, as life continued. Yes, the future would be a place of rest, of peace, and of joy. Who could think otherwise? The future would eclipse the past, the joy of living would bury the darkness that pursued him. How could it be otherwise?

But the darkness did come back, came back with a fist of iron that pulverized Jacob and strangled his dreams.

Jacob waited expectantly in the hospital waiting room. He waited and paced as soon-to-be fathers do. Then a nurse came to talk with him. "There has been a complication, but nothing to worry about. The doctors have it all under control." He waited again, for two hours, and was soon called through the double doors. A doctor, bloodstained and sweating, met him around the corner. Yvonne was dead. It was as simple as that. Yvonne was dead and the baby boy was alive. Jacob listened to the doctor talk of hemorrhaging, of severe blood loss, of breech, of uterine deterioration. He listened, but all he could think about was the blood on the doctor's scrubs—the last remnant of Yvonne's life. And then, suddenly, he felt the slow closing of immense and impenetrable doors.

The funeral was held in a cemetery outside of De Panne. He and some neighbor friends gathered around the open mouth of the earth, gathered and said little. Jacob held Asher in his arms and swung him back and forth. His mouth was dry, words hollow and meaningless.

The terrible doors swung closer together.

He watched as the shiny mahogany casket was lowered into the ground, the edges snagging on the inadequately dug grave.

The terrible doors swung closer together.

He watched—cradling the crying Asher in his arms, blocking the cold autumn wind with his back—he watched as the rabbi and the gravediggers tried to nudge the coffin down the yawning mouth of earth. Soon the coffin was tilted in such a precarious position he knew Yvonne was now balled up at one end. The rabbi said a blessing as the gravediggers held the one end from dipping any further.

The terrible doors of his past shut tight.

Life was a cruel joke. Never again would Jacob give his heart completely to anyone or anything. So were his thoughts as the rabbi pronounced the blessing, as the gravediggers held up the end of the coffin, as the autumn wind blew across the cemetery. To survive the war, the Nazis, the darkness, only to be crushed again—this was too much for any human to endure. Yes, Jacob would go forward, one step after the other, now with Asher, but he would wait for the blow to hit again. Yes, he would raise his newborn son, but it would be his way. He would teach the boy to endure, to win. This was all that mattered now. Life had kicked him in the teeth. He would kick it back, harder and with more calculated blows.

The door of his past was sealed. So be it.

And that is what he was thinking when he boarded the *St.*

Martin, a one way ticket to New York City, the Empire State Building, the Statue of Liberty. This is what he was thinking as he caressed his son Asher, as he stared out the porthole and into the terrible gray of the ocean. But his tears and his dark nights told a different story, a story that would never let him forget he was now alone on his journey, that now only two would reach the promised land. And that land, that land of milk and honey, seemed as dry and fruitless as the greatest desert.

1

The fool says in his heart there is no God. And at the moment Jacob Horowitz saw the light in the doorway, heard the man's voice, heard Hans Kraemer's voice, he was no fool. For how else could he explain that on a night as black as coal, a constant rain pouring down from the abyss above, his sister close to death—how else could he explain that open door, that beam of light. Was it chance? Was it blind luck that had just so happened to turn in his favor? Or was it God, a God who suddenly and quite miraculously brought a desperate woman and her children to the doorstep of Grace?

Yes, he wrestled the rest of his life with the nagging questions of destiny, why some and not others? Why did God snatch up his father and uncle and all the other Jews hiding in the apartment? Why would that same God allow such evil to take them all away? Yes, Jacob wrestled with that angel every night after Liza's death. How could he justify one and not the other? How could both be true? He asked his rabbi, he asked his Jewish friends, he even asked Lereau, the Christian. Yes, the questions remained all of his life, but from that moment at Hans Kraemer's house, Jacob believed the verse in the book of Psalms that says, "The fool has said in his heart there is no God." Jacob was no fool.

The doctor has just left little Sarah after giving her some medication that will cure her pneumonia. She will have to rest for at least a week. Jacob is sleeping in a warm bed upstairs in Hans Kraemer's house. Rachael and Hans sit around the kitchen table. It has been three days since they met in the rain.

"I will follow up on a lead I have with someone in Charleroi," says Hans rubbing the outside of his coffee cup. "Every day you stay in Antwerp is a day closer to your capture."

Rachael is silent. She has been silent for most of the three days. The memories of her husband are flooding around her, and she is powerless to stop them. When she was out in the forest, hiding from the Germans, when there was a focus, a goal, she was able to suppress the terror and do what must be done. Now all she can think about is her husband's misfortune. Why not every one of them? Why weren't all saved or all taken away? She is suddenly lost in that terrible loop of empty answers. Though she knows she should not think about the past—the vacations, the joys spent in each other's arms, the silly moments between them—she is powerless before them. And so she is silent, for if she opens her mouth she will sob like a little girl.

"I know you've been through a lot, Rachael, and you are still in great danger." Hans's voice is hesitating and concerned. "I am afraid that what was behind is only a fraction of what is ahead."

Rachael observes Hans's features, his pitted face, beak nose, and small round glasses. He is so kind, so trustworthy. It is God who transforms the insignificant souls into significant ones. Hans and his family pray every night for each other and for their new arrivals. They are deeply committed to the small church on the outskirts of Antwerp, a congregation of only fifty souls. Rachael remembers Ruben laughing at the lanky man and his absurd habits of church and prayer. Hans was always helping the down and out. Ruben never understood his compassion, but deep inside Rachael knew her husband would trust this man with his life.

"What needs to be done?" Rachael whispers.

"I will make contact with several friends of mine who are connected to the Underground in Charleroi. I believe one of them can help you. I'm afraid it will take some time, however. We must hide you upstairs as long as we can until it is safe to move you."

"I understand."

"Rachael..." But Hans does not finish his question and looks down at the table. He looks back up at her, his long face racked with emotion. "I tried to warn Ruben about—" He cannot continue and Rachael takes Hans's hand and squeezes it. "I tried to..." And then in a shaking voice he says, "Oh, Rachael. What has happened? He was my best friend, my mentor, my—" He is once again unable to finish, and Rachael steps over to him and hugs him. He wipes his eyes with his large, lanky hands, fingernails clean and sculpted. "I am sorry. You don't need such outbursts right now."

"You are a good man, Hans Kraemer. You did all you could for him, and now you are doing all you can for us. Ruben would be proud of you."

Mary Kraemer walks into the kitchen. She is large and abounds with flesh. Her face, a puffy mask, is wrinkled with concern and compassion. Mary pours a cup of coffee and joins them at the table.

"Sarah is tossing quite a bit upstairs. I put the blanket back on her and tucked it under her legs."

"Thank you, Mary. You and Hans have been so kind."

Mary reaches out her fleshy hand and grasps Rachael's thin arm.

"The children concern me most," says Rachael sipping her coffee. "Jacob will not show his emotions. He keeps them all inside. I fear for him sometimes."

"He's a strong boy," Hans says. "He has his father in him. I see it in the way he carries himself." Hans pulls his glasses from his face and rubs it, then replaces his glasses. "He will have to be strong for what lies ahead. You will all have to be very strong."

Jacob rests upstairs, eyes wide, peering into the darkness, ears straining to hear the conversation below. Even he realizes that to stay in Antwerp is to join his father and uncle. Belgium suddenly seems as infinite as the sky and at the same time, while his family hides, it is to him tinier than the head of a pin. The house is strange, the room unknown and filled with looming shadows. But the bed smells of laundry soap—clean and perfumed, dry and comfortable. The mattress snuggles around him, pulling his arms closer to his side. He is in the womb of safety, and all around the spears of the enemy threaten to puncture through.

Suddenly, Jacob sees Dr. Aaron Feldman hunched over his little fire, sitting alone in the cave, dry goods and candles on the rock mantel. He smells the mildew mixed with smoke from the many fires. How many Aaron Feldmans were there out in the darkening world? How many were hiding and wandering, scared and alone. And suddenly Jacob feels very small, trapped and afraid. The black hand of the Nazis stretches and roams across the world. Who can stop it?

A car squeals its tires as it turns a corner. Jacob sits up and pulls his knees to his chest. "I must be like Papa," he says to himself, the gooseflesh now covering his arms and legs. "I must be like Papa. Papa wants me to be strong. I must be strong like

Papa." He can hear the shouts of the guards as they rush into the apartment where his father is. He sees the flashes from the machine guns. And all the while the one in charge calmly smokes his cigarette as if contemplating a mountain landscape.

Jacob pulls his knees closer and chants his mantra faster and faster. He sees his father coming out in the line of Jews, sees him shuffling his feet one after the other like some convict on a chain gang. And Jacob continues to chant his mantra over and over. He sees his father reach for Uncle Benjamin, stoop down to help him up. He sees the guard's gun stock slam into his father's scalp and his father, like a rag doll, slumping to the wet ground. "I must be like Papa, strong like Papa." He sees his father stand up, a glob of red, like paint, now showing on his head and face. And he sees his father disappear into the back of the truck—forever. And all the while the tall officer smokes his cigarette and stares emotionless at the horror before him.

Something strange, something almost calming happens to Jacob. He suddenly directs all of his attention onto the tall officer smoking his cigarette. And like a snake shedding its skin, Jacob sheds the old memories from his mind.

This night that man who stood smoking his cigarette becomes the symbol that replaces all the pain, replaces the screaming guard and the horrible Nazi flag from Jacob's dream. Now there is a single focus—the Wolf. And a controlled rage boils deep within Jacob's heart. He does not realize that as he falls asleep, he has fists of sheet and blanket in his hands.

Since the first roundups, Belgium has become a giant prison camp within the terror of the Nazi regime. Roads are blocked off and detoured so anyone coming into the country must first go through the major checkpoints. The North and the South sections of Belgium have become one unified prison. The Germans roam the streets, take what they want, harass whom they want—all the while working with the Black Brigade to flush out the remaining Jews.

No one is safe, and Hans Kraemer is more and more aware of this. The Gestapo has been seen on his street. Do they know something? Do they suspect Hans and his family? Every day on his way to work, Hans expects to be hauled down to Brussels to Gestapo headquarters for questioning. On his return trips from the garment shop, he expects his house to be empty—the Horowitz family taken away to the death camps.

Soon Sarah is well enough to move, and Hans is relieved though they are not yet able to leave. Hans is waiting on false papers for Rachael, papers that identify her as Hans Kraemer's cousin. Hans learns that the family that forges papers is under surveillance. They have decided to stop after this last job. They still think they may have been discovered. It would be best for these last set of papers to go far away.

Finally the papers are ready and Hans gives them to Rachael. The papers include an identity card, a birth certificate, and occupation information. She is now not a mother of two, wife of one—all of that has been erased by words on a page. She is now a single woman who cleans houses for a living.

The time has come for them to make their way to the southern part of Belgium, the French speaking part—to the town of Charleroi one hundred and five kilometers away. The plan is straightforward and every detail is worked out. Hans and Rachael will take the garment truck, loaded with coats and other paraphernalia, along with Jacob and Sarah, and drive to Charleroi. They will leave during the evening hours and arrive at an abandoned barn just before midnight. Once there, they will be met by several members of the Belgian Underground. Hans will return home, and Rachael will be told what to do.

Everything is secure, and the truck sets out at seven o'clock in the evening. The roads seem to be empty. The truck makes its way out of Antwerp and hums toward their rendezvous. Hans has been warned to bypass Brussels, for it has become the Nazi head-quarters in Belgium. He turns the truck down several dirt roads that seem endless and winding, the headlights only illuminating twenty feet before them. They drive on and on. The map Hans has been given shows the route least likely to be guarded by the Gestapo. But soon the truck is plummeting into an abyss of back country roads where nothing is marked, each turn seemingly the wrong one, each stretch of road a path to danger.

Then just up ahead, as the truck turns a sharp corner, just beyond the headlights stand several guards with machine guns, several German trucks and a closed gate blocking the road.

"We'll be okay," Hans says to Rachael. "I have secured the children in the back so that no one will find them. Remember who you are."

A helmeted guard waves the garment truck to a stop. "May I see your papers, please?"

Hans smiles weakly, and pulls out his papers and hands them to the guard. The guard reads through them and then looks up.

"Where are you going?"

"To Charleroi. I have a special order of garments I need to get to my other shop."

"To Charleroi?"

"Yes…to Charleroi."

The guard peers into the cab and sees Rachael. "May I have your papers also, please?" Rachel takes them out and hands them to Hans who hands them to the guard. "Wait in your truck please." The guard walks away from the truck and disappears into a small building. Hans and Rachael stare ahead through the front window. The headlights illuminate the gate and several guards are now walking around the truck. The guard steps out of the small building. He is accompanied by someone else, an officer. As the officer steps closer to the truck, Rachael gasps.

"Is there anyone else with you?" Wolfhardt Becker says, his small round glasses reflecting the light so that his pupils are undetectable.

"No," Hans says. "We are carrying a load of garments to Charleroi."

"Yes, so I have been told." He smiles. "To Charleroi."

Rachael stares ahead, not daring to look over at the Wolf. She feels his eyes piercing her and fights back the urge to run. She stares straight ahead in fear, in panic, in silence.

"And who is with you?" says Becker, shining a light into Rachael's face.

"Look," Hans says suddenly and with a burst of emotion that startles everyone, "I have to get these garments to Charleroi by midnight or I will lose a whole lot of money. Will you kindly quit playing games with us and allow me to pass. I still have a long road ahead if I am going to make it to Charleroi on time."

The Wolf smiles and then stares at Rachael's papers. He looks up at Hans, his face serious and menacing.

"You see, Mr. Kraemer, my job is to find Jews. I find them in all sorts of different places and at different times. That is why we have these road blocks keeping those people in Brussels who should be kept in and those out of Brussels who should be kept out." He hesitates again and looks at the papers, then back up to Hans. "You tell my guard, Mr. Kraemer, that you and your beautiful cousin must hurry to Charleroi to deliver garments. And yet, you are headed out of Brussels and toward Antwerp—the opposite direction."

"What are you talking about?"

"You are heading toward Antwerp, Mr. Kraemer. Do you not know where you are going?"

Hans looks over at Rachael. He is at a loss.

"Please, sir," she says as the Wolf shines the beam on her face, "we are in a hurry and obviously lost. If my cousin does not get these clothes to my father in Charleroi, it will mean his job. I know you have greater goals than helping a man keep his job, but I assure you we are not Jews, we know no Jews, and we desperately need your help if we are to make it on time. Now could you please give us directions and allow us to pass." This is not a question but a command.

The Wolf clicks off his light. He gives back the papers to Hans and places his hand on the truck door. "One does not find in such a backward country, Miss Kraemer, a woman with such pronounced German traits—beauty and fire. You are a credit to your race." He smiles again, showing his young age, and turns to the guard. "Give them directions around the checkpoints in Brussels." And with that he walks back into the little building.

"You have come far, Madame Horowitz," says the short, thick man with only a wisp of hair left upon his head. He is dressed in a black leather jacket and dark army fatigues. Rachael is alone and now sitting in a wine cellar in Charleroi.

Hans had dropped her off several hours before at an old barn outside the city. There she was met by two men, one smoking a pipe and dressed in a long coat, as if out for a stroll. He had stepped right up to the barn where she was and asked quite casually, "The sky is full of stars, Madame, no?"

Rachael was tired, scared, but she remembered the response: "Yes, Orion's belt is quite visible." Then from out of the shadows stepped another man dressed in a black leather coat, black turtleneck, face blackened like the night. He had appeared just to the side of Rachael, pistol in hand, barrel pointed right at her. She gasped, but the young man, only sixteen or so, hulking and tall, calmed her, putting his finger to his lips and returning the gun to his shoulder holster.

The man with the pipe grabbed Rachael's hand while the other dashed around the corner of the barn. He returned in a matter of minutes, and they all three rushed into the field of tall grass that surrounded them. Soon a car was visible just beyond the field, and Rachael and the man with the pipe got inside. With a wave of his hand, the young man, pistol now drawn, suddenly disappeared into the night, vanishing as though he had never been there at all. The car ride was short, for soon they parked and traveled on foot down a path in the woods. They picked up another car, a black Mercedes, elegant, hardwood paneling, and leather seats. The man in the long coat put on dark leather gloves and they soon were off into the night. Nobody spoke a word.

Rachael was afraid. Was this the way it was supposed to go? Nobody had told her anything.

And then, the car pulled up to a black metal gate. The man with the pipe flashed his lights three times and the gate swung open. They arrived at an old brick estate. The man with the pipe opened the door for Rachael and hurried her to a side entrance which led to the wine cellar.

And then she is alone. She thinks she hears whispers, but it could be only the wind. A door creaks, a large oak door from the side of the room, and in steps the older man with a wisp of hair, cracks and lines in his weathered face. He is thick, strong, hands fleshy and used. And after a moment of silence he addresses her with a voice filled with passion and warmth.

"Yes, you have come far indeed. Can I get you a cup of coffee to warm you up?" Rachael nods. He turns away and then turns back. "Would you care for a warmer coat, or perhaps a blanket?"

"A blanket would be nice, thank you."

A woman steps out of the shadows—she too dressed in army fatigues and a dark sweater—and the balding man whispers something to her. She disappears into the shadows again, but Rachael can hear a door creaking open and closed.

"My name is Rene, Madame Horowitz," says the balding man reaching out his hand. She shakes it and then sits back down. "I apologize for this meeting place, but it is secure—a bit cold, but dry and out of the way of prying eyes and ears."

The door opens and in steps the woman dressed in fatigues. She smiles warmly at Rachael and hands her first the blanket and then the cup of coffee.

"Merci," Rachael says. The woman smiles and again steps into the darkness.

"I only hear a hint of Flemish in your accent, Madame Horowitz. That is very good. Certainly not enough for you to worry about." Rene hesitates and then looks around him. He rubs the stubble on his chin and then screws up his face. "Now for the facts, Madame Horowitz. You are under the care of the Belgian Resistance. You must do whatever we say, whenever we say, or many people will die. Your life is now intricately tied into all of ours, and one wrong move could destroy the whole apparatus. You will know only what we think is important to your well being. All else will be kept from you. It is for your protection and your family's protection."

"My children—"

"They are safe, Madame Horowitz. You will see them shortly." Rene picks up the cup of coffee next to him and sips it; he makes a face but gulps down the rest anyway. "Is your coffee satisfactory?" Rachael nods and takes a sip. Rene smiles at her. "This is scary, I know. But you are a strong woman, Madame Horowitz. Hans has told me a great deal about you. That is good. You will have to be strong, stronger than you think you are able to be at times." Rene rubs his hands together and then checks his watch. "Time is short, so I will be brief. From now on you will have to forget everything that has happened to you. You must forget your husband, your brother-in-law, even your children."

Rachael shakes her head back and forth. "You cannot ask me to forget my children. They are—"

"No, you are right, Madame Horowitz, I cannot *ask* you—I *command* you. From now on you are not a mother, not a wife. You are stepping out of this wine cellar and into a new existence. That is the way it must be. There is no other way."

Rene stands up. Rachael thinks to herself, *He has killed before.* This thought is quick and fleeting. She sees the compassion in his grooved face. He is a man who will die for what he believes, will die for her and her children if need be. And Rachael nods in acknowledgment of all of this.

"Good. I see you understand. From now on you will see your children when we say you can. They will be hiding in houses throughout Belgium. They will be hiding with sympathizers who understand who you are and the risks involved. There are many, Madame Horowitz, who hate the Nazis as much as you. They are good people who are willing to risk death to help you. Remember that. There will come a time when you will think you can make it on your own. When that time comes, when you begin to believe all of this is not worth it—remember your husband, Madame Horowitz, remember what happened to him." Rene steps over to Rachael. "From now on you and your children are in great danger, but you are much safer now than before. You see, Madam Horowitz, you are now not just hiding alone. You are now part of a vast network—all of Belgium is trying to help you survive, pulling for you every day. And we have committed our lives to that cause."

Suddenly all of the fear, the taking of Ruben, the escape into the woods, the despair—all of this crashes upon Rachael. She covers her face and sobs into her hands. "Why?" she whispers. "Why are you helping us?"

Rene crouches next to her and rests his thick hands upon her shoulder, pulling the blanket tighter around her. "There are many reasons, as many as there are people participating. I don't know about the rest, but for me it is clear. We serve the same God, Madame Horowitz. My Savior died so all men may be free. I believe that with all of my heart. As long as I have breath and strength in my limbs, I will fight against the evil that has taken over our country and the world. Yes, we all have different reasons for fighting the Nazis. This is mine."

The oak door creaks again, and in walks the woman dressed in fatigues. Rene stands up. "It will be time to go shortly." He helps Rachael to her feet. "Now I must tell you the rest. A place has been provided for you in La Louvière. You will live and breathe among us. You may see me passing you on the street. Do not look at me or say hello. There are many eyes watching, some evil. You will be briefed on what you should do and where you should go, who are your friends and who are your enemies."

"What about my children?"

"It is better for now that you do not know where they are or who they are with." Rene puts his hand upon her shoulder. "But you will in time. They will be split up and given to different families and rotated as their safety demands. They will not be allowed to see each other or you for some time. They must, as you must, get acclimated to their new existence. The more they forget their old life, the better it will be for all involved." Rene squeezes Rachael's shoulder. "Don't worry, Madame Horowitz. You will be able to say good-bye. That is where we are going now."

The room where Jacob sits is musty and filled with the smell of old dreams, old memories, scaly books, and thinning hair. When he walks into it for the first time, the odor overwhelms him, and he gags. This bedroom, makeshift and hidden away on the first floor, creaks and groans under the weight of Jacob's feet. And that noise and the decaying smell force Jacob to stay put on the bed—hands on his knees, the dampness of his palms seeping into his pants. He can hear the younger sister—younger compared to her sister who is now eighty-plus—hobbling above him. The wooden floor creaks and shudders—now a thump, now a scrape, the distinct grind of the phonograph as it revs up to play, and then the scratchy lull of a violin concerto sifting through the dust-laden vents, around the lead pipes and through the floorboards.

Jacob is now in hiding. His first stop is with the Vineau sisters, Rita and Margaret. The oldest, Margaret, lies upstairs a withering husk, bone strung to bone, face hollow and sunken. Rita moves patiently around her sister's room, the room that was once their mother's and her mother's before her. They are spinsters, alone in a darkening and forgotten world. And yet, the will to help is strong. Rene had only to put the question to Rita and she responded with complete delight. But Margaret is dying, and the house smells of stale soup and confinement.

Toys and books so neatly stacked against the far wall, flow over onto the floor nearby. It is a gesture which shows how much Rita cares, and yet the books are tattered, the toys dilapidated and childish. What is Jacob to do? Again he hears the floorboards groan under Rita's hesitant strides. Jacob remains on the bed, forcing his mind to concentrate on the now, desperately wanting to be anywhere but where he is.

He remembers his mother greeting him. He remembers her words of encouragement. "Now you must be strong like Papa, Jacob. Now you must be the man of our house. I shall come to see you as soon as I am able, but that may be some time now. There is so much I want to say to you, so much I have left undone. But there will be time enough for those words later, when we see each other again." Rachael held Jacob's shoulders and squeezed them in her hands. "Your name is Tany now. You are visiting from England, and you have been trapped here by the war. Tany. Can you remember that? Good. I don't know where they are taking you, but you must trust them. Every house you stay in, every family that takes you in, everyone who helps is your friend. But remember, you can trust no one completely. No one, I tell you."

Rachael pulled Jacob close to her, cheek to cheek. "Never forget who you are, my little lamb. Never forget who your father and mother are. Never forget you are a Horowitz, and no matter what name you hide under, that name will be precious to you—your secret. You are a Jew, my lamb. You are chosen by God. Never forget that. They can strip you of your name, of your humanity, but they can never take that from you."

Jacob could feel the forceful breath on his ear, could hear the passion in his mother's voice, but he was unable to understand all she said. Who were "they"? What did she mean by "humanity"?

He reached out for her and held on to her with all of his strength.

"Oh, my baby, my baby," she whispered in his ear. "I will be back for you soon." She pushed him away slightly and looked at him once again. "Remember, always remember that I love you, Jacob. Never forget that."

And then she was gone. Jacob was placed in an unfamiliar car, driven by a man in a trench coat who smoked a pipe. The car pulled up to an unfamiliar house, and the man introduced Jacob to Rita and her dying sister, Margaret Vineau.

And here he sits listening to the creaking of the boards and the scratchy violin concerto as it drifts through the dusty house.

The bedroom door suddenly swings open and there stands Rita Vineau. She is a cornstalk of a woman, baggy white and faded red-checkered housecoat, tattered slippers fraying out like deformed toes, her face, sunken in and pale, small spectacles positioned precariously upon the bridge of her nose. She suddenly claps her bluish hands—dark from veins and age spots—together in a silent gesture of mock astonishment.

"Tany," she proclaims, but her voice is as hollow as her face and eyes. "My dear little Tany. You have not even touched the toys I set out for you." Jacob stares over at the old wooden soldier, the small pushcart, the tops and blocks. He wants to reply, "I am eleven. What can I do with those?" He thinks it best to remain silent.

Rita Vineau hobbles over to the pile of toys, bypasses the pile and reaches down for a book. Jacob hears her spine creak like the floor, like the door, like the very house itself. She places one hand on her lower back and forces herself with an extraordinary act of will to straighten. And then she hobbles over to the bed and sits next to Jacob.

"Would you like me to read you a story, Tany? This used to be my favorite story. My mother read it to Margaret and me every night before we went to bed."

"Yes, please," Jacob says, suddenly scared and desperately trying to push down the feeling of displacement surging around him. All he can think about, all that circles in his head is—how long? How long until the war is over? When can I see my family again? He has been in his new home for only one hour.

Rita Vineau lifts the thin picture book up to her eyes to read the title out loud. And then she struggles to separate the thick cardboard pages. "Ah, there we are, Tany."

They both stare at the first page in the dim light of the room, curtains only partly open, sun now drifting below the horizon. There are twelve words on the page, big words thick and black, simple words for the beginning reader. Rita Vineau has a difficult time reading them, for she continues to adjust her glasses—her large brown eyes sealed over by glaucoma.

"Can you read that, Tany?" she asks.

"Yes, ma'am."

"Please, Tany, call me Auntie Rita."

"Yes, ma'am. I mean, Auntie Rita."

Auntie Rita smiles. "Can you read this for your Auntie Rita?"

And Jacob slowly—for he thinks the occasion calls for it—reads out the words: "Mary is happy with her new friend. She is very, very happy."

It takes Auntie Rita nearly thirty seconds to separate the thick pages. Jacob notices her spindly fingers, yellowish nails. The palms of her hands are veiny and disrupted with wrinkles. She turns the page. Fewer words than the last page, but the picture is done in deep primary colors. Jacob reads the next page: "Suzanne is Mary's new friend."

Auntie Rita struggles again with the thick pages, so much so

Jacob decides to divert her attention.

"Auntie Rita?"

"Yes, Tany," she says, still concentrating with all her effort on the pages.

"Can I go outside tomorrow?"

Auntie Rita looks up from the picture book, dark eyes peering above the rims of her glasses. "Oh, well, Tany. We will just have to see about that later." She places the book next to her and stands up. "Right now, I think it is time for all of us to go to bed."

Jacob looks out the window trying to guess the time of day. His stomach is empty, but he is afraid to ask for dinner for fear of a reprimand, so he remains silent. Auntie Rita stands up with a creak, the bed creaking, the floorboards beneath her feet creaking, the entire house exhaling a sigh of exhaustion. She walks toward the door, then stops.

"Oh, Tany, my dear. There is a towel on your dresser for your bath tonight. You can hang it over the tub when you are finished. I will be upstairs reading to my sister. Please let me know if you need anything." She walks to the threshold of the door, then turns around again. "We are very pleased you are here, Tany." And she closes the door behind her.

Jacob hears her step up the stairs, hobble across the floor, and close the door. He is alone in a strange forgotten world of leftovers. Perhaps this was a mistake. Perhaps the driver dropped him off one house short of where he was supposed to go. Perhaps, perhaps, perhaps. He sits in the room and looks around once again. Then, for the first time, he climbs off the musty red bedcover and explores his new world.

Near the wall is an enormous dresser, towering above him. He cannot believe anyone could reach the top drawer. Near the bed is a nightstand, drawers empty save for a Holy Bible. He creeps across the floor and ventures out the door.

The house seems alive, a bubbling and gurgling surge of energy as it pumps fluids through the old pipes. The bathroom is just down the hallway, and Jacob takes his towel and walks over to the tub. He turns on the water and allows the cast iron to fill up. And just like that, Jacob is transported back to his old house, the house in Antwerp, the empty husk of a building where poison seeped in through the pipes. He had struggled to control his fear, struggled to contain the growing terror working its way up through his feet and legs. But now the cast iron tub filling with water releases the gate that holds back the panic. Once again he huddles on the floor, knees drawn up to his chest, huddles and sees his father hurrying out of the apartment with Uncle Benjamin—sees his father slump to the ground when the butt of the rifle slams into the back of his head—sees him stand, wobbling, and disappear into the truck—forever.

He turns off the water just in time, the rim a thin lip holding it back from the floor. And then he thinks of the officer standing before his father, watching him, calmly smoking his cigarette. This is enough to harness the fear. This single thought smashes the voices and images back into a fold of memory. Jacob allows half of the water to filter down the drain. He undresses and bathes in silence. *I will do whatever it takes to survive,* he thinks. *Whatever it takes.* And he slaps the water in anger. The soap feels strong and coarse, and he enjoys that feeling as he washes away the dirt, the fear, the doubt. Yes, he will survive, no matter what. He pulls the rusted chain that unplugs the drain and stands toweling off as the water gurgles down into the abyss of pipe below. He steps out of the tub, walks down the hall and back into his darkened room. Secret pacts are made with God and his family, and then he drifts off into a dreamless sleep.

Jacob awakes with a start. He takes several minutes to remember where he is, what he is doing there, and that he is safe. The house is silent. He has no idea what time it is, so he opens up the curtains. Sunlight bursts into the old room. He sits back upon the bed and watches the dust particles dance and drift within the beam of light. He dresses and steps out into the world before him.

The house is still dark; drapes are closed in the living room and sunroom. Jacob walks into the kitchen and sees a large butcher-block counter, crumbs, and dirty silverware strewn upon it. Next to the sink is a loaf of bread and some butter. Jacob cuts and butters several pieces of bread, then sits down at a table near a large window. The light from the morning shines through and warms his face.

There is nothing but the groans of the house for quite some time. Then Jacob hears the creaking and thumping. The soft, scratchy sound of violin filters again through the house, and the strange world of the Vineau sisters is once again in motion. Jacob waits after finishing his bread and butter, waits for Auntie Rita to walk downstairs to greet him, but she does not come down.

Jacob wanders about the house, creeping here, stepping there, opening this—hesitating to see if anyone is coming down—sliding that. No one does come down, not for lunch, not for most of the afternoon. Jacob is so bored, the life in this house so inconceivable and tiresome, that the silence and creaks transform into an oppressive, all-consuming sound. He steps up to the stairwell but is unsure if he should shout, should walk up and tell Auntie Rita he would like to go outside, or should just be quiet and go outside without a word. He walks up several stairs, each creaking and groaning under his little weight. As he nears the midway point, he is surprised to hear a door close and there stands Auntie Rita at the top of the steps. At first she looks very upset with Jacob's sudden intrusion, then she whispers, "What is wrong, Tany?"

Jacob feels like laughing, then screaming, "What do you think is wrong?" But he says, "Auntie Rita? I was wondering if I may go play outside for a bit?"

Auntie Rita looks behind her as if spooked and then turns toward Jacob. "That will be fine, Tany. But be careful out in the field. Don't go anywhere but into the field, Tany."

"Yes, Auntie Rita."

And Jacob walks back down the stairs in a hurry, thumping and skidding with joy.

The field is large and overgrown. At one time it may have provided wheat or corn for the Vineau family but not anymore. The brown grass has gone to seed and is rolling and pleasant to run through. Jacob runs for some time, holding his hands like wings of an airplane, allowing the dry seeds to smack and scrape against his fingers. And soon he is crouching in the field listening: birds, a distant tractor, the wind whipping and moving the stalks. He stands and follows his imagination further and further into the field. And to his surprise, before him lies a clearing. It is large and round, several stumps from the nearby forest upright like seats around a small stone fire ring.

What is a boy of eleven, alone and in a place seemingly abandoned by the world, supposed to do but build a fire? But how? He would need to gather wood from the forest just beyond. He would need matches and maybe some paper to start the flame. It wasn't long until Jacob had piled some dead branches near the fire ring. He decided he could roll the log seats into the ring once the fire got going a bit. Now all he needed was matches. Auntie Rita would not mind lending him those. After a quick glance at the fire ring and the neatly stacked wood, Jacob runs back through the field and to the house.

Again, he is struck by the aroma of decay, of must and stagnation. The house is a sepulcher. The darkness of the house juxtaposed with the sunny field is stark and overwhelming, and for a split second, Jacob wants to run away and live in the field. But his eyes adjust to the shadows, and he walks into the kitchen for matches. Before he searches through the drawers, he steps over to the stairwell. The house is quiet, no violin concerto, nothing. He wants to call out for Auntie Rita, but is afraid that in such silence even a whisper may shatter the house like a fragile porcelain vase. And then he thinks, "They have gone. Everyone has gone! The Nazis have taken them away!" He stands, petrified, legs stiff and unyielding. The silence of the house is overwhelming, like his house in Antwerp—sinister and cold, a poison oozing and drifting over the floorboards and through the vents.

And then there is a creak, that wonderful shifting of weight upon the old wooden floor. Auntie Rita is there, yes she is there. With a sudden turn of the handle, the scratchy violin concerto once again floats through the stagnant air of the house. Jacob's knees relax, bend, and he cautiously backs into the kitchen and plunders the drawers for matches.

The small flame crackles and sputters to life, consuming the thin and yellowed newspaper, turning it black. He watches with delight as the smoke curls up above the field and then is scattered by the autumn wind. And he tosses several twigs, large sticks, and finally a log right in the middle of the flames. Soon, he is not a small boy of eleven in south Belgium hiding for his life from unrelenting evil. No, he is at peace. He is captured for the moment by the fire, the wind, and the swaying grass—a moment that is a gift from God to the weary pilgrim who does not know where to go, how to get there if he did, and how to calm the terrible fear that threatens every thought. He sits with mind clear of anything save the glow of the flame, the deep smell of carbon, and the coming of winter.

The evening shadows drift further and further across the field, until a gray darkness is everywhere. The small fire is now only embers, and Jacob's mind reels from all that has happened to him in the past several months. This darkness, this field, this abandonment suddenly feels as oppressive as the musty house with the dying sister and the scratchy violin concerto. He leaves the embers still glowing and runs like a madman—tall grass a barrier to freedom—tripping, rushing headlong to the house.

He enters through the back door only to find the house as dark as night. He walks into the kitchen and turns on the small lamp—counter still strewn with crumbs and silverware, dishes in the sink (those are new), a pot on the stove, still steaming. Near the pot is a bowl. The house is silent, save for the slurping and groaning of pipes and the wind now picking up outside. There is no one downstairs to greet him from his adventure, no one to ask him how his day went, nothing to stamp the experience of the fire, the hiding, even Auntie Rita into the world of the real. No, it all is part of the whole, a dream that does not seem to grow better or worse, a perpetual existence.

Jacob ladles out a bowl of soup and walks it to the counter. There he sits in shadow and sips the broth. This is too much for him, the house too large, open, and strange. And so he walks his bowl into his room and closes out the emptiness behind him. The wind whips against the wooden siding and soon a torrent of rain and hail punish the worn wood and the old tar shingles. The soup bowl is soon empty, and Jacob huddles under his covers trying to focus on anything that would stave off the coming terror. He hears the creaking of the floorboards and what seems to be a sort of sigh—or was it a groan? The rain hurls against his window, and he is not sure if the noise was from outside or from within. Again the floorboards creak, and Jacob is sure someone is crying. He lifts his covers off, goes to his door, and opens it up. Soon he finds himself at the bottom of the stairs, the house dark, rain pounding outside. But he cannot go up. There is no more crying, no more movement. He rushes back to his room, closes the door behind him, and huddles against the headboard until a thick blanket of sleep settles upon him.

The next morning he is greeted with the same: house empty, nobody downstairs, and the soft, scratchy violin concerto Jacob has learned to hate. He does not ask this time but goes out to the field, to the fire ring, and builds a fire. As he returns for lunch, he notices a car pulling into the driveway. It rolls to a stop, and a tall man with a raincoat and pipe steps out from the automobile. He wears a short-rimmed hat and spots Jacob immediately. It is the man who brought him here, the same man who promised to check on him in a few days.

"Hello there, Tany," says the man smiling, pulling the pipe from his mouth and reaching out his hand.

"Hello, sir."

"And how is it going, lad?" asks the man, now squeezing Jacob's shoulder, firm, powerful.

"Fine," Jacob whispers. He wants to tell the man about the house, the sisters, the silly books, and the dark rooms, but he says, "Fine" once again as if repeating it makes it so.

"Are the Vineau sisters inside?"

"Yes."

The man looks Jacob over and then rubs the young boy's head with affection. They both walk into the house. The man looks at

Jacob and then at the silverware, the pots, the crumbs on the counter.

"Is this like this every day?"

Jacob nods.

The man steps into another room and calls out, "Hello! Anyone here?" There is a creak in the floorboards upstairs. "Hello?" he says again, this time with more force.

Jacob is soothed by that voice, powerful, penetrating, unafraid. The man looks at Jacob and then up the stairs.

"Do they stay up there a lot?"

"Yes, sir."

"Have they ever come down? I mean…" The man looks up the stairs then over at the kitchen counter. "Wait here, Tany. I will be right back."

The man bounds up the stairs and takes a right turn. Jacob can hear him knocking on the door. He knocks again. "Mademoiselle Vineau? Hello?" Jacob hears the door open, hears a cry of astonishment, the forceful voice as it rumbles through the room and drifts down the stairs: "How long has this been? Good heavens, woman! Why did you not call?" Jacob cannot hear anymore because the sobs from Auntie Rita are drowning out the man. The door shuts and the man races downstairs. He flies past Jacob and goes to the phone.

"Hello? Jacques here. We need to move the parcel. I will be in with the parcel in a few minutes. Make the necessary arrangements." He pauses and wipes his brow. "And send someone to the house. There has been a death in the family." The man puts down the phone and pats his forehead with a handkerchief. He looks up and sees Jacob frightened and alone. "Let us leave this place. Come, Tany. Gather up your belongings, and we shall leave. Quickly!"

And the two exit the house. The man sits Jacob in the seat next to him. He reaches up to start the car but pulls the keys away and looks at Jacob. "Did you ever see Mademoiselle Vineau?"

"Yes, sir. She came down and read me a story my first night."

"Have you seen her since then?"

"No, sir."

The man looks at the house and then back at Jacob. "Were you frightened, Tany?"

"Yes, sir."

The man puts his pipe in his mouth, clenching his teeth. "This will not happen again, Tany. Do you understand? This sort of thing will not happen to you again."

"Yes, sir."

The man turns the ignition and the car rumbles to life. The tires spin before the wheels catch traction and the car heads down the long dirt road and away from the house. Jacob looks back and watches the field and the house disappear. He thinks of Auntie Rita, and imagines her huddled over the bloated and stiff body of her sister as the scratchy violin concerto drifts through the dusty vents, the thick stagnant air, the dark and silent house.

Jacob is soon back in Charleroi, at Rene's house. It is evening and Jacob is sleeping comfortably in a clean, warm bed, the smell of coffee thick in the air. The man with the pipe and Rene discuss what had happened and what must be done. Very soon they hear the knock on the door, the knock both have dreaded. It is Rachael Horowitz.

They give her coffee, sit her down, and explain the misunderstanding. Rachael goes immediately to her son. She wakes him up and holds him tight.

"How could this happen?" she hisses to Rene. "How could you allow this to happen?"

"Let him rest now, Mrs. Horowitz," says Rene calmly. "It is all over with now. He is okay." He walks over to her and lifts her to her feet. "Tuck him into bed. We must talk."

Rene walks out the door as Rachael kisses Jacob's head. "Oh, my little lamb. My poor little lamb."

They sit sipping coffee around the kitchen table: the man with the pipe, Rene, and Rachael.

"There is nothing to be said." Rene has a very serious look on his face. "All I can say, Mrs. Horowitz—Rachael—is this sort of thing will not happen again."

Rachael wants to say something but sees the furrowed brow of Rene and realizes the alternatives are worse, that there really is no recourse, that she should be thankful they are not all dead. "Now what happens?" she asks.

"Now we relocate your son to an available household."

"That will not be easy," Jacques says. "We usually need several weeks notice before we place a parcel—I mean a family member."

"I think I know of a place," Rene says. "Tany will stay here until we can arrange it." Jacques looks up with great concern on his face. Rene lifts his hand in order to stop the inevitable words before they come out. "Yes, Jacques, I know it is unwise. But this child has been through too much. He needs rest and food. I will keep him here for only a few days. If all goes well, maybe not so long as that."

They sip their coffee and Jacque smokes his pipe.

"Is there some sort of procedure," Rachael asks, "a requirement the families must pass before the children are given to them?"

Jacques smiles and looks at Rene. Rene does not smile, but looks solemnly at Rachael.

"The only requirement, Mrs. Horowitz, is that the family does not turn your son or daughter over to the Gestapo. No matter what happens to them beyond that is irrelevant. I think on that we can all agree."

Rachael nods her head. There is silence.

"How are you getting along in La Louvière?"

"I have settled right in. Your contact there has set me up with an apartment, with a job as a seamstress. I am doing well." Rachael hesitates, then blurts out, "How is my daughter doing?"

"I am sorry, Rachael. I can only tell you she is alive, that as far as we know she is fine." Rene reaches out his hand and places it upon her forearm. "I will tell you more when it is safer for you to know. This is for your own good and hers."

Rachael nods and wipes a small tear from her cheeks.

"All of Belgium has been sealed tighter than a drum," Jacques says. "The Nazis are squeezing the life out of us. Soon, I am afraid there will be no more life to squeeze."

"There is more life in one Belgian plant than in all of Germany," Rene says. "We will survive." He looks at Rachael. "You will survive, Mrs. Horowitz."

Rachael smiles politely and finishes her coffee. "Could one of your men drive me back to La Louvière? I'm afraid it is getting late, and I need to make it back before curfew."

"Yes, of course," Rene says. "I will give you the necessary papers with my signature in case you are stopped." He looks over at the closed bedroom door where Jacob is. "You may want to say good-bye to your son, Mrs. Horowitz. This may be the last time you see him for quite some time."

The room is warm and Rachael stirs the drowsy Jacob out of his sleep.

"I am leaving, Jacob," she whispers. "I will not see you for a while. I pray God keeps you safe until we may see each other again." She strokes his head and hair with her long, callused fingers.

Her work in La Louvière is hard, taxing, the boss an ogre, the hours nearly unbearable. But it is work and safety and her children are protected. She kisses Jacob on his cheek, on his forehead, and then once on his lips. He is still in the land of fairies and does not fully comprehend the visitation.

Outside the wind picks up and Jacob wakes to the sound of rain beating against the window. He stirs from his sleep and for an instant he is back with the Vineaus, in the dark house with the dirty dishes, the crumbs, the stagnant odor of decay. He sits up and the wind whirls about him, ears straining for any recognizable sign: the creaking floorboards, the sucking and pumping pipes. But all is quiet. A waft of coffee still lingers in the air, and something else, something strangely familiar. He looks into the darkness of the room and cannot place where he is or what has happened to him. He has been cut free from the mooring of location, of place, everything a kaleidoscope of sense memory. But one recollection supersedes all the others—the old woman, the silly book, the haunting violin, the cryptlike house—one sense overrides them all: his mother's perfume. And as Jacob pulls his pajama top closer to his nose, he sucks in deeply the fragrance of things lost, forgotten.

But Jacob cannot now remember his father's face, cannot remember his sister's face, cannot remember the dog they once owned. In the small house, in the city of Charleroi, as the rain and wind pelt against the window—that night Jacob sits in his bed and tries to recall anything that will secure him to the boy he used to be. And at that moment, a time he will revisit over and over throughout his life—at that moment the eleven-year-old boy is no longer a boy but a tired soul adrift on an ocean disrupted by a world at war.

13

J acob stood in line at the small café just across from Barnes and Noble in concourse B of Cleveland Hopkins International Airport. In one hand he held his worn and faded black leather wallet; in the other, his son's latest novel, *The Tombs of Anakim*. He could hear the steamer froth the milk for the customer in front of him. *Yes,* he thought, *a cappuccino is just what this occasion calls for.*

Within five minutes he was sitting at a reddish table trimmed in oak, sitting down and opening one of his son's novels—for the first time ever. He half expected the heavens to part and a voice to come out of the abyss above: *This is thy neglected son with whom you are so displeased.*

He opened the hardcover to the first blank page. He flipped it over, creased it, and turned over the next page: copyright notice, Library of Congress information, and he flipped and creased that one. It was a good time for a sip of his cappuccino—wouldn't want to start down this road without plenty of rewards. The cup was next to him, and he reached for it, fingers tipping it ever so slightly. Then he recalled the young woman professor and her catastrophe, coffee dripping off the table. He looked up from the page, and grabbed his cup firmly in his hand.

It was then that he glanced down at the dedication:
For my father.

He looked up with surprise at a fat woman suddenly gurgling and spitting with laughter. He looked down again. Still there.

For my father.

And this time he took his weather-worn hand, age spots and veins now all too apparent, took his hand and gently smoothed the page, rubbed the dark ink, the simple inscription—over and over and over. He pursed his lips and took another sip of his cappuccino. And he turned to chapter one.

In the heart of madness, in the very depths of chaos, Lawrence Fairborne found the strand of sanity that would keep him alive.

He still was unhappy with the opening sentence, too overwritten. No critic had yet to pick up that thread, but it was still early in the game for them. He began to read further into the opening scene.

Jacob had read furiously when he was young. Something marvelous and magical happened every time he opened a book, something so elemental his father and mother rarely found him without one. But the world and its vines of worry and thorns of despair snuffed out that desire, placing it in a folder and labeling it "when I have time." And yet he could still remember hiding somewhere in the recesses of an old library, opening *Treasure Island,* and disappearing into the text. He had forgotten how powerful the magic of words could be, a magic so potent as to arrest all he was doing, eclipse all that was around him and take his thoughts captive, sometimes kicking and screaming in the process. He had forgotten the basic and fundamental connection between the reader and the word.

And quite unexpectedly and by no effort on his part, Jacob Horowitz was transported from the chaos of an airport to the lost, ancient Inca ruins somewhere in Peru. He was pushing against a smooth stone wall with Lawrence Fairborne, desperately trying to press himself free from the stone sarcophagus around him. The hand on his shoulder immediately brought him back to Cleveland.

"Well," burbled the enormous man before him, "I never thought I'd see the day when Jacob Horowitz was reading Jack Oxford." Herman laughed. "And that's not even his best work, my friend."

"Herman, what are you doing here?"

Herman sat down, with little effort for such a large man, and placed his huge paws upon the table. "Stuck here, just like you, my friend. The rain has delayed my New York flight." He shook his head and rubbed his bearded face. "Good for you, Jacob. You truly are taking all of this seriously." He looked around the small café. "Where's Isaac? Is he here?"

Jacob placed his coffee receipt in between the pages and closed the book. "No. He has not shown up. Maybe he will not come at all."

"Nonsense, he'll be here. The roads are a mess. I just went out for some lunch not too long ago, and the orange barrel brigade is in full march."

The two were silent for some time, but it was a comfortable silence.

Herman Bergman had met Jacob when he arrived in New York City from Belgium in 1951. Jacob was living in a tiny apartment over his aunt's garage and took the bus into the city each day to open up his even tinier garment store in Brooklyn. One day as he was working on a suit for a well-known Jewish businessman, Jacob noticed a thin, wraithlike figure standing near his window, back toward Jacob. The man was dressed in an old and fraying suit, muffler around his neck, dilapidated short-brimmed hat upon his head. Jacob put down his needle and thread and stared at the man's back for quite some time. Who was this guy? What was he doing at his business? But that was all the thought he gave it and went back to work. As the morning progressed he looked up periodically to check on the stranger, and around noon he saw that the man was gone. Jacob walked over to the window and was surprised to see the man still there, sitting cross-legged on the sidewalk. And still Jacob did not think much about it. He ate lunch behind the counter, sipped his coffee, and worked the rest of the day. When he left his small shop for the evening, the man was not there.

For several days after, the man would appear at his window, back to the shop, sit down in the afternoon, and disappear before Jacob closed the shop. On the fifth day of this routine, Jacob went outside to confront the man, and was surprised to find that the thin cornstalk of a soul was in fact not a beggar at all. No can, no nothing. The man sat there staring out into the road. Jacob approached and said in a gruff voice, "Hey, you. No begging here in front of my store."

The man did not respond, only blinked several times.

"Listen, buddy, I don't mind you sitting around, but why not go to the park. This is my storefront, and I want you to sit somewhere else."

The man sat staring straight ahead, blinking every now and then.

"I'm going to call the police if you don't move within the next half hour," Jacob said in a voice much more angry than he actually felt. He walked away and went back behind his counter to sew. He did not call the police, did not even think about calling the police. No, there was something about this man that connected with Jacob.

About an hour later, Jacob poured a cup of coffee and walked out the door. The man was still there.

"I brought you some coffee. You can drink it or not—either way it makes no difference to me." He reached out his hand, but the man did not respond. Jacob placed the cup next to him and walked back into the store. He spent several hours in the back room, and when he returned, the cup was empty.

"I have some more, if you want it," Jacob said.

"Thank you," the man replied in a whisper of a voice, a voice that suddenly crashed down upon Jacob like a fist. He recalled the man in the woods, the man who had helped his mother and sister and him to hide from the Nazis. But this man was not Aaron Feldman. This man was no older than Jacob. He held up the coffee cup to Jacob. "Yes, I would like another cup, if you please."

"Yes, yes, indeed," Jacob said hurriedly. And then he stooped down. "Please, sir, come inside out of this cold. Come and sit in my shop. I will make you more coffee."

The man blinked and stared out at the road, then turned his face toward Jacob. "Yes, that would be most kind."

His clothes were mildew stained and rotted at the elbows, his pants patched with what looked to be pieces of underclothing. When he took off his short-brimmed hat, Jacob could see the frayed hair and a deep scar that ran from his eye to his chin, a pinkish streak outlining his jowl. His eyes were clear blue, a translucent and hypnotizing blue. Jacob had him sit at the counter, and he filled his cup with coffee. A long silence ensued, but it was not an awkward silence. Jacob stitched a sleeve onto a suit coat while the man sat sipping his coffee, breathing in the aroma, allowing the heat of the mug and the steam to seep over his face.

"My name is Jacob Horowitz," said Jacob, not looking up but

concentrating on the project before him. There was another round of silence. Jacob stopped sewing and realized the man's cup was empty. "Would you like more coffee?"

"Yes," the man whispered. "Yes, that would be very nice."

Jacob went and filled his cup. They sat in silence for about an hour, the man drinking coffee, Jacob going about his business. About twelve o'clock, Jacob went into the back room to get his lunch. When he came back, the man had gone.

The next day, the man was sitting in front of his store again, head to the window, translucent blue eyes staring across the street. Jacob brought him out a cup of coffee. "You can come inside to get warm if you want. I have the pot of coffee filled." This time when the man came in, Jacob had a sandwich for him. The man thanked Jacob in his whisper voice, and as with the coffee the day before, he seemed to revel in every bite of the sandwich, every swallow, every sip of the bitter liquid. This pleased Jacob to no end, and while he sewed, the man sat—both silent and about the business in their own minds.

And then, the man said, "My name is Herman Bergman." This was all that needed to be said. They sat all day this way, Herman sipping coffee and watching Jacob sew and stitch his garments. Every day after, Jacob would open his store and Herman would come inside.

One day after Herman had his cup of coffee, Jacob said, "I made that suit for you, Herman. See if it fits. I can let it out or take it in as need be."

Herman looked over at the rack where a single suit hung. It was charcoal gray and finely stitched.

"Here," said Jacob stepping around the counter, "allow me to see if it fits you."

He walked over and took the suit off the rack and pulled the jacket from it. Jacob stepped over to Herman and with a gentle touch pulled the tattered coat off him. To Jacob's surprise, Herman was wearing only a short-sleeve shirt underneath. As he pulled the coat from his arms he noticed the blue numbers inscribed across one forearm. Gently, Jacob stood Herman to his feet and fitted the coat as though he were the most prestigious of customers.

"We can take it in a bit here," Jacob said, chalking a streak here and there. He pulled on the back of the coat and marked again. He reached over to the sleeves and pulled them down. "Yes, that will do nicely." He walked in front of Herman and scanned the coat and the absurd and comical figure standing before him: beautiful wool coat juxtaposed to the weather stained and patched pants. "Now, Mr. Bergman, if you would kindly step into the dressing room and try on the pants, I can fit them as well." Herman obeyed and Jacob chalked and pulled at them. "Well, Mr. Bergman, if you would allow me to take these from you, I think I could have them ready for you while you wait." Jacob paused. "Please, if you would allow me to take your old clothes, I will give you something temporary to wear while I do the alterations."

By the end of the day, Herman Bergman was wearing a brand-new tailored suit. Jacob had fitted him with shoes and a shirt, a belt, a tie, and even a new hat. Jacob set up a cot for him in the back of his store, coffee pot filled, plenty of bread and meat for sandwiches. When Jacob locked up to go home, Herman was fast asleep, and for the first time in months, warm and well fed.

Herman stayed at the store for several weeks, and then one day he was gone. Jacob asked around, but was unable to find him. Months went by and Jacob lost himself in his business. Then out of the blue he received a letter (addressed to the store) from Herman.

Dear Jacob Horowitz,
Please meet me at Storeman's Deli for lunch. I will be there
this Thursday at 12:00.
Sincerely,
Herman H. Bergman

When Jacob met Herman, he hardly recognized him save for the suit. He was now plump with ruddy cheeks and a nicely groomed beard. As they ate their lunch, Herman told Jacob about the camps, about his escape under the barbed wire that lacerated his face forever, about the long, lonely stay in the forests of Poland, and of his displacement to America. Jacob was the first soul to offer him a kind word, clean clothes, and warm food. "Yes, it was you who brought me back to the land of the living. It was you who made me realize life was worth living again." Herman wiped his eyes, those wonderful translucent blue eyes. "Forgive me, my friend. It is the first time I have told my past to anyone. It is the first time I have considered all that I was and all that you did for me."

Jacob was silent, thinking of his own past, his own demons that whipped about to poke and jab, to gloat and chortle over him.

Herman explained he had gone from Jacob's store with a new purpose. He left the garment shop and walked over to his uncle's jewelry store and asked for employment. Now he had a steady job and was making the most of the life God had given him to live.

Jacob and Herman saw each other every week after that. It was Herman who encouraged Jacob to marry again, to have children, to live life. He was there when Isaac was born. He was there when Isaac left. He stood in the crowd as Liza's casket was lowered. It was Herman who finally persuaded Jacob to seek reconciliation with Isaac.

Herman was the first person Jacob told about his prostate cancer. It was a cool evening, and Herman sat out on his screened-in porch, sipping coffee and reading the sports page. Jacob came in and sat down. He remembered the cool air, the creaking of insects, the shadows of night approaching. It all seemed to him unreal and subjugated to the doctor's news.

"The doctor says a year, maybe two."

Herman carefully folded the paper and placed it on the floor. He stared long and hard at his friend.

"We—you and I—have lived long, good lives, Jacob. We should not fear death, for God has blessed us more than we deserve." He paused. "I am truly sorry for the news."

Jacob stared into the darkness and whispered, "I know you are, my friend. And I know you are right."

They were silent for some time.

"I have decided to go ahead with what we discussed," Jacob said. "I will call Isaac and ask him to go to Belgium with me. We are all leaving this world now, it seems."

"You must call him, Jacob. You cannot leave your family without a legacy. No, you must go through with it. It is the right thing to do."

"Yes," Jacob whispered. "Now that there is no time. It is now or never."

And here they were sitting together in the airport waiting for the sky to clear.

"I think crazy thoughts sometimes," Jacob said suddenly. "I keep thinking all of this is just an absurd and useless gesture by a dying man. And then that nut, Lereau, his words revolve around in my head."

Herman laughed. "You're not thinking of converting, old man! That Christian has us all screwed up. Every time we play handball, I come away with another question for my rabbi. The rabbi likes my religious pursuits, but I will leave theology for him to work out. I go to temple, I say my prayers. That's enough. What did Lereau say?"

"He told me reconciliation is the starting point for both Jews and Christians, that God reconciled with man and man must reconcile with each other. I believe him. I must take those steps with my son. This is the start of something—where it will lead I don't know."

"Yes, it's wise counsel. He'd make a good Jew, that Lereau. He'd make a good rabbi even."

Soon they were laughing and talking of handball, of kill shots and the next weeks matchups. They talked and planned as if both had all the time in the world.

14

It has been several weeks now, and Jacob is settling into his new life with the Delvaux family—an older man and his wife. Jacob has slept in the upstairs room, well furnished and cozy. Philip Delvaux, an accountant, leaves for work in the morning and comes home like clockwork at five-thirty every evening. Jacob stays around the house and helps Alice Delvaux with the chores.

The Delvauxs live in a small town south of Charleroi called Cerfontaine. It has a bank, a post office, a petrol station, and a grocery store where farmers bring in their fresh vegetables and meats. It is a poor community, one that has felt the war, has felt the occupation by the Germans. But it is also a town hidden far south from the prying eyes of the Gestapo.

On this particular morning, Jacob is awakened by a rustle across the hall. He has heard that same noise every morning since he arrived. This time he goes to the door and listens, creaks it open ever so slightly and sees Mrs. Delvaux leaving the room across the hall and closing the door behind her. She is startled when she sees Jacob in the doorway, wipes her eyes and smiles politely.

"Well, good morning, Tany. Are you ready for some breakfast?"

"Yes, ma'am."

She smiles warmly at him and walks downstairs.

As he dresses he thinks about that room across the hall with its door always closed, and he wonders if Mrs. Delvaux goes in there often. This is soon pushed from his mind, for today he will travel to the market with Mrs. Delvaux and get food for a party this Sunday afternoon.

He is greeted by Mr. Delvaux who is sipping coffee and chewing on a piece of toast reading a passage from his Bible.

"Good morning, my little Tany," he says smiling.

"Good morning, Uncle Philip."

"I pray you slept well last night," Mrs. Delvaux says as she stirs some eggs in her pan. There is no sign of tears now, no hint of sorrow.

"Yes, Aunt Alice."

Aunt Alice walks over to Jacob and scoops a heap of eggs onto his plate, soon followed by two slices of crisp toast.

"Listen to this, Alice, Tany," Uncle Philip says as he puts his fingers upon a verse in his Bible. "It says here that, 'After all, if you were cut out of an olive tree that is wild by nature, and contrary to nature were grafted into a cultivated olive tree, how much more readily will these, the natural branches, be grafted into their own olive tree.'" Philip looks up from his book and adjusts his glasses. "I see you are at a loss, my little Tany. Forgive me." He smiles and takes a bite of his toast, sips his coffee, and scoots closer to Jacob. "Well, my friend, this passage tells me there are two types of branches God cares for. There are those that are the well-cultivated and natural branches and there are those that are not from the natural branches and must be grafted in."

Jacob eats his eggs and toast and tries to follow Uncle Philip's explanation. He is used to these by now, for every morning the two Delvauxs pray and read each other passages from the Bible.

"I see you're still unclear about this," Uncle Philip says rubbing his smooth face. "What it says, if I may paraphrase the good Book, is that you, my little Tany, are so special, so unique to God that He has made you and all the Jewish race the natural olive tree. That's what he calls all Jews who believe in Him. Aunt Alice and myself are not natural branches at all, so we are grafted onto the olive tree."

"Why were you not part of the olive tree?" Jacob asks.

"Well, Tany, that's a question for God alone. But if you remember your Torah, you'll recall that out of all the people in the world, the God of the universe chose the Jewish people to be His own. Aunt Alice and I are not Jewish, not as special as you. Well, God devised a plan that would make everyone, Gentile and Jew, just as special. That's why Jesus came. That's why He died for our sins and for your sins too—so that we could all be special to God. Someday, when you're ready, maybe we could talk about it some more." Philip smiles and rubs Jacob's head with affection.

Jacob sips his milk and takes a bite of his toast. Then a strange thought occurs to him.

"Uncle Philip?"

"Yes, Tany."

"If I am so special to God, then why do I have to hide? Why are the Nazis looking for my family? Why did they take my father and uncle if we are so special to God?"

Alice and Philip look at each other, then Philip looks back to Jacob.

"There is a power upon this earth, my little Tany, that wants nothing more than to destroy God's people. He will do anything to get at them. That is why you are hiding, Tany. That is why your family is separated and your father was taken away."

Jacob sees Aunt Alice turn away and wipe her eyes.

"But, Tany, there are those who are willing to give their lives so that enemy will not be victorious." Uncle Philip stares out the kitchen window. "Yes," he whispers, "some have given their lives so that you may live." And again he turns toward Jacob with a warm smile. "That is why you are special, Tany. Never forget that. Promise? Good boy." He rubs Jacob's hair again with affection, looks at his watch, and gulps down his coffee. "I must get to work. I hear your aunt is going to take you someplace special today."

"We're going to the market."

"And are you going to make your special apple pie, mother?"

"If Tany and you are good boys, I will," she says with a smile.

"Well, Tany, you heard her. I guess I'll have to be good today." Philip gets up from the table, puts on his jacket, and kisses his wife good-bye.

On the way to the market, Jacob suddenly takes hold of Aunt Alice's hand. She pulls it away, then places her arm around Jacob's shoulder.

"Do you miss your mother, Tany?"

"Sometimes very much, Aunt Alice. Sometimes I cannot even remember what she looks like. Is that bad?"

Alice looks away, trying to wipe the tear from her eye. "No, Tany. No, it is normal for you to feel that way. It is also quite normal for you to forget as well. It is God's way of helping us cope with something we—" But Alice is not able to finish and looks away again. They walk the rest of the way to the market in silence.

When they get back home, Alice starts on her apple pie while Jacob occupies himself in the garage, a weather-worn building that houses all of Uncle Philip's tools, a workbench, and odds and ends. And then to Jacob's surprise, he sees a bike leaning against the stone wall. It is faded blue, grease around the frame where the chain droops brown and powdery. Jacob lifts it from the wall, wiping the cobwebs from between the handlebars, smashing the black spider now crawling up the corroded metal. He looks around for something to wipe the rest of the dirt and cobwebs away and finds a grease-stained rag. Jacob wipes away the dirt, wipes away the webs, wipes away the years of neglect. He had forgotten about his bike until that moment, forgotten all the memories associated with it. But now! Now he remembers the hills, the wind, the clatter of playing cards clipped to the spokes.

He pumps the tires up and soon it is ready for a test ride. He leans it over so as to get one leg over the seat. Then, very slowly, he tilts the bike up to its starting position. One handlebar has streamers, the other just an empty hole—a home for an unwanted insect. A push, and another—and suddenly he is wobbling out of the garage and onto the driveway. Wobble, wobble, wobble and then glide, legs pumping. And for the first time in a long time, Jacob is smiling. He hears and feels the autumn wind blowing through his jacket. His eyes tear with the contact of the air—a droplet streaming down his reddened cheek. Now he is flying; now he is circling and swooping from side to side.

And then, suddenly, Aunt Alice races out the side door, rushes out with apron still tied around her waist, apple juice and flour smattered all about. Jacob smiles and waves—one hand and then the other, his back to her. Then he circles around and heads right toward her. He looks down at the dip in the driveway and then back up at Aunt Alice. With a sudden start, he realizes she is not happy. She is racing toward him and she is screaming at him now.

"How dare you! How dare you just take that out of the garage like that!" She reaches out to the bike, stopping it with a sudden jerk. "Get off of this! Do you think you can just take things like this! Do you?" Her face is red and swollen from crying and she is shaking with rage. "Get off, I tell you!"

"I'm sorry, Aunt Alice.

"Get off, do you hear me! You have no right! It is not yours! It is not yours!" Jacob is trapped between the seat and the handlebars. He leaps from the bike, catching the side of the frame with his thigh, a rusty barb scratching into his flesh. He is crying now. Aunt Alice is stooped down over the fallen bike and sobbing uncontrollably. Jacob does not hear or see any of this. He is racing for the woods, and soon he is hiding behind a large oak—leg bleeding, gasping for breath. What had he done?

The rest of that afternoon, Jacob huddles behind the smooth bark of the oak. He ignores Aunt Alice's pleas for him to return. She walks the edge of the woods calling out to him. He is confused and terrified.

Evening begins to settle upon the land. At five-thirty Uncle Philip pulls into the driveway. Jacob can hear Aunt Alice crying, her voice muffled. Soon Uncle Philip is walking out toward the woods.

"Tany? Tany, it's your Uncle Philip." He continues to head toward the darkness of the woods. "Tany, it's okay, son. You can come out. Everything is okay now. Aunt Alice is so sorry about what happened." And Jacob rushes from the trees and into Uncle Philip's arms.

"I'm sorry for taking the bike," Jacob cries into Uncle Philip's chest. "I didn't mean to hurt anyone. I'm so sorry. I didn't mean to hurt Aunt Alice. I didn't mean—" But he cannot say anymore, for his fear and anxiety is caught up in his chest, then his throat. All that comes out are choking gasps for breath.

"There, there, Tany, it's not your fault, my boy. Shh. It's not your fault." Jacob feels the strong hand on his back, on his head.

He is safe with this man. He is a good person.

Uncle Philip walks him over to the side door, the same door Aunt Alice had stormed out of hours before. She opens the door for them and hugs Jacob.

"Forgive me, Tany. I'm so sorry for what I did this afternoon." She hugs him and shakes her head. "I just don't know. I just don't know." She wipes her eyes. "Sometimes it just overwhelms me, and I am powerless."

Philip helps Aunt Alice to a kitchen seat and walks Jacob over toward the stairs.

"Tany," he says gently, "I want you to come with me for a moment." He leads Jacob up the stairs and right in front of the room where the door is always shut. They pause. "Go ahead," Uncle Philip says, "open it."

The room is filled with pictures. Some placed on the wall, some propped up on the dresser. There are airplanes hanging from wires on the ceiling and a Belgian flag on the wall. All the pictures are of one man, one boy, one baby.

"This was our son's room, Tany." Philip walks over to a picture and lifts it off the desk. It is a picture of a dashing young man, dressed in an officer's uniform. "He was killed fighting the Germans no more than six months ago." Uncle Philip smiles, but it is thin, worn, a mask of agony just below the surface. "Just six months ago," he whispers. He sets the picture back where it came from, gently and with great care. And then he turns toward Jacob. "It was his bike you took from the garage." He raises his hands to stop Jacob from apologizing. "No, Tany, do not worry. You had every right to take it out and ride it. It's just that Aunt Alice has not quite gotten over all of this yet. It is hard on her—hard on us all." He suddenly stops and takes a deep breath. "Well, that is not your concern, my little Tany. You were not at fault, and Aunt Alice is deeply sorry for what she did." He walks Jacob from the room and closes the door behind him. "In fact, I have a surprise for you. But you cannot have it until the morning. Okay?"

Jacob nods his head, and they walk downstairs where Aunt Alice has set the table and is stirring the pot of vegetable stew.

The next morning Uncle Philip takes Jacob outside. Aunt Alice walks up to the door and watches from the stoop.

"Well, go on in," says Uncle Philip, pointing to the garage.

Jacob opens the large door and steps inside. There sitting upright, freshly painted and shined, is the blue bike.

"Go!" Uncle Philip laughs. "Get on and see if she works."

Jacob looks over at Aunt Alice.

"Your Uncle Philip has put a lot of elbow grease into that silly bike, Tany. You better jump on before he takes it for a spin himself."

Jacob smiles with delight and races over to it. He straddles the frame, the seat positioned just right, and soon the well-greased chain is spinning the gears round and round. Jacob races to the end of the driveway and then back toward Aunt Alice and Uncle Philip who are smiling, arms around each other. And it is then, that scene, that moment that the young Jacob Horowitz realizes he has erased—just for that segment of time—the loss and pain of a lonely and hurting couple.

Jacob has now become a part of the Delvaux family. The routines that seemed so out of place, so odd—praying before every meal, a devotion in the morning, church every Sunday—all of these have become not only expected but, in the back of Jacob's mind, even comforting.

And this interest in the Christian faith is the reason on this Sunday afternoon that he and the Delvauxs travel to the small

Catholic church to see Father Jean Gilbert. Father Gilbert is a stern man, short and bulky, his belly protruding, pushing out the baggy robe he wears, making him grunt as he sits down and grunt when he stands up. His intimidating figure is in the doorway as they enter his small office. Jacob is so fearful, so awed by him that he does not respond when Father Gilbert says hello. There is silence as the Delvauxs sit in the three wooden chairs before the large desk. Father Gilbert grunts and drops into his own.

"So, this is Tany." Father Gilbert smiles, his puffy, watery eyes stabbing into Jacob's head and heart. He places one fleshy hand upon the desk and then the other. "This is Tany." He rubs his chin and settles back in his swivel chair. "Why do you want to be baptized, young man?"

The question catches Jacob off guard. This whole event did not just happen over night. No, it all started—like a tiny pebble rolling down a mountaintop—this avalanche of emotion all began when he first stepped into Father Gilbert's church. He did not realize it at the time, but the elements of the service—the silver cup and the small wafers, the kneeling and chanting, the large broken man, gaunt and bleeding on the cross—all of these buried themselves deep inside his conscience.

That night, Jacob's dreams were filled with a collage of images, some directly from the stations of the cross, others of Father Gilbert waving his hand and chanting Latin. All of these rushed forward toward a single image: that nine-foot figure wounded and bleeding, that skinny, haggard man with arms stretched out and nailed to the cross.

The next morning Uncle Philip explained who he was, that he was Jewish just like Tany, that though innocent he was persecuted and killed so young men like Tany could go to heaven. The following Sunday, Jacob viewed the crucifix as something different—a man who suffered like he was suffering, a man hunted down and killed, just like all the Jews in Europe. If becoming a Christian would stop the pain, the terror, the suffering, if that was all one had to do—stop being a Jew, a clean slate—why not do it?

And now as he sits before the huge priest with bloated chin, Jacob contemplates Father Gilbert's question.

"There is something you need to know, Father," says Aunt Alice, blushing ever so slightly. She looks over at Philip and then back to Father Gilbert, who motions for Philip to close his office door.

"Go on, Mrs. Delvaux."

"Tany—well, this young man is not really a relative of ours."

"He's not?"

"No."

"Then who is he, Mrs. Delvaux?"

There is a pause, and Alice and Philip look at each other.

"He is a young Jewish boy in hiding, Father," Mr. Delvaux says.

Father Gilbert stares blankly at the family across the desk. He grunts to his feet and hobbles over to the door, opens it and peeks out into the hallway. Then, carefully, he closes it and hobbles back to his seat, grunting as his weight settles into the wood frame of the chair. He rubs his jowls, his watery and puffed eyes.

"So," he says, placing both hands on the table before him, "Tany here is not really Tany at all." And after a long stare at the boy, after rubbing his face once again and leaning back in his swivel chair, Father Gilbert's stern demeanor becomes one of compassion. "What do your father and mother say of all this?" He raises his arms, palms out, and whirls them around, as if to say, "This Christian church stuff."

"His father has been taken to the camps, Father Gilbert," Mrs.

Delvaux says. "His mother and sister are all that is left."

"So what does his mother say to all of this, Mrs. Delvaux?"

"She does not know about it—yet."

"It may be wise to ask her, Mr. and Mrs. Delvaux. Such conversions are serious and with serious repercussions. I suggest we wait until this young man's family has thought through all the implications. Once that has happened, Mr. and Mrs. Delvaux, then we will proceed to the next step."

Jacob starts to walk out of the office behind the Delvauxs, and Father Gilbert places his large hand on his shoulder. He turns Jacob around so they are face to face.

"You are safe here, my son. The darkness will not follow you here." He pauses and then lifts his hands. "May the Lord bless you and keep you, my son. May He make His face shine upon you. May He give you His peace." Father Gilbert makes the sign of the cross once again and smiles warmly.

Several weeks go by, and Jacob is riding his bike up and down the driveway, down the winding road, and onto a dirt path headed into a field and next to a forest. This bike riding has been a great gift to him, for something strange has happened, all of a sudden and without warning. It was after leaving the room with the pictures, when the door closed behind him, at that moment Jacob felt the oppressive weight of all those who had given up their lives to save him.

That night while lying in bed, he recalled his father playing chess with him in the apartment. He remembered his father's winning move, his explanation of that move, and the intense anger that spread through Jacob as he realized he had been defeated. And now his father was gone. His mother was gone. His sister was gone. All he had left were memories, and he huddled against the headboard all that night hoping and praying tomorrow would never come. And that was the morning Uncle Philip had presented him the bike.

Soon Jacob turns the bike and wobbles onto another dirt path. There, to his surprise, he sees a young boy crouched by the side of the road.

"Hello!" Jacob cries out.

The boy looks up and places the magnifying glass to his side.

Jacob pulls over and straddles the frame. "What are you doing?"

The boy does not respond.

Jacob glances down at the sandy dirt in front of the other boy's knees. "What are you doing?"

"Burning bugs with this magnifying glass. That's all."

Jacob jumps off the bike and lays it down on the road. "Have you fried any yet?"

"No, they're so small and move so fast I can't keep the light on them long enough."

Both boys stare at the dirt like physicists contemplating a chalkboard filled with equations.

"They're just too small," the boy says.

"Hey, why don't we find something else to burn?"

The boys look around and soon see a large spider in the midst of a web strung between long stalks of grass. They huddle around it, and the boy focuses the light upon the spider's abdomen. Within seconds the spider is smoldering and trying to move, then falls from the web. The two boys search out other victims—some moving, some burning, most able to escape unscathed.

"My name is Michael," says the boy reaching out his hand.

Jacob smiles. "My name is Tany."

"There are no boys to play with around here, and I'm lonely most of the day. Are you from around here?"

"I live with my Aunt and Uncle Delvaux. I'm visiting from England."

Michael lifts up the magnifying glass and hands it to Jacob. "You can play with it, take it home if you like. I can get it back from you tomorrow."

"We can meet here."

"I'll meet you here tomorrow," Michael says with a smile.

And just like that, the two boys part company, Jacob peddling back down the dirt road happy to have found a new friend near his own age.

Several days go by, the boys meeting and playing at that same spot. Then one afternoon Michael invites Jacob over to his house.

"My mom will give us cake and some milk. She asked me to invite you." The boy looks eager. "I told her all about you, where we met and what we did. She says she wants to meet you."

Jacob hesitates and then decides it will not hurt to visit the lonely boy and his mother. They walk down the dirt path toward the old farmhouse. When they get inside, an older woman with graying dark hair is standing at the door. She is worn looking, creases under her eyes. Jacob thinks of his mother.

"Come in," she says gently in a raspy, smoky voice, "come in." She scoots into the kitchen grabbing a pitcher of milk and some cake. She is a nice woman, warm and eager, cigarette propped between two fingers. Jacob feels comfortable with her, and soon she is asking questions.

"So where in England are you from, Tany?"

"London," he whispers, groping for a name familiar to him.

"Do you speak English?" she suddenly says in English with a smile.

Jacob chews on his bit of cake, and she repeats the babble again. Jacob realizes he is getting into deep waters where he will not be able to swim back. He fidgets on his seat and sips his milk.

"You don't understand me, do you, Tany?" she asks in French.

Jacob looks at his friend Michael who is eating his cake and looking on expectantly. "No, ma'am," Jacob says.

The woman stands to her feet and walks over to the door, locking it. Jacob's face registers panic, and he searches around the room for a way out. All exists are blocked, windows closed, curtains drawn.

"Stand up," the woman says with an edge to her voice. "Stand up and come before me."

Jacob does not know what to do. He is caught, like his father, like Uncle Benjamin. He thinks of his mother and of his sister. They will never know what happened to him. His mother will come one day and he will be gone.

"Come on," says the woman, "do what I say."

Jacob stands up and walks before her. Michael sits up and looks on with anticipation, a strange gleam in his eye. The woman pulls Jacob before her and roughly grabs his arm. Then she says the unthinkable.

"Unzip your pants."

Jacob does not respond.

"I said, unzip your pants, Tany. Come on, come on!"

Jacob does so, and the woman pulls down his trousers and underpants.

"I knew it!" she cries out with triumph. "You are a Jew!"

Jacob grabs his underwear and trousers and pulls them up with a sudden terror. He backs away toward the wall like a trapped animal.

"Oh, Tany, Tany, Tany! Don't be frightened, Tany. We are Jews!

We too are hiding from the Nazis! When my son told me about you, I knew you had to be one of us. I just knew it!" She steps over to Jacob and hugs him. "I had to be sure, Tany—or whatever your name is. I had to be sure you were one of us. We have been so lonely out here. We have heard not a peep from anyone. Oh, we are dying from boredom, from loneliness." She sits at the table and lights a cigarette and inhales deeply. "Yes, yes, yes," she says in her husky voice. "I knew you must be one of us."

Jacob finishes his cake, says little, but in his heart he feels comfortable and safe with this new family of castaways.

"Do you promise to come back and see us, Tany?" the mother asks.

Jacob nods his head yes.

"Good. I will give you more cake and milk if you do. We are so lonely, so very lonely." And then she looks around. "I will not tell a soul—no one. This will be our little secret, Tany. We will have you over for dinner and lunch and even breakfast if you want."

She stands up and hugs Jacob once again, her smoky breath filtering up his nostrils. And then he is riding his bike down the long and winding dirt road back home to Uncle Philip and Aunt Alice.

"I received a letter at work today," Uncle Philip says in a matter-of-fact way as they sit at the dinner table. Alice smiles and looks at Jacob. "It was from Charleroi."

Jacob stops eating and looks up.

"The letter was from a friend, explaining how he would like for Tany's aunt to visit this weekend. I wrote him back, Tany, and explained that we would be delighted to have your...mother... come to see you and to stay with us for a few days."

Jacob drops his fork and runs over to Uncle Philip with such excitement he can barely contain himself.

"I will arrange everything, Tany. She will be here Saturday morning when you wake up."

The days drag on with such a long and arduous stagnation—each minute, each hour as if chiseled from granite. Jacob spends his time with the old Jewish lady and her son Michael. One day comes and another day goes. Finally it is Friday night. Jacob lies in his bed and thinks about all that has transpired since last he saw his mother. He has a hard time imagining her face. He panics and tries to conjure up photographs of his family, of his sister and his mother.

Mama! Won't she be surprised when she finds out there are other Jews hiding in the area. Won't she be excited about his pursuit of Christianity! Oh, that the morning would come!

15

When Jacob awakes late the following morning, it soon dawns on him his mother may be already downstairs. He splashes water on his face, combs his hair, dresses, and nearly skips five steps on the last leap to the bottom floor. His mother is indeed there, but as Jacob rounds the corner, he sees the Delvaux family and his mother hunched over the kitchen table discussing something important. And then, just like that, the mood shifts to one of jubilation and reunion.

"Oh, my little lamb! How you have grown! How much like your father you look!" Rachael runs to him and they hug, a deep, all-consuming embrace that leaves both breathless. "I have missed you so much, Jacob!" says Rachael, now holding his cheeks in her hands, pressing them gently, rubbing the tears away with her thumbs. She straightens up, suddenly aware of where she is, how dangerous the world is, how close the enemy is to finding them out. "Why don't you eat some breakfast, Tany," she whispers to him. "We will have time to talk later."

Jacob joins them at the table, and listens in as the discussion resumes.

"What are we to do?" Alice Delvaux asks.

"We wait, be patient," Philip says.

Rachael watches him squeeze his wife's hand, and for a moment she thinks of Ruben—the simple note on the table—and just as fast it is over. She clenches her fist as if that pressure will somehow dissolve the guilt, the anxiety, the terrible worm of doubt that gnaws at her every day.

"We do not wait," Rachael says. "We do not sit and do nothing while my son is in your house. If it is not safe here, then we will move him."

"But, Madame Horowitz, where will your son go?" Philip says. "If the Black Brigade is about, as you yourself have said, then it will be safer for us to wait until things quiet down."

"They will not quiet down, Mr. Delvaux. That is what we have thought all along. That is what we thought when they captured Belgium. That is what we thought when they erased our identity. That is what we thought when they took our homes, our businesses." She puts her hands over her face for a brief moment and then whispers, "That is what we thought as they took our families to the death camps."

"Yes," Philip says, "I am sure you are right. It is better to move and keep moving than to wait for them to come."

Rachael suddenly looks over at Jacob. "Eat up, my little lamb. We will go on that walk in just a little bit." She rubs his head, just as Ruben used to do, and this too clenches her heart in a moment of reflection. When Jacob finishes his breakfast, Rachael asks him to leave.

"Tany, go out and ride your bike," Alice says. "Your mother will be out to see you soon."

Rachael looks at Alice, a look full of emotion—a longing to be the mother she should be. Alice smiles warmly, recognizing the pain.

"Would you care for some more coffee, Madame Horowitz?"

Rachael nods and watches her son go out the door.

"How is your other child?" asks Alice as she pours the coffee.

"Thank you. I don't know. I have not been able to see her. Rene is working on that for me. Right now the family has not responded to any of his inquiries. Until that time comes, I am helpless. Either they are being pursued by the enemy and are being cautious, or something else altogether is happening."

"What is your concern?" Alice asks. "Do you think a domestic problem?"

"That is my worry. I know I should be thankful for any help they can give me, but what if the enemy is not from without?"

"Now is the time to be patient, Madame Horowitz," Philip says. "We fall into the enemy's hands when we begin to doubt, when we make careless moves, when fear grips our lives. Let us be patient, that is what God wants us to do. Trust Him, Madame Horowitz." Philip smiles and then stares at her for a moment. "Are you a practicing Jew, Madame Horowitz?"

Rachael looks away, watching Jacob out the window; he is happy, content, pumping his legs and riding about like any child on any autumn day. "No," she responds still looking out the window. "No, we were not practicing Jews, Mr. Delvaux. And perhaps that is why my family is in hiding."

"Never think that, Rachael. God is watching you as surely as you are sitting at this table. He has brought you here, brought your son into our house. He has saved you from the very jaws of death. No, Rachael, He cares for you more than you know."

"I am sure you are right, Mr. Delvaux." Rachael wipes the tears from her eyes, the words from this sincere man like an arrow to her heart. "I am sure you are right." And then she stands. "And now I am going to spend time with my son."

"If you go down the trail that leads into the field and beyond, you should have all the privacy you desire," Alice says.

Rachael nods and walks outside to Jacob. They walk down the

road and take the path that leads into a field. Jacob squeezes his mother's hand and swings it with affection. For a brief moment they are not two displaced people hiding for their lives but mother and son—one of countless other mothers and sons walking the earth on that day. Yet, skirting and weaving about the borders is the fear and terror only the hunted know.

They walk together for quite some time in silence, absorbing each other's presence, acclimating to each other's smell, walk, breathing.

"Have you been safe?" Rachael asks to her son. "Have they been treating you as they ought?"

"Yes, Mama, they have been very nice to me."

Rachael stops and turns toward her son. "Have they hurt you in any way?"

"No, Mama. What's wrong?"

Rachael hesitates and looks away to wipe her eyes. "It's nothing, my little lamb. No, nothing." She pauses again and looks at the trees, the field of grass. "Sometimes we cannot control what happens to us." She is not in front of her son now but in front of a tribunal that has accused her of negligence. "How could I have known my daughter would be given to such a place. They did not know. How could I?"

"Mama?"

"I'm all right, Jacob. It is your sister, Sarah." She pauses, choosing her words carefully, deciding to swallow some. "I am not able to see her right now, but I will, Jacob. Don't worry, my little lamb. She is fine. I will be over to see her in a while. Don't worry. You must worry only about yourself, only about Jacob, only about staying alive. Do you hear me? You cannot afford to think of anything else. You will be strong. You will banish any fear that comes over you, and you will survive. Do not think this fun, this bike, this family is anything but a hiding place." She hesitates, then pulls his face close to hers. "The Germans are all around you, Jacob, pursuing you with hounds and guns. They want to take you away from me, away from your sister. They want to kill you. Do not forget that. When you lie down, when you rise up, write it on the forefront of your mind. You must escape. You must do whatever it takes. Whatever it takes." She pulls him close, close, as if they were one. "You are my life, my love. You and Sarah are the reason I get up every morning. Never forget that, Jacob." She whispers, "Tell me you will never forget that."

They separate and walk down the trail hand in hand. They sit beneath a tall shade tree on the edge of the forest and look out over the swaying fields. Rachael produces an apple for each of them, and they suck and bite the juicy pulp.

"Why are you so pensive, Jacob?"

"I have been thinking about a lot of things."

"Oh?"

"I have been thinking about baptism and Christianity."

"Have you, now?" She looks down at him and then lifts his chin so he is looking into her eyes. "Have the Delvauxs made you think about such things?"

"Well, yes. But—"

"You have forgotten." Her voice is cold.

"No, I haven't. We went to see a priest. Father Gilbert. He said that—"

"You have forgotten what I have told you."

"Father Gilbert said that—"

"I don't care about Father Gilbert. I don't care about the Delvauxs. I care about the Horowitz family, if we will live to see tomorrow, if we will eat today. This is what I know. This is what I care about. You have forgotten why you are here, Jacob. You have been bewitched by the Delvauxs and Father—"

"No, Mama. No, I haven't."

Rachael takes one last bite of the fruit and tosses the core into the field just before them. She is silent for a while.

"We will tell the Delvauxs and Father…"

"Gilbert," Jacob whispers.

"Yes, Father Gilbert. We shall tell them we cannot make such a choice at present, but will wait to hear from your father about such matters."

There is a sense of loss mixed with a renewed sense of vigor—a pursuit of God, of who He is, of who Jacob is, of what it means to be Jewish. And then Jacob remembers the other news he was so excited about.

"I have met a friend, Mama."

Rachael turns suddenly and looks down at her son. Jacob sees the concern and continues rapidly.

"I met him in this field, down the road the other way. We played together, and then he said his mother wanted to meet me, wanted me to come to the house. So I did, and she gave us cake and milk. She's a Jew, Mama. She told me she was hiding just like me, just like we are hiding, Mama."

"When did you see them last?"

"Just yesterday. They only live down the road. Shall we go and see them?"

"No!" cries out Rachael with more force than she intends. "Where do they live?"

"Just that way," and Jacob points down across the field and behind them. "She told me we could come over any time. She said no one visited them anymore. She said they were lonely, Mama."

Rachael is standing up and pulling Jacob down the road with her. She decides they would be better off in the field. She grips

Jacob's arm tighter and tighter, pulling him through the tall grass, all the while putting the pieces together, piece by piece. Time is running out.

Rachael leaves Jacob standing on the porch near the blue bike. She runs inside to where Alice is making dinner. Alice turns to her with a smile, but the smile fades as she sees Rachael's expression.

"What is wrong, Madame Horowitz?"

"We have been compromised!"

"What are you talking about?"

"Are you such a fool as to allow the boy to go off and play at a stranger's home! Are you so stupid and careless as to jeopardize my boy's life? To compromise the entire Underground apparatus? Stupid woman!"

"What are you talking about, Madame Horowitz? Who did Tany see? What has he done? I don't understand?"

Rachael rushes over to the phone and picks it up. "Send for my cab immediately! Call Rene to pick us up. Hurry!"

"But...but I don't understand. What is happening?"

"Call! Just make the phone call! Tell Rene we need to be picked up immediately! Call! Call now!"

Alice dials the number with trembling hands. Rene is on the other end. He soon realizes the danger. Alice puts the phone down. "The cab is on the way."

"Tany!" Rachael screams. "Tany, get in here, now!" Jacob runs in and sees the panic on Alice's face. "Go upstairs and pack your things. Hurry, we do not have much time." She turns to Alice. "Where is your husband?"

"He was just called away."

"What do you mean called away?"

"Someone called him and told him he needed to meet with him."

"Who called?"

"I don't know who it was—"

"Was it the police, a neighbor…who?"

"Business. It was a client of his, a new client."

Rachael runs to the bottom of the stairs. "Hurry up, Tany! Hurry up!" She looks out the window half expecting to see Wolfhardt Becker and his troops marching down the road. Jacob comes down the stairs with his suitcase. He puts it down on the floor and walks over to his mother. She turns to him and kneels down.

"Okay, Jacob, it is time for you to be strong. Can you be strong for me?"

Jacob nods.

"Good boy. I want you to take your suitcase and start to walk by the road. I don't want you to walk on the road but in that field we just walked through. Do you understand? Good. You will see a cab coming down the road. When you do, I want you to wave it down and get in. I want you to tell the driver the house is compromised and he is to stay where he is. Tell him I will meet him further down the road." She stops and looks him straight in the eyes. "Do you understand all I said to you?"

"Yes, Mama."

"Good. Now hurry along. No time for good-byes. No time for anything except what I just told you."

Jacob hugs Alice and then runs out the door. He thinks he can hear the German shepherds, the guards with gnashing teeth and flashing machine guns. He runs faster and faster through the field. Evening is coming quick. Jacob drags the suitcase along, his arm burning from the exertion. Don't look back. Don't look back. You must be strong like Papa. And then the feeling that had so gripped him in the old woman's house—the emotion that had sustained him through the stale odor and the long dark nights—this feeling erupts in his heart: anger, hatred, revenge. He is running not from the German army, not from the Nazis; no, it is from one man: a tall spectacled man who smokes cigarettes, who watched his father get knocked to the ground. And if he had not at that moment seen the headlights from the taxi, he would have stopped, turned around, and run into the very twilight screaming for him to come and face him.

"This place is crawling with Gestapo," says the bearded driver. "I don't know how your mother knew it, but today is not a good day to be in this place."

Jacob huddles in the back seat as told, huddles against the seat and shakes uncontrollably. His bravado, his sudden burst of courage is now squirming somewhere in his bowels, ready to release itself at any moment. The taxi driver backs the car up and turns off his lights. The darkness is now thick and nearly impenetrable. He pulls forward and slowly begins to creep up the road. His window is rolled down, and both he and Jacob can hear the unmistakable rumble of trucks. Dogs bark in the distance.

"This is too hot!" the taxi driver whispers. "This is way too hot. I can't stick around here. We will all be caught!" He begins to increase his speed.

"You can't just leave my mother!" Jacob screams. "She said she would come! She said it!"

"I believe you. I believe you. But if we don't get out of here right now, we are not going to get out at all. It may already be too late." He has made up his mind and pushes on the accelerator.

Jacob looks through the back window into the darkness. "Mama," he whispers. "Mama." Suddenly he is thrown forward, his head smacking against the back of the front passenger seat. The driver screams out in panic and hurriedly gets out of the car.

It is Rachael. He has nearly run her over. He helps her into the front seat and closes the door.

"Stay down, Jacob," she commands in a sure, strong voice. "If I tell you to get out of the car and run—you do just that. No questions. Understood?"

"Yes, Mama," Jacob whispers.

The car speeds off into the night, gravel and dust flying and smacking into the wheel wells.

Wolfhardt Becker would write in his report later that night that all suspects died while trying to escape. Headquarters was used to that, used to his methods, the brutality that was necessary to purge the virus that was the Jews.

It was by accident he even found out about the farmhouse, the Jewish mother and her son hiding out in it. One day a Brownshirt—bless their souls but they are diligent in their wanting to please him—a Brownshirt who just happened to be a postal delivery man had delivered a package to the wrong house. That was all it had been, a simple mistake.

"You have the wrong house," said the worn and frightened woman who came to the door.

"Is this not 1345 rural route 3?"

"No, I am sorry. This is 1342."

The postman had smiled—they were so good at what they did, and Becker liked that diabolical aspect in all of the Brownshirts, the homegrown spies of Belgium—he had smiled, thanked the woman, but all the while remembered the fear, the haggard look. He reported it like any other suspicious activity.

Becker receives thousands of such reports a week—most unconfirmed, most just empty interrogation vomit. The Belgians, when they did crack, when they did finally break under torture, usually gave false information. The Underground resistance did not tell their people enough to threaten the entire operation. Only a few Underground members have such power. But Becker chooses this particular house above other particular houses as one to investigate. If it is false, then it is false. The war will last long enough; he has time on his side. Belgium is small, and his power is increasing daily.

The first step in all of his operations is to find out who the neighbors are. Once they are assessed, their records checked, any suspicious or anti-German tendencies discovered, then they are called into the office one at a time, preferably at night: snatch them from their homes when they least expect it. A phone call, a letter delivered personally, a strange car pulling up in the driveway. There are as many pathways to fear as there are people to frighten.

It is, once again, by sheer luck that he strikes gold. The neighbors, a Mr. and Mrs. Delvaux, are keeping a young boy of eleven or twelve with them—trapped here by the war, it is said. This is not unusual, for many family members from overseas were trapped by the sudden and swift blitzkrieg. But all leads must be exhausted. Becker decides to plant an agent into Philip Delvaux's life. He poses as a wealthy businessman who needs financial help. He compiles a complete dossier: stay-at-home wife, son killed in the resistance, devout Christians. This in itself is enough to haul them in for interrogation. The Wolf hates Christians, at least the born-again type. All of Germany is guided by God. The Führer is God's agent. Jews killed Christ. This is pounded into the heads of all young Hitler youth (Becker being one). The born-again Christians seem to be against everything Herr Hitler stands for. They are zealots and Jew sympathizers. The Delvauxs fit into that category. The trap is set.

Several weeks go by and Becker stakes out the old farmhouse. Yes, there seems to be little activity, only the mother and the boy. The boy is seen playing with the Delvaux child, in a field. The day is scheduled; all is ready.

Becker strikes the first blow with a simple phone call to Mr. Delvaux from his new business friend, the Gestapo agent. Delvaux shows up and is immediately arrested and brought to the interrogation room. Without hesitation and with no warning, the Wolf smashes a brass knuckled fist into the unsuspecting Delvaux's face.

"I will say this one time," says the Wolf in an emotionless voice. "Who are you working for?" Before Delvaux can respond, the Wolf smashes his face again. Delvaux's hands are handcuffed behind his back. He sways forward from the pain and the terrible onslaught.

And what is this? Good heavens! Is he actually praying? The Wolf grabs his hair and pulls his bloody face up toward the intense light.

"Your God cannot help you now, Mr. Delvaux." He yanks Delvaux's face back once again by the hair. The man, cheekbone shattered, nose flat and puffy, blood streaming down his lips and chin, dripping onto his lap—this man is already breaking. He whispers something through his swollen lips.

"What is that?" the Wolf says. "Speak up, Mr. Delvaux, I can't hear what you say."

Delvaux whispers the same thing once again.

"What is he saying, Fritz? I cannot hear him. We cannot hear you, Mr. Delvaux. If you want to confess, you must speak up."

Delvaux says the same thing once again, his voice is dissipating in the surge of pain. The Wolf bends closer, nearly putting his ear to Delvaux's lips. Delvaux repeats his words:

"I forgive you," he whispers. "God forgives you."

The Wolf steps back and smashes Delvaux in the face once again and again and again. Each time Delvaux whispers, "I forgive you." The Wolf grabs the guard's gun and places it against Delvaux's head.

"Give me names. I want names!" he shouts in a rage. But Delvaux repeats the same words, his voice a gurgle of blood and vomit. And just like that, the Wolf pulls the trigger.

They leave the cell, the husk of Philip Delvaux slumped forward and angled to one side.

They wait until dark and then move fast and furious. The trucks rumble down the road, while SS troops surround the farmhouse. One guard breaks in, then another. There is a scream of fear. The mother yells to her son: "Run! Run for your life!" But it is too late; the mother is cut down with a single pistol shot. They take the terrified boy and throw him into the back of the truck. And they move toward the Delvaux house.

They pound on the door. Alice opens the door, clutching her Bible, and lets them in.

"Madame Delvaux, you are under arrest for treason against the laws of Germany," the Wolf says. "Where are the Jews? Search the premises!"

The guards thrash about, capsizing this, throwing that. A pair of pants is brought to the Wolf.

"Where is the Jew boy?"

"I don't know what you are—"

The Wolf slaps her to the floor. "Where is the Jew boy?"

She too begins to pray.

The Wolf screams out, "Find the Jew boy! Find him now!"

Alice Delvaux is huddled upon the floor, praying and wiping her eyes. She does not stop praying and reciting Scripture even as the cold steel barrel is placed to her head.

"Love your enemies, do good to those who hate you, bless those who curse you, pray for those who mistreat—"

She does not finish.

Herman sat with Jacob at the airport on that rainy day in Cleveland, both waiting to see if Isaac would show. And then, just like that, while Jacob was recounting a handball story to Herman, Isaac stepped up to the table and sat down next to his father.

At first Jacob continued his story about the unbelievable shot Lereau had pulled off, but that was cut short by Herman's redirected stare and the solid mass in Jacob's peripheral vision. He turned his head. There was Isaac—New York Mets baseball cap pulled over his forehead, scrubby beard, small round glasses on his face—a completely different figure than the cardboard cutout that stood at the entranceway of most major bookstores. In fact, the man sitting next to Jacob was not his son—no, at first glance he would have missed him altogether. Perhaps he had. Absurdly enough, he was looking for an Indiana Jones hat and leather coat. It was silly, but that was the truth. There was a moment of uncontrolled joy, a joy that seemed to encapsulate all of Jacob's face. But that moment was for the trained eye, for it lasted only a second; the eyes refocused, the burden of time, pride, and guilt collapsed upon him, and he struggled to maintain civility.

"Hello, Pop," Isaac said, his small lenses catching the hub's light. "I'm sorry I'm late. The roads are a mess." He paused and looked around. "And it doesn't look like we're going anywhere soon." He turned to Herman and smiled. "Hello, Herman. Fancy meeting you here."

"I'm flying to New York, Isaac." Herman placed his paw of a hand upon Isaac's forearm and squeezed.

What followed was unbearable silence on all sides. Then Jacob sighed, stood up, and without another word hobbled off to the bathroom.

Jacob had tried to prepare himself for this very moment, had contemplated his first words; but all of a sudden his head was empty, his mouth sucked dry of all moisture, a stopper in his throat not allowing him to say a word. So he sighed. And since he could not cover it up or did not wish to explain it, he promptly stood up and walked to the bathroom.

As he walked out of the restroom, he breathed in and then breathed out. *Okay,* he thought, *I must let things fall in place. I must allow the pieces to drop. I started this, I can go through with this.* He stopped at the café and bought three coffees before walking back to the table where Herman and Isaac sat whispering to one another.

"I bought us some coffee," Jacob said. He did not look at his son but at Herman. "I don't know what you want in it. You will have to get that yourself." Jacob put the cups down in the middle of the table.

"Well," Herman said, "I like cream and sugar—the half and half kind, not the creamer." He stood up and walked to the café counter.

Jacob and Isaac did not look at each other.

"I like cream in my coffee as well," Isaac said, standing to his feet. "Yep, sounds good."

Isaac and Herman soon returned, and an astounding scene began to unfold. One would have thought Herman Bergman was some sort of high official, a sage of wisdom and mirth. Neither Jacob nor Isaac said a word to each other—only to Herman.

"Yes, Herman, the traffic is something. Isn't it?"

"Is your coffee hot enough, Herman?"

"I wonder when our flight will depart. Have you any idea, Herman?"

"Yes, yes, yes, I see what you mean about the surface of this table, Herman. It is smooth. Yes, indeed."

"By the way, Herman, do you have the ability to transport me out of this situation?"

"Oh, yes, Herman, yes. Oh, you are the sole of wit. Indeed."

It was Herman who remedied the situation. He decided to say good-bye—say good-bye and leave these two miserable people to work out their own reconciliation in fear and trembling.

"Well, I am off to my plane."

"No, Herman," Jacob said, but he then caught himself. "I mean, so soon?" Jacob smiled a thin smile as if to say, *Please, dear, dear friend. Please don't leave me alone with my son.*

Herman reached out and squeezed Jacob's shoulder. "You will have to send me postcards from Belgium." He looked at Isaac and winked. "And you better be on your best behavior. You may be famous, by I can still knock you around."

And then Jacob and Isaac were left sitting by themselves. Both shifted and then picked up their empty coffee cups, jiggled them to confirm they were indeed empty, and placed them back down.

"I thought I would never see the day Jacob Horowitz read Jack Oxford."

"Well, yes," Jacob said, rubbing the cover with the palm of his hand. "That was to my detriment."

"Have you read any of it yet?"

"The first sentence is so overwritten I cannot imagine reading any further than I did. Has the taste of our culture degenerated so much?"

Isaac pulled off his glasses and rubbed his face. "I see you're going to dish out the same stale and cold meal." He stood up. "I don't need this, not now, not from you. You were the one who invited me here. If this is the way you—"

"Wait." Jacob raised his hand and motioned for Isaac to sit back down. "Please, please," he whispered. "I am sorry. Forgive me. I didn't mean to upset you." He sighed deeply. "That is the last thing I wanted to do, Isaac." And for the first time in ten years, father and son made direct eye contact, sustained and penetrating.

Yes, thought Jacob, *Yes, I am different. I am not the same man I was.* And with a Herculean effort he grasped the closing door and heaved it open inch by inch. Time was running out. He must go all the way. No stopping, not now, not ever. It's to the finish tape. This was for all the ghosts: his mother, father, and sister; the Delvauxs, Yvonne, Liza, Pierre.

"Please, sit down, son. The time for anger and bitterness is over."

PART THREE

17

The tone of the meeting had changed. Jacob could see it in his son's face. Isaac sat back down in the chair opposite his father and rubbed his stubbly chin. He took off his small, round glasses and held them up to the light.

"Isaac," said Jacob, still in that defeated tone, "I'm glad you came."

Isaac looked at his father. "I'm glad I came too, Pop."

Jacob was about to respond when he noticed a young woman hovering behind Isaac. She had been there ever since Isaac had appeared. She shifted her weight impatiently from one foot to the other, as if waiting for the right time to approach. She had scooted closer, inch by inch, as Jacob prepared to speak to his son. Finally, he looked up at her and then back at Isaac, then back up at the woman. Isaac turned to see who was behind him.

"Is that someone you know?" Jacob asked.

"No," Isaac said.

"Excuse me, Mr. Oxford," she said sheepishly, her red ponytail swinging from side to side. "I knew it was you when I saw you loitering around the gate about an hour ago. That beard and glasses can't fool me."

Isaac smiled, but his face showed his embarrassment. "Well, I haven't been here that long."

"Oh, I checked my watch," the woman said. "I've been here for some time now. I told my boyfriend, Peter, I said, 'I'll betcha that's Jack Oxford!' He didn't believe me." She stopped and turned around and then turned back to Isaac and Jacob. "He's over there. He said I was going to make a fool of myself. I told him to wait over there and watch." She stopped again and turned around— this time waving at Peter. "Could you humor me, Mr. Oxford, and wave at Peter for me?"

Jacob looked on in bewilderment. Of all the times, in all the situations—just when he had managed to suppress all of his old feelings about his son and what he had done—now he was being force-fed this Jack Oxford heresy right in front of the watching world. He looked away in disgust.

Isaac waved to Peter and smiled politely.

"Do you think you could sign Peter's copy of your new book, Mr. Oxford?"

"Certainly," said Isaac, looking up at his father and then taking out his fountain pen.

Jacob acted as though none of this were happening. And suddenly, he stood up. "Excuse me…Jack. I'll be back in a moment." And he walked away.

By this time Peter had scooted over to the ponytailed girl. They were both laughing nervously, talking in puffs of air and with long pauses.

It wasn't that Jacob minded his son being famous. He was very proud of Isaac's accomplishments. But it was obvious it was not Isaac who was actually famous. It was a figment of Isaac's imagination. He had created a persona that was nothing like the real man. And every time the name Jack Oxford was invoked, Jacob immediately thought of the war, of all he had endured to save the Horowitz name. What a cost! What a sellout! The more he thought of his past, the more he hated Jack Oxford and what his son had done.

By the time he made it to the restroom, he was so angry it took all he could do to calm himself down. He stood in front of the mirror, in a long row of mirrors with white porcelain sinks beneath, and turned on the cold water.

Oh, how much he had changed. It was obvious in his son's expression when he first set eyes on him. He could tell that he, Jacob, must not be the same man he once had been. Expressions, at least unprepared ones, tell stories politeness and manners would never allow to be told. This was a story of deterioration. Ten years and a bout with cancer has an effect on a person's soul, on his appearance. He stared at his reflection, at his drooping chin, his watery eyes, his creased and wrinkled neck. For a moment he lost his direction and had the sensation of displacement, the same displacement he had felt when standing in front of the mirror just before leaving for the airport. His mind raced for contact with the real, with the image in the mirror, and slowly, it made the connection. He stooped down and bathed his hands and face in the cold water from the tap. He felt the pressure building down below, that uncomfortable feeling that told him the cancer was eating him up, and he bathed his face again.

He walked back to the hub, then suddenly stopped near one of the pillars that bordered the open space now filled with people. He leaned up against the concrete as though he were just another weary passenger waiting for his flight. And then he turned and watched his son still sitting in his chair, now facing the red pig-tailed girl and her friend Peter. Jacob watched as his son nodded and smiled, gestured with his hands. Yes, he waved it just the way Yvonne had many years before. But how could that be? It was not a genetic thing, not a biological connection Isaac carried away from her—no, this was Liza's child. And yet, Isaac was more like Yvonne than Asher could ever be. Maybe that was why Jacob had such a problem with Isaac's betrayal. Yes, Isaac had Liza's hair, her cheekbones, her delicate hands. But his temperament, his creative urge to explain the world through art—this was all Yvonne. And this was a special bond Jacob had never allowed himself to nurture. Those memories from his past were sealed away. He was no longer that person. But that gesture, that simple movement of Isaac's hand—sweeping of the arm, turning of the palm upward—had eroded decades of carefully placed barriers.

The pigtailed girl was still laughing, still talking. Peter was now doing the same. Isaac looked around, and that was when Jacob decided to come to his rescue.

"Well, Jack," said Jacob with a smile, "shall we be off to that place you were telling me about?"

Isaac turned suddenly, a look of relief on his face.

"Jacob, yes, yes, indeed." He paused and looked at his father, then back at his overambitious guests. "Well, it was really nice meeting you both." Isaac stood up and adjusted his baseball hat, pulling it further over his eyes. Jacob and Isaac were just about to walk away when the red-haired girl grabbed Isaac's hand.

"Oh, Mr. Oxford, you forgot to sign *my* book! You signed Peter's but not mine." She opened her copy of *The Tombs of Anakim* and brandished it like some sacred text.

"Yes, yes, of course."

Jacob watched as Isaac scribbled his name, scribbled the canned message under it, watched as the girl suddenly clasped the book to her heaving chest.

"Oh, Mr. Oxford. This means more to me than…than…" Peter took her by the arm and walked her away.

Jacob grabbed his empty cup of coffee. "Well," he said, "how about getting out of here?"

Isaac looked embarrassed and relieved at the same time. "What about our departure?"

"We can check with the desk and then go somewhere quiet."

"There's a bistro close to the airport. I know the owner. We could get a place in the back—he will be so happy to see me. He's followed my career since the beginning."

Jacob took the last phrase full force in the heart.

A couple who had overheard the conversation was now whispering to one another. Jacob and Isaac grabbed their trash and headed to the desk to check on their flight.

The plane was delayed for at least two more hours—it had yet to leave New York. And so Jacob and Isaac hailed a cab and told the driver to take them to a small bistro just beyond the hotels and car rentals. The rain had finally stopped, the severity of the storm now drifting off to the southeast—black cumulous clouds rumbling and glowing with power and electricity. The two sat silently in the back like strangers who meet for the first time and will soon depart, never to see each other again. The cabdriver, an Indian with a pelt of black hair, quietly sat in the front—eyes every now and then glancing up at his passengers and then to the side mirror.

"Here we are," said the Indian with an inflection that made his statement an interrogative. Isaac paid the driver a healthy sum, and the two entered the restaurant. Sam's Taste of New York was an upscale eatery that appeased finicky taste buds and the miser's pocketbook all at one time. When Sam learned Isaac had arrived with his father and was sitting in the back, he rushed out to see him. "Your father! Your father is in this store!" cried Sam, suddenly hugging Isaac and then a resistant Jacob. "Mr. Horowitz, you are indeed an honored guest here in my bistro!" Jacob looked surprised, glancing at Sam and then over at his son. Sam hesitated and looked with half a smile at Isaac.

Isaac smiled, "Oh, don't worry about it, Sam. My dad is probably impressed you know me by my real name."

"Of course I know you by your real name, Isaac. Good heavens! A man cannot be separated from his name. A name is everything. A name is culture, is history, is how we see the world. A name is—"

"How about something to drink, Sam?" Isaac said.

The owner blushed, his greasy face glistening red with embarrassment. And he hurried off to the back to get a bottle of water that had just come in from the Netherlands.

Liza Horowitz and her son Isaac had a bond that far exceeded any bond between Liza and Asher. Jacob could tell this right away. At first, when he had met Liza and she realized he had a little baby boy to take care of, she immediately took on the role of mother— even before they had married. But at that time Jacob was an emotionless wreck of a man. He had started to put his life back together, and Asher was just one more piece of the puzzle he needed to fit somewhere. Liza was that fit. Jacob guarded his heart and willed his affections with great effort. He was a used up man by now. Yes, at the age of twenty-six he had lived a lifetime, had seen too much death, had started to separate himself from all that could hurt him again. He did not love Liza in the way he had Yvonne, but he needed her. Liza accepted this. She was not very attractive, and yet attractive enough. She knew it, Jacob knew it. They married and another piece of the puzzle fell into place.

But when Liza became pregnant, Jacob noticed a change.

Jacob would catch her looking at Asher, now nine years old, looking at him and rubbing her stomach. "He does not have your nose, your hair," Liza said one day while they were all sitting at dinner.

"Who?" Jacob said.

"Your son."

Asher stared at his plate in silence. Jacob watched as Liza rubbed her stomach. Asher stood from his chair and ran upstairs. Jacob stared at his wife in disbelief.

When Isaac was born, Liza cuddled him and swooned over him. Asher was scolded for treating the baby too hard, for not paying attention to the baby, for being forgetful to pick up the baby's toys, to wake up mother for the baby's feeding. In fact, Asher became a symbol for all that Liza despised. Jacob watched as his son Asher became the other, the product of the mysterious woman who so plagued Liza's life.

Jacob did not tell Asher he was the son of another relationship, a former relationship where love and passion had controlled all the couple did. No, Jacob said nothing to him, and commanded that Liza treat him as her own flesh and blood. But a command is easily circumvented when the commander is never home. Soon it was clear who was the golden child and who was the outcast. Jacob, ultimately, was the cause of this, but he was too wounded and sick to recognize his sons cries for help.

The terrible truth about both his sons—a truth Jacob had only recently recognized—was that they were both Jacob. Their temperaments and their outlooks on life, their drives to succeed, their high ambition, and their willingness to cut off all they knew and loved for the sake of emotional survival—these were the traits Jacob had passed on to his sons. It was a heritage that haunted him all his life.

Sam returned with the bottle of water shipped from the Netherlands and two crystal goblets.

"This is such an honor, Mr. Horowitz," said Sam tilting the bottle as though he were pouring an expensive wine. "You and your son in my restaurant. Such an honor." He stood erect and stepped to the side like some archaic waiter.

"Is there a problem, Sam?" asked Isaac after several minutes had passed.

"No problem, Isaac."

"Then why are you standing there?"

"I am waiting for you to order. Take your time. Act like I am not even here." He stayed still, eyes watching the father and son's every move. Isaac waved him over, bade him bend close to his ear.

"We wish to be alone, Sam. Order us two Reubens with slaw on the side."

Sam stood up and hurried to the kitchen, his clump of thinning hair blowing straight up like an absurd dorsal fin.

Jacob stared out the window, then suddenly turned on Isaac. "This man calls you Isaac. This man knows how important a name is. This owner of a restaurant treats my name better than my son does."

Isaac tipped back his hat and rubbed the newly grown beard. "Is that what you think, Pop? You think I abandoned the name to spite you?"

"Why else would you do such a thing?"

"Have you ever heard the term *pseudonym,* or are you being obtuse?"

"I can see trying to break into the market with another name. But all these years, all these books? What am I to think of such a thing?"

Isaac smiled sardonically and looked out the window.

"You can't answer that, can you?" Jacob was animate but whispering for fear of casting attention upon himself. Isaac shook his head in disbelief. "Tell me then, Isaac. Tell me why you kept Jack Oxford if it was not for spite?"

"You have a short memory, Pop."

"What do you mean, short memory?"

"You really do amaze me, you know that."

"What? What are you getting at? I am right and you are not man enough to admit it to me."

"Listen to me," Isaac hissed. "I did use the name to break into the market. Yes, I did. But you were the one who made me use it for all the other books. You. Or have you forgotten our one-way discussion on the phone when I called you after my first novel was published."

Jacob pulled back from the table ever so slightly.

"All I wanted was a word of praise, a word of encouragement. Just one word to tell me I was doing okay. No, no, that's not how it went." Isaac leaned over the table and pointed his finger at Jacob. "Once again, all you could see was what you wanted to see. Well, I had had enough of that. That night I swore I would have nothing to do with you again. If you did not want to be a part of me, then I wanted no part of you."

Sam came walking back with their lunch. "Here you are, Mr. Horowitz. Sam's special sauce and sauerkraut nestled under enough corned beef to kill a lion." He vanished quietly and with much haste.

Neither man touched his food. Jacob chewed on his son's words. Once again shortsightedness, his not wanting to be hurt, his holding on to things that should have been forgotten—all of these were dancing before his eyes like nightmare ghosts. He had single-handedly marred the lives of his sons, and he was truly sorry.

When Isaac turned from looking out the window, Jacob had his head in his hands, and he was sobbing. The table shook. Isaac reached out to his father, but Jacob pulled away, embarrassed for what he was doing, embarrassed he could not control himself, embarrassed it had taken this long and the end of his life to bring him to this point. He turned to face the window and shook again, placing the back of his fists tightly against his eyes as if that would stop the flow of tears.

"Pop," Isaac whispered. "Pop, I—"

But Jacob pulled himself from the table, turned his back to Isaac, and hobbled off to the men's room.

He went into a stall and closed the door behind him. He plopped down on the closed toilet seat and again lost all control. Ten years of anger, of sadness, of pain, and the guilt of his childhood, all of this exploded through his body, shaking it, convulsing him like a seizure.

"Oh, Pierre!" he sputtered out through open mouth and closed eyes. "Yvonne! What have I done?" And this was all he could say, for the force of the torment was so great nothing else could come out. He mouthed those names over and over again. The final pieces of his man-made wall crumbled to the ground and he was left naked and exposed for the first time since Yvonne's death.

It was Isaac who finally came to the bathroom stall, like a father to his tardy son, and tapped on the door.

"Pop?" said Isaac gently.

The door clicked and then swung open. Jacob's face was red and swollen from his earthquake. Isaac stared at him for only a moment and averted his eyes to the floor.

"Why don't you wash up and come and eat. Sam is making new sandwiches as we speak."

Jacob nodded and then wiped his nose with his hand. Isaac left without another word.

And once again, Jacob Horowitz was staring at his face in the mirror, eyes swollen, reddened, and watery. And for the first time, he did not have that feeling of dislocation. No, he *was* the man starring back at him in the mirror. He reached up and touched his face and rubbed his cheek gently. Then he reached out and touched the image in the mirror. Yes, this was Jacob Horowitz the Belgian Jew who hid for five years from the Nazis. Yes, it had been a while, but he had returned. Now he must finish what he started. He turned on the water and bathed his face with it, wiped it with a towel. He blew his nose several times and then once again looked at himself in the mirror. And then he walked out to meet his son.

He was greeted with a hot steaming Reuben, the pungent smell of sauerkraut. Isaac poured his father some water and Jacob thanked him. They began to eat in silence, but there was a fresh sense of hope hovering about them.

"Did I ever tell you, Pop, about the woman who tried to track me down for an interview? She wanted me to discuss some theory she had concerning my books. It was the craziest thing. She called it sub...substantial...substan—"

"Subversive textualization?" Jacob said.

Isaac looked at him in stunned surprise.

Jacob took another bite of his sandwich; he was suddenly famished. "Are you going to eat that coleslaw?" he asked Isaac, who was still looking at him. "What? What's wrong?"

"How did you know about subversive textualization?"

"I know a lot more than you could possibly imagine, Isaac."

18

The first time Jacob meets Pierre Chabot, he is standing near a fence post staring out at the cows in the field. Pierre is an enormous young man, neck and back a wedge of muscle, large forearms and thick farmer's fingers. Jacob walks up to him and says hello. Pierre's eyes glaze over in a stupor. Again Jacob says hello and then tells Pierre his name. The young man of seventeen stares out at the cows, silent. He seems to be in another world, one of the ones children who never reach beyond the age of four or five go to. Jacob walks back to the house.

The Chabot family owns a four hundred acre farm outside the little town of Charleroi. It is a peaceful place with fences and animals, the smell of hay and the sound of farm machines. Every day is a routine, everyone has their chores to do. And routine is what Jacob so desperately needs in his life. Every day he begins to understand how close he had come to capture. Jacob has learned through Rene that the Delvauxs are dead. Jacob's friend, the little Jewish boy who showed him the magnifying glass, has been taken to the death camps. The house where he had ridden the bike, where he had learned about Jesus, where he encountered the God-Man, now sits abandoned—an empty dark husk—a sacrifice to the gods of war.

"What is wrong with Pierre?" asks Jacob to Mrs. Chabot.

The round, worn woman smiles so that crow's-feet appear in the corners of her eyes. "Oh, I suspect he will warm up to you by and by." She winks at Jacob in an odd fashion. "You don't worry about Pierre. How about you snap the ends off those beans and put them in the pot for me?" She points to a large metal pot and then to the pile of beans on the counter. Soon Jacob's thoughts are consumed with the task at hand, and that seems to please Mrs. Chabot more than anything.

Mr. Chabot was killed several years earlier in a car accident. The full details were never disclosed. The oldest son, Philip, was killed during the first onslaught of German troops: a single bullet through the neck. Pierre is a large dumb brute who seems to stand in one place when he is outside. Yvonne, gangly and energetic, is too involved with her chores, with helping out in the house—involved in everything but befriending Jacob. *Fine,* Jacob thinks. *I must be my own person anyway.* And he spends his days walking the cows out to pasture, walking them back in to milk, and cleaning their stalls at night.

One night he is pitching old hay and waste into a wheelbarrow when Yvonne walks up to the stall opening. She stands before him, her shadow darkening half the stall, which is funny and ironic to Jacob, for she is a skinny rail of a girl. And this is the first time he sees that gesture.

"Are you afraid to be here?" she says waving her arm, palm upward and sweeping it across her chest.

Jacob stops what he is doing and puts the pitchfork into the hay.

"No," he says, trying to be more of a man than he truly is, as if that will impress this girl he suddenly finds attractive. She is pretty in a tomboyish way. She had cut her own hair—short and at places uneven. Her long legs and long arms give her such a gangly appearance Jacob thinks of a marionette.

"If I were in hiding and separated from everyone I knew, I would be scared." That is all she says. She turns her back on Jacob and walks out into the night. He finishes cleaning the stalls, and then hauls the water bucket out to a pond near the barn.

The autumn has slowly drifted into winter, and Jacob has been with the Chabot family since early November. Snow and rain has drizzled down for at least two days now. Christmas is about a month away. There is a sense of peace about this family and this place. Jacob has seen only Yvonne and Mrs. Chabot for any length of time. Pierre keeps to himself. That does not seem to bother anyone, however, and since it does not bother the Chabots, it does not bother Jacob.

In all the chaos that is the war, peace comes in small, sporadic doses, little moments of routine—what you are doing, when you must do it, and satisfaction in doing it well. Oh, there are drills Jacob has to learn, moments of panic when he is told to hide in the barn, bury himself in the hay, and wait for the "all clear" signal from Mrs. Chabot. Jacob slowly forgets the Wolf. He concentrates on the now.

One day while Jacob is outside and Pierre is sitting on the grass playing with some rocks he had collected from the fields, two men drive slowly by. The car stops and one of them walks over to where Pierre is sitting, a split rail fence separating them.

"Hey boy!" hollers the man with a bit of a sneer. Pierre does not even look up. "I said, hey boy!" The man turns to his buddy in the car and then back to Pierre, this time smiling a bit. "Is this the Chabot farm?" asks the man again. Pierre does not move, does not even acknowledge them. "I only want to know how far we are from town, boy." The man spits and looks back at his buddy in the car, then back at Pierre. Yvonne walks up to Jacob who is watching this from the barn.

"What do they want, Tany?" she says.

"I don't know. They seem to want directions or something."

"You better get into the barn," Yvonne says with an air of motherly protection about her. "I've seen this kind of thing before. The Black Brigade comes in all shapes and sizes." She pauses and then shoves Jacob from the side. "Get going, Tany."

Jacob enters the barn and peers through a crack as Yvonne walks out to the men and her brother. The other man is out of the car by now, both with a foot up on the lowest rail, hats pushed back in a cocky nature.

"He doesn't hear you," says Yvonne, her long legs and gangly arms moving in a rhythm all their own. "He's stupid—dumb—retarded since birth. What can I do for you?"

The two men look again at Pierre and then over at the young girl walking hastily toward them.

"We were just asking directions to town, little missy."

"Well," replies Yvonne with hands on hips, standing nearly on top of Pierre who is still sitting down and playing with his rocks, "if you go straight that way and then turn left at the first road you come to, that will take you into town."

"Rumor has it, missy, that your brother there is smarter than all of us combined." And with that the man who arrived at the fence first takes a pebble and tosses it playfully at Pierre. The pebble hits him right on the cheek. He slowly reaches up to his face as if a mosquito has bitten him.

"What are you doing!" Yvonne shouts. "How dare you throw rocks at my brother!" She steps in front of Pierre. "This is Chabot property, mister. You and your friend are not welcome here."

"How about that, Pierre? Is this Chabot property?" He takes another pebble and throws it at Pierre. "Where were you last night, Pierre? Where were you at, say, 2:30 in the morning?"

Pierre suddenly turns around, left lip drooping to one side, tongue out like a dog. He holds up the rocks to the two men and then playfully smacks them together. He does this several times and then turns away from them.

"Ya, ya, ya," sneers the man. "We know your game." The man turns toward Yvonne. "Oh, don't worry, missy, we'll be back. Yes, indeed. We will be back." And he points defiantly at Pierre with his finger.

As the car drives away, Yvonne takes Pierre and walks him toward the barn. Jacob stands in the doorway, trying to sift through all that has taken place. He watches them come up into the shadow of the barn and that is when Pierre stumbles, looks directly into Jacob's face, grins like a Cheshire cat, and winks. Then he walks slowly back to the house with Yvonne, her head darting this way and that, scanning the yard for any more signs of intruders.

That night Pierre comes up to Jacob's bedroom and closes the door behind him.

"I never had a chance to welcome you to the family, Tany." His muscular body fills the door frame, the single light in the room casting half of him in darkness.

Jacob sits up and pushes his back against the headboard in fear.

"I thought you were...were..."

"A little slow, thick in the head?" says Pierre, now walking over to the bed and sitting down near Jacob's feet. "You were the ultimate test, Tany. If I could fool you, I could fool them."

"Who's them?"

"Oh, the Black Brigade, the Nazi scum, any German that comes snooping about." He laughs. "You saw it with your own eyes this afternoon. I know, it's just a matter of time. But time I don't have."

He stops what he is saying and looks at him. "Yvonne says you're not afraid. I like that. It's a good trait to have in such a war."

Jacob cannot help the feeling he is dreaming all of this: the darkness, the sudden transformation of Pierre, the late hour. But no, there on his bed sits Pierre Chabot—stronger, more intelligent and articulate than any seventeen-year-old Jacob has known.

"Why do you put on that act?"

"Labor camps. I would have to work in the camps every day. I have bigger plans for the war than that."

Jacob thinks of Mr. Chabot and Pierre's older brother who have both been killed in the war. He looks at Pierre again and thinks that deep inside, Pierre is a coward for putting on such an act. Others have died, the Delvauxs the most recent, in order to stop the Nazis. Pierre has chosen to stay alive through artifice.

"What are the camps like? Are they that bad?" says Jacob suddenly.

"Well, Tany, let me tell you, there are many ways to fight the enemy. I have my own way." He smiles and pats him on the shin. "Get some sleep." And just like that Pierre walks out of the room.

Later that night, around 3:00 or so, Jacob wakes up. For a moment he cannot place where he is, then the moorings are secured and he pulls himself back into the real. There is a commotion downstairs. Several people are whispering. Jacob steps out of bed onto the hardwood floor. It creaks. The voices stop. Jacob stands perfectly still, the cold seeping through his feet and traveling up his legs. After a few moments, the voices begin once again. Jacob is fearful for his life, for the Chabot family. He gathers up his courage and takes another step. A creak. The voices stop, and suddenly a door opens and shuts.

The next morning Mrs. Chabot is reading the local paper, its major headline:

Underground strikes again
Another ammunition train hit by late night attack

Pierre is sitting next to Yvonne sipping coffee and scooping up loads of eggs into his mouth, a residue of yoke in the corners of his lips.

"Good morning, Tany," says Mrs. Chabot with a smile. "Would you like me to serve you some eggs?"

"Yes, ma'am." Jacob sits across from Yvonne. She is dressed in a blue jumper, and Jacob looks at her awkwardly, the sunlight striking the side of her cheeks. She is beautiful.

"What are you looking at?" she says with a playful smirk.

Jacob turns his head and asks Mrs. Chabot for a glass of milk. He can feel Yvonne's eyes upon him, boring into his skull and neck. He will not look at her.

"Eat up, Yvonne," Mrs. Chabot says. "You don't want to be late for school."

"Will I go to school here, too?" Jacob asks.

"No," Yvonne says tartly. "How are you going to go to school?"

"Yvonne!" Mrs. Chabot says. "Let's remember that Tany is our guest." She turns her head toward Jacob and smiles warmly. Her smile is beautiful, refreshing, reassuring. "I will teach you at home, Tany. It is just too dangerous for you to go to school right now."

Jacob looks at Yvonne and then at his food. He wants to be with her, but at the same time wants to prove to her that he doesn't.

"Did you sleep okay, Tany?" Pierre asks.

"Yes." Then he remembers the voices. "I heard someone downstairs late last night. I got out of bed to check who it was, but—"

"Oh, that was just me, Tany," Pierre says.

"But who was with you?"

Pierre looks at Yvonne and then over to his mother with a look of surprise. "No one, Tany. I got up to get some milk. I couldn't sleep. Must be the moon or something."

"But I heard two voices."

"Don't you remember, Pierre," Mrs. Chabot says. "I came down to let Blacky out." She laughs. "That dog. He can keep you up all night." There is a moment of silence and then: "Eat up, Tany. Those eggs are going to get cold."

It is now five o'clock and Yvonne has been missing for three days. She has not returned home since that morning she left for school. In fact the principle of the school has told Mrs. Chabot she did not arrive at all. Pierre is nowhere to be found. It is just Tany and Mrs. Chabot. They are sitting in the living room next to the phone, Mrs. Chabot every now and again pacing across the floor. A door opens and Pierre's large frame enters the room.

"What is it?" Mrs. Chabot asks.

"It's what we have feared, Mama." Pierre rushes over to his mother and holds her tightly in his thick arms. "It's okay, Mama. I have a plan."

She pushes him away. "What are you talking about?"

"I know where she is, and I know how to get her out."

"That's foolishness, Pierre. I will not allow you to risk your life like that. The war has already claimed your father and brother. I won't allow it to take you."

Pierre is fired up, mad, crossing his arms and storming around the room.

"If I don't get her out, she will die, Mama. You know that. Is that what you want?"

Mrs. Chabot places her hands over her face and shakes her head.

"Okay, then. It's settled."

"But how are you going to get into the labor camp? There are guards and dogs. Pierre, it is too risky." Mrs. Chabot hurries over to Pierre and grabs him by the arms.

"Don't worry, Mama. I will get her out. I have a plan."

"Oh, Yvonne," Mrs. Chabot whispers. "Sweet Yvonne."

Pierre runs upstairs, scurries around, and then heads out toward the barn. Jacob looks out the window for several minutes but does not see him reappear.

The night drags on. Mrs. Chabot has tried to read to Jacob, but she is too nervous. The story is cut short, and she soon is pacing once again. A fire crackles in the fireplace, the blues and reds and the soothing warmth hypnotize Jacob, make his eyelids droop. He opens them suddenly as the situation, the danger, settles down upon him once again. What happened to Yvonne? Would the Nazis claim yet another soul? He thinks of his father, of his mother, of Uncle Benjamin, of Sarah. The idyllic world he had constructed has once again crashed about him. Those he loves are in danger. A little while later he once again becomes sleepy and his eyelids close shut.

Then, like some mythic warrior from the netherworld, Pierre bursts through the door. In his arms, wrapped in a blanket, is the scarecrow figure of Yvonne. Mrs. Chabot bids Pierre place her by the fire. Yvonne looks worn and sickly. She has been in the labor camp only three days and two nights, and her new blue dress is mud-stained and torn.

"Pierre, get her some hot tea," Mrs. Chabot commands.

Pierre disappears into the kitchen. Jacob looks at Yvonne, and even though the dirt and matted hair changes her complexion, he thinks to himself something he will never forget the rest of his life: *I love you, Yvonne.* The voice vanishes just as fast as it has come, but the thought drifts in his mind. Pierre comes back with a cup of hot tea and some bread. As Mrs. Chabot cares for Yvonne, Jacob glances up at Pierre. His face is serious and stern as he looks at his sister.

It is not until later that night, when Jacob is in bed nearly half asleep, when all of the excitement has dissipated, that he realizes Pierre had been dressed in black: black turtleneck, black pants, black stocking cap. His face had been smeared with black grease, so that when he spoke his teeth were as white as snow. And then he remembers the gleam from the metal revolver tucked into Pierre's belt.

On a cold winter afternoon, snow falling, St. Nicholas Day now a week behind them, Jacob and Yvonne are sledding down a large hill deep within the forest that borders the rolling fields. The hill is hidden quite well. To get to it the two had to cross the field, make their way through the frozen marshland, and then climb ever upward until they came to the pine forest. The trail is barely noticeable even after years of use, but several runs down on their toboggan and that problem will be solved. The hardest part is getting to the top of the steep hill.

"Come on!" shouts Yvonne playfully. "What? Are you afraid?"

This taunt bolsters Jacob's courage, and he pushes Yvonne down into the snow. She gets up and chases him. She jumps on his back as he is trying to drag the toboggan up the hill. They both tumble to the ground and shove the powdery snow into each other's face. The weight of the clothes, the exhausting climb up the hill, all of this drains their energy, and they both lie back into the deep drifts of snow. Above them is a cloudy, gray sky.

"This moment," she says as her hand sweeps across her chest, "is the greatest in all the world. The most peaceful. I want to capture it forever." There is a long silence. She turns her head toward Jacob with an adolescent anticipation. But Jacob is faking he is dead, and Yvonne grabs a handful of snow and shoves it into Jacob's face. They explode with laughter and empty threats, and scurry up the slope as fast as their bundled bodies can take them.

After several runs down the hill—and after turns are carved, embankments created—Jacob sees the parachute.

"Look!" he cries from the top of the hill.

Yvonne comes over. "What? What do you see?"

Jacob points out into the gray skies, but Yvonne is unable to see the white chute against this backdrop. Jacob points it out again. It is just a single dot against an enormous panoramic landscape of woods, streams, buzzing cars off in the distance, and a thin string of railroad cars making their way toward Brussels.

"There!" Jacob cries out. "Right there!" And he takes Yvonne's arm and lifts it up like the barrel of a gun.

"That's a parachute! That's a parachute! The Germans must have shot down a pilot." She suddenly turns around and looks in all directions into the sky. "Look!" She points to her left. "See that vapor trail? That's from the plane."

Soon she has abandoned Jacob and the toboggan and is running and stumbling down the steep hill, Jacob close behind her.

Pierre is already out in the yard, standing in a stupor, but Jacob suspects Pierre is calculating the drop spot. Yvonne runs up to him, and they both stand by the split rail fence. Pierre says something to Yvonne that Jacob cannot hear, then she moves, quite nonchalantly, across the snow and walks by Jacob.

"Come with me. Hurry or they will see you."

But Jacob decides he will not stay in the network of tunnels below the stacked hay bales in the loft. He waits until Yvonne has pushed the bale behind him, waits until he hears the large door roll shut. And then with little effort he shoves the bale from the entrance and slides out of the tunnel. Something is driving him, telling him to watch the unfolding events.

Yvonne runs over to the house and in her hands she holds a pair of binoculars. Soon she disappears into the house and then within a minute she is opening a large window on the top story, climbing out on the roof, and sitting on one of the gables nearly fifty feet above the ground. She looks through the glasses and sweeps the entire field for any intruders. Jacob sees Mrs. Chabot race the pickup truck toward a small reddish dot. The truck speeds away, but the dot runs into the forest.

The enemy comes just at that moment. Jacob watches as a black dot steps out of the car, gets back in, and follows after Mrs. Chabot. He sees Pierre and the pilot come from the woods and make their way into the mass of dairy cows circling up on the other side of the split rail fence. They are closer now. Jacob makes out Pierre's clothes, sees the bright red hair of the downed pilot.

Pierre looks around, then motions instructions again to the obviously noncomprehending, carrot-topped English pilot. He grabs the pilot by the shoulders, then pulls out a stocking cap from his back pocket. Pierre takes his hand and rubs the young pilot's head and then points to the hat. The pilot puts it on.

Jacob can still see Yvonne up on the roof, poised precariously as though at any moment she will fall. Once again, out of nowhere, the thought floats through his head: *I love you, Yvonne.* He looks over across the large open yard and spots a car coming up the driveway. It is the Gestapo. Yvonne backs down the roof and disappears into the house. Jacob runs to an open window and steps to its side. He lies on the hard, cold floor of the loft and watches as the driver gets out of the car. It is Yvonne who comes out to meet him.

"Is your father home?" questions the man clothed in a long black leather coat.

"He was killed by the Nazis," Yvonne says.

The man smiles politely and pulls the glasses from his face, looks at them in the sunlight, and places them back on his nose. The little round lenses catch the light. He smiles again and repeats the question, this time asking for the girl's mother.

"She is out chasing a cow."

"Do you mind if I look around?"

Yvonne steps in front of him as he nears the barn.

"You just can't come on our property and do what you want."

"Out of my way, peasant." The man steps around her and heads toward the barn.

Jacob cannot move his legs, cannot move his head even from the window. Coming toward the barn is the Wolf. He is coming for Jacob. And that terrible Nazi guard, the one he had so handily walled off deep within his consciousness—this guard bursts out, yelling and cursing, screaming at the top of his lungs. At that moment Jacob's bladder releases. He knows he will die.

The Wolf stops suddenly and looks into the sky. "Have you seen a parachute today, little girl?"

"No." Her voice is empty, almost a whisper.

"I'm going to ask you this one more time, little girl. Just once. Did you see a parachute come down around this property?" Before she can answer, she is knocked to the muddy snow with one powerful back hand by the Wolf. He lifts his hand to smash her again, but his arm is jerked backward. It is Pierre.

The rage in Pierre's eyes is even apparent to Jacob who is

watching from the loft window. It looks to Jacob as though Pierre is about to bludgeon the Wolf with his fist, but he does not. He poises the hammer as if ready to strike, but instead of retaliating, Pierre growls deeply like an animal, and then starts screaming and crying like a lunatic. He flings the man's hand away and dances around like some deranged ape.

The Wolf steps back. "What is the matter with him?" he cries.

"He saw you hit me," Yvonne says. "And if I were you, I would get out of here as fast as I could before I tell him to get you."

The Wolf slips out his gun and puts it to Yvonne's head. Jacob nearly screams out to her. Pierre suddenly stops.

"Now what are you going to do, retard?"

Pierre moves closer. Yvonne stiffens. "No, Pierre! No! It's okay. Don't do anything foolish."

"Tell him to back away," Wolfhardt Becker screams. Pierre obeys. "Now, little girl," he says calmly, but his breathing is erratic and his hat has fallen from his head and several long strands of his hair hang over the bridge of his nose. "Now tell me, where is the downed pilot that parachuted onto your farm?"

Yvonne does not answer.

Becker suddenly pulls back the chamber on his Luger and points it back at her head. "I am going to count to three. That is all. One…two…"

But at that moment several things happen at once. Jacob suddenly screams from the barn door, "Don't shoot her!" And Mrs. Chabot, along with several other farmers sitting in the bed of her truck, comes roaring around the house and into the driveway. The Wolf turns toward Jacob and points his gun at him, then flings around to face his new enemy.

He lowers the gun as Mrs. Chabot runs over to where they are.

"I'm going to give you five seconds to get off my property or those men will start shooting!"

Becker turns to face two shotgun barrels pointed directly at him. He holsters his gun and makes a quick sweep of the scene. And then he walks back to his car, slowly, deliberately.

Yvonne collapses into her mother's arms and sobs. Pierre stares at the black car as it rolls out of the driveway, then he turns and sees Jacob standing in the doorway. For a moment the two stare at each other, eyes fixed on the other. Then Pierre nods his head as if to say, "You truly are not afraid." And he quietly and quickly disappears around the barn.

The weight comes upon him slowly, layer by layer. At first a thin veneer of despair that can easily be shaken off, but soon the layers have stratified, and Jacob is trapped beneath them. He has always felt that desperate sense of urgency—fleeing from the apartment in Antwerp, fleeing from the decrepit Auntie Rita's house, and fleeing from the Delvauxs. What is new, what is nearly unbearable, is the weight of all those souls who are keeping him alive—one simple boy, a boy of twelve who does not truly even comprehend what is happening. No, there is just that thickening feeling that soon becomes unbearable.

At first he wants to find his mother, to run to her, for she has been his focus, his sense of identity through the shifting landscape. But she will not come, for it is too dangerous. And why exactly is he being selected as a scoundrel, a traitor, a rodent that must be eradicated? He is being hunted because he is a Jew. This is the sum total of all reasons. His mother and father have never been practicing Jews. Oh, on occasion they would go to temple, but those were few and far between. No, he is no different than the Protestant or the Catholic who goes to church at Christmas or Easter. Who is he? What does it mean to say he is a Jew? If the Nazis hauled him off to the death camps—killed him by fire or with gas or by a bullet to the back of the skull—if any of this were to happen, he would still be no closer to an answer to that question. There is nothing so empty as to die for something you do not believe—or worse yet that you have just not gotten around to investigating. This is what surfaces and resurfaces in Jacob's mind. This is the reason for his sudden withdrawal from the Chabot family. And this is why, one evening, Mrs. Chabot walks out to the barn to talk with him.

"It is not your fault," she says, lifting a bucket of water and clipping it to the fence post. "All that is happening is out of your hands, Tany." She keeps herself busy while he sits silently staring through the open barn door and out into the darkness of night. "We wake up every day and ask—at least I do, maybe you don't— I ask what will I do today that will make a difference. Just one day, that is all we can ask for."

There is a long silence, and she reaches over to a bale of straw and begins to break it up with her hands, separating it and spreading it around the damp earth. "When my son died, I cursed God. But it was my husband—God bless him—who decided that instead of despairing he would make a difference. Well, the difference he made was to leave a daughter and a son fatherless. You see, Tany—" she stops and looks up at him—"my husband believed in something. He believed with all of his heart that the Nazis were evil and that God wanted him to do something about them. I believed they would kill him for it." She puts one hand on her hip, the light of the single bulb encasing her features in shadow. "Funny. We were both right. I learned then that this war was bigger than any one of us, any one family, any one cause. This war is a million causes, every day, all moving in a direction we cannot see. Once I learned this, I changed forever. Every day when I get out of bed I say, 'Help me to be strong and to not sin against you, O Lord.' That's all any of us can really say in the face of this nightmare. Questions seem empty when your family is killed, the life you once knew forever lost."

"But I don't believe in God," Jacob says. "I mean, I don't know what I believe. I don't even know who I am. People are dying all around me. I know I am connected. I know I am to blame."

Mrs. Chabot drops the straw and walks over to Jacob. She reaches out her arms, but he moves away and leans against the frame of the door.

"You are just a small part of the whole picture, Tany. I know you think you are causing this pain, but it is not you."

"But wherever I go, the Nazis go. They are following me. I would feel better if I believed in whatever they accused me of believing. But I don't." Jacob looks over at Mrs. Chabot and is quiet. Then he asks her, "What do you believe in?"

Mrs. Chabot sits down on a hay bale. She rubs her pants to keep her legs warm. She too is quiet and then looks at Jacob, eye to eye.

"Like I said, when my husband died I cursed God. But you see, Tany, I really didn't even know what God I was cursing. The god I believed in was one I made myself—a god that would make everything healthy, happy, and fun. That is not the God I believe in now. My husband, Jacques, died because there are evil people in this world that want to do evil things. I can't explain the peace that I have. And listening to me talk about it makes me realize how unbelievable it sounds. But it is true in my life. My husband is dead, and I miss him every day. My son is dead, and I miss him as well. But I know God has spared me for a reason." She smiles at Jacob. "That reason, Tany, just might be you."

For a moment Jacob wants to run into her arms, bury his head in her chest, feel her hands stroking his hair. But she is not his mother, and his separation is growing.

"Is that what Pierre believes? Is that what Yvonne believes?" His voice is not without an edge. Mrs. Chabot smiles and then walks over to the stall and begins to toss around the straw once again.

"Pierre is driven by something completely different than I am. He is driven by revenge, by hate. From the moment he wakes up until the moment he goes to bed, he is thinking about the Nazis and what he can do to get them back. I'm not saying he does not have a place in this war. He does. But when hate drives a man to action, he will eventually become empty, and those actions will be bitter and petty. Pierre wants to kill because his brother and father are dead. When that is the only reason, evil and hate perpetuate, and the cycle goes on unbroken." She begins to toss the straw about, kicking some into place with her foot. "Yvonne does not know what she believes or why she does what she does. I think someday she will. Some day when all of this is over, she will meet a man who will teach her to believe in something. Who knows—" she smiles and winks—"that man could be you."

"I want to believe," says Jacob. But this is all that comes out, and after several moments of silence the conversation shifts to something more earthy: fill this bucket, shovel that over here, call in the cows.

Jacob suddenly stirs out of his sleep and sits up. It takes several moments to orient himself to the now familiar room where he is staying, but once he does he hears the voices downstairs that night after night, awaken him out of deep slumber. He cannot hear what they are saying, but the sentences are short, followed by long pauses. Every time he has tried to listen to them, they have stopped. Every time he has come to the staircase, they have vanished. This time he reaches over to his nightstand and opens the drawer. He has stashed a pair of socks there, and he pulls them on, pulls on a pair of pants and a shirt, and quietly sneaks to the edge of the stairwell. He can hear a buzz of commotion. He creeps closer and closer to the rail, trying to peer over it. It is nearly 2:30 in the morning—who could be up at this time?

He steps on one stair then the next, the next and the next. He stops as a door opens and then closes, the whispers fading. As he rounds the corner into the kitchen, he smells the bacon, the biscuits. He creeps closer and closer to the basement door. The sound of voices is growing louder and louder. He places his ear against the cold wood: yes, he hears Pierre's distinct accent. And then, suddenly and without hesitation, he opens the door and walks down into the cellar.

As he descends, he cannot believe his eyes. In the dim candlelight, which flickers and bounces off the dark metal, he sees an assortment of machine guns, rifles, and various other weapons lining the old stone walls. Set in the middle of the open space is a candlelit table filled with eggs and biscuits, sausage and bacon. Seated around it, shadowy and ill-defined, are about a dozen men, some speaking in their native tongues, some speaking in French. Jacob scans the group. He spots the carrot-top pilot eating and laughing quietly with the shadow man next to him. Then the pilot looks up, and Jacob and he make eye contact. He stops talking and motions with his chin toward Jacob. One by one those at the table look up, and they too stop talking—a kind of uncertainty masking each one. It is as if they were all caught preparing to do something painful and hard. Pierre cuts off his heated discussion with the men next to him and looks up as well.

"Tany?" He looks at the men at the table, looks at Jacob. "Come in. Come in, Tany. Come and join us." He stands up, his muscles bulging beneath the black turtleneck. "Here," he says as he walks over to Jacob and grabs his hand, "let me introduce you to everyone." Pierre points to each man around the table, explains what country they are from, and gives Jacob their first names only. He comes to the carrot-top pilot: "This is Michael. He's from England." Michael nods and begins to eat once again, sopping up the egg yoke with another biscuit.

The men are in black. Some have their faces painted with grease, others do not.

"Welcome to the Belgian Underground, Tany." Pierre pats Jacob on the back and smiles. "Here we defeat the Nazis one train, one officer, one traitor at a time."

Jacob notices for the first time that Pierre is not much older than he. Pierre is big, muscular, but compared to the worn and seasoned men sitting around the table he is just a boy playing with guns. Jacob follows him to his seat and sits down. Pierre starts up his conversation with the man next to him once again, a ragged looking Russian pilot, skin burned from the sun and wind, face creased and wrinkled from anxiety.

"I tell you, Pierre, tonight will be a night to remember. But I must confess, I am feeling a bit under the weather. My stomach. It feels queasy."

Pierre suddenly laughs and smacks Jacob on the back. "You see, Tany, even the Underground is not without its cowards." The Russian looks away and then back at Pierre, anger smoldering just below the surface.

Jacob glances around the room, trying to act as though he did not understand or did not hear what was just said. Pierre's end of the table is quiet, all hands tense and ready to move. And Jacob thinks again of Pierre's youth. He looks more and more like a large, muscular boy playing an adult role.

A large shadow next to Jacob nudges him. It is another Russian. He is bald, the dim candlelight shining off his scalp. He smiles at Jacob and pats him on the head. Then he pushes a glass over to him. It is filled with a steaming liquid.

"Good," says the Russian, smiling and patting him on the head once again. He points to the drink. "Good." Jacob takes the cup and sips it. The contents burn his throat, and Jacob grimaces. The Russian laughs and slaps Jacob on the back. "Good?" Jacob nods and is made to take another drink. More than a gulp pours down his throat and he nearly gags. The Russian shoves his friend next to him and they start to laugh. "Good," says the one to his comrade. "Good," replies the other. They return to their food and drink and ignore Jacob once again.

Pierre's conversation with the Russian is over, and he nudges Jacob's side and motions to the other room. "Let me show you my world, Tany. Let me show you the world of a patriot." Pierre glances around the table and then back at the Russian with disgust.

The adjacent room smells of acid and sulfur. Glass milk bottles, one after the other, line the tables. A thin, black-haired man with goggles is pouring something into tiny glass tubes. Then once they are filled he places a cork in the top to seal it.

"That's acid he's pouring in those tubes, Tany. The tubes have a special cork with a tiny hole at its top. We place a thin wick of paper inside the cork and voilà! We have created a time-delayed fuse. As soon as we get to our destination, we take those milk jugs that are filled with an explosive mixture and place the glass tubes upside down on top of them. The acid saturates the wick, drips into the explosive, and we have created a bomb that can wipe out a whole platoon of Nazis—several bombs and we can blow up an ammunitions dump."

Pierre smiles and shakes his head as though the whole process amazes him.

"And what are those?" asks Jacob pointing to the wall where large prongs stick out of a V-shaped metal base.

"These," says Pierre, walking over to one and lifting it from the table, "these are the saboteur's greatest weapon. We place the base next to an automobile tire, and when the wheel rolls forward, the prong punctures the tire and this—" he points to the odd angled prong—"then rotates and cuts the outer wall of the tire to shreds." He turns the thing on its head and then back again as though demonstrating how it works. "The Nazis hate these things. It's just one more weapon we can use to get out of trouble." Pierre turns toward Jacob and puts his hands on his shoulders. "I know you think I should be fighting in the army, Tany. Well, I am. Like I said: I fight in my own way. I want to kill every Nazi, every member of the Black Brigade, every single traitor that has forced you to hide and has forced our great country to its knees. Slowly, over time, we will win. And when we march all the traitors to the wall, line them up to be shot—then I will celebrate. Not until."

There is a disturbance in the other room, and Pierre hurries back into the room where several men are standing, the table a barricade between fists.

"What is wrong?" Pierre says.

"What is wrong," growls the weathered Russian, "is that I will not stand for this mockery. I am the one who planned this mission. I am the one who should make the final decisions. If I cannot go, then I cannot go."

"You knew when you got involved, Ivan, that this would be a dangerous mission," the British pilot says.

"I will not go tonight. I will go the next time. It is all planned. There should be no need to worry."

"You will go," says Pierre, now walking over to him.

"I am their superior officer, and I say, I will not go. My head and stomach may threaten the mission. This is the way it must be."

The men around the table have now all stood up. Some are poised, some are relaxed, all watching Pierre and the Russian.

"Why am I listening to this—this boy!" the Russian says. "What experience does he have in such matters? I will not walk into a vulnerable situation—or lead my fellow comrades into one—all because of a boy."

Suddenly and with no warning, Pierre unholsters his revolver and places it against the Russian's head. The men around the table step back.

"You are a coward, Ivan. It has taken me this long to realize how much of one you really are. You see, you miscalculated the hearts of these men around the table."

"You will kill us all," whispers Ivan.

"Yes," replies Pierre gritting his teeth. "Yes, Ivan, I believe you are right. The mission you would have us go to is suicide. A setup. You would actually have allowed your fellow comrades in arms to be killed? You are more of a coward than I knew. Well, Ivan, your friends in the Gestapo will be a little upset with you when we don't show up for the fireworks." He pushes the gun harder into Ivan's temple. "Tiger, what time is the train?"

"1500 hours, sir," says a solid voice from the table.

"Shark, are the others ready?"

"Yes, sir."

"Red?" says Pierre still looking straight into Ivan's eyes.

"Sir?" says the pilot in his thick British accent.

"Do you have the papers in order?"

"All in order, sir."

"Tiny?" A large man steps from the shadows. He has been sitting there without a word.

"Sir?" he says in a deep resonant voice.

"Did you bring what I asked you?"

"Yes, sir. I have it right here." The large man dressed all in black steps forward. Pierre has not taken his eyes off Ivan, gun still to his head.

"Tie him up," Pierre says suddenly.

The other Russians at the table do nothing but look the other way. The large Frenchman manhandles Ivan and soon the Russian is immobile and sitting awkwardly in a chair.

Pierre holsters his gun and steps back. "Ivan Denysovich, I charge you with treason and spying for the Gestapo and hereby sentence you to death."

"No, comrade. No. You are mistaken." The Russian turns his head to the other Russian pilots. "Comrades! Please, you must believe me. Who do you believe, your commander or this...this boy." One of them (the one who gave Jacob the drink) walks over to him. "Fydor," Ivan says, "we have been together through it all. Comrade, untie me and we will go back to Russia together."

Fydor stares at Ivan for only a moment and then suddenly and ruthlessly smashes him across the face. "Traitor!" he hisses. And he spits on him.

"Please...Pierre? Comrades? Please—"

"Gag him and take him outside," Pierre says.

Several men surround Ivan and cover his mouth. Jacob watches as he sobs in shame and defeat. He has become a tiny child, fearful and terrified of his future. They haul him to his feet and shuffle him out the secret exit.

"All such traitors will be cut off," Pierre hisses. "Agreed?"

"Agreed," cry the voices in unison.

"Now, gentlemen, we know what we must do." Pierre pauses and looks at each man in turn. "For Belgium and for the defeat of the Nazis." And the men disperse and gather their belongings for the night's activities.

"I want you to go upstairs now, Tany. I wish you did not have to see this tonight." Pierre reaches out his large arm and squeezes Jacob's shoulder. "But what you witnessed will make you stronger. It will make you realize how committed all of us are to you and to our country."

Jacob looks into the eyes of Pierre and no longer sees a young man, a boy of seventeen. No, he sees a seasoned warrior who will lay down his life for what he believes. And at that moment, Jacob commits himself to Pierre and to being like him.

"What will happen to the Russian?"

"Of such matters you must not concern yourself, Tany. He will not be able to hurt you or us ever again."

As Jacob ascends the stairs he once again hears the whispers, but this time they are audible and coupled with snapping and clicking of buckles and weapons. Mrs. Chabot is sitting at the kitchen table sipping coffee when he closes the door behind him.

"What you have seen tonight, Tany, you must never repeat to any living soul while the war is on. If the Gestapo finds out about this operation and that Pierre is its leader, we will all be killed." Her voice is mild and emotionless. She sips her coffee again and cups it in her hands.

Jacob is silent and pensive, trying to assimilate all that has happened.

"Go to bed, Tany. I'll stay up and wait for them to return."

Jacob drags himself upstairs and falls into bed. His last thought is of Ivan and his pleas for mercy.

When he awakes, he walks downstairs to the smell of bacon

and the crackling of eggs. Yvonne is sipping a glass of milk; Mrs. Chabot is busy at the stove; Pierre sitting relaxed and stretched out reading the paper.

"Good morning, Tany," Mrs. Chabot says with a smile. "I have some eggs ready for you."

Pierre shakes the paper and turns the page. He crumples it down and winks at Jacob who takes his seat at the table.

"How did you sleep, Tany?"

"Fine," whispers Jacob as he sips his milk. "I don't think I even dreamed."

"Hurry up, Yvonne, or you'll be late for school," Mrs. Chabot says as she scoops out the eggs onto Jacob's plate.

It is a morning like all other mornings in the Chabot house, a beginning to a new day, an ending to an old night; all a little more tired of the war, of the threat of danger, a little bit closer to each other. As Jacob spoons some eggs into his mouth, he glances at the paper Pierre holds before him.

Underground Strikes Ammunitions Train Killing All Onboard

He sips his milk and asks for another piece of toast.

H ow's your sandwich?" Isaac asked.

"Fine."

"The corned beef is one of the state's best. Did you know that—"

"Where is your owner friend?" Jacob said. "I need some more of that overpriced water."

Isaac caught Sam's eye and motioned him over to the table.

"About time," Jacob mumbled. "Please, fill up my glass with your expensive tap water."

Sam looked at Isaac who shook his head slightly as if to say, "Don't worry about him." Sam looked at both and then walked away.

"Tell me, Pop, how is the garment factory in Belgium doing these days?"

Jacob looked up with surprise. *Yes*, he thought, *I must remember why I am here. Yes, the garment factory, the trip to Belgium, my secret life he does not know about.*

"Yes, the garment factory. Well, it seems to be doing quite well—not the one I started all those years ago, mind you. That one's abandoned now. But it's something I would like you to see. Asher and his family have seen it several times. They have always enjoyed the trip. Did you know he has now opened up more stores in California and Connecticut?"

It was Isaac's turn to call Sam over. "Some coffee for me, Sam," he said curtly.

"Yes, sir, Isaac. Coming right up."

"I was just out in California on a book signing tour: San Francisco, Los Angeles, even toured the Napa Valley."

"Well, the stores are small, but they have great potential. It seems that in San Francisco, there is a real need for—"

"Where in San Francisco exactly? I mean what street? I may know a bookstore close by there."

Sam came back with the coffee. His guests were now jovial and smiling. He walked away again, shaking his head.

"Asher has really taken the business to the next level," Jacob said. "When you go to Belgium with me and see the old garment factory, you will be amazed at what he has done."

Isaac waved Sam over to the table. "More cream, Sam. You know I take cream in my coffee. I've been here enough for you to know that."

Sam hurried off for the cream, hurriedly placed it down, and hurriedly fled.

"I think of when I was a young man," said Jacob, "just off the boat from Belgium, I think about what I had to go through to make it. And then I think about Asher, and what he has accomplished. It is truly remarkable."

"Did I tell you, Pop, what my agent told me? I guess Paramount wants exclusive rights for my next three novels. You know I never dreamed of this type of success when I was a struggling writer in New York."

"Yes, both of my sons have had to go out and grab what they wanted. Asher was told once by his business professor at Harvard that he had the mind to be a great economist. I sometimes wonder what would've happened if he had traveled down that road.

Books and lectures, teaching and respect. I'll bet any publisher in the business would have offered him a contract." Jacob smiled politely. "I'm sure he wouldn't have made the money you have made with your novels, but with important books comes more than money. I'm sure if Asher were to go down that road, he would have had to make some serious decisions about such things."

"But he didn't take that route," Isaac said. "He decided to run your store. I'm sure if he had become a professor he would've done quite nicely. How is Rebecca? Is she progressing down the right road? I was very saddened to hear she has Down's."

Jacob stared out the large glass window and watched the traffic as it headed toward the airport.

"She is doing very well, Isaac. She is growing and developing just the way she should. She is so precious, and you will be so excited when you see her." Jacob's face beamed with pride. "I have pictures of her, you know." And he pulled out his wallet and opened it up over the table. A piece of paper that had been folded several times fell out. Isaac reached over and picked it up and unfolded it.

"What are you doing with this franc?" he said.

"Hmm?" Jacob stopped flipping though his wallet pictures and looked up. "Oh, that. That's from the war. It's nothing really." He took the franc from Isaac and put it back into his wallet. "Look at this one. Isn't she just a beautiful baby?"

Isaac took the wallet and looked at her. She was adorable, slanted eyes, outstretched tongue. Right across from Rebecca was a family picture of Isaac, his wife and his children. It was the most recent one. "She really is beautiful, Pop."

"You know," said Jacob, "she crawls around now and pulls herself up. Gets into everything." Jacob took the wallet back and put it into his pants. He looked out the window again and then back to Isaac. "How has your writing been going, son?"

"The traveling gets to me after a while. I miss the kids and Laura."

"Are you gone a lot? I thought writers holed up in small cottages like recluses—deep into the book they are writing."

Isaac laughed. "Not in the twenty-first century. Once that book is complete, I'm off to book signings and interviews. They're all nice, but it's getting to be too much."

"I thought you were happy with all the fame and fortune."

"I am. I'm not complaining. But the books I'm writing are...well..." Isaac stopped and sipped his coffee. "You don't want to hear about my books, Pop." He chuckled, but his words had an edge. "If I talked about them, you wouldn't even know what I'm talking about. I know you've never read any of them. How can I tell you I'm tired of writing this fluff when you don't even know what fluff I'm talking about? I write every day, all day, the same old, same old. At first what I was writing was okay, it paid the bills. I took on the pseudonym and pumped out the books. One every year—keep the publisher happy. But my heart wasn't in them." He paused and looked out the window as though weighing whether he should continue down the road he'd started. "I know this doesn't mean anything to you, but I tried to write a book that was from my heart, an explanation of who and what I am. I took three years to write it, three years, day in and day out. It was the hardest book I have ever written. It was an exploration of my Jewishness, my heritage.

"When I was finished, I knew I had discovered something about myself I had never known, something about our people, something about what it means to be Jewish and American. It was the first work of art I have ever produced, and when I was finished with it, I collapsed and had to stay in the hospital for some time." He sipped his coffee again, but the cup was empty. He put it back on the saucer and looked at Jacob. "It was called *The Golden Calf*. It was nominated for some awards. I was really proud of it, but the industry is a machine, and they don't want awards. They want bestsellers.

"*The Golden Calf* did the exact opposite of what the publisher hoped. My readers felt betrayed, like I had turned highbrow or something. In order to not break contract I had to write *The Tombs of Anakim*. That was the worst book I have every written, because I knew it was a sellout."

He caught Sam's eye and asked for more coffee.

"Pop, I have lived my whole life as someone else. I have been Jack Oxford for ten years, but that's not necessarily true. I've been him for as long as I can remember—him or someone I don't know. I don't want to be him anymore. I want to be Isaac Horowitz. But I don't know who Isaac Horowitz really is. I feel like my life is displaced, like I am not who I should be. I have separated myself from you, from Mom, from Asher. I basically closed you out and ran away. Just like you did with me."

Jacob listened to all of this, and his first impulse was to reach out and pull his son close. But he did not. Both sat silently in their cocoon world of regret.

"Why did you give up on me, Pop? Why did you just…let me go?"

"You turned your back on us," Jacob said. "You are the one who forsook your name, your Jewish heritage."

"What Jewish heritage? We were never practicing Jews. We never observed the law. We never even went to temple, save for special occasions. How can you say I turned my back on something I never even knew?"

"Being a Jew is more than going to temple." Jacob was passionate. "It is your blood. You just can't say you are or you are not a Jew. It doesn't work like that. Don't you have any idea what we as a people have gone through?"

"I'm stunned you are now so fervent about your heritage, Pop. But that has nothing to do with how you treated me ten years ago. You may be a practicing Jew now, but back then you weren't. Back then you were the same old, same old."

"I know. I know that now. I know. This didn't make sense to me back then." He stopped short and decided this was not the time for his confession. "I can't explain it to you, not now. You wouldn't understand." He looked away. "I don't understand all of it myself, Isaac," he whispered.

"Why such a reaction to my using a pseudonym, then?"

Jacob's head started to pound. He could feel the pressure building inside. He rubbed his forehead roughly—back and forth with the tips of his fingers.

"I hung up on you that night," Isaac said, "and I swore I would never, ever talk to you again. I convinced myself I didn't need your blessing, didn't need your accolades. It was Mom who stirred me back to you."

Jacob stopped rubbing his head and looked up at his son.

"Yes, Pop, that's right. Mom talked with me on the phone almost every week. She sent me letters of encouragement after each book. Mom read every book I wrote. Right up until her death."

Jacob cleared his throat. "If you were so close, then why didn't you go to her funeral? I can see being mad at me, but your mother—God bless her soul—she was your own flesh and blood. You were bone of her bone, Isaac. You were all she had in this world. And you did not show up at her funeral."

"Of course she was bone of my bone and flesh of my flesh. She was my mother! What kind of statement is that? Asher was there. Herman told me Asher was there."

Jacob breathed out suddenly in a great exhalation. It seemed all of his anxiety and fear, all of his pent up frustration and guilt just fluttered out his lips and into Sam's restaurant.

"Let's order some more coffee, shall we?" Jacob said.

"No. I want to know what you meant by that comment. I loved Mom. I loved her. I was far away, but I loved her. I wrote her letters. She talked with me on the phone—"

"Asher is not her child," said Jacob suddenly, calmly.

"What?"

"Asher is not her child. You are."

"I don't understand."

"My words are not difficult, Isaac. Liza is your mother. She is not Asher's."

"But who—"

"It is a long story. One I hope to tell you on our way to Belgium."

"I don't want to know later. I want to know right now! Good heavens, I don't believe this! You have the audacity to—"

"Please, Isaac. Calm yourself. I will tell you everything. Just sit down. Please—"

"Don't touch me! How could you lie to me all these years. How could you hide such a thing from me?"

"What are you so upset about?"

Isaac looked around in bewilderment as though something in Sam's restaurant would give him some mooring. "No wonder I've spent all of my life so displaced and so lost. My childhood and my life was a big lie. Unbelievable. This is—" Then he looked up into Jacob's eyes. "I get it. You brought me here to confess this. You brought me here so you could tell me the truth about all your stu- pid lies. Oh yeah, I get it now. This is some special father and son bonding time. You wanted to drop your guilt on me and then have me tell you it's all okay." He pulled himself up so that his chair flung back into the table behind him. "No way," he said pointing his finger at Jacob accusingly. "No way." And he walked hastily out of the room.

Sam stepped up politely. "More coffee, Mr. Horowitz?"

Jacob nodded yes. Sam poured the coffee and hurriedly escaped.

Jacob sat rubbing his forehead with the tips of his fingers. None of this had gone the way he had planned. The way he had planned? He had no idea what it was supposed to go like. And he had barely begun the story. All of this fluttered through his head, and to stop himself from thinking about it, he rubbed his fore- head with the tips of his fingers. How did he expect his son to react to such news: "Gee, Pop, that's swell. Tell me all about it. I am so excited about your life and that you lied to me all these years."

Jacob thought about calling a cab and heading home. He could cancel the tickets later. Who was supposed to benefit from this smoke and mirrors show? Was all of this to purge the sins of an old man riddled with guilt?

He reached over to his cup with a shaky hand and brought it to his mouth. Isaac was right for storming away, was probably on his way back home. *What a fool I am*, thought Jacob. *What an old fool.* When the grave is dug so deep, and the shovelfuls are so many—after so much time has passed, it is better to just go down to silence. It is better to just shut up and step into the pit.

He called Sam over to him. "I'll take the bill, please."

"Oh, that is quite all right, Mr. Horowitz. Your son has already paid. I will give you another refill of coffee if you like?"

"No. This is fine, thank you."

Jacob breathed out again, then pushed himself from the table.

"Wait."

Jacob turned to the voice.

"Sit down for a minute, Pop."

Jacob settled back into his chair. Isaac was sitting across from him, eyes wide and concentrating. The two looked at each other without blinking.

"Is that what your beef with me is? Is that why you have shunned me all of this time? Because I was from a different woman?"

"I shunned you, Isaac, because you had forsaken my name."

"Horowitz? What is so special about this name? How can you be so angry at me for taking another last name? I don't understand."

"You wouldn't."

"I know I wouldn't, Pop. I wouldn't. I don't. I never will. Why are you so bent out of shape over this?"

"I told you, you wouldn't understand, Isaac."

"Try me! I'm a lot brighter than you think. What? Is there some famous great, great, great, great grandfather you have not told me about either? What? Some Jewish man who saved the world? Some great rabbi who—"

"My father died in Auschwitz. My father, his brother, along with his family. Every one of them—shot or gassed to death."

Isaac blinked in stunned silence. Jacob looked away so his son would not see the moisture in his eyes.

Jacob has been with the Chabot family for nearly a year. He has become very attached to Mrs. Chabot, helping her in the kitchen as she prepares for the late night guests. Jacob has begun to develop a sense of who he is—defined by the long talks with Mrs. Chabot, Yvonne, and Pierre.

Wolfhardt Becker has tightened the noose on all Underground activity. His method is simple: utter brutality. More and more citizens are taken in the middle of the night. More and more are murdered. And more and more informants emerge, for it is better to inform than to be tortured.

Because of such a hornet's nest of activity, Jacob's mother has visited only twice—Mrs. Chabot always sneaking her in at night and Pierre always sneaking her off the following night. Those days when Rachael does visit, she is sad and weary. Life in the city has been extremely trying. There is little food—potatoes and every now and then some meat—and because of this, Mrs. Chabot stocks Rachael up with canned vegetables and dried meat when she leaves.

Jacob's sister has been with the same family for as long as they have been in hiding. She is nothing more than a slave. Rachael cannot complain, cannot say or do anything, for to act would be to place Sarah's life in jeopardy. It is better for her to be a slave and alive than be put to death in one of the camps. Sarah is resilient, young. She will survive.

Rachael is worried about Jacob, for he is asking questions about Jesus, about the Christian faith, how Judaism and Christianity tie together—if they tie together. Rachael tells Jacob he is special, that it is not the religion but the blood that makes him Jewish. She warns him to be careful around the Chabot family, to thank them for their kindness but to be wary of their religion.

Jacob sees Pierre—bold, strong, fearless, committed to revenge—and what Pierre stands for, and he longs to be like him. But he sees another influence in the Chabot household. Many nights Jacob has walked the house and found Mrs. Chabot kneeling at the coffee table or head bowed at the kitchen table, one time even prostrate on the floor.

"I am praying for every soul that comes into harm's way tonight," she says one night as she stands up with a groan, knees creaking and popping.

"You mean," asks Jacob in his nightshirt and bare feet, "you are praying for Pierre and his band of men?"

"Yes, them, and all those men he shall come up against."

"What do you mean? You aren't praying for the Germans, are you?"

Mrs. Chabot walks over to the kettle on the stove and pours a steaming cup of tea. She sets it on the table and sits down. "Yes, Tany. That is exactly what I mean."

"But how can you pray for the very people who could kill your son?"

She sips her tea. "Would you like a cookie? I just made them."

Jacob sits down at the table and takes one from the plate. The raisins are still warm from the oven, oatmeal chewy.

"When I get down on my knees before God, Tany, I don't pray for what I want. I pray for what God wants. Men will die. They die every day and every night during wartime. Pierre will kill tonight. I know all of that. I accept it. But that does not mean God does not want the soul of every man, woman, and child on this planet. His desire is for everyone—Nazi or Belgian—to come to know Him. That is what I pray, Tany." She sips her tea once again. "The Germans will go back to their families, after the war is over. They will go back to their churches, their synagogues. As soon as someone wins and someone loses, we will all be human beings once again. And God will not let me forget that. I can't explain it, Tany. That's just the way I feel in here." She places her hand on her chest.

They are silent for quite some time. Jacob reaches for another cookie.

"I don't feel that way, Mrs. Chabot," he says without any emotion. "I think of my father. I think of my mother and my sister, of my Uncle Benjamin and his family. I think of them, and I want to kill anyone who had a part in this. I don't feel anything in here," he says, pointing to his chest. "I don't feel anything at all. And every time I try and feel what you tell me, I cannot. I can't explain it either, Mrs. Chabot, but sometimes I feel like what is inside me is building and tearing me apart. It needs to come out. It needs to be released."

"I felt that way, Tany. I felt the same way when Jacque died. I wanted to run straight to Brussels, go up the steps, and take somebody's life. I am no saint, Tany. I still feel as though I could do that. And that is the very reason I fall on my knees and pray with all of my heart. I pray evil will be overcome with good, that the Nazis will fall, that my son will not be killed tonight. And as I pray these things, I pray for the souls of all men, women, and children who are caught in such times and in such places that they have not the strength to overcome. I pray for you and your family, Tany. I pray every day God will show you His will for your life, and that you will take the steps He commands you to take." Mrs. Chabot smiles warmly at Jacob and then walks her saucer and cup over to the sink. "It's late, Tany. It's time for bed."

The plan has been laid for several weeks. By this time, Jacob knows the routine, knows how the men of the Underground work, prepare for their missions. Jacob has decided in his heart it is better to be Pierre, to fight against the Nazis, than to pray for his enemies. "Blood for blood," he tells himself. As Pierre and his men eat and talk down in the cellar, Jacob dresses and creeps downstairs. Mrs. Chabot carries a large pot of soup from the kitchen to the cellar door. When she disappears into the cellar, Jacob hurries out the front door. He knows where they appear, knows the secret entranceway to the cellar. And so, for several hours he waits crouched beneath a bush.

He has painted his face with black grease, covered his white skin, so only his teeth and eyes stand out. He has taken—over the course of several weeks—dark garments: a pair of pants, a sweater. The sweater has light patches on the elbows, but he can always hide them somehow.

Night after night, Jacob has sat up and looked out his window, waiting for the human shadows to disappear into the woods or the fields. Each night he has waited to hear the clanking of pots, the pouring of soup, the crackling of bacon. And on these nights his heart has soared, because finally he is engaged in an effort. He is no longer passively waiting to do something—no, he is, vicariously, striking at the heart of the Nazi machine. Jacob does not think about the danger, about the fear and terror of capture. Each night the men leave the house, he leaves the house. Each time they come back, he comes back.

And now, he waits in a thicket for the shadow men to emerge from the secret entranceway. And he waits and waits and waits, his eyelids growing heavy. Finally, he hears the door creak open, a dilapidated cellar door with bent and rusted hinges. The shadow men emerge: black faces, black turtlenecks, black pants. The leader—it must be Pierre for his body is massive and he dwarfs the others—crouches like a lion, turns his head one way and then the other; and with quick and rapid movements, he waves the rest of the group out of the hole. They creep right by Jacob, some even brushing against the branches above him. He pulls his knees up and leans back into the thicket. He hears the branches scrape the metal of the guns, scrape and snag the wool pants, the gloved hands. And as the last one trails off into the darkness, Jacob steps out of the thicket and runs silently behind.

He keeps his distance, through the fields tall with grass, into the dark woods. They are silent, like cats, swift and agile. As Pierre stops, they stop. As Pierre goes, they go. They are a unit of one, fingers on a terrible hand of hate and revenge. Soon, they stop—everyone falling to the ground. No one moves. Jacob strains to see, but the woods and the darkness hide the group. A fog has settled down upon the low lying areas and Jacob is soon surrounded by a cloud of mist.

He does not hear his attacker, only feels the swift blow to his spine. He is thrown to the ground, a razor sharp blade held to his throat. And then the knife pulls back in a moment of astonishment.

"Tany?" Pierre says. "Tany! What are you doing out here? Why are you following us?"

Jacob pulls himself up to his knees, the wind still seeping back into his lungs. "I...I wanted to come with you."

"That's crazy!" Pierre looks ahead of him. One of the group has come back to check on their leader. It is the carrot-topped Brit.

"A stowaway?"

"Not for long," Pierre growls.

"We can't take him back, and we sure can't leave him here. This place will be crawling with Krauts after our mission is completed."

Pierre looks at the mist, looks up ahead and then behind. He shakes his head at Jacob. "This is a dangerous and stupid thing you've done, Tany! Stupid! Don't you realize I could have killed you just now—let alone the danger you have put us all in?" Pierre grips his hands into a ball as if he is ready to strike the nearest tree.

"I'm sorry, Pierre. I just wanted..."

Pierre looks down at Jacob with a scowl. "What did you want, Tany?"

"I wanted...to do something. I can't sit back and wait for them to find me, Pierre. I needed to do something."

Pierre looks around one more time and then back at Jacob. His face has softened. "Come on. Follow me."

They join the others who are now in a combat formation. Pierre holds up his right hand and points to the Brit and waves him off to the right. The Brit takes eight men and disappears into the fog.

"You will stay right by my side until I tell you to lay low." Pierre reaches over and grabs Jacob with his large saucerlike hands. "And when I tell you to lay low, Tany, you do exactly that. Understood?"

Jacob nods yes, and soon Pierre and his group of seven men

are filing through the woods one after the other. The group comes to a clearing. Pierre motions three of the men to take their places. He crouches down with Jacob near his side. Beyond the tree line is a railroad bed. The fog has become a thick cloak in which they will work. Several of the men take wire and snake it down the track. Another group takes out the explosives and attaches them to the rails at various locations. Jacob watches as they work, silent, quick, each with a purpose and a confidence all his own. They are trained experts who pick their battles strategically—like surgeons cutting away the cancer as it spreads.

Pierre checks his watch and glances down the track. He rushes over to the rails and places his hands on it, feels the vibration. He whistles to the others who are still on opposite sides of the track. Pierre slides to the bottom of the rail bed and whistles again. He edges closer to the track to check the location of his men. Two are still setting the explosives. He waves to them, but they do not see him.

Pierre grabs Jacob and shoves him back into the woods just as a flood of bright lights illuminate the track. A beam of light from the train locks on one of the men, a dark hump huddled on the ground. Several shots are fired, rocks and dirt spraying the stranded man.

"Stay back!" shouts Pierre to Jacob, as he flattens to the ground. "It's a trap! It's a trap! Abort the mission!" he screams out into the bright lights. Several more shots are fired from the train.

"I'm hit! Pierre, I'm hit!" It is the man on the rails.

Pierre rushes over to Jacob. "Tany, you must run! Run as fast as you can. Follow the trail the best you can. Don't stop, just keep running!"

"But I'm afraid. I don't know where to—"

"Run straight that way." He points into the woods. "I will find you. If you stay here you will die. Now run! Run!"

Jacob runs for just a few steps and then stops and turns around. Pierre's hulking figure launches into the bright light. Shots ring out as Pierre vanishes over the tracks. Jacob senses evil, the very evil he felt when hiding in the barn as the Wolf walked toward him. And then he is running blindly into the fog and darkness. More gunfire echoes through the night. There are shouts and screams, commands. And then Jacob hears the dogs. Why did he come out here? What was he thinking? Another branch snaps him in the face, another thornbush snags his clothes and hands. Still he runs, runs for his life.

Where is he going? The thin trail has vanished, and Jacob is running blindly and furiously toward a destination he does not know.

A terrible blast erupts to his left—a brilliant flash of light and power. He hears metal crunching metal, screeches and groans as the integrity of the steel is compromised. Another blast forces Jacob to huddle near a tree. He watches the skyline as it flickers and dances between the darkness and the brilliance of the fires. And still another blast erupts. This one larger than the other two. The ground beneath Jacob shudders. Another blast, this time smaller and concentrated several yards down the tracks. Gunshots are fired, then screams and shouts of horror. More gunshots, more explosions, more and more flashes of light.

Jacob can see his direction was off. Given enough time he would have run right back to the tracks. He listens to the groans of wounded men. Pierre must be dead. The Nazis have beaten him. He looks in the opposite direction of the explosions and rushes headlong into the darkness and fog—away from the enemy, away from Pierre and the others.

Soon it is apparent he is lost. The woods, the trees, the lay of the land is all unfamiliar to him. The lights from the explosions have dwindled, so he is not sure if he is headed toward the Nazis or away. He stops altogether and soon is crouching near several large moss-covered boulders. To move is to die. To stay put is to die. And then he hears the dogs! He can't move. He can't think. He stays put and shakes, limbs useless and uncontrollable. And he suddenly thinks of his father and uncle—how they were taken away in the truck. "I am coming, Papa," he whispers. The dogs close in, howling and snarling.

And then out from the fog bank rushes a huge figure dressed in black. With one hand he holds a revolver, the other is open and sweeping toward Jacob.

"Get up!" Pierre screams to him, his right hand grasping Jacob's shoulder. "Get up, Tany, and run!"

Jacob is hauled to his feet and is soon running alongside Pierre. Jacob begins to lag behind, for he is unsure of the terrain, unsure of his footing.

"You must run faster!" Pierre screams from in front.

The dogs are zeroing in on Pierre's wounded leg, blood dripping onto the forest floor.

They come to a pile of boulders, large, rounded, and stacked one upon the other, jutting out into the darkness.

"We must descend to the bottom of the ravine, Tany." Pierre wheezes trying to catch his breath. He grits his teeth and then suddenly slaps the rock with his open hand to release his anger and the horrible pain in his leg. "If we can make it to the bottom, I can get us to safety. There is a stream down there. It will take away our scent. The dogs will not be able to follow. The only way down is to jump over this rock. You will fall about ten feet and then slide to the bottom. We have no choice, Tany."

He heaves himself from the rock formation and they both

scramble their way up to the ledge. Jacob can feel the wind whipping around, can feel the open expanse of darkness before him. He cannot see where he is jumping, cannot see what he is jumping onto.

"I can't!" he screams. "I can't jump. I'm scared, Pierre."

Pierre is already crouched and ready to jump. He looks over at Jacob. He can hear the dogs approaching. And with a sudden and terrible effort, Pierre groans out as he leaps into the darkness—pulling Jacob by the arm. They tumble into the night, into the empty air and disappear.

Jacob screams and tries desperately to stabilize his descent. His buttocks and back smash against the severe slope; then his feet catch in the loose rock and mud, catch and catapult him head over heels, tumbling down, down, down. He falls and slides forever. Rocks and branches bounce off, the force of his momentum sweeping them out of the way. He feels a sudden sharp pain, as a broken branch rips into his side, scraping the length of his body. And then it all stops. He is just barely conscious as the rubble gathered by the fall rushes over and around him.

The dogs bark somewhere in the distance, an abyss of night and emptiness separating them. He lays still listening to his short and rapid breathing, his heart as it races. A low moan soon disrupts the seconds of peace. Jacob sits up, bending and stretching the deep scrape on his side, and he falls back to the ground. He hears shouting above them, far off, up near the top. The Nazi officers are ordering their men to descend.

"Pierre?" whispers Jacob, his eyes trying to pierce the darkness. "Pierre?"

"Over here, Tany." Pierre's voice is weak, full of agony. "We must get into the river, Tany. I need your help to walk. I think I broke my foot."

"I can't see you, Pierre." Then Jacob notices a hump off to his left. They had fallen nearly together—sliding side by side all the way down the steep ravine. He crawls over to him and feels for his body.

"Ow! That's my leg!" Pierre gathers himself to a crouched position. "Here. Help me to my feet."

Jacob stands up, and soon Pierre is leaning heavily upon him, so much so that Jacob nearly collapses. They hobble forward as the guards shout out more orders.

They wade into the stream, the water now up to their calves, then to their knees, and make their way laboriously down it. Soon they are one hundred yards away, then two hundred.

"I must rest for a moment, Tany." Pierre drags himself over to the edge of the stream and sits down in the shallows near the steep bank. The water is cool and soothing to their wounds. "We just need to go about another three hundred yards or so, and we will be safe. There is a place, an old cave where I can see to my wounds." Pierre grimaces and then shakes his head to clear it, an obvious struggle. "Just a few hundred yards, Tany. We can make that. We can make a few hundred yards."

Pierre has become, once again, a young man not much older than Jacob. The light, reflecting off the dark, smooth surface of the water, reveals his pale and hollow features. There is another moment of deep struggle, and then Pierre says, "Okay then, let's go."

Jacob pulls him up to his feet and they slowly make their way downstream. They come to a large rock island, and Pierre wades to shore and crawls up onto the embankment. Both young men collapse from exhaustion.

But Pierre soon says, "We must continue." He is standing on one foot. "If you can help me walk—we can make it to the shelter in about fifteen minutes."

How peaceful is the night! The trees swaying in the spring breeze, the echo of the stream as it meanders onto large rocks and boulders further down. Jacob is conscious of Pierre's labored breathing, his sudden spasms of pain. They hobble up an incline and then down a mild slope. Pierre points to another rock formation, a hidden cave. They make their way up to it and then around several boulders covered with moss and enter the cave.

"There is a light on the ledge," whispers Pierre as he leans against a rock and slides his body to the dirt floor. "It's okay to use it. No one can see it down this far. We're safe for the time being." He grunts as he tries to tighten up his bootlace. "You're going to have to help me with my boot, Tany. I need you to pull as hard as you can, lace them up as tight as you can. Give me the light. Now—" A spasm of pain shoots up his leg. "Easy, easy…"

"I can't get it any tighter, Pierre."

"That's…that's fine, Tany." Pierre grits his teeth and stiffens, a low growl comes out of his mouth, and he clenches his fingers into fists. Several minutes go by, Pierre leaning his head against the wall, eyes closed. Then, "Okay, Tany. You need to do exactly what I tell you. Go over to the ledge and grab the metal box. Bring it over to me."

Jacob does so and opens it up.

"Now shine the light on my upper thigh."

Pierre unbuckles his pants and pulls them down to his knees. He has been shot in the leg. The bullet has entered the front, missing the bone, taking a chunk of flesh with it.

"Okay. I want you to hand me that medical kit, Tany."

Jacob watches as Pierre first cleans the wound with packages of sulfur, placing pressure on it to help stop the bleeding. Next he takes several cloth bandages from the kit and places them over the gaping hole. "Hand me that roll of gauze, Tany." But before Pierre can bandage up the wound, the blood has soaked through the pieces of cotton cloth. He takes the cloth off, calmly, with controlled breathing, and asks for more. Jacob hands him a wad. Pierre folds them and places them over the wound. He applies pressure to it, leaning his head against the wall and closing his eyes. Jacob gags from the sight of all the blood.

"You get used to it, Tany," says Pierre, smiling and opening his eyes. "When you have to do it all the time, you get used to it."

After ten minutes have drifted by, Pierre looks down at the wound. "Hold the light steady, Tany. That's it." He grimaces again as he lifts the bandage up. "Good. Okay, hand me the gauze." Pierre begins to wrap the bandage layer upon layer around his thigh. Over and over he wraps the strips until he is satisfied with the amount of cloth and the pressure it exerts. "Almost got it." He cuts the strip with his knife and then ties off the end. "Now, that wasn't so bad, was it?" Pierre looks up into Jacob's white face and slaps him on the shoulder. "One night with me will make a man out of you, eh, Tany?"

They sit quietly for some time, and Pierre leans his head against the rock walls once again. Jacob knows he is in great pain, can see the sweat pouring down his forehead and cheeks. He also knows they are far from safety.

"Okay then," says Pierre. He crouches with the wounded leg stiff and straight. Then he pulls himself up and leans against the cave wall. He places his bad foot on the ground, and sucks in air.

The night has moved on quietly, the forest peaceful and serene. The darkness and fog still give them cover, still allow them to take advantage of their dark clothing and grease-stained faces.

Pierre rubs mud onto Jacob's white elbow patches, and they disappear into the forest like two wrecked vagabonds.

22

The going is slow, for Pierre must stop every now and then to rest his leg. Jacob supports him on one side while the walking stick supports the other. After several hours in the darkness, the large trees suppressing any light the stars and moon can give, they come to a clearing.

"Let's rest here for a moment," Pierre says. And once again, Jacob has the sense that this large young man is really only a boy playing with guns and war.

"What happened back by the railroad tracks?" asks Jacob, now kneeling and then sitting near a large fallen tree. He leans his back against it, as Pierre has done. They both look up into the night sky—the myriad stars, tiny dots of light filling the abyss above.

"Somehow the Nazis found out about our mission. I don't know if they just got lucky and were out on routine patrol or we have a mole among us." He breathes out a long sigh. "Whatever the case, they didn't stop us. We blew the tracks, blew the ammunitions cars on the train. It was quite a show." He moves his leg to the left and sucks in breath through his teeth. "We lost some good men back there."

"How's your leg?"

"Ah, it's just a scratch," Pierre says, but Jacob can once again see the pain exploding across Pierre's face.

Jacob feels a fear building all around him. If Pierre is unable to walk, they will be caught. All of his hiding, the rotations, the lives given up to save his own—all of this will become just one more ironic moment in a seemingly futile war.

"Why did you get involved with the Underground?"

Pierre rubs his face with his hands as though this would pull his thoughts back to the present. He adjusts his leg and again leans against the log.

"I took it over after the Nazis murdered my father. He was the leader before me. My father decided to get involved after my brother's death. He masterminded the entire operation, connecting to Antwerp with a father and a son there who became his link to England. They would use their radio to contact London. London would send messages to Antwerp, and they would send those orders to my father. Soon we became the leader of a network, an Underground railroad system that would transport orders, refugees, and even downed pilots to various locations throughout Belgium." Pierre suddenly sighs with another long and exhausted breath.

"But the Nazis finally caught up with him. It wasn't long until the network was infiltrated with double agents. One of them, a pilot who faked he had been shot down—" Pierre nods to Jacob. "Yes, Tany, that's right. The man had faked he was shot down. The Germans do it all the time. They confiscate one of the English or Russian planes, fix it up and send it over France or Belgium. They shoot it down themselves, and the pilot parachutes out. It's really a diabolical scheme. That pilot then is brought into the system and becomes a mole for the Nazis. It doesn't happen all the time, but it happens. Remember that Russian pilot, Ivan, the one you met when you came down to the basement that night?"

"He was placed there by the Nazis?"

"Yes. But he won't be bothering us any longer." Pierre smiles and chuckles. "Anyway, the Nazis found out about my father, and one night he was taken from his car. We don't know where, when; we don't know anything. But he never came home. We had to shut down the network for several months to see how deep the infiltration was. The spy was caught, killed, and we started it up again." Pierre grimaces as he readjusts his leg.

"It is a most remarkable network. England can send targets from aerial reconnaissance missions, and we can eliminate the target within twenty-four hours of our orders. It is a well-oiled machine, Tany. We provide shelter for Jews in hiding. We rotate downed pilots through the country and back into service. The Nazis would do anything to find us—to find me. And that is why we must get out of here and back to the farm as quickly as possible." Pierre pauses and breathes deeply once again. "But we will not leave just yet." He looks to his left and then his right as if that confirms what he is thinking. "We're safe from patrols. At least for the moment."

They are silent for a while, and then Jacob says, "You know, Pierre, you really didn't answer my question. Why did you get involved?"

Pierre turns his head and looks at Jacob with a peculiar smile. "Let me guess, Tany. You have been talking with my mother."

"Yes, actually we have had some very long talks."

"Long and boring, you mean. I can't tell you how many times I have heard her say: You must give your life to Christ. You must repent of this anger inside you. You must give it to God." Pierre mocks his mother in a sarcastic, high-pitched voice. "All of that talk should be thrown on the manure pile where it belongs." He spits to emphasize his point. "I do what I do because I want to kill those men who killed my father. That is that. I don't believe in fate or God or anything of the sort. The world is hard. It hurts us, but we can give back as good as we get."

"But why do you do this? Why do you help blow up bridges and save helpless Jewish boys?"

"Because it is the right thing to do. That's why, Tany. It's just the right thing to do."

"What makes it the right thing to do, if you don't believe in God?"

Pierre laughs. It is warm and full of love. "You will not leave me be, eh, my little rabbi? Well, I'll tell you something. Since there is no God, I am god. And I think helping you is the right thing to do. How is that for an answer to your question?"

Jacob suddenly and with great passion misses his father and mother. His head is filled with images and words from that forgotten life that seems an eternity away. It happens all of a sudden, but with great ferocity. His mother is cutting roses in her garden. His father is smoking his pipe and reading a book. Sarah is playing with her dolls. And then, as fast as they arrive, they vanish. He is left with only an aftertaste, left with the cool night wind, left sitting with Pierre somewhere in the south of Belgium.

"You see, Tany, if I believed in God, I may not be able to do what I must: kill the enemy. If I believed in God, then I would have to stop murdering the scum that killed my father. And I cannot do that. I let my mother pray for my soul. She can pray all she wants her empty prayers, but at the end of the day it is I who will have satisfaction. It will be I who have avenged my father's death. She thinks you can keep turning the other cheek, Tany. But when does it stop? When is it enough? When is justice exacted, meted out? I say it is now. With the life we have, in the days we are given, we must take those scales and use them ourselves."

"But what if you use them wrongly?"

"What does that mean?"

"What if you take someone's life out of hate and not out of justice? What if you use the scales wrongly?"

Pierre looks again at Jacob and then smiles. "Remember what I told you, Tany. I am god. So however I use the scales, it is the right way to use them." He laughs and then tries to sit up on the log.

Jacob watches him, and he looks more infantile and helpless than at any other time Jacob has known him.

"What have Christians done to help your cause, Tany? Tell me. What is peace and forgiveness to do with war? What is love to do against a Nazi who would *love* to put you in a death camp. You can't stop hate like that—with love. You stop it with this." Pierre pulls out his revolver from a side holster. "This is the only thing that stops a Nazi—a bullet to the head."

Jacob suddenly remembers his conversations with Mrs. Chabot, and then another image comes crashing into his mind: Mr. and Mrs. Delvaux sitting around the kitchen table discussing Bible passages. And the words just come out of his mouth: "What makes you any different than them?"

Pierre turns to him, but his reaction is cut short, for just at that moment a caravan of trucks rumbles through the woods. Pierre pulls himself over the log with a grunt, clenching his teeth as his leg falls like a brick to the ground. Jacob is in front of him—both lying face down in the moist dirt. It isn't that the caravan is actually coming through the forest, but the clearing where Pierre and Jacob have stopped is right next to an old dirt road. The fog and the darkness have obscured it.

A German staff car is leading the procession, and as it drives by its lights explode over the fallen log where Jacob and Pierre lie. Each truck in its turn does the same thing. Jacob looks up at Pierre, who puts his finger to his lips and spreads out his palm in a gesture to Jacob to remain calm. He glances over to his other hand and motions with his head at the revolver. Jacob closes his eyes and puts his face to the ground. The roar of the trucks, the laughing guards, the dust from the road are a violent intrusion into the peaceful world of the forest. One by one the trucks drive by, lights exposing the fallen trees, and one by one they disappear around the bend further up the road. Soon the interval between trucks grows longer, until the last one drives by.

Pierre motions for Jacob to stay put. He peeps over the log into the night, and then he pushes himself up onto his elbows and flips his legs around so they are straight.

"Okay, Tany. It's safe."

Jacob crouches on all fours, and then he too sits against the log. But the peace is short lived.

"Down!" hisses Pierre, shoving Jacob face first into the dirt. He lunges sideways just as a car comes up the road. There is a terrible thumping noise coming from it. The thumping grows louder and louder as the car approaches, until finally the driver pulls it over to the side. Somebody curses. Then curses again.

"I told you, Becker," says a slurring voice filled with mirth. "I told you we could not make it back to town with the tire like that."

"Oh, shut up, Fritz!"

"I am only telling you the truth, my friend. The vodka has not dampened my ability to tell you the truth." The man explodes with laughter. "Here, Becker, take another drink. It will calm you down. You know, my friend, you really are strung too tight."

"Driver," Becker says, "get out of the car and fix that flat!"

"But sir, I told you earlier we have no spare."

"What? No spare!"

"That is right, sir."

Fritz laughs. "Well then, what shall we do about this situation?"

"Driver!" Becker yells.

"Yes, sir?"

"How far is it to town?"

"About five miles, sir."

"Driver!"

"Sir?"

"Get going!"

"What do you mean, sir?"

"I mean, get out of the car and get us a new tire!"

"You want me to walk to town, sir?"

Becker starts to laugh. "We have a most brilliant driver, Fritz. He must have been educated in the best university in Germany. See how smart he is?"

"Would you like a drink before you go, driver?" Fritz asks politely.

"Absolutely not!" Becker says. "If he gets drunk, then he won't find his way back to get us, you idiot. You see, Fritz. If he drinks the vodka two things will happen: We will have no more to drink and we just might become sober, and he may wander off into this godforsaken land and get lost. Now get going!"

The driver gets out of the car and begins to walk away.

Jacob hears them laughing, hears them slapping each other and joking, cursing, and drinking again. Pierre lies silently near his head. To move is to be seen, for although the engine is turned off, the lights are shining onto the fallen log. He thinks once again of the irony and futility of his situation. All of this just to be captured and killed by two drunken officers. He can only lie there and listen. Pierre seems all but dead.

"You know, Becker," Fritz says, "this war is driving me mad. I mean, how long can we stay in this puny little country and how long can we hold off the Allies." Fritz's tone becomes sullen. "I miss my wife, Wolfhardt. I miss my kids, my hammock in the backyard, the smell of the lake." He swigs the bottle of vodka and hands it to Becker. "I miss good German beer!"

"You mean you would rather be there than fulfilling the great mission of our leader?"

"What is the great mission? To kill all the Jews? To take over the world? I have seen enough death to last me an eternity. I'm sick of death. I'm sick of war."

They are silent and contemplative in their drunken stupor.

"I saw a young Belgian boy of five, Becker. I saw him cut down by a grenade. He was shattered in so many pieces. So powerful was the explosion that the blood and water in his body just evaporated. And why, Wolfhardt? Why? What did this little Belgian boy do to deserve such a death? What did his mother do to deserve it? They were in the way. That is all. They were in the way," he whispers.

They are both quiet again, then Fritz explodes with laughter. "You were something tonight with the ladies, Wolfhardt? Eh? Who was the blond, eh?"

"I met her in France, if you can believe it. I can't believe she is here in this hick country. I met her at university. She was studying political science. Can I tell you something?"

"What?"

"Come here. I have a secret to tell you."

"What?" says Fritz loudly. "I couldn't understand you."

"I said, I lost my virginity with her."

They both start laughing hysterically.

"Yes, yes, yes. I kid you not. It was in a woods just like this one. In fact, it was in a place just like over there. A clearing in the woods."

"In the woods?"

"Yes, in the woods."

They laugh again, but this time it is forced and quickly stagnates into silence.

"I loved her very much, back then," whispers Becker. "I asked her to marry me after that. And then the war came and we drifted apart. I wrote her all sorts of letters. She responded to the first ones, but those too stopped. It was good to see her tonight, Fritz." He pauses for a moment. "It was as though the war did not exist. For a moment anyway."

Silence.

"Women!" Fritz says. "Who needs them!"

"Well," Becker says, "it would probably be a good idea to turn off these lights. We don't want to draw unnecessary attention to ourselves." He reaches over the front seat and pushes in the knob. The forest returns to darkness.

"I need to relieve myself," Becker says in a stately manner. He lumbers out of the car and staggers out into the darkness of the woods. He begins to sing. The singing fades as Becker walks farther and farther away.

As soon as the lights are off, Pierre slowly moves in a circle so his face is pointed at Jacob. "Tany?" he whispers in Jacob's ear. "Don't move. I will be just over there." And Pierre slides away from the downed tree and into the thicket of the woods. Several twigs snap.

"Who's there?" Fritz says, laughing.

The wind sways the trees, creaking them, branch upon branch rubbing together.

Fritz suddenly turns on the lights of the automobile. "Who's there? Becker?" Fritz yells over his shoulder. "Probably passed out somewhere in the woods, the idiot." Fritz opens the door and stumbles out. He gathers himself up and wobbles toward the illuminated area—toward Jacob and the fallen tree.

Then Fritz is slammed to the ground and screams out a couple of words before he is silenced by thunderous blows to his face and side.

Pierre clicks the hammer back on his gun and places it to the officer's head. "Get up!"

The officer responds groggily to the command. Soon they are both standing, Pierre leaning on one leg more than the other.

"Tany, get up." Jacob does not move. "Tany! Get up and turn off those lights!"

Jacob stands up and runs toward the car, his shadow huge and ominous.

"I am not going to hurt you, sir," says Fritz, his voice almost a whisper. He steps away from the gun and in a split second kicks Pierre in his broken ankle and begins to run away.

Jacob hears the officer speak, and turns around just as Pierre is screaming in pain, grabbing his leg and falling to the ground. Pierre sits up and fires his revolver: once, twice. The German falls in a heap of coat.

"The lights! The lights!" Pierre screams, his voice more of a yelp than a command.

But as Jacob turns around to push the knob into the dashboard, he hears Wolfhardt Becker running out of the woods.

"Whose there?" Becker screams. "What is happening? Fritz! Fritz?"

Jacob huddles on the other side of the car, moving as the German officer moves, keeping the automobile between them. Then suddenly, in a fit of rage and terror, as though all of the tension for the past years of hiding suddenly explode from him, Jacob rushes headlong into the officer and knocks him to the ground. Jacob beats the man over and over again in the head, pounding the side of his face and neck. Jacob realizes the officer is reaching for his weapon and suddenly knees him in the kidney with the full force of his weight. The officer releases the gun. Jacob takes it in his hand.

Pierre is over by the other officer. He puts the gun to his head and pulls the trigger. The sound tears through Jacob's soul.

The officer beneath Jacob is silent, his face badly beaten and bloody.

"Kill him!" screams Pierre. "Use his gun and kill him."

Jacob takes up the pistol and points it at the back of the officer's head. But then Jacob hears another sound. It is Pierre, collapsing in pain, now lying on the ground—passed out.

"Get off me, and I will allow you to go free," the officer whispers through swollen and bleeding lips.

"Shut up!" Jacob screams, and he pushes the gun hard against the officer's skull. "Pierre?" he says, then catches his voice in horror as he realizes the information he has just given away. There is no response.

Jacob pulls back the hammer to the gun and places his finger on the trigger. But something strange happens to him. He thinks of the conversation once again with Mrs. Chabot. He thinks of the conversation this officer had just had with his friend. He thinks of all of this in a second and pulls the gun away. Then he lifts the gun high into the air and brings it down on the back of the officer's skull. He hears the metal crunch the bone, feels the tension in the officer's body slip away. He jumps up and runs to Pierre.

Pierre is regaining consciousness, and Jacob lifts him up to a sitting position.

"Come on, Pierre," Jacob says as he shakes him. "Come on! You need to get up. We need to get out of here." Pierre is back with him, and Jacob stands him to his feet. "Good. Now take this stick and lean on me." Jacob looks around. "I need to know the way to the farm."

Pierre points off into the distance, and they begin to straggle away from the car, away from the dead and wounded officers, away from this event in the woods that will affect them for the rest of their lives.

saac had not spoken a word to his father in an hour, other than to say, "When we get to Chicago, I'm getting off."

Jacob sat in a slouched position, head back against the seat, hands on his thighs. There had been no easy way to tell Isaac about his past, there was no sugar to coat the pill. No, had he waited any longer, he would never have done it. So, at the restaurant, he just blurted it out, "My father died in Auschwitz." It was a simple statement, but the ramifications to Isaac were enormous. *Displacement.* That was the word Jacob was looking for. He had known it all of his childhood. Isaac was now adrift in an ocean he did not know, with no oars or sails and no place to drop anchor. The rug had been pulled out from under him. Jacob had pulled it, and his son was writhing on the floor.

At first Jacob didn't understand Isaac's reaction: a burst of laughter, then he got angry, pointing his finger, palming the table with his delicate hands, fisting them, palming the table once again. And next, a Horowitz family trait, he completely withdrew and had not been back since. Jacob and his son were so close together—a secret between them that no one else knew had been revealed—and yet they were further apart than at any other time in their relationship. They sat elbow to elbow in the first class seats on their way to Chicago, but that two-inch space might as well have been a chasm the size of the Grand Canyon.

Jacob looked past his son and out the window at the dark clouds, the murky air, the streams of white running over the wings. And when the plane ascended above it, Jacob felt liberated, as though the plane itself were a symbol of freedom—that he had made it out, intact, able to breathe. And yet there was this terrible wall between them. He knew his son was in shock, that his son would indeed get off at Chicago's O'Hare airport, and that he would probably never speak to him again. In desperation, he reached for a ledge, fumbled for a hold, and leapt.

"In 1992 you published *The Moon below the Earth*," Jacob mumbled slowly and with great patience. "And the critic James Calhoon of the *Boston Globe* proclaimed it a breakthrough in adventure fiction. Helen Fitzpatrick from the *New York Times Book Review* hailed it as a fresh new voice, one that would be around a long time. Scott Dempsey from *Publisher's Weekly* proclaimed it…" And so he began, from top to bottom, from first to last, every book, every critic he could remember, all of it—Jacob began the oral history of his son's career.

When Jacob said the name Helen Fitzpatrick, Isaac turned his head toward his father.

"In 1994 you published *Buried* which the critics smashed to powder as a cheap play on the *Taloned Necklace* which came out a year before. Dempsey said it would be better for Jack Oxford to 'take a couple of years and come up with a new story idea, to recapture the voice that has been silenced, or to give up writing altogether.'" Jacob turned to his son. "A brutal review that was unnecessary and vindictive." He then continued with the list, again in order, starting where he had left off.

Isaac looked back out the window, then back at his father. "Okay, Pop. Okay."

"Last year you finally published *The Golden Calf*. It took you three years to write it, and when it was finished you spent several months in the hospital recovering from bronchitis and pneumonia. Helen Fitzpatrick said that—"

"Said if she wanted to read complex narratives she would pick up a copy of Don DeLillo." Isaac looked at his father in silence, and then said, "Why, Pop? Why the secret all these years, when you obviously cared more than some of my fans?"

Jacob looked across the aisle and through the small portal on the other side. "I don't know," he whispered. "It meant more to keep it inside, perhaps."

"What happened to my grandfather?" Isaac asked. "How did he end up in Auschwitz?"

Jacob turned his head back toward his son and smiled gently. He shook his head and explained what happened when he, his mother, and his sister went to the post office that one afternoon.

"Did you ever see him again?"

"No," said Jacob, shaking his head in a matter-of-fact way. "We searched for him, checked the registries. A man we ran into years later said he had come across a Ruben Horowitz, but that he was shot with others when the war was coming to a close." Jacob looked away again, turning that memory over in his head. It had been such a long time since he had thought about it. "Dr. Aaron Feldman was the man who told me about my father." He rolled the name around his mind again. "He was a dentist, I think. I met him at a bistro one day in New York. Mother and sister and I had run into him during the war." He rubbed his chin and paused in contemplation. "Funny how the webs intertwine and mix together. It's funny."

"And Grandmother Horowitz? What happened to her?"

Jacob looked into Isaac's eyes and then patted him on the thigh. "Does this mean you will still go with me to Belgium, my Isaac?"

"Yes, I will go with you to Belgium. But there is a world of people and places that I need. And you must tell me everything."

"I will tell you everything, Isaac. I will tell you everything without leaving anything out. But not right now." Jacob turned to the stewardess as she pushed her beverage tray to them.

"Coffee for me," Isaac said. "A little cream."

"I will just have water, thank you," Jacob said.

They sat with their drinks and their peanuts and munched in silence, staring out the window at the clouds below.

"I really studied Jewish history, the founding of Israel, the political nuances and subtleties of their relationship with the Palestinians during my writing of *The Golden Calf*. I could have written a doctoral dissertation with what I discovered. I tried to put it into a new and exciting narrative, and it nearly killed me. What the pneumonia left, the critics attacked. It was probably the biggest mistake of my life. Give the people what they want. I should have learned that a long time ago."

"No!" said Jacob suddenly, seriously, with great passion in his eyes. "That is not how one becomes all they can be, my Isaac." His tone was gentle and fatherly. "If I make a suit, and I make it cheap, then my customers will expect that. But if I want to take a customer and bring him to a place where he can appreciate a good suit, pay for a good suit because now he understands a good suit is worth the money—then I have done my job." He sipped his water to wet his suddenly parched and hoarse throat.

"There was a time when I had to make a decision. Would I make the cheap suit and sell by volume, or would I make the best suit I could and try to win over a new customer base? I decided on the latter. Herman told me I was crazy. The Gentiles would not buy from me because they could pay that kind of money at the larger department stores. I thought about it and decided that to make the cheap suits would be to sell myself short. I would rather spend the hours laboring over something I was proud of and allow it to sit on the rack, than make something I wasn't and sell it to the first customer who came along."

"Well, Pop, it looks like you won out."

"But, my Isaac, my Isaac, that is how it looks now—now with hindsight. No, no, no. I made that choice in the face of all contrary advice, and I suffered for it. Customers came in and said the suits were too expensive. They walked out without buying anything." Jacob sipped his water again and smiled a large smile. "But you see, my Isaac, they did not leave empty handed." He liked saying his son's name, liked the flavor in his mouth, a drop of water after a long and painful drought.

"I thought you said they didn't buy the suits?"

"Yes, yes, indeed, they did not buy my suits. But each one left with something else: an education. I gave them a demonstration, showed them the way the suits were made. I showed them the stitching, taught them a lesson on quality sewing, told them what would happen with a cheaply made suit. They left without buying my suits, but they left with an education. And eventually, guess what happened?"

"They came back?"

"Yes, my Isaac. They came back. They bought my suits, and they told others to do the same."

"So what are you saying about *The Golden Calf*?"

Jacob's face soured for but a second. He patted Isaac on the thigh once again and smiled the anger away. "You have finally written something you are very proud of. You spent three years researching and writing it. You yourself have said it almost killed you. The critics didn't know what to say because they had never seen such writing from you before. How were they supposed to act? No, my Isaac, you have started down that road and you must continue. You are educating your public. They have had McBurgers for seven years. They don't know what filet mignon tastes like. When they eat it, they can't appreciate it. You must teach them."

"You mean, you want me to write another serious novel?"

"Yes."

"My agent will have a fit."

"Let her."

"The public—who pays my bills I might add—will burn me at the stake."

"You will be surprised at the resiliency of your followers, my Isaac. Give them a taste of filet mignon, teach them what they are tasting, and they will crave it beyond anything in the world."

"But I don't know what to write about. The well is dry."

"It won't be for long. Have patience, my Isaac. You must have patience."

They arrived at O'Hare International Airport just as another storm front was passing through. The plane rocked and swayed to the runway, landed with great effort, and rolled through the torrent of yet another downpour. Jacob and Isaac stepped off the plane and walked through the gate. They made their way to the ticket counter and were told that again they would have to wait—for an hour at the most. Their plane to Belgium was delayed—refueling and a crew replacement.

Isaac seemed to have withdrawn since the plane landed. He was short with Jacob, and after twenty minutes of moping around the gate area, he decided to call home.

Jacob looked outside once again and watched the rain roll through. He enjoyed Chicago, knew that Isaac was a big star in the city, and suddenly wanted to take him around to show him off.

What was eating him? What was not! But they were at least heading in the right direction. Suddenly Jacob felt that all too familiar pain in his lower abdomen. He stood up slowly and hobbled toward the men's room. When he returned, Isaac was sitting down waiting for him.

"You okay, Pop?"

"Yes, fine," he said with a thin smile. "The plane ride was a bit long. The family is okay?"

"Yes, yes, they are all fine."

A young man with blond hair, a beak nose, and a small diamond earring crept up to Isaac.

"Excuse me...but are you Jack Oxford?"

Isaac looked up and adjusted his small round glasses. "Yes, I am."

"Would you be interested in—"

"Sure." Isaac listened to the name, spelled it properly, and gave the book back to the young man.

"We don't have time to go anywhere, Isaac," Jacob said when he saw his son's agitation.

"No, I guess you're right."

"We could go to another gate, somewhere with less people." Isaac still looked anxious. "Is there some place you want to go?"

"No," Isaac breathed out in a long breath. And then, "Yes. Let's get out of here." He stood up, pulled his hat further over his eyes, and walked along the window, then led the way through the security gate and down another concourse. They came to an empty gate, save for a single attendant behind the podium. Isaac walked over to the window. He was now very agitated, hands in his pockets then out of his pockets, now sitting down, then standing up. He turned suddenly and said, "Is there anything else you want to tell me, Pop?"

Jacob cocked his chin down as if to say, "What is wrong with you?"

"Is there anything else?"

"Only about Belgium—"

"I mean about you, your life."

Jacob shook his head and wondered what his son could be getting at.

"I know, Pop," he said. "I know about you and the doctors."

Jacob glanced up with wide eyes, confused eyes.

"Herman. Herman has been in touch with me for nearly all my years in New York, Pop. He has told me about the cancer. He told me how long."

Jacob looked outside. The rain had passed, a sense of newness and beginnings lay just on the other side of the glass. But not for him. He sat down in a cushioned seat and did not respond.

24

It is the latter half of June, 1944, and Wolfhardt Becker is furious. It is not enough that his best friend, Fritz Von Kirchbach, has been murdered by members of the Belgian Resistance. That is just one festering wound. It is now all too clear the Allies have invaded the coast of France, not where the great Führer had suspected, but at Normandy. And with every passing day they push deeper and deeper into France. Soon they will be at Belgium's doorstep. Both these factors grind Becker's insides to powder. He strikes out the only way he knows: a rampage of terror across the farmlands and the backwaters of Southern Belgium. But there has been an unforeseen breakthrough: A Brownshirt in Charleroi has uncovered a potential Underground headquarters—a farm several miles from where Fritz Von Kirchbach was murdered. And so, Becker spends his nights and days planning what will become his final assault upon the unsuspecting Chabot family.

"It has become too dangerous," says Mrs. Chabot, her lips twisting down on both sides of her mouth. "Somebody has found us out."

"Impossible!" Pierre smacks the armrest of his chair. His leg is propped up on a cushion more for sympathy than comfort. His plaster cast, gray and dented in, has seen more activity than his doctor would ever suspect.

"Impossible?" says Mrs. Chabot. "Pierre, you know it is by the grace of God we were told about this letter. Imagine what would've happened if it had not been intercepted!" She tosses the envelope onto the coffee table and walks over to the window. The summer breeze is blowing the dark green trees, limbs swaying. This countryside, verdant and teeming with vitality, has not seen the forces of man, of his armies, of his bombs and cannons.

"It won't be long now," says Pierre, rubbing the worn armrests with his palms. "The Allies will be here soon, and Belgium will be liberated."

Mrs. Chabot turns around. "That does not mean anything. What good is liberation when the Nazis have killed Tany and all of us! What good is freedom then?"

"We must hold out a little longer. I know, Mama. I know you are worried. Just a little while long—"

"But we may not have that long, Pierre." She sits on the windowsill and continues to stare outside. "You still haven't told me what happened that night you and Tany were out late."

"I told you already. I told you the mission had to be aborted. We were separated from the rest, and it took us a while to find our way back."

Mrs. Chabot leans her head against the window, feeling its cool, smooth surface on her forehead. She turns around and watches Jacob and Yvonne on the other side of the room. She sees their hands separate as they realize she is watching them.

"I pray you did not jeopardize this that night."

"What is that supposed to mean?" says Pierre, now standing to his feet. "I told you what I know. That is enough."

"And I tell you, Pierre Chabot, that this threat—" she points to the letter on the coffee table—"this is what I know. Someone has information on our family and on our doings. They are sending letters to Brussels, and we are in great danger."

"But it didn't make it, did it?"

"But the next one will. Or the next one."

Pierre takes his cane and starts to limp out of the room.

"I spoke to Thomas, Pierre! He told me what happened in the woods!"

Pierre stops and stares straight ahead.

"Thomas told me what happened, Pierre!" continues Mrs. Chabot, her voice bordering on hysteria. "Why an officer? Why didn't you just walk away! Why is there so much anger in your heart that you kill without thinking, that you would jeopardize this family?"

Pierre turns, his face solid, lips pursed. He stares straight at his mother and whispers, "I have no more to say about it." He turns around and hobbles into the kitchen.

Jacob and Yvonne have grown considerably closer since that night when he all but carried Pierre through the woods and back to the farmhouse. Once they were distant observers—each captain on their own ship watching the other from a spyglass. Now they are eating and talking together, planning and working. At first the walls of fear and doubt encircled them, but slowly those walls begin to fall apart, crumble each and every time either one would catch the other silently stealing a glance, a secret pat on the shoulder, a touch of the hand lasting longer than was needful. Soon, for no reason, one follows the other out into the woods, both sitting by the lake or under a large tree. And they talk—about everything. They are in love, and the war-torn world is suddenly fresh and new, like the first world, like the first couple in the first garden, isolated and fearless, together.

"What is it like to be a Jew?" asks Yvonne with that gesture of hers, palm upward, sweeping her hand across her chest.

Jacob stops walking, realizes he has stopped and decides it is better to walk. "I don't know. I don't think about it."

"But, I mean, the Germans want to kill you. Why?"

This time Jacob does stop. The question intrigues him. That someone is willing to hunt him down, seek him out for the sole purpose of destroying him—this makes him quiet, stills his breath for but a moment. "Maybe it's in my blood or something."

Yvonne laughs. "Let's see."

"What?"

"Give me your penknife."

"What?"

"You heard me. Give me your knife."

"No."

"Come on, you baby. If it's in your blood, then we should be able to see it."

"Of course it's not in my blood."

"But how do you know," she smiles with a grin Jacob will come to love as he grows older. "Come on. Give it over."

Jacob reaches into his pocket and pulls out his knife. Yvonne opens and touches the point, then the edge.

"Is it sharp?" she asks.

"Sharp enough."

"Well, let's see how Jews bleed."

"We bleed just like Gentile girls."

"Let's see."

"You first."

Yvonne takes the tip and slowly, methodically, hand shaking just a bit, cuts into the palm. "Now you."

Jacob hesitates, then takes the knife and swipes it across his hand—the blade never touching the skin.

Yvonne laughs. "You baby."

Jacob takes the point and cuts his palm as well. A thin line appears, and then the blood is seeping out. Yvonne giggles. They watch the blood gather in the creases and grooves.

"Let's make a love pact."

"What?" says Jacob in a whisper.

"Tell me your real name, Tany."

"But…"

"What is your real name? How can we make a love pact if I don't know who you really are?"

Jacob looks at his palm, looks at her palm. "Jacob," he whispers. "Jacob…Horowitz," the breath catching in his throat.

"Jacob," whispers Yvonne back to him, slowly. She grabs his hand and places hers onto his and squeezes tightly. "On this day, June 24, 1944, Yvonne Maria Chabot and Jacob Horowitz swear a blood oath to each other. They swear they will never forget this day. Never, ever." She pauses and looks at him. "Do you swear, Jacob Horowitz?"

Jacob looks into Yvonne's eyes, and he is thunderstruck. "Yes," he says, squeezing her palm, and then placing his other hand over hers. "Yes, Yvonne Maria Chabot, I swear."

Yvonne smiles and then pulls her hand from Jacob's. The warm summer wind is blowing through the forest, but neither one is aware. Yvonne reaches over and takes Jacob's hand, palm upward. And she kisses the patch of smeared blood so that when she pulls away, the blood is on her lips and the tip of her nose. And then as if none of this ever happened, Yvonne suddenly turns toward home.

"It's time for dinner, Tany. I bet I can beat you to the house."

When Rachael comes up the porch stairs, Jacob is shocked at her appearance. Her movements are slow, careful; her face gaunt and wrinkled. Has it been that long since last he has seen her? Or perhaps the year has not been kind to her. Rachael has learned that the Germans have taken all meat and vegetables for themselves, the inhabitants forced to survive on beans. Dogs and cats have begun to disappear.

There is a hatred, blatant and uncontrolled, toward all Belgians, toward any sign of resistance—for any reason at all. Shops are burned to the ground, citizens taken at gunpoint in the middle of the night and beaten. As the Allies move closer toward the Gestapo headquarters in Brussels, the intensity of the brutality increases.

Several times, Rachael has been brought before the local magistrate. Her beauty and her poise make her an object of desire, in an occupied country a reason for abuse. The Gestapo officer begins to frequent the local garment shop in La Louvière where she sews. One day, he closes the door behind him. Rachael knows she is in grave danger. He explains to her his power, his authority, his benevolence for those whom he desires. When his advances are thwarted, he beats her. When she resists further, he calls for help. Rachael becomes one more nameless casualty on a list of statistics.

So, when she walks up those porch stairs, Jacob is horrified at the woman she has become—her dignity intact, her soul intact, but her body revealing the hardships of her life.

Mrs. Chabot sits her at a table and feeds her bread and cheese. She munches on it slowly, methodically, like her movements, like her life—second to second—don't think of the past, only the now. Every now and then, Rachael looks up at her son and smiles,

smiles and lifts her hand to touch his face, the beginnings of whiskers around his chin and upper lip. She smiles at Jacob and whispers to him, "God is good, my little lamb. God is good."

Rachael looks at Jacob for several moments. The contrast between Jacob and Sarah is unimaginable. Sarah is now sickly and used up. She has been locked down in the cellar, forced to sleep on a plank of wood in a flooded and moldy basement. Her imprisonment (for that is what it is) has taken such a toll on her she has developed the first stages of tuberculosis. At first the family allowed her to stay upstairs, but soon it was clear she would be better off away from the family: Jews have a bad influence on the young. Once she was found to be a good housecleaner and laborer, she was treated as such. And after every hard day's work, she would go back to the wet cellar with the black mold. And this is how she spends most of the war.

It is Rachael who finds her out, who steals away to the farmhouse unbeknownst to the residents there, who pulls out the metal bar securing the outside door, who creeps down the broken and missing stairs and sees her daughter—silent, huddled on the wooden plank that is her bed. The decaying rodents, their bloated bodies floating in the puddles, the pungent mold which spreads like a disease across the stone walls—these make Rachael gag and vomit. Sarah awakes. Is it a ghost, a figure from her dreams? She is unable to distinguish the real from the imaginary. And just like that, Sarah is taken from the house, taken from the family in the dark of night, taken out and secured in another location in the city of Liège.

"Would you care for more cheese?" asks Mrs. Chabot with a soft smile. Rachael glances up at her with a sense of fear, and then relaxes. She takes the wedge and nibbles at it along with her thick slice of dark bread.

Silence seems to ease its way upon the uncomfortable scene. Pierre looks down at his newspaper, Yvonne places her knuckle against her cheek to wipe away the tear, Jacob stares out the window.

"Where will you go?" asks Pierre suddenly, his face a mask of concern.

"He will stay with a family in Liège," says Rachael, still nibbling on her bread. "His sister is already there."

"If Tany stays here, he will—"

"No," Mrs. Chabot says. "You know how dangerous it has become, Pierre. With the Allied invasion, who knows what the Nazis will do."

Yvonne suddenly stands up and rushes out of the room. Rachael watches her leave and then carefully watches the expression on her son's face. Yes, he is in love with her. A mother knows these things. Poor child. Hasn't he been told the dangers of Gentile women? *No, he has not. I have not been here to tell him.* And a sudden and complete grief settles upon Rachael quite unexpectedly. She bites a piece of bread to settle the emotion as though it were a bout of gas. No time for the petty. No time for emotional, Gentile women either.

Jacob looks around the table and then at the door where Yvonne has exited. He pushes his chair away from the table to follow her.

"Wait," says Rachael with no emotion and a quick, clawlike hand to her son's shoulder. "I need to talk with you, my lamb."

Mrs. Chabot motions to Pierre with her eyes. They excuse themselves from the table and leave Rachael and her son alone in the kitchen.

"Look at me, Jacob," Rachael whispers.

It takes a moment, but he eventually pulls his eyes from the floor. "You have forgotten what I told you many months ago. Do you remember?" She purses her lips and pulls Jacob's chin up so his eyes meet hers once again. "You must be strong, my son. You must fight everything that is inside you, everything that pulls you from your main objective. Do you remember what that objective is? Do you? Look at me." Her voice has turned raspy. "You must survive! You must do whatever it takes to walk away from all of this and survive, Jacob."

He averts his eyes to the floor once again. "Yes, Mama. I know I should not, but—"

"But nothing!" Rachael hisses. "How can a Jew marry a Gentile?"

"Marry?"

"What else do I see before me but a young man who is following his heart down a road he knows he cannot travel. How can you marry a woman who does not understand who you are, what you are, all you are hiding from, all you are running toward? How can you think of such a thing?"

"She does understand, Mama. She does. We have talked about—"

"Talked about nothing! You don't know what you are doing, Jacob. When all of this is over, when there is no more adventure and death, only the mundane rituals of work and children—when all the glitter has fallen away, you will be trapped in a relationship that will kill you."

"But how do you know she will not convert—"

"Pah!" and Rachael begins a soft, hoarse laugh.

"You may think that, Mama, but I know her heart."

"You would turn against your family? You would mock our God? You would mock your father who is dying in a concentration camp? You would turn your back on me, your mother? All for this Gentile girl? If you go down this road, I will disown you! You will no longer be called my son!"

Jacob is silent. He again looks down at the floor and blinks the tears away. Rachael pulls him close and caresses his hair and his cheeks with her long fingers.

"Oh, my baby," she whispers. "Oh, my little lamb. I know it is hard. I know, I know." And she mouths that over and over again without a sound.

2
5

"Tany, be a good boy and go get Gaston," Therese Delvigne says with a smirk as she places the last of the dirty dishes into the tub of hot soapy water. Sarah is sitting quietly in the corner of the old wooden house, the August breeze blowing the drapes into bloated sails. The two Horowitz children have been in Liège for one month. Sarah looks considerably better (if one with tuberculosis can indeed *look better*). She has come out of her shell with each passing day, but as she heals from the years of abuse and neglect, the disease thrives and spreads into her lungs.

Gaston and Therese Delvigne are a paradox as well. She attends Mass every day and, Jacob has learned, prays for her husband's soul and for the two refugees who now darken her doorstep. Gaston, on the other hand, proudly proclaims, "I am not a religious man!" as he pounds his barrel chest and sucks down another pint of ale. "Religion makes one weak! A man stands on his own two feet! Yes! On his own two feet he stands and faces the world!" And it is usually after that boast that he falls into an empty booth (or not empty) and passes out for the night.

Jacob has added Gaston to the other characters in his storytelling repertoire. Gaston—with his large walrus mustache, his high-waisted pants, oily bald scalp rising like the crest of a wave and then dipping and dripping with long strands of coarse hair over his collar—could have been right out of a Charles Dickens novel. The name "Gaston" fits the old codger's personality, but something more playful like Mr. Bagmouth or Slobdrink, or even something like Nobhead would have sufficed nicely. Nobody at the Wild Goose listens to Gaston, for he is always talking; and people who always have something to say never say anything important. And so, while he raves up and down in his drunken stupor some laugh, some slap him on the back to egg him on, others ignore him as though he were nothing but an annoyance soon forgotten.

When Gaston has spent the afternoon at the Wild Goose, Therese glances over at Jacob and sends him off to the tavern to bring home her irascible husband.

And on this occasion, it is no different. The town is safe from prying eyes; in fact, rumors abound that any Nazi still in the village will not be there for long. The Allies have moved further into the continent, and the people of Liège are expecting liberation by September. Jacob walks the dirt street of the small, rural town and turns right down the road that leads to the Wild Goose. As he approaches the tavern, he hears the booming voice of Gaston and the thumping of his large hairy hands upon the wooden countertop of the bar.

"I tell you," he slurs and shouts with bravado, "that in all my years, I have not seen such a coward as you, Monsieur Gobier! You and your stupid wife and your stupid kids and your stupid dog! You are all cowards! I stand here—" Jacob walks in, just as Gaston slips on a wet spot of ale from his own glass, hits his chin on the countertop, and slumps to the floor.

"Gaston!" shouts Jacob with a slap to Gaston's head. The whiskers beneath his large pockmarked nose tremble. Limp and drenched with the head of his last lager, they look more and more like those of a sea lion or an overgrown schnauzer. He sees Jacob peering over him and he smiles—his mouth a wreck of teeth. Why pay money for something you can take care of yourself? Toothache! Bah! A little whiskey and there is no more toothache.

"Tany, help your Uncle Gaston to his feet." The pudgy man rises slowly and with great exertion, face red, eyes red, nose red, every corpuscle nearly busting from the strain. He blows out a stale breath of peanuts and lager, wipes his walrus whiskers with the back of his hand, and peers menacingly around the room. Gobier has settled back into his seat. All is well.

"Come on, Uncle Gaston. Aunt Therese wants you back home."

Gaston belches so that his lips gather and puff out, smiles warmly at Jacob, and pats him on the back with his thick-fingered hand. "You are a good boy, Tany. A good boy, indeed." He rubs his rounded and bloated belly, and they walk out of the Wild Goose and down the road toward home.

Jacob has attached himself to this man for reasons few could articulate. Gaston is so unlike Jacob's father, a tad like Uncle Benjamin, and nothing like any other man in the boy's life. Jacob's world has been superseded by danger, by driven people who want more than can be expected at any given moment: Be aware! Be watchful! Trust no one! But Gaston is different. Gaston is kind, gruff, but most importantly, oblivious. Gaston talks big about the Nazis, about the Germans in general, but he is ignorant on world affairs. He has become a sort of respite for Jacob, and the city of Liège an island among the ocean of pain and sadness.

"Woman!" Gaston says in a loud obnoxious voice as he enters his small house. "Where is my dinner!"

"You drank it down at the tavern, you drunken old coot!" Therese yells back from the kitchen.

"Well, if that's the case, old crow, then I might need second helpings—because I'm sure not getting any nourishment here!"

"There's some nourishment on the end table, old man," Therese says.

Gaston sits down with a thud in his favorite chair. He greedily looks over at the table for the waiting plate of food, but finds only a large, black leather Bible. He curses under his breath, and then crosses himself as if that will somehow undo the blasphemy. He kicks off his shoes and stares at the large hole where his big toe protrudes like some grotesque knob—nail yellowish and lined with dirt. It does not take long until he is passed out in his chair, sonorous snorts fluttering the long mustache.

It is during these nights that Sarah and Jacob once again bond. As Sarah sits holding her small rag doll, red yarn hair spindly and clumped, Jacob takes a place beside her, and they stare out the window into the forest or up into the blackness of the sky. Jacob talks to the doll as though it were Sarah. Sarah sits quietly and then whispers to the smudged and dirty cloth face so Jacob can hear. They begin to talk of their mother, how much they miss her—how all the world is strange and uncertain. Every now and then Sarah coughs, a dry cough, a cough that seems to pull at her insides, tug at organs and bone. She wipes her mouth and holds her doll. Day after day, night after night this story is repeated.

It is Yvonne who brings the war back to the tranquil home of the Delvignes. She has changed, her face gaunt, dark rings around her hollow eyes. As she sits at the kitchen table, Mrs. Delvigne fixes her some beans and bread.

"Oh, Jacob," she cries and falls into his arms. Only for a moment is she able to compose herself, then again, sobs and clutches at Jacob.

"What has happened, Yvonne? Why are you here?"

"They have taken Pierre, Jacob." She looks at him with a blank stare and then her face explodes in grief. "Mama…is dead. She's dead."

Mrs. Delvigne comes in and brings the plate of food.

Yvonne has been in the woods, hiding from the Nazis for over a month. Her clothes are damp and stale, a musty odor Jacob remembers from his time spent hiding with Dr. Aaron Feldman. The beauty and the innocence has disappeared. The war has claimed yet another soul.

"It's okay, child," soothes Therese Delvigne. "Eat all you can." She leaves the table to prepare a place for Yvonne to sleep. The poor girl is exhausted, for she has traveled nearly a hundred kilometers to find Jacob. This alone catches his breath as he thinks about the journey, the commitment. And it is now that he falls deeply in love with her—yes, this wretch of a young woman, scrawny and hollow, pale skin and thin lips. He watches her inhale the beans and bread, watches as she takes another helping and yet another. And then, as though she were a tiny infant, she nearly falls asleep where she sits.

Wolfhardt Becker is not sure who he actually has in his grasp. What he does know, is convinced of beyond a shadow of a doubt, is this man is an important part of the Underground. And he is also convinced the large village idiot is nothing but a sham.

"What is your name?" the SS guard hisses once again. The Wolf sits smoking a cigarette and casually flicking the ash into the clay ashtray—a nice ashtray from the fatherland. Written across the base: *Staatl Hofbrauhaus, München.*

The large man, lips drooping to one side, sits silently, his face registering nothing. They have been at him for nearly four hours. The accused has said nothing, slurred some inarticulate grunts, but all in all the session has been unproductive. Still the Wolf sits silently by. The SS guard, a blond-haired, blue-eyed Aryan, tall and well built, wipes the sweat on his forehead once again. He has slapped the large man, yelled at him, kept him from sleeping, beat him until his face was black and swollen with blood. Nothing has worked.

Now the Wolf stands up and commands the other officers to stop.

"We are through for the day," he says calmly. "Let our friend, the village idiot, think about his predicament for a while. Solitude will be his worst enemy."

The men look at each other and then back at their superior, then at the large man sitting at the table, his face blank.

"Now!" the Wolf says. "We are through. Take him to his cell."

Pierre is alone in the darkness. His mind is reeling against the fear that threatens his every thought. His insides are a wreck, bowels releasing out of reflex, but in case any are watching, he sits stoically, feigning stupidity. How much time has passed? He cannot tell. He fills his mind with rage, with an uncontrollable anger which feeds off the fear until he is a resolute, impenetrable stone of resistance. They have killed his mother and probably his sister. *I will wait, hold out, and kill them all. I will not give in.* His cheekbone is shattered, his nose flattened against that same cheek. As he sucks in small breaths through his swollen lips, he recounts all the events that will fortify his hatred toward these people. No, if this is as bad as it gets, he can go farther, last longer. He will survive!

The cell door clanks open. In the doorway is the SS officer. *I thought I was through for the day.* He is hoisted to his feet by two other guards and walked to another part of the complex. He enters the room and sees a bathtub filled with water. Near it stands Wolfhardt Becker. Pierre grunts in fear at the empty room, the cold draft, the tub filled with water. As the guards step him up to the tub, he catches something horrible out of the corner of his eye: *Nerf-de-Boeuf. O God,* he whispers deep inside his mind. *O God, not this.*

He has heard rumors of such a torture. The few who survived were never the same. Two guards hold him on each side, and even though he is magnificently strong, his struggles against the guards are futile. His head nears the tub of water. In the tall SS guard's hand is the Nerf-de-Boeuf, the long hard rubber club now swinging in the officer's hands. Pierre holds his breath as his head plunges into the water. *I will drown,* he thinks as the oxygen slowly seeps from his brain, from his body. How many minutes? And then his head is pulled from the water. But just as he sucks in air, just as he gasps, the hard club slams into his back, into his arms, over and over. Someone is shouting, but he cannot understand them. And before he can take another breath, his head is submerged into the water once again.

And this is repeated over and over and over. On the fourth or fifth time, Pierre does not hear the shouts, does not feel the club as it cracks his ribs and bruises his kidney. No, he suddenly does not care about any of this, for he sees a man before him. "Papa?" he yells to the figure as it walks away into the terrible light. "Papa, wait for me!" But he cannot go any farther, for the light will not let him. Another figure appears. It is someone he does not recognize.

"You cannot go where he is going. Not yet." And then, "I will show you how much you must suffer for My sake." And then, "I will be with you even to the depths of Sheol. Don't be afraid any longer—just believe!" The voice turns into a shout. Pierre thrusts himself into the light, but his head is yanked out of the water, and he feels the numbing pain that is the club against his broken ribs.

Once again Wolfhardt Becker sits silently at his table in the back of the interrogation room. The village idiot has not given up the facade. After the near drowning, after the severe beatings—nothing. The muscular young man, now reduced to a black-and-blue pulp, has remained a simpleton. *But how?* thinks Becker at his table. *How can someone withstand such pain and fear? No, there is something more here. I will break him to pieces.* He pulls out another cigarette and lights it, then realizes he has one already smoldering in his favorite ashtray—the one with Hofbrauhaus written across it, the one his lover had given him as a gesture of her affection.

But there has been a change in this brute of a man, this fake idiot. Yes, there has been a change, but it was not the one expected. The unrelenting pressure to break his will has somehow given him peace. Oh, this has happened many times before—but just before death, just before the final blow. This man was not dead, far from it. And there was a moment when Becker actually thought the man mumbled a prayer!

Again, Becker sucks on his cigarette, breathes out the smoke, and sits in the dark in silent contemplation of these things. He does not hear the tall SS officer come into the room.

"What are you doing in here all alone?"

"Hmm? Oh, I am thinking," Becker says.

"What shall we do with the retard?"

Becker sucks on his cigarette. "Goethe?"

"Yes, sir."

"Do you really believe this fraud?"

Goethe hesitates for a moment. "Uh, I don't know, sir. No one has ever survived such a beating. I don't know if a liar could withstand such abuse."

Becker sucks his cigarette down to the nub and smashes it out in his clay pot. He stares straight ahead, lips tight with rage. "Bring him back here," he whispers.

"Sir?"

"You heard me. I want the retard brought to me." He pulls out his cigarette case and lights another one, allowing his will to regain control of his emotions. "I said bring him to me now."

Goethe leaves the room. A few moments later he appears with the hump of flesh that was Pierre. The two guards drag him to a chair across from Becker.

"I will say this one more time, my friend," Becker says with a slight grin on his face as he leans up to him. "Who do you work for? Where is the location of your Underground headquarters? Who is involved?"

He pauses to allow the words to sink in. And then after sufficient time, he stands up and goes to a cabinet in the corner. When he returns he is holding a hammer in his hands. He lays the hammer in front of the broken man and sits down again in his chair.

"So, you are retarded? Is that it? You have no sense? No brain cells in your head? You cannot register what I am saying or doing? Well then…"

Becker picks up the hammer with a quick, fluid motion, and smashes it down upon the large man's head. The man slumps to the desk.

"Every day," Becker whispers into the unconscious man's ear, "every day from now until you die, retard, I am going to smash this hammer into your head. Every single day, day in and day out,

I am going to beat your brains until they come out your skull. You will either tell me what you know, or you will become the retard you pretend."

And with that Pierre is dragged from the room and thrown into his cell.

J acob's visit with his doctor was short. He respected his friend enough not to carry on like others may have done. Jacob knew he was in trouble when he was invited back to the doctor's office and not the examination room.

"I'm afraid I have bad news, Jacob," the doctor said.

"Yes, tell me all you know."

"The cancer has spread into your lymph nodes. There isn't much we can do." He sighed. "If you would have come in sooner— Well. I would say the cancer is inoperable and you have at the most two years. This type takes a long time to progress, but once it starts, it attacks rapidly and severely."

And that was that: rapidly and severely. Those words revolved around in his head as he drove to the empty house, as he sat by himself in the large open great room, as he lay in bed that night watching CSPAN. Rapidly and severely. Who else could have survived what he had survived, could have lived the life he had lived—in Belgium, in the United States? Rapidly and severely. Yes, he knew the final bookend had been set in place. Like Scrooge hunched over the large granite marker in *A Christmas Carol*, his only thought was remorse and regret for how he lived.

All night long he reviewed his mistakes. And each time he had experienced the failure, an image would appear, the one he had seen in Father Gilbert's church, the broken Jew, gaunt, with head drooping, body drooping. Before him was the crucifix and the God-man upon it. And as the visions continued, his fear increased. He shouted in terror, *Who are you? Who are you? Who are you?* The image was silent, convicting. He saw again the faces of the Delvauxs, saw Father Gilbert praying over him, Mrs. Chabot hunched over her kitchen table. And a voice said, "For you. All for you. I will lay down My life…for you."

When he awoke from the terror of that world, that very morning he received the letter from Micheline Chabot about Pierre and his illness. And that morning he knelt at the foot of his bed and prayed to God, a God he was just learning to understand, a God who was bigger and more complex than he imagined. That morning he again pursued the questions that haunted his childhood— Why am I a Jew? Who is this Jesus? What do I believe and why? It was that afternoon that he made his way to temple to speak with the rabbi. That afternoon he would ask Lereau to explain his conversion. And it was that night he picked up the phone and called Isaac and invited him to Belgium.

"Everything is different now, Isaac," said Jacob, still looking out the window. "I don't know what you want me to say to you. Yes, I am dying. No, I didn't tell you because—well, what difference does it make?" Jacob turned his reddened eyes up to his son and then again out the window. "What is, is what is."

Isaac pushed the bill of his hat up onto his head and sat down next to his father. "Is this why you wanted to take me to Belgium?"

"Partly. I am sure my cancer has a lot to do with every aspect of the rest of my life. People who have not been a part of my life, must now be a part of my life. Reconciliation is what the rabbi calls it. It will be good for my soul."

"You're seeing a rabbi?"

"Things change, Isaac."

"Yeah, but that much? You must be serious."

"I have never been more serious in my life, my Isaac." And Jacob locked onto his son's eyes and did not blink.

Isaac pulled his glasses off, rubbed his eyes, lifted his lenses to the light, then put them back on his face.

"You know," Jacob said, "I think about my first wife a lot these days. Sometimes I am ashamed I ever married your mother—as if somehow I have betrayed Yvonne."

"I don't know anything about her, Pop. I don't know how to respond to such a statement, because I don't know anything about her."

A wave of passengers streamed by them. As the last one waddled away, Jacob spoke again.

"I met her in Charleroi. At the time...well, at the time I was hiding from the Nazis. I can see her yet, at that kitchen table ready to go off to school. She was lanky and boyish back then. Back then... It seems to me another life."

"I don't know if I want to hear about this right now. I don't know if I'm ready to talk about this." Isaac stood up and turned to look out the large pane of glass. Then he faced his father. "You're dying, and you feel the need to expunge your soul, but I don't think that is your right. You can't take me with you to Belgium in order to purge this from your life. I don't know if I can do this, Pop. I just don't know if I can take such a hit. Not now. Not now." Isaac turned and walked away from the row of padded seats.

Jacob was once again alone. Is this what all of this was about: a dying man's purge? Who was he fooling? To drop such a bomb and not expect major casualties—this was sheer bad decision making. And yet, he had been driven to do so. Liza's death drove him, Rebecca's Down's syndrome, the letter about Pierre, his own cancer—all of these were weaving and spinning a web he could not control. There was no doubt about what he had to do. He had to get his son to see what he had been through—who he really was deep inside. And wasn't that what this was truly about? Wasn't this a sort of cathartic moment that would finally make things right? Perhaps. He could not tell anymore. He had become mad with his plan, mad with his journey to Belgium, mad with his passion to reconcile with Isaac.

He felt that all too familiar discomfort and decided to find a restroom. When he returned, Isaac was sitting on one of the cushioned seats. Jacob sat next to him.

"The plane will board in half an hour," Isaac said.

"Good."

"We aren't going to Belgium to visit your old garment factory, are we?"

"No."

"You have some other reason behind all of this—this calling me up and asking me to go, this reconciliation your rabbi talks about, don't you?"

"Yes."

"When were you planning on filling me in on the details?"

"When you were ready to hear the details."

"Why me?"

"It can only be you."

"What does that mean?"

"It means that all that has happened so far in my life has been meant to happen, and you are the one who was meant to be a part of it."

"I don't understand."

"You will."

"I want to understand now."

"Are you ready for the truth, my Isaac?"

"I wouldn't be back here if I wasn't."

"It will hurt me to tell you about it. It will hurt you to hear about it. It will be painful for you to remember all you see and hear when I am gone."

"I don't follow."

Jacob placed his hands to his face and rubbed his eyes and then his forehead and then his hair as if this finally allowed him to say what he had been meaning to say ever since he first saw his son. When he spoke, his voice was shaky and unsure.

"It is not the dead who praise the LORD, those who go down to silence; it is we who extol the LORD, both now and forevermore." He again wiped his eyes with his palms. The emotion was coming too quick for him to stop it. "That is what I had to tell you, my Isaac. It is from the book of Psalms. My rabbi quoted it to me when I came to see him. It is a word from God Himself. I cannot die until I have given this gift to you, my son. I must give it to you—only you. I have blocked out my past with every ounce of my will. When Yvonne Chabot died, I decided I would start over, but this time I would not be the same man I was in Belgium. No, I would make a new self, create it from sheer force of will. I could not go back. To go back would be to face death. I knew if I were to start digging into the graves of my memories, I would die. Well, I am dying anyway." Jacob suddenly reached out his hand and grabbed his son's arm. "I will not go down to silence, my Isaac, without a promise from your lips."

"I don't understand, Pop," Isaac whispered with a plea in his voice. "What kind of promise could you possibly want from me?"

Jacob squeezed his son's arm harder. "You must promise me

you will write down all that I tell you. You must promise that my life, my story, will not be in vain."

"You want me to write a book about your life?"

"Yes. I want you to come to Belgium and see the world I had forsaken for all these years. I want you to see Pierre and Micheline Chabot. I want you to follow me into my thoughts and help me to purge it forever."

Isaac looked again out the large pane of glass.

"I will start now if you want, Isaac. I will do whatever you want me to do, but I must know you will not forsake my one wish."

"No, Pop. No, I won't forsake your wish. I will go with you to Belgium. We will face it together." Isaac checked his watch. "It's time we were off to the gate. We don't want to miss the flight."

Isaac helped his father up, and they slowly made their way back.

The line was small, and since they both had E-tickets, all they needed was to show a picture ID. Jacob opened his wallet but was unable to find his driver's license. He searched through the small pockets, the secret compartments, and as he opened it up, a piece of paper fluttered to the floor. Isaac bent down and picked it up and put it in his shirt pocket as his father continued to fumble through the wallet.

"Are you sure you didn't put it in your pants pocket?" Isaac asked.

"No," said Jacob shaking his head with frustration and embarrassment. "No, I distinctly remember putting it in my wallet just before Asher pulled up in the driveway." He paused and put his hand to his forehead. "I was standing in the foyer of the house, staring at the mirror, when I heard him pull up outside…" He started to search his pants pockets, and to his astonishment there was his license. "I don't remember putting it into my pants, Isaac," he said, shaking his head. "I really don't remember putting it there."

"Never mind, Pop." Isaac grabbed the ID and gave it to the lady behind the podium. She looked at both pictures and then looked at Isaac with intensity.

"Excuse me, Mr.—" She glanced down at her computer screen and then back at Isaac. "Mr. Horowitz? Did anyone ever tell you that you look a lot like—"

"The adventure writer Jack Oxford?" Isaac said with a smile. "Yes, people tell me that all the time." He smiled again at the woman and then walked Jacob over to another seat to wait for boarding.

The first class seats on the 747 were luxurious. Jacob had made sure that he bought the best money could buy. They would leave Chicago at 5:40 in the evening and would not arrive in Belgium until 7:10 in the morning Belgium time.

"My name is Kaitlin," the flight attendant said. "Can I get you anything to drink before we take off?"

Isaac looked at his father who was busy searching through his wallet again.

"Pop, do you want something to drink?" Then he turned toward Kaitlin and smiled. "We'll have two glasses of Dom Perignon, please." The flight attendant nodded and left. "Looking for this?" said Isaac pulling the piece of paper from his pocket.

"But where did you find that?" said Jacob, grabbing it from Isaac's hand and opening it up, then folding it the way it had been.

"It fell on the floor. You never did explain the importance of that franc to me."

"Maybe another time." Jacob put the note back into his wallet.

Isaac suddenly reached out and held Jacob's hand and his wallet at the same time. "Now is not the time for secrets, Pop. Now is as good a time as ever to start your story. If you want me to write about what happened, I need to know everything." Jacob began to pull his wallet away, but Isaac held it firm. "Everything, Pop. From beginning to end."

The waitress interrupted them. "Your champagne, gentlemen?"

"Thank you."

"Champagne?" Jacob said with a start. "I didn't order champagne, Isaac. You know I can't drink that stuff. It will—"

"Here is to new beginnings. New beginnings and happy endings."

Jacob looked at his son and then at the plastic cup with effervescent bubbles popping above the rim. "Yes. Yes, to new beginnings…and happy endings."

They clinked the plastic together and each took a sip.

"Now," Isaac said, "we have a long trip ahead, and I can't sleep. How about telling me the story concerning the five-franc note."

Jacob sipped his champagne once again and then gave the rest to Isaac, pulled out the note and unfolded it. The note was creased and faded, to the point it looked like a small rectangular piece of cloth.

The captain's voice came over the loud speaker explaining the trip, the time, the procedures. The flight attendants saw to their routine, and soon the plane was racing down the runway. Up and up and up it ascended, banking left, straightening out, and vanishing into the darkening sky, the white beacon in a rhythmic and hypnotizing pulse of light.

"Belgium was liberated by the British Twenty-first army group on September 3, 1944. At the time my sister, Sarah, and I were staying with an old man and his wife—Gaston and Therese Delvigne. Gaston was a good man, but he liked to drink and fight too much. He and Therese were always bickering—a lot like your mother and me, I guess.

"Anyway, there was a field outside of town where Sarah and I would go to play. Yvonne was living in Liège with us." Jacob put his hand up to stop Isaac's question. "You want to know everything, I will tell you everything; but I will tell you it in my own way." Isaac lifted his now half empty cup of champagne and toasted his father.

"If you know your history, then you know all of Belgium was liberated by September 15, 1944. You never saw such jubilation! People were dancing in the streets, people were lining up outside to wave flags and salute the British and American troops coming through town. Therese Delvigne had knitted special scarves for us that looked like American flags. It was a great time.

"Well, by St. Nicholas Day—their Christmas—we were trying to get our lives back together. My mother was still in Charleroi finding a place for us to live. Sarah was sick, and she needed to be near a hospital.

"I'll never forget the snow that day, the twenty-seventh of December. It was light and fluffy, and there seemed to be layers and layers of it, drifts up to my waist. Yvonne and I sledded down a certain hill we found, while Sarah sat in the snow with her favorite doll, watching us. She was like that. I'll explain why later.

"Anyway, on that particular day when we had all we could take of sledding and snow angels and snowball fights, Yvonne, Sarah, and I made our way back to the village." Jacob stopped and looked out the window for a moment. He shook his head. "I will never forget the people. They were all lined up, hundreds of them, lined up alongside the mud and snowy roads waving flags and shouting."

"Why were they lined up like that?" Isaac asked.

"The final counterattack—the Battle of the Bulge—had just ended. The Germans were retreating in all directions, fleeing toward the German border. The Americans were in hot pursuit.

"Well, like I was saying, Yvonne, Sarah, and I were heading back to the Delvignes' house when we saw the crowds. We started to walk across the road to join in the fun, when of all people Gaston comes racing on his bicycle, wobbling every which way you can imagine—he comes racing toward us screaming at the top of his lungs for us to go.

"I thought he was drunk as usual; so did everyone else in that crowd, I assume. But the old codger wouldn't stop yelling at us. The bike hit a patch of ice and sent him flying into a snowdrift. It didn't take him long to get out of the snow and rush toward us. Still, he was yelling for us to leave, to get to safety. Next thing I know, the old man had grabbed Yvonne and Sarah around their waists and hoisted them off the ground. The people were still shouting and waving flags, and I was not sure what to do. Gaston suddenly turned toward me and screamed in his raspy voice to follow him. 'Quick, Tany! Quick!'

"I ran after Gaston, who was still carrying Sarah and Yvonne, and followed him through a gate and around a stone wall. Immediately he dropped the two girls and grabbed me by my coat, throwing me to the ground. 'What are you doing?' I shouted at him, but he did not heed me. He toppled me onto Sarah and Yvonne and then with a great heave, covered us with his body.

"'I can't breathe!' I shouted. 'Gaston! You are crushing us!'

"'Silence!' he screamed. 'Keep your head down!'

"And then I heard the tanks and the trucks. It was the same sound I had heard all of my life. The same trucks that took my father away, the same machine guns that killed all those I loved."

Jacob turned toward the window and said no more for several minutes.

"What happened, Pop? What were the trucks?"

Jacob faced his son and there were tears in his eyes. "They were German trucks and German machine guns." He paused again and pursed his lips and closed his eyes. He opened them again and wiped his cheek. "All those people lined up to greet the liberating armies were suddenly struck down by the escaping Germans. They fired at whatever they could. The bullets ripped into the crowds, catching them completely unaware. No one had time to hide. That old drunk, Gaston—bless his soul—saved our lives."

"I don't understand. Wasn't Belgium already liberated?"

"Oh yes, but since the German army pushed forward in that last offensive, some of them were cut off from the rest of their troops. Platoons were scurrying everywhere to get back to the fatherland. They just happened to storm through our village just as the people were lined up in celebration—lined up expecting the Allies." Jacob shook his head and smiled sardonically. "It was the last great irony of the war. Expecting liberation, they are killed in cold blood. They had all survived a brutal occupation, only to be murdered on the very last day of the war."

"So where does the five-franc note come in, Pop?"

Jacob smoothed it out in his hand and held it up. "This was given to me by an American tank driver. When the Allies finally did come through our town, they stopped and allowed us to celebrate. Well, I went up to this man and asked him for some chewing gum. That was the only English I knew. He didn't have any, so he put his helmet on my head and took me inside his tank. Instead of a piece of chewing gum, he gave me this five-franc note. I guess in all my travels, I hoped to one day find that man and show him I kept his memento."

"Unbelievable," Isaac said in a whisper. "You were actually there when they liberated Belgium."

Jacob excused himself and went to the restroom. When he returned, Isaac asked, "What happened to your sister and Yvonne?" He put his hand on his father's leg. "You don't have to say anything about it now if you don't want to, Pop. I was just curious."

"Well, it is complicated. Sarah, my mother, and I went to Charleroi, then to Brussels for a bit. Sarah was dying of TB and there was little anyone could do. She finally passed away at the end of 1948. I will never forget the coughing, the blood. It was a terrible thing. Terrible."

"And Yvonne?"

"Hmm? Oh, Yvonne. Well, my mother did not think it fitting for a Jewish man to marry a Gentile, so I told her I could never see her again. Mother and I left for Antwerp for a short time, and then I left for the coast shortly after that."

"Did your mother go with you?"

"No. No, she did not. My mother was changed by the war. I think she came to a point when there was nothing left to give to anyone. She was placed in a home in Antwerp, a sanatorium. She withdrew from everything and finally could not even recognize me any more." Jacob looked out the window and into the darkness. He was quiet for a long time. "I saw a little piece of her die when my father was taken away. I saw more and more of her die when Sarah took ill. When the war had ended and Sarah died, I think she finally gave up—she snapped out of survival mode and that was that." He paused again and looked out the window and then turned back toward Isaac. "She was the greatest woman I have ever known. She saved my life, Isaac. If not for her courage, I would have died in the same camp my father died in."

The flight attendant appeared and gave them each a dinner menu. They ordered, and after their meals were served, they ate and spoke only when necessary. Jacob did not finish his meal but ordered a pillow and blanket for the remainder of the flight. Isaac finished his meal and sipped an after-dinner coffee.

Jacob turned toward the window and did not turn back around, though his eyes were wide open. The dark window became a screen on which the story of his life was played over and over and over again. And in each scene he saw his mother, Sarah, and Yvonne. They were ghosts that danced and whirled, round and round and round. He saw them laughing and making fun. He saw them huddled down in the dirt bunker in the middle of the freezing winter. He saw his mother crying in Hans Kraemer's arms, in the pouring rain, once again finding safety in the chaos. And he saw her silently sitting in the chair on the porch of the sanatorium, sitting and staring into space. What visions, what images cascaded about her mind? He saw her gaunt face, used up and sunken in, the lines of her once beautiful features now the lines of her skull. And she sat silently, only now and again blinking.

The night screamed by, the plane hurtling across the ocean below. And as it did, Jacob revisited all of the ghosts. He thought of Pierre, of his great sacrifice. He thought of the terrible price all the families had paid to keep him alive. And then, silently and with great restraint, teeth clenching the white cotton pillow, he began to sob.

"Make me worthy," he whispered into the pillow. "O God, make me worthy."

In the morning, when Jacob returned to his seat after a trip to the restroom, Isaac was still sleeping. So Jacob ordered a cup of coffee, then reached into his shirt pocket and pulled out the letter from Micheline and scanned the simple lines over and over. Then he turned to look out the window at the cotton layers of clouds far below. The noise of the airplane cabin made it easy for him to drift off into the past. It was Isaac who interrupted him from his thoughts.

"Good morning, Pop," he said, yawning and then stretching his arms stiffly before him.

"Ask the flight attendant for a warm towel," said Jacob, smiling. "Does wonders for the eyes and face."

Isaac got up in search of the towel, and while he was away, Jacob ordered him a cup of coffee, which was an excuse to get himself a refill. He sipped his cup, and sipped some more, but his son did not return. The muffled sound of the cabin and the comfortable seat eased him back into a contemplative moment.

When the war had finally ended, after the German's horrifying massacre of the townspeople of Liège, after Yvonne had told Jacob of what had happened to her family—mother murdered, brother taken away—after all of this, it was time to put the pieces back together.

Rachael took Sarah to a sanatorium where she could receive whatever help they could give her. Her parting words to Jacob were cold and without pity. "If you go with this Gentile girl, you will be cut off from us. Oh, you don't see it now, but she can only cause you pain."

Jacob looked at his mother's worn and gaunt face, her spindly hands. The beauty was nearly used up. The war had creased and wrinkled her, had swollen her cheeks and painted dark rings around her eyes. But more horrible than all of that, it had snatched her will to love.

"I know what I am doing," Jacob said. "Pierre must be found. I owe him everything. I owe him more than I could possibly give him."

"And what do you owe your mother?" Rachael hissed. Then she smiled and said, "You have grown up, my little lamb. I do not know how to speak to you anymore."

"Things have changed," whispered Jacob, looking out the small hotel room where his mother was staying. "The war changed me—changed you—changed all of us forever. I need to do this," he said with vigor, turning around and facing her eye to eye. "I need to find Pierre, and I need to look for Papa. This is all that concerns me now."

"But what about Sarah? What about your mother?"

"I will come and join you later."

"We will be dead by then," she said without emotion.

"I must do what is in my heart. I can't explain it. I owe Pierre at least that much."

And that was that. Jacob and Yvonne went to Brussels to find Pierre, and Rachael took her sickly daughter to Charleroi.

It took several weeks of misdirection and false leads to finally locate Pierre, now a dwindled and shattered man: face scarred and swollen, head wrapped in bloodstained bandages. It was months before they learned what had happened to him and how he had escaped.

Pierre had survived three weeks of torture few could imagine. As he lay dying on the cold stone, he heard several loud booms. The floor shook. Another loud boom—this one closer still— shifted the cell door off its frame. No one had come to bring him to the interrogation room, no one had come (and they did like clockwork) to open up the thick steel door, grab him from his corner, and drag him down the hall. Another tremor knocked him against the wall, then tremors and booms followed one after the other until his simple mind reeled in fear. Powder sifted down from the stone ceiling above. It was as though the world were falling to pieces. Someone pounded on his cell door. Several loud bangs, and then soldiers broke into the dark cave. Pierre could not understand them, their syntax was strange, the words undecipherable. As the soldiers lifted him to his feet, he screamed and grabbed his head in pain. And that is all he remembered.

Jacob and Yvonne found Pierre in a British-run hospital. It would take him years of hard work to once again speak in full sentences. Even these were jagged and at times unintelligible. But he was alive! Pierre had survived, like all of them—he had made it out with his life.

Yvonne stayed with her brother and nursed him back to health. It was clear Jacob was a third wheel, and he decided it would be best to find his mother and spend some time with her. When he arrived in Charleroi, his sister was already dead, his mother's health declining rapidly. He stayed with her until she too passed away. That is when he fled to the coastal city of De

Panne—escaped and tried to forget all that had happened to him. That is, until Yvonne Chabot tracked him down.

Jacob had kept in touch with Pierre and his wife Micheline only by letter—secret notes at holiday time, always with his office's return address. This was a private relationship he wanted nobody else to participate in. As the years passed, his conscience pricked him—tiny barbs that soon imbedded themselves deep into his present. It would be a good thing to return, he told himself one day while driving to work. And so he did. At first under the auspices of business, he traveled to Belgium and to Liège and to the farmhouse where the Chabot family had lived. It was there he met Pierre working on a split rail fence. Pierre was changed, his face worn and haggard, but he smiled and talked in his fragmented French. They fell silent. Jacob wept. Pierre wept. Words lost out to gestures.

They would see each other every year from that point on until Jacob's family grew up, were old enough to uncover his secret. And when that happened, he once again closed off his life in Belgium. Again he sent letters with his business as his return address. He decided to take his family to Belgium, but something deep inside would not allow him to go anywhere near Charleroi (where his sister and mother were buried), or to Liège to see Pierre. No, he took his family to De Panne and to the little shop where he started his garment business. It had been many, many years since he had seen Pierre and Micheline. And then the letter arrived.

What must Pierre look like now? he thought as he stared out the airplane window.

"Pop," Isaac said as he slumped into the supple leather seat beside his father, "you won't believe who I just ran into on my way from the restroom."

"Hmm?"

"You okay, Pop?"

"Yes, yes, I am fine." Jacob smiled and sipped his coffee. "What was that you were saying, Isaac?"

"I'm on my way from the restroom, right. And suddenly I'm stopped by none other than Robert Slazenger from the *New York Times Book Review*. He wants an interview right there and then. Unbelievable." Isaac took the coffee cup from the armrest holder and sipped it. "Unbelievable. I wake up thirty thousand feet in the air and am asked for an interview." He laughed.

"He's an important friend if you decide to write this book."

"That guy has hounded me ever since *The Golden Calf.*" Isaac rubbed his chin. "You're right, maybe it would be the prudent thing to do."

The flight attendant appeared and they both ordered breakfast—Jacob a bran muffin, Isaac the same. It was now 6:30 Belgium time. They were already on the descent to Brussels.

On the corner of Jacob's tray sat the letter from Micheline. Isaac saw it and picked it up.

"Will Micheline be at the gate when we arrive?"

"Yes," Jacob said.

"Will Pierre be able to be there?"

"No." Jacob's lips trembled as he tried to explain his answer, but then he fell silent and turned to look out the window.

"I'm sorry," said Isaac, staring at the beautiful script of the letter. "You know, I wish I knew something about him—Pierre, I mean." He stopped himself short and then plunged ahead. "Pop, I want to know all of this. I want to feel it in my bones. If you want me to write your story, then I need to know every detail. I need to—"

"Be patient, my Isaac. You will see more than your heart and soul can endure. There will be time for all of your questions later. Pierre was the bravest man I have ever known. You will know why very soon. Be patient."

"Is he still living?"

"I don't know," Jacob whispered. "It has been some time since that letter arrived. The blame is completely on me, for my delay. It is my own fault. I suspect we will be greeted by Micheline only."

Jacob stared out the window and watched the clouds rip over the wing like phantoms, like phantoms from his past, layer upon layer of memories. This would be the hardest trip he had ever made, and this fact was beginning to sink deeper and deeper into his mind. *Why,* he thought, *why did I not jump on a plane immediately and fly to see this great man before he died?* He envisioned the arrival, stepping into the gate area, surveying the crowd only to find the thin frame of Micheline, her large lips and nose protruding in an elegant way, small brown eyes—surprised eyes, like tiny dots of coal—these eyes would be filled with tears as she told Jacob of her husband's passing. They would stand awkwardly before each other, and the guilt and remorse would go with Jacob to his grave. Oh, the mistakes! How terrible, how final.

The captain's voice came on the speaker explaining the weather conditions. He spoke in French, then in Flemish, then in English. They put their trays up and fastened their seatbelts, Jacob staring at the country that had so long haunted all that he was.

The plane bounced upon the pavement and shuddered to a slow crawl as it taxied toward the gate.

"Let's grab our bags, Pop," said Isaac, still waiting patiently for his father to realize they had stopped and could depart the plane. "Is everything okay, Pop?"

"Mr. Oxford?" Isaac looked up at the flight attendant hunched over him with a look of concern. "Does your father need some assistance?"

"No, he's fine. Ready, Pop?"

"Yes, yes, Uncle Philip, I'm ready to go," Jacob says as he hobbles past Isaac and past the flight attendant and toward the door of the plane.

Isaac turns to follow, but just as he does, the flight attendant pushes a copy of *The Tombs of Anakim* into his face.

"I've been waiting all this time, Mr. Oxford, to have you sign a copy of your book. I didn't want to bother you, so I figured this would be the best time."

Jacob does not grab his carry-on bag. When he finally hobbles into the openness of the airport and hears the hum of forgotten languages, he nearly collapses. He scans the crowd just as he had imagined, his eyes focusing on just who he thought he would see, and he hobbles toward that inevitable conclusion.

As he walks up to the throng of people—kissing, hugging, speaking rapidly and so elegantly in French and Flemish—when he steps up to the mass of colors, he stops and scans the crowd. The ghosts from his past are free, the chains that for seventy-plus years had kept them at bay suddenly disintegrate, and they dance and whirl before his eyes. He blinks several times trying to wake from the memories.

He sees the Delvauxs sitting at their table reading their Bible. He glances to his right and there is Father Gilbert making the sign of the cross. Just to the left of Father Gilbert is Yvonne—that gesture, that beautiful gesture. And there just beyond her are his father and Uncle Benjamin.

What? his mind screams through the roar of all the voices. *What is that you say? I cannot hear you. Jacob. Jacob?*

"Jacob?"

Jacob blinks again, and before him stands the thin and frail Micheline. She is just as he has imagined.

"Oh, Jacob, it is so good to see you," she cries in French, hugging his broad shoulders, squeezing him back into the present.

He pushes her away so he can see her. Her skin is puffy and full of wrinkles.

"There you are, Pop," Isaac says as he drops the heavy carry-on bags at Jacob's feet. He looks up and is accosted by Micheline.

"It is so good to see you, Isaac Horowitz," she says, hugging him with strong arms. "Pierre and I have waited a long time for this moment."

Jacob's smile leaves his face. "What do you mean, have waited? Pierre is—"

"Oh, I left him over there. The crowd was too much for him. He doesn't see well now, and loud noises drive him mad."

Jacob turns to where the old woman is pointing. There, off to the side like a discarded coat, is a thin wraith of a man, hunched up in a wheelchair, blanket over his emaciated legs. Jacob leaves the others and walks over to him. "He's alive," he whispers. "Oh, God in heaven, he is alive. I am not too late."

"I told him he should not come," he can hear Micheline explaining to Isaac in her broken English, a tinge of anger and frustration bordering her words. "I told him, but he is a stubborn man. 'No,' he says to me. 'No.'"

Pierre's head is bald. Across his scalp—grotesquely lumped and hardened—are the scars from the hammer blows. His eyes are hollow, face bony and pasty white. The once bold and bulging shoulders are now like two bat wings, pointed and ugly, humping up on either side of his neck. He does not move.

Jacob steps up to the chair and then drops to his knees. He whispers Pierre's name, but the old man does not respond. He whispers it again. "Pierre. It is Jacob. I have come back. I have come back, Pierre. I have brought my son Isaac." His words are beginning to break apart from the overflow of feeling deep within. "I have come back, Pierre."

Then Jacob hears a commotion to his left.

"Jack Oxford," a woman says. "Jack Oxford, could I just stop you for a moment…Jack Oxford."

Pierre's lips twitch, and then gibberish comes forth—squeaks and tiny unintelligible chirps.

"Yes, my friend, yes. It is Jacob. I have come back."

The commotion next to Jacob is louder, the woman more obstinate. Jacob reaches over to Pierre's lap, takes his clawed hand, and gently squeezes it.

"Mr. Oxford, could you please sign my copy of your latest novel?"

"I don't know what you're talking about," Isaac says. "Please, leave me alone!"

"But Mr. Oxford. Just a simple signature. What's the big deal?"

"I'm not who you think I am," Isaac says.

The woman tugs at his shirt. Isaac turns around. "My name is not Jack Oxford, lady. You are mistaken. My name is Isaac. Isaac Horowitz."

At that moment Isaac steps up to Jacob and Pierre, and Jacob takes Isaac's hand and places it over Pierre's.

"Now, my Isaac. Now I will tell you a story."